ABOUT THE AUTHOR

Carol Westron is a successful short story writer turned novelist. Fascinated by psychology and history, Carol writes crime novels set both in contemporary and Victorian times. Her books are predominantly set in the South of England, where she now lives.

Crime Series set on the South Coast

The Mia Trent Scene of Crimes and the Serious Crimes Team form an overlapping series of police procedurals where characters and events from one series interact and impact on the other, mirroring real life, where police personnel often work over a large area within their county.

Books in the Scene of Crimes and Serious Crimes Team Series:

The Terminal Velocity of Cats
(Mia Trent Scene of Crimes) published 2013.

About the Children
(Serious Crimes Team) published 2014.

Karma and the Singing Frogs
(Mia Trent Scene of Crimes) to be published 2015.

Tyranny of the Weak
(Serious Crimes Team) to be published 2016.

The books are separate and all stand by themselves.

About the Children

Carol Westron

To Nina
Keep on writing
love
Carol
x x

pentangle
press

ISBN 978 149523 210 7

Book design by The Art of Communication www.artofcomms.co.uk
First published in the UK 2014 by Pentangle Press www.pentanglepress.com

To Peter, with love.

Thank you for taking me to Paris,
where I saw a girl with jewelled teardrops painted on her face,
sitting on a bench beside the Seine.
It was that scene that triggered this book.

Acknowledgements

As always, my family for their love and support. I couldn't do any of it without you. Thank you Peter, Jo, Paul & Claire, Alan & Lyndsey, and my wonderful grandsons, Jack, Adam, Oliver, Henry and our new baby, Thomas.

Chris Hammacott and Wendy Metcalfe, my writing friends and colleagues in Pentangle Press and the newly formed panel, Criminal Tendencies. Thanks to both of you. It has been a great year and we're getting better all the time.

Thanks to Art of Communications for another incredible cover. The bar's so high now, I can't wait to see what you produce next time.

Thanks to all my writing friends for their encouragement and support, especially my incomparable fellow Deadly Dames.

Last but by no means least, a heartfelt thank you to Mystery People for supporting me so generously. Thanks to Jennifer Palmer for giving me my first review, and one that I will always treasure. Above all, thank you to Mystery People's founder and editor-in-chief, Lizzie Hayes; I will never forget how you helped me back on my feet when ill-health had knocked me down.

Prologue

"People died here. Hundreds of them." The boy's voice holds an exulting note. "The Druids killed them."

He reaches out and strokes the gnarled bark of the ancient oak, once a giant, now cut off at six-foot and pinioned in place to support the Play Area zip wire. "They tortured them first. That man who's written a book about it came into our class and told us."

He finds a roughly carved heart encircling initials. He wishes he had a knife with him. He'd carve out his own message.

"Don't keep talking about death." His brother's voice is shrill. He turns away. "I don't want to think about it."

"You're pathetic." He knows what he wants to write, stabbing through to the tree's core. "It's awesome."

Chapter 1

The two boys lay sprawled and broken, like fledglings that had tumbled from the nest. Tyler looked, and carried on looking until he could process the details of their deaths.

They were young… under twelve years old… both had brown hair and both wore jeans and sweatshirts. One child had fallen into shallow, muddy water. A knitted hat lay near to his right hand, its red wool mottled with a darker stain. The other boy must have tried to get away, marks of blood trailed for several feet.

Both boys had been shot.

Sheltered by the Scene of Crimes tent, they lay close to the stump of the ancient oak, Stone Park's last link to its dark history.

"Superintendent Tyler?" A slim, fair-haired woman entered the tent. "I'm Gill Martin, your replacement DI."

"Yeah, the ACC told me." He couldn't manage welcoming but he thought he'd hit neutral. It wasn't her fault his regular second-in-command was on sick leave. "This is a nasty one."

"Yes, sir. SOCO has processed this area and the pathologist should be here to move the bodies soon," said DI Martin. Her voice was brisk and Tyler didn't know if she felt more than she was letting show. "It's lucky you got here in time to see them."

He wondered what sort of luck that was, good, bad, or totally lousy. "Yeah."

"Are you okay, sir?" She must have picked up on the sarcasm in his voice.

"Of course." That was a lie. After a gruelling conference in America, his plane had been diverted because of freak weather conditions, tripling the travel time. He'd dropped in at the Station with some paperwork and found himself catapulted into becoming SIO in a child-murder case. "Tell me exactly what we've got."

"Five victims. Three dead; a woman and these children. Two wounded, a man and a young woman. The adults were in the formal garden, quite a way from the kids. The emergency call was logged in at 13:55. It was anonymous, a male voice said, *'Park... all shot.'* We've got the phone. It was lying next to the bodies. It belonged to one of the victims... the dead woman."

"Any connection between the two sets of victims?"

"Not that we've found, sir. The shootings were in two different locations in the park. They've taken the survivors to hospital but we left the dead in place for you to see."

Tyler thought, at some point, his life had taken a wrong turn. Normal people didn't get a mini-massacre as their welcome home package after a conference. "Any witnesses?"

"Only the two wounded and they're not fit to talk. We've secured the park and we're doing house-to-house in the area. We've got armed units available in case more trouble breaks and we've warned the public to stay indoors."

"Right. So are we looking for a gunman who was targeting one of the people in the park or a random killer who ran out of bullets?" Tyler was thinking aloud, not expecting a response.

"I don't know, sir."

"No, of course not." Great! Just what he needed, they'd given him a DI who answered his rhetorical questions. "Have we got the weapon?"

"No sir," her tone was apologetic.

He sighed. "You got any more good news for me?"

"We've got IDs for the adult victims but not these boys yet."

"What do you mean you haven't got IDs? The whole case could rest on what we find out about these children."

"It might not be about the children." Gill Martin sounded defensive.

"In murder it's always about the children. Even if they were only in the wrong place at the wrong time. Everyone feels things more intensely when kids are killed." After twenty-five years as a cop he'd seen a lot of evil but the death of children still filled him with outrage. "So what have we got to identify these kids?"

"All we've got to go on is this small rucksack and a football."

The contents of the rucksack had been laid out on a plastic sheet. Three cartons of orange juice, three packets of crisps, a tube of cough sweets and a small, spiky, blue, plastic block.

"What the hell's that?" said Tyler.

"A sticklebrick, sir... it's a kids' building toy."

He wondered if she'd got children. It could come in handy if she had. One of the strong points of his long-time DI was the knowledge and understanding Roy had earned by being a devoted husband, father and grandfather. Sometimes Tyler wondered what it would have been like to have kids. His ex-wife had loathed the thought of having children. Occasionally he'd regretted that, but he knew he'd have made a lousy father. He'd never let anything get in the way of his career.

"You got kids, Inspector?"

"No, but I was with a friend when she bought some sticklebricks for her grandson."

"I see." Perhaps that was as well. Whatever the politically correct propaganda claimed, it was still tough for a woman to get to the top of the police force when she was juggling job and family. "So we've got two kids who're school age here in the middle of Monday afternoon. What do you think they were they doing? Skiving?"

"Most kids who bunk off school head for the shops or the amusement arcade. Unless they were into drugs, glue sniffing or something."

"Maybe. Until the post-mortem it can't be ruled out. But

the cough sweets could mean the kids have been off school with colds. If they were almost better, whoever's looking after them might have booted them out for a while."

"In that case someone will be missing them pretty soon."

"Yeah but we can't wait for that. Get descriptions of the boys taken to all the local schools. Start with the nearest, St Ignatius, the private one just down the road. And, if anyone gets an ID, tell them to check if there are any other kids off school. Especially someone the teachers would expect to be with these two."

"The three drinks and packets of crisps? You think there was a third kid here?"

"What the hell do you think?"

He saw her face tighten into wariness and read her thoughts: she knew she'd screwed up and was waiting for him to give her grief. He thought she deserved it; she should have guessed there were three kids from the moment she'd looked in the bag. There could be a kid out there in desperate need of help. If she'd deployed the search teams with that in mind they might be a lot further on. But what was done couldn't be altered by him yelling at his DI. It would do no good to undermine her confidence and, from what he'd seen, she'd done a reasonable job setting up, not easy when dealing with an unfamiliar team.

"I want this park searched quickly and thoroughly. And I want divers in that lake."

"Yes sir. We've already got people searching but I'll get more onto it, and I've requested divers." She hesitated, then asked, "Do you really think there's another victim?"

"I don't know." To Tyler, at this moment, every scenario seemed more evil than the last. "It's possible there's a child lying bleeding somewhere, unconscious or too scared to call out. But, of course, this third kid, if there is one, may not be a victim."

She stared at him. "You think a child could have done this?"

14

He shrugged. "It happens." He turned as the pathologist slipped quietly into the tent. "Afternoon Doctor."

"Good afternoon, Superintendent. If Scene of Crimes are ready I'd like to move the children as soon as possible."

"Of course." Tyler stepped aside to allow the pathologist and her assistants access to the bodies. "Come on, Inspector, let's get out of here."

As they left the tent, the light made Tyler wince, although it was a cloudy October day. He wasn't fit to take on a case like this. He should have refused the Assistant Chief Constable's request to 'at least go down and take a look.' He'd taken a look and now he needed to go home.

They stripped off their scene of crimes' protective suits. They'd need to put on fresh suits before they entered the other crime scene to avoid cross-contamination.

He paused a moment to consider the position of the Children's Assault Course in relation to other features in the park. On three sides the playground was bordered by undergrowth and sheltering trees. Within easy reach there were two exits, one leading through allotments, the other onto a quiet, residential road. Three hundred yards away, over to the west, he could see the grey shimmer of the lake.

Five years ago, this park had been the scene of the first serious assault he'd investigated, when he'd returned to Saltern as SIO of a new hand-picked Serious Crimes Team. Stone Park had always had a strange reputation... and a strange feeling. Like there was something under the surface; something cruel. Sunlight pierced the grey clouds, briefly bathing the park in pale light. *'The darkness crumbles away – it is the same old druid Time as ever.'*

Tyler hauled his attention back to his DI. For a ghastly, embarrassed moment, he thought he'd spoken the words out loud but Gill Martin didn't seem to have noticed anything odd, so he hadn't given himself away. Reading good literature helped him to make some sort of sense of all the ugliness, but it must never intrude into his work. Private life

15

should be kept private. He'd got his camouflage. Down the pub he'd listen to the football talk and maybe throw in the odd comment from the sports news he'd looked up for that purpose.

He summoned up a brisk tone, "Give me a minute or two will you, Inspector? I've a call to make."

"Of course, sir." Gill Martin withdrew and headed across the park towards the other crime scene, where a second SOCO tent concealed death from public view.

Tyler dragged his mobile phone out of his jacket pocket. The display panel was unresponsive. It seemed the phone had completed the journey back in marginally worse condition than he had. He summoned a nearby constable. "Have you got a phone?"

"Yes sir." The young man handed him a police issue mobile and moved dutifully out of range.

Tyler felt profoundly grateful that, when it came to technology, he was a belt and braces kind of man. He checked his ipod, in which he'd recorded key phone numbers, and phoned through to the Assistant Chief Constable. "Sir, it's Tyler. I'm in Stone Park."

"Yes Kev? How bad is it?"

"Very bad. Someone else should deal with this."

"I'm sorry but I need our best SIO on this one. That's why I sent your team down there straight away."

Tyler felt no gratification at the compliment. Beneath the drag of jet lag he was aware of a deeper weariness, the on-going exhaustion of continually witnessing the results of violence and trying to deal with them.

"Please Kev. Otherwise I'll have to pass the case to DCI Aron. He's a very conscientious officer but…"

Tyler sighed. The ACC did not need to complete the sentence, they both knew Stephen Aron wasn't up to dealing with this.

"All right, sir."

"Thank you. Let me know if there's anything you need

and keep me informed of developments."

"Yes sir." Tyler keyed off and handed the phone back to the constable.

"You're welcome to hang onto it if you need it, sir."

"Thanks."

"It was lucky I happened to spot you in the car park, sir."

Tyler wondered why everyone else's definition of luck didn't seem to tally with his own. If this young constable hadn't sprinted after him with the ACC's message, he'd have made it home and into bed, and nothing would have woken him.

The boy looked bloody young and too bloody eager. Saltern boasted as much violent crime as most other large towns in Southern England but Tyler was certain this youngster hadn't yet encountered a murdered child.

"This your first murder case?"

"Yes sir."

"Have you ever seen a dead body?"

"Yes sir, a few." For a moment the boy looked puzzled then comprehension dawned. "But they were accident victims. I guess that's different?"

"Yeah. It shouldn't be, but somehow it is. What's your name?"

"Jones, sir. Ryan Jones."

Tyler got out his wallet. "Right Jones, there's something I need you to do for me." The only hope he had of staying focused was a large coffee, strong and sweet.

PC Jones set off at a gallop and Tyler stood, resting his shoulder against a tree and waiting for the much needed caffeine to arrive. Gill Martin was directing impatient looks at him. He wondered if she was in a hurry for him to inspect the other scene of crime or hoping that he'd head back to his office. That was the official role of senior cops, but it wasn't his way of doing things.

As soon as the coffee arrived he gulped it down, ignoring the way it burnt his mouth. Then he strode across

17

to the second crime scene, a formal garden bordered by a wide circle of seats. The paving slabs were creamy white, except where they were strewn with autumn leaves. A patch of brighter colour caught his gaze. Someone had lost a scarf. It was delicate, rainbow-beaded and woven in silver thread.

The vivid strands had filled with blood and, as Tyler looked, the outline of the scarf lost definition. Before his tired eyes the sparkling shapes transformed into a grotesque mosaic, the symbol of some primitive sacrifice.

Chapter 2

Gill had been warned that Tyler was a tough bastard and, as he approached the second crime scene, she thought he looked like one. Around six-foot, broad shouldered and muscular, his brown hair closely shaven, he looked more like part of the SAS than a top detective.

She saw his lips tighten as he paused by the bloodied scarf but he just said, "Were the adults shot first or the kids?"

"I don't know, sir. We haven't got a time-line yet."

A constable handed Tyler a fresh coverall and he clambered into it.

Gill led the way into the second SOCO tent. A smartly dressed, middle-aged woman was sprawled on the bench, head thrown back, mouth gaping. A blossom of bright blood adorned the neck of her white shirt.

Tyler rubbed a hand across his forehead. "You said the triple-nine call was made by an unknown man? Could it have been the guy that was shot?"

Gill shook her head. "He was too badly injured. I suppose he could have shot the others and then made the call before he shot himself, but there's no trace of the gun."

"Any idea what calibre bullets we're talking about?"

"No sir, not yet."

"It doesn't seem like you've found out very much."

Gill felt a spark of anger. "Unfortunately the bullets are still in the victims, sir."

Her former boss, DCI Aron, would have reproved her for her insolent tone but Tyler said, "What's happening with the search for the gun?"

"DS Warden is directing the search for material evidence."

"Fine. Luke Warden doesn't miss much."

"And Inspector Rowner's leading the house-to-house."

"Well done. It's good delegation, putting a uniformed officer in charge of that."

Gill was ridiculously pleased by this moderate commendation, and ridiculously embarrassed when she realised this.

"You said we've got IDs on these victims?"

"Yes sir." Gill flipped open her notebook. "They all live here in town. The dead woman is Colleen Holebrook. She owned a dress shop and lived in a flat above it at 37 High Street. The injured girl is Sophie Hughes of the same address. The injured man is Joshua Fortune of 14a Bengal Street."

"Joshua... Josh Fortune? That name sounds familiar. Not one of our customers?"

"No. Someone said he was a singer-songwriter, some sort of poet. Perhaps that's where you've heard of him." She waited for Tyler to tell her poetry was for poofs.

"Possibly. I think I heard him interviewed on the local radio not long ago. It might be useful if we want a voice sample to check it wasn't him that called triple nine."

"Yes sir." She made a note of that.

He turned to survey the spread of blood where Josh Fortune had lain and the smaller pool that marked Sophie Hughes' place. Gill saw his gaze return to the limp figure on the bench. Death had drained Colleen Holebrook of colour; the only brightness about her was her lipstick and the blood on her shirt.

"How old is Sophie Hughes?" he asked.

"According to her driving licence she's twenty."

"And, if that scarf's hers, she's a stylish sort of kid?"

Gill recalled the brief view she'd had of Sophie as they'd loaded her into the ambulance. "Yes and beautiful in an unusual sort of way."

"She and Colleen Holebrook were in a lesbian relationship?"

Gill shrugged, instinctively defensive. "They shared a flat but that doesn't prove anything."

"No, but someone kissed Colleen on the lips and nuzzled against her neck."

Gill followed his pointing finger and focused on a speck of dark purple on Colleen's red-painted lips and another mark above the collar of her blouse. Both spots were very small but she felt annoyed with herself for not seeing them. She of all people ought to have noticed a thing like that. She also felt wary, although she told herself not to be a fool. Her personal life was well hidden. No-one in the police force knew about her and Isabel. There was no way Tyler could have sussed it out.

"How badly is Sophie hurt?" he asked.

With an effort Gill pulled herself back on line. "One bullet grazed her head, another went into her shoulder. Josh Fortune's in a bad state. They reckoned he'd taken at least two bullets in the chest."

"And how were they lying?"

"Colleen as you see her. Sophie down by her feet. Josh along here, half beside Sophie and half on top of her. We're not sure, but the Forensics Team think one of the bullets… the one that grazed Sophie's head… also killed Colleen."

"We'll need all the forensic help we can get."

Gill thought Divine Intervention would come in useful too but she didn't say so, Tyler didn't look like a man who'd appreciate flippancy.

Fifteen minutes later Gill looked round the crime scene. Considering their limited manpower and her new status on the team, she thought she'd done okay, but Tyler made her feel edgy, like she had to justify everything she did. And she'd screwed up big time, not working out there'd probably been a third kid on the scene. She could tell herself she'd been harassed, trying to do too much in too little time, but excuses didn't get you anywhere. High profile cases and getting good results was what got you to the top. Along with working all the hours God sent and not pissing off your bosses. And not making really stupid mistakes.

"I see the Bossman's turned up. Might have known he wouldn't resist the chance to head a big case." Detective Sergeant Kerry Buller joined her and glared across the park at the Superintendent.

Gill shrugged. "They wouldn't leave a DI in charge of this."

"You watch Tyler. He's a bastard to women he thinks might make it to the top."

"Is he?" Gill tried to keep her tone neutral. A major reason for leaving DCI Aron's team had been his obsessive jealousy of any promising junior officer, whether male or female. She hoped she hadn't leapt from frying pan into fire.

"Yeah. God knows there's plenty of chauvinist pigs in this job, but with him it's personal. He's got it in for women ever since his divorce. Mind you, his ex is a stuck-up bitch. He's better off without her."

Gill wondered if Kerry had actually met Tyler's ex-wife. If she was stuck-up, surely she'd have avoided junior cops? She didn't ask. She shouldn't have encouraged even this much gossip about the SIO. "Back to work," she said.

Kerry returned to the second crime scene and Gill waited impatiently for Tyler to live up to his reputation as the best SIO around. Despite her reasonable words to Kerry she felt exasperated and harassed. Here she was buzzing round like a blue-arsed fly on speed while the SIO stood drinking yet another take-away coffee. The chances were high that the more enterprising newsboys had already found a spot to train their long-range cameras on the park.

She worked her shoulders trying to loosen the knots that tension had put in them. This should have been her day off. This afternoon she'd planned to run on the South Downs. She loved hill running: the feeling she was pushing herself to her limits; the deep steady breathing; the solitude and the knowledge she was totally in control. Isabel didn't share her love of running but she accepted it without complaint and was proud when Gill ran marathons. Isabel fund-raised relentlessly for whatever good cause they'd chosen to support. Gill sighed. She was booked to run the Snowdonia Marathon at the end of the month. It was one of the most exciting and difficult marathons in the UK and she couldn't slack off her training.

"Inspector!" With a jolt she realised Tyler was calling her. She hurried to join him. He said, "We need more men."

You didn't need to be a superintendent to work that out. "I know, sir. I've requested more help, but the divers haven't even turned up yet."

"Right." He got out a mobile. "Superintendent Tyler for the Assistant Chief Constable... Sir, I need more manpower, urgently."

Fascinated, Gill watched his face as he listened to the ACC's response; she thought she'd never seen anyone look so icily implacable.

"Yes sir, I appreciate that, but, as you know, we've got two murdered children, a dead woman and two others badly wounded. We've got a shooter out there and, as far as we know, this person is still armed. Above all we've got the possibility of another child victim who could be hurt or being held hostage. And, on top of everything else, we've got a deep lake no-one's looking in, either for the third kid or the weapon. As my DI requested, we need divers and more manpower down here, and we need them now." He listened for a few moments and then said, "Thank you."

He put the phone away. "We're getting reinforcements from other divisions and the divers will be here within the next half-hour."

"Thank you, sir." Gill had to admit Tyler wasn't afraid to put himself on the line.

A brief relaxation of his dour expression made her wonder if he'd read her thoughts, but, if so, he didn't call her on it.

"I was trying to remember the details of some trouble

23

here, centred round that bloody oak," he said.

"What sort of trouble, sir?"

"A few years ago. The oak tree got dangerous. When the council had it cut down some loonies made threats. They claimed it was on some sort of sacred, historical site. There was an archaeologist who wanted to dig next to it. That got really nasty... death threats and violence. The archaeologist was badly beaten up and the bloke who'd orchestrated the campaign went to prison."

"Do you think that's relevant?" Gill couldn't see any connection at all.

"Probably not. I'm just opening up possibilities, however incredible they sound."

Gill's mobile rang. She answered, listened and said, "Hang on a minute, let me write that down. Okay. No, stay there for the moment. I'll get back to you." She keyed off. "That was Stuart Farrow. You called it right, sir. It seems the kids did go to St Ignatius' School. They've have been off with flu. Their names are Barnabas and Timothy Quantrull. Parents are Ian and Jasmin Quantrull. At least he's the father, she's their stepmother."

"What happened to the biological mother?"

"The school told Stuart she died three years ago. I've got the address, sir."

"We'd best get on with it then." Tyler drained his coffee, threw away his mangled cup and thrust his hands into the pockets of his leather jacket. His shoulders were hunched and his jaw clenched, as if he was feeling cold. "Any ideas on the third kid? Was there another brother at the school?"

"Stuart says not. And none of their friends are missing. He got them to do a roll call to make sure no-one had gone walkabout."

Tyler was staring across the park. "Luke Warden seems to want us over there."

As they approached the shrubbery near one of the park gates, the search co-ordinator said, "We've found something

24

you ought to see, sir. In there. We haven't touched anything." His tone was tense but brisk. It was clear whatever was in the bushes it wasn't the body of a third victim.

Tyler took the torch the sergeant offered and hunkered down to peer inside a child's makeshift den. "Oh shit!" He stood up and his face was even grimmer than before.

Gill's stomach tied in knots. "What is it, sir?"

"Take a look." He passed her the torch.

She squatted and played the light across the dark hollow. A multi-coloured pile of sticklebricks and a child's picture book lay abandoned. Thomas the Tank Engine beamed up at her from the crumpled pages.

She edged back and stood up. She met Superintendent Tyler's eyes; they were the colour of amber and just as hard.

"So now we know," he said. "The missing child is a toddler."

Chapter 3

"Nice houses," commented Kerry Buller, "Millionaire's row all right."

Neither Tyler nor Gill Martin replied.

Tyler was sitting in the back of the car, leaving DS Buller to drive and DI Martin to check on house names as they moved slowly past the most expensive range of dwellings in the town. He was trying to focus on the task ahead of him. Gill Martin glanced over her shoulder at him. She looked anxious. He forced a smile and she turned back, apparently satisfied.

Through half-closed eyes he considered her: mid-thirties, fair-haired and attractive in a quiet sort of way... and ambitious. He'd been ambitious himself and he recognised the signs.

She must have felt the pressure of his gaze. Again she turned to look at him. "Are you all right, sir?"

As his second-in-command he owed her the truth, but not with Kerry Buller listening in. "Yeah, I'm fine."

Of all the lousy jobs a cop had to do, the worst was telling parents their kids were dead; especially children dead by violence. But when a kid had been missing for days or weeks there was often an element of relief when the family was informed. The start of closure came with the ability to hold a funeral.

This was hideous. He had to tell these parents their boys were dead when they didn't even know anything was wrong. And he had to find out about the other one; the infant who was probably out there in the power of a lunatic.

"This is it, sir." Gill Martin's voice was sharp with controlled tension. Tyler didn't think worse of her for that. Compassion was fine, as long as it didn't compromise performance, and it was a damned sight better than Kerry's abrasiveness.

It was one of the poshest houses in a very posh cul de sac. The wrought-iron gates stood open and they drove in and parked outside the elegant house. The rose-coloured brickwork glowed softly and the front garden was a medley of autumn tints. Outside the garage stood a gleaming Range Rover.

"Very nice," commented Kerry and, despite their errand, he could have sworn there was envy in her voice.

Tyler quelled her with a look and rang the ornate bell.

The woman who opened the door was a small, slender redhead, as expensive and decorative as the house. Her flowery perfume wafted over them.

"Mrs Jasmin Quantrull?"

"Yes?" She had a high-pitched, rather childish voice.

Tyler held up his identification. "I'm Detective Superintendent Tyler. This is Detective Inspector Martin, and Detective Sergeant Buller. May we come in, please?"

"Of course." Her blue eyes were wide with fear. He'd avoided saying they were from the Serious Crimes Team but his rank must have warned her his business was serious.

The carpets deadened all sound of footfalls. They were white shag-pile, impractical for a household that had contained at least two football-playing boys. The air was scented and there were flower arrangements on every side table.

"What can I do for you, Superintendent? Is there something wrong?"

"May we sit down?"

She led them into the living room. It was as brightly lit and handsomely furnished as the entrance hall. The pot-pourri was even stronger and the flower arrangements more magnificent. A wood fire augmented the radiators and the room was stifling.

"Is your husband here, Mrs Quantrull?"

On cue, there was the sound of the front door closing.

"That's probably him now." Jasmin Quantrull raised her

voice, "Ian, can you come in here, please."

A tall, dark-haired man entered.

"This is my husband. Ian, these are detectives… Superintendent… I'm sorry, I've forgotten your name."

"Detective Superintendent Tyler. Would you like to sit down… both of you? I'm afraid we may have some bad news for you."

"What is it?" Ian Quantrull remained standing, his shoulders braced.

"You have two sons, Barnabas and Timothy?"

"Yes. What's happened?"

"Do you know where your sons were this afternoon?"

"The park," said Jasmin. They've been away from school, ill, but they're a lot better and I sent them out to get some fresh air. I warned them to be careful crossing the road and I told them to take their mobiles, but they forgot." Her voice was rapid, as if a barrage of detail could fend off his news.

"Could you tell me what they were wearing?"

"Jeans and sweatshirts. I think Barney's was green and Timothy's dark blue."

"What's happened?" Ian Quantrull's manner allowed no further delay.

"There was a serious shooting incident in Stone Park this afternoon. Amongst the dead are two young boys who answer the descriptions of your sons."

Jasmin screamed. Ian's colour drained. He stood like sculpted grey stone. Even his breathing seemed to halt.

Tyler said, "Was another child with them? A younger child perhaps?" This information couldn't wait.

"Charlie, their little brother. What's happened to him?" Jasmin sobbed the words.

"I'm sorry, we haven't yet located him."

"So he could be okay?" said Ian.

"We're doing everything we can to find him. His well-being is our top priority." There was nothing more positive

28

that Tyler could say. "We need a full description. How old is Charlie?"

"Nearly four... three and ten months but he seems a lot younger," said Ian. "He's still in nappies and he doesn't talk very much." He bit his lip then said quietly, "There's a photo on the sideboard. It was taken last month at our daughter's christening."

Tyler crossed the room and picked up the photograph. It showed a brown-haired, hazel-eyed child, sitting next to a fair-haired, lace clad baby. Charlie was his father's image; as were the two older boys, portrayed in a succession of photographs.

"Is it them?" Ian spoke raggedly.

"I believe so, sir, but we'll need DNA to be sure." The clothes matched but the ravages of the bullet wounds had made visual identification impossible.

He selected the most recent pictures and turned to ask, "May we borrow these? I'll return them as soon as possible."

Ian nodded.

"Would you like to sit down, sir?" It was always better to get bereaved relatives seated, to minimise the damage if they collapsed.

"No." He pushed the suggestion away with an impatient gesture of his hand.

"What was Charlie wearing?" Tyler directed the question to Jasmin.

"A blue, hooded top and jeans, like his brothers. He liked to dress like them. He worshipped them. He wanted to go with them." She cast an appealing glance at her husband.

"You sent them to the park to get them out of your way." Ian's voice was savage. "And you sent poor little Charlie with them because he'd whinge if he was left here alone. Well they're out of your way now... for good."

Chapter 4

'Grief fills the room up of my absent child.' As he looked at Ian's face that most poignant expression of loss echoed through Tyler's mind. These were the moments that stayed with a cop all their lives. For him it had never been the bereaved who screamed and wailed that hurt the most; it was those who stood silent, turned to stone by pain.

Jasmin had covered her face with both her hands. She sank down onto the sofa and began to sob. Gill Martin moved to sit beside her.

"What time did the boys leave here, Mrs Quantrull?" Whatever pity Tyler felt was subordinate to his need for information as soon as possible.

"About half-one."

"And do you know which route they'd take?"

This time it was Ian who answered. "There's a cycle path. It runs past the back of the house and along to the park. The boys would have gone that way. There's only one road to cross. On foot, with Charlie, it would have taken them about ten minutes."

"Thank you, Mr Quantrull. Please understand these questions are just routine, but I have to ask where you were between one-thirty and two-thirty this afternoon?"

"In my office."

"And where's that?"

"Quantrull Constructions."

"And can anyone confirm your presence there?"

Tyler expected a protest but he said, "No... at least my PA may have seen me."

"I phoned my husband," said Jasmin. "Around half-past one."

"I see. Thank you. And Mrs Quantrull, where were you this afternoon?"

"Here. Looking after Polly."

Tyler glanced again at the forest of silver-framed photos. "That's your daughter? How old is she?"

"Four months. She's had the flu too. The doctor was scared of pneumonia and I can't take her out. That's why I sent Charlie with his brothers to get some air."

"Jas, I'm sorry for what I said," Ian spoke huskily.

Still crying, she reached out a hand. He took it and sat on the sofa next to her.

"And did anyone see you, Mrs Quantrull? Any phone calls or visitors?"

"No, but I was upstairs with Polly most of the time. I heard someone ringing but I couldn't answer the door. When Polly cries she starts to cough. It wasn't something to do with the boys, was it?"

"That's unlikely. One last thing, was Timothy wearing a red, knitted hat?"

She nodded. "I told him he ought to keep his ears warm. That hat was a bit small for him but it was his favourite."

"I see." That was no surprise. It had been unlikely the hat was the property of the killer. "Three adults were also victims. Do the names Colleen Holebrook, Sophie Hughes or Joshua Fortune mean anything to you?"

They both thought for a few moments, then shook their heads.

Tyler stood up. "We'll let you know as soon as we have any news."

This was decision time. He realised Gill Martin planned to leave Kerry here as the Family Liaison Officer, but he knew she was the wrong person for the job. "I'm going to leave DI Martin here to look after you." He caught Gill Martin's outraged glare and held it. "It's very important you talk to her. Tell her everything you can about the boys. Even if you don't think it matters tell her, she'll sort out what's relevant."

He was already in the entrance hall when Ian Quantrull's

voice summoned him back. "Just tell me one thing. My boys, did they suffer?"

Tyler remembered the two limp bodies and the way one boy had tried to escape after he was wounded. He, at least, must have known pain and fear.

'Suffer the little children.' The words came to him even though he'd never been religious. He wondered how anyone in his job could believe in a caring God.

"It must have been over very quickly." He longed to say something that would offer comfort and understanding but he couldn't find the words. More than ever he missed his old DI. It had always been Roy's role to comfort bereaved parents.

In the car he phoned through to report the name and description of the missing child. That done he called Luke Warden to check out the state of play back at the park.

"No luck yet, sir. No gun and no kid."

"Anything from the house-to-house?"

"Not a lot. Reg Rowner told me they'd turned up an old girl who said, over the last few weeks, there's been a young man hanging round the park, lurking in the bushes and taking photographs. She said she'd thought about asking what he was up to but decided not to in case he turned nasty."

"The local cops haven't had any complaints about stalkers or flashers have they?" Tyler cursed himself for not having checked before.

"No sir. DI Martin made sure of that straight off. Stuart's finished at the school and gone to the Council offices to see if they'd had any complaints."

"Good idea. Any word on the victims?"

"Not that I've heard but Nikki was trying to contact you. She's still at the hospital."

"Right." Tyler rang off. Within seconds he was through to Detective Constable Nikki Anderton. "Nikki? Tyler. You wanted to speak to me?"

"Yes sir. I wanted to tell you we haven't been able to

track down any next-of-kin for Colleen Holebrook or Josh Fortune but we've got an address for Sophie Hughes' mother. Do you want me to go and tell her or send uniformed?"

"What condition are the victims in?"

"Sophie's sedated but they say she'll be okay. Josh Fortune's still in surgery and no-one's giving good odds on him coming out alive."

"You'd better stay there. Where does Sophie's mother live?"

"20 Larch Grove, Wallend. Her name's Rhiannon Hughes."

"We're not far from there. Kerry and I'll take that."

"Rhiannon, that's a funny name," commented Kerry as he relayed the news.

If Tyler remembered correctly Rhiannon was Celtic and meant goddess or maybe priestess. He had a vague feeling she was the goddess of the moon. A bit too appropriate considering the legends of ancient sacrifice that surrounded Stone Park.

"It's Welsh."

"I might have known."

Tyler had to admit the one good thing about having Kerry around was that dark clouds of prophecy didn't stand a chance.

Rhiannon Hughes was beautiful. When she opened her front door Tyler was amazed by how stunning she was and how aptly she was named. She could have carried off the role of Moon Goddess without any aid from Make-up or Wardrobe. She was tall and statuesque, with dark hair and a pale, luminous complexion. She was wearing casual jeans and sweatshirt but Tyler thought she'd still turn heads as she walked down the street.

He introduced himself and Kerry and asked permission to come in.

She stepped back to let them enter, demanding, "What's

33

wrong?" Her voice had a soft Welsh lilt.

"I'm afraid we've got bad news for you. Your daughter, Sophie, was injured in a shooting incident early this afternoon."

"Sophie? A shooting?" She stared at him. "How badly is she hurt? Is Colleen with her? Oh God, tell me…"

Tyler glanced at Kerry but she was clearly not going to offer comfort or reassurance. He put a hand on Rhiannon's forearm and felt her shaking. "The doctors think your daughter will be okay. We'll take you to the hospital now if you like."

"Thank you." She dragged on trainers and grabbed up coat and bag.

"Have you got your keys? And is everything secured?" It caused a lot of hassle when distraught relatives returned from hospital to find themselves locked out and even more if they discovered they'd been burgled or vandalised.

Clearly impatient, she checked her bag and nodded. Tyler slammed her front door and led her to the car. He put her in the back seat and got in the other side to sit with her.

"Does Colleen know?" she demanded. "Her partner, Colleen Holebrook. Is she with her?"

"Ms Holebrook was with her when the shooting occurred. I'm afraid she's dead."

"Colleen's dead?"

"I'm afraid so. Do you know the whereabouts of any of Ms Holebrook's relatives?"

"She didn't have any close relatives. No brothers or sisters and her parents are dead."

"Do you know of any enemies Colleen or Sophie could have made?"

She shook her head. "I can't imagine either of them having enemies who'd shoot them. But I haven't seen them for months. Where did it happen? At Colleen's shop?"

"No, it was in Stone Park."

"In the park? There's no way Colleen would be out of

34

the shop in the afternoon."

"We've been wondering about that ourselves," said Tyler. She'd put her finger on something that had been in the back of his mind.

She shook her head. "It makes no sense. Why would anyone shoot them?"

"We're not sure yet whether they were the target or if they were in the wrong place at the wrong time," said Tyler.

She stared at him in bewilderment, then understanding dawned. "You mean someone else could be the target? Other people were hurt as well?"

"Two young boys were killed and a man was badly hurt."

"Children!" She shivered. "Was it a family dispute? A father killing his children and turning the gun on himself?"

"No, the children had no known connection to the man who was wounded. In fact he was found lying beside your daughter. His name is Joshua Fortune. Do you know him?"

Her blue eyes clouded and her face bleached. Tyler thought she was about to faint.

"Yes," she whispered, "Yes, I know Josh."

Chapter 5

Just before seven that evening Gill walked into the Serious Crimes Team Office, now doubling as the Incident Room. She saw the display board had been extended to its full length although they were only five hours into the case. It was good to have so much information, not good to have so many victims.

She didn't linger on the photos of the three young boys; in the past few hours she'd seen enough images of them to haunt her dreams. Instead she inspected the pictures of the adult victims.

Josh Fortune, singer-songwriter and music teacher, was forty-two. He had strong features and his hair and eyes were brown. Apparently he'd been facing the shooter. He could tell them what had happened in Stone Park. If he survived.

Colleen Holebrook was forty-four, dark-haired and handsome. The picture showed her smiling and yet there was something defensive in her look. Maybe it was due to loving a much younger woman and one so exquisite. Gill had seen the same anxious, yearning look on Isabel's face when she didn't know Gill was watching her. Bel was in her fifties, nearly twenty years older than Gill. She knew Bel was afraid that one day the age gap between them would turn into a gulf and Gill would fall in love with someone else.

She thrust the thought away. This wasn't about her and Bel. She forced herself to focus on the last picture on the board.

Sophie was enchanting; slender and delicately made with raven-dark hair and ivory-pale skin. Her beauty was emphasised by her extraordinary make-up, with heavily decorated eyes and pearly tear-drops painted on her cheeks. But there was something else, something intangible, an air of elusiveness.

"You enjoying your day off?"

Gill jumped, then turned to face Kerry Buller. "It goes with the territory." She wondered how Kerry knew it should have been her day off. For the first two weeks in her new post she'd been glad of Kerry's friendliness but it was beginning to feel intrusive.

"That was a lousy trick, leaving you to liaise with the Quantrulls. I guess the Bossman decided you were doing too good a job and wanted to screw you up."

Gill didn't answer.

"It's true," insisted Kerry. "He's always giving me and Nikki the lousy jobs he wouldn't give a guy. But she daren't moan, she's got three small kids, so she's got to keep him sweet. He lumbered me with looking after Sophie Hughes' mother for hours this afternoon. Look out, he wants us to shut up."

Tyler had appeared from his office and was clearly impatient to start the briefing. He'd changed his shirt and was freshly shaved. The removal of the dark stubble from his cheeks seemed to emphasise the black shadows beneath his eyes.

"Right, you lot, settle down." The immediate silence reminded Gill of draping a blanket over a birdcage.

"This isn't a full briefing. A lot of people are still out in the field, including the searchers and officers doing the house-to-house. We've got to move cautiously. The killer could still be armed."

He referred to his notes then continued, "At 13:55 this afternoon a call was received by the emergency services." He flipped a switch and sent the gasped words, 'Park... all shot,' whispering round the room.

"It took a few minutes to locate the relevant park but a patrol car got to the scene at 14:06." In a voice drained of all emotion he described the scene of carnage in the park. "The only man still on the scene was another victim, Josh Fortune. We've accessed recordings of his voice and he didn't make that call."

He paused but no-one offered comments or questions so he continued to describe what was known about Colleen Holebrook's life and death.

He rounded up his summary with the simple statement, "She was a lesbian."

Gill thought she saw a reaction amongst the team. Not exactly hostile but possibly an element of 'well that explains it.'

Tyler continued, "Her partner is Sophie Hughes. She works in Colleen's shop. Sophie was shot in the shoulder and a bullet grazed her head. We haven't been able to question her yet, but she's likely to be our best bet as an eyewitness."

"Is she being guarded?" demanded Gill.

The tawny eyes flicked over her in a look she could only interpret as contempt. "Of course she is." He turned back to the team, "So's our other survivor, Josh Fortune. The chances are he won't live to tell us about it but if the gunman struggled with him there may be some forensic evidence on his clothes."

"I got them bagged up and sent to the lab, sir." Nikki Anderton had been the first of Tyler's team to reach the hospital. "But I don't know how much use they'll be. In A&E they were more interested in saving his life than preserving evidence."

"Did SOCO check whether there was any trace on Josh Fortune's hands?"

"They did what they could but both his hands were plastered in blood."

A mutter ran round the room but Gill was unimpressed and so, by his expression, was Tyler. "He probably clutched his chest as he went down. But I want to know more about Josh Fortune and his relationship with Colleen and Sophie. Sophie's mother, Rhiannon Hughes, damned near fainted when I told her he'd been found, wounded, lying beside Sophie in the park. I tried to talk in the car but we reached the hospital before I could get anything out of her but I'm sure she knows more than she was letting on. Kerry, you spent the afternoon with Rhiannon, did you find out anything?"

"No sir."

"Nothing?"

"Rhiannon Hughes isn't like her daughter, she can't be bothered to talk to other women."

The insolence in her voice was finely balanced, possible to ignore but clearly there. Gill saw Tyler's lips clench. "We'll have to find you some duties you can cope with, sergeant."

He directed his next words at the entire team, "Rhiannon did tell me that, as far as she knew, none of the adult victims owned or had access to a gun; but she hasn't been in close contact with them for some time. The bullets were heavy calibre. They were fired from a handgun. We can't be precise about the make because it's still missing. So far the divers haven't found anything in the lake but they'll be back at it first thing tomorrow."

He fumbled with some papers on the desk beside him, frowning as he stared at them. At last he carried on, "The only other thing about the crime scene where Colleen died is that SOCO found a trainer print in the blood, and a smudged area, as if someone had fallen, within a few inches of Josh Fortune. We don't know who this person is, whether it's the gunman or the person who made the triple nine call, or if they're one and the same. The rain held off this afternoon, but now it's pissing down. SOCO's working all out on this and our search teams are hunting through the night. At the moment our priority is the missing child."

Chapter 6

"The missing child's the brother of the other victims…" Mid-sentence Tyler felt himself lose momentum, what long-distance runners call hitting the wall. There was a sickening moment of blank dizziness. The sea of faces shimmered before his eyes. He knew he'd pushed his luck too far and his brain had taken itself to bed without him.

He tried again, "…two young boys. Barnabas and… DI Martin has been dealing with the family, she'll tell you about this."

Carefully he made his way to the edge of the room.

"Here sir." Someone had vacated a chair for him. He sat down. There was a bee colony buzzing in his brain. Somebody put a cup into his hand. He sipped. Instant coffee, heavily sugared. It tasted vile but he drank it anyway. The act of swallowing brought him partially back to life. He saw Nikki looking at him anxiously and realised she must have supplied the chair and drink. Nice girl and a bloody good cop. She could make it to the top if she wasn't tied up in her domestic life.

He tuned into Gill Martin's briefing. She must have covered the information about the state of the bodies and the missing toddler. She was telling the team about the family. "Barney was eleven, Timothy was ten and Charlie was… is almost four but he's got developmental problems and trouble communicating. I've requested an appointment with his paediatrician so we know exactly what we're dealing with. Their mother died over three years ago."

Tyler roused himself to ask, "When did Ian Quantrull marry Jasmin?"

"About six months ago."

"And their baby's four months. Is it a happy marriage?"

"I don't know, sir. It's an old-fashioned marriage. Ian

runs the family firm and Jasmin does the house. At least she does the flowers and the entertaining and looks after her baby. But they've got a girl who's a sort of nanny, she does some housework and looks after Charlie, as well as a gardener and a woman who comes in every day to clean."

"How the other half lives," commented Kerry Buller.

Tyler glared at her as ferociously as his aching head would allow.

Gill Martin said icily, "We're not here to judge their lifestyle, we're here to find out who murdered their kids." She turned back to Tyler. "It's hard to judge how good their marriage is. At the moment they're deep in shock and grief and crazy with worry about Charlie."

"Any sign of jealous lovers on the scene?" asked Luke.

Gill Martin shook her head. "Not so far."

"Any known connection between the two groups of people who were killed?" asked Nikki.

"None that we've found, except Jasmin Quantrull said she's bought clothes in House of Colleen occasionally."

"In where?" asked Luke.

"That's Colleen's shop," said Kerry. "Over-priced, pretentious, pseudo-designer wear."

"You mean out of your price-range?" retorted Luke.

Gill felt control of the briefing slipping away from her and was grateful when Tyler roused himself to ask, "Anything on the search of the grounds, Luke?"

"No sir. We've still got search teams out with flashlights. God knows what clues they're trampling but…"

"Finding Charlie's the thing that matters," impatiently Tyler finished the sentence for him. "What about the house-to-house?"

"Reg Rowner has still got men out. They're doing the house-to-house enquiries and searching nearby gardens in case Charlie's hiding somewhere. There's a set of allotments on the route between the Quantrulls' house and the park and they're going over them. All they've turned up is a sighting of a red car parked in a lay-by outside Stone Park." He came forward and pointed out the relevant entrance on the map.

Tyler said, "That's the exit near where the kids were killed. We got any other details about the car?"

"A middle-sized one, no make or licence number." Luke sounded apologetic.

Stuart Farrow chimed in, "Sir, remember the guy in the bushes the old lady mentioned?"

"Yeah?"

"I checked with the Council and they said they'd commissioned a sculptor to do some work in Stone Park, sort of posh it up."

"And?"

"He's got a red car and he's been hanging round Stone Park." Stuart flicked through his notebook. "His name's Daniel Peters. He's twenty-seven. He lives in the village of Crossbrook."

"Got money then," said Kerry.

Tyler ignored her. "Did you check him out?"

Stuart looked uncomfortable. "I sent uniformed but they reported he wasn't in. I'm sorry, sir, I didn't think he was a priority."

Tyler considered hurling a thunderbolt but it was too much effort. "Check him out and do it properly. Did you get anything useful from the Quantrull boys' school?"

"Not really, sir. Just that Tim, the ten-year-old, was the sharper one of the pair. No-one wanted to talk to me. I got the impression a constable who'd been to the local comprehensive was too common for them." Again he added, "I'm sorry, sir."

"That's okay." Tyler made a silent vow to see what the obstructive teachers made of a Superintendent who'd been to the local comprehensive. "The Press are co-operating in keeping quiet about the missing toddler."

"Miracles will never cease," commented Luke.

"The newsboys will toe-the-line in kidnap cases. They

42

don't want to cause the death of an abducted kid, or at least they don't want the public to think it's their fault. As far as we're concerned, the less the public knows the better."

"Are you sure that's a good idea, sir?" asked Stuart. "If the public are alerted it's more likely someone will spot the kid."

"Possibly, but we've got to weigh that against the likelihood of the guy who's got him deciding he's a liability and killing him. That's assuming Charlie's still alive. Remember this person has killed two kids already. We don't want to spook the bastard and we don't need any heroes walking in on a gunman and getting themselves and Charlie killed."

Kerry muttered something.

Tyler said, "You got anything you want to add to that, sergeant?"

"With respect, sir, you keep saying the 'gunman' and 'he', but is there any indication the person we're after is male?"

The temptation to pitch something at her smugly enquiring face boiled up within him. He overcame it. "For the extremely politically correct among us, I would like to amend that to gunperson and he/she. Now get on with your work."

He forced himself to his feet, cleaved his way through the dispersing cops, and went straight to his office, slamming the door behind him. In a case like this the first twenty-four hours were vital and he'd fumbled through six of them.

There was a knock on his door. He yelled, "Come!" The sound reverberated painfully in his head.

Gill Martin entered, looking nervous. "I've sorted out the work for the team but have you got any specific orders for me, sir?"

He stared at her helplessly. He knew he should have but he couldn't think.

"Do you want me to go back to the Quantrulls, sir?"

"Do you reckon they need you tonight?"

"I think they'd rather be left on their own. We've got men outside the house and we're monitoring their phones in case there's a ransom demand, even though the landline's ex-directory."

"Then leave it for tonight." Tomorrow he'd appoint a new FLO for the Quantrulls, his DI ranked too high to be sidelined.

Apparently Gill Martin had also been thinking about the Family Liaison situation. "Sir, I think we should take Kerry away from Rhiannon and Sophie Hughes. She won't get anything out of them or support them."

"Yeah. I only put Kerry in as a temporary measure because the others were already tied up. More fool me for thinking she'd get some useful background from Rhiannon Hughes. In future, at the start of a case, put her in charge of finds or collating statements, she's good with anything involving computers. Just bear in mind she's better with things than people." He knew he ought to tell her why Kerry was being so lairy but, at the moment, he didn't feel inclined to explain a decision he knew was right.

Gill nodded. "I'll ask Nikki to support Sophie and to deal with Josh Fortune if he makes it. Kerry can take on computer checks and help Luke with material finds."

Tyler had planned to tell Nikki to take on Jasmin and Ian Quantrull but tomorrow would do for that. Tonight he'd reached the end of the road. He forced himself to his feet. The room swooped and swayed around him. "You're in charge for the next few hours. Call me if anything major happens and make sure you run any dealings with the Media past the Press Office."

"Yes sir, of course. Where are you going?"

"Home." He managed to unhook his coat from the peg but he didn't attempt to put it on, two arms and two sleeves were likely to prove too challenging.

He was almost out of the building when a voice called,

44

"Sir, do you need a lift?" Nikki caught up with him. "I'm going back to the hospital. I'm sorry but I don't think you ought to drive."

As he'd mislaid his car, this seemed to Tyler to be eminently practical. "Thanks."

"It's cold tonight, sir." She took his coat from him and helped him put it on.

As they drove, she said, "Do you think there's hope of finding that little boy alive?"

"I don't know." Tyler thought he'd said those words more today than at any other time in his working life.

"It's scary. My husband often takes the kids to Stone Park. Thank God, today they were at the big *Save the Children* charity party in the Town Hall."

As her words flowed round him, Tyler felt a surge of panic. He couldn't remember what orders he'd given. "The lake... they are searching it for the gun or... anything?"

"Of course sir."

He felt like an idiot... a sick, thick idiot who was losing his grip.

"It's okay, sir, you just need a few hours sleep."

As she pulled up in front of his house he said, "Thanks Nikki." He got out and slammed the car door and, with approval, heard her click the central locking on.

The house was dark and chilly. Tyler fumbled for the light switch and pressed it. Nothing. He touched the hall radiator. Cold. Swearing he groped out the torch he kept for such emergencies and made his way into the kitchen. He stepped in a puddle of water and realised the fridge and freezer had defrosted. Stoically he sloshed his way to the sink, filled a glass with cold water and drank. Then he went upstairs, kicked off his shoes, dragged free of his coat and crawled into bed.

Chapter 7

As she opened her front door, Gill checked her mobile for messages and was glad to find none. It was only half-nine but it felt later. This had been a long day and, before she worked through the night, she needed some time-out.

She ran upstairs. Voices from the kitchen told her that Isabel's sister was visiting her. Disappointment lanced through her; she'd wanted Bel to herself.

"Hi." She switched on a bright smile as she entered the room.

Isabel jumped to her feet. "You must be shattered. I'll get your dinner."

"Sorry, no time for that. I'm just passing through but I could do with a cup of tea."

Isabel filled the kettle. It was clear she was anxious and Gill felt an overwhelming surge of love. She put her arms round Isabel and hugged her.

"Are you working on that murder in the park?" Bel sounded as worried as she looked.

"Yes."

Alana, Isabel's sister stood up, rescued the kettle and plugged it in. "I'll be off."

"No Lani, don't go." Gill knew this was perverse when she'd wanted to be alone with Isabel, but in a few minutes she'd be going back to work and Bel would be left alone to fret. "It just swept over me how you never know what's round the corner."

Lani nodded. "It's always worse when you think 'that could have happened to me.' When I heard the news, the first thing I did was phone Carys. I felt everything inside me churning until I heard her voice and knew she and Jack were safe." Her green eyes were troubled as she relived the fear she'd felt for her daughter and small grandson.

"How much detail is there on the news?" asked Gill. Spending so long with the bereaved parents had left her feeling isolated from the world.

"Just the bare facts." Again it was Lani who answered while Isabel busied herself making tea. "I expect there'll be more on the next news broadcast."

"Yes. I'm sorry Lani, I probably won't make it to your dinner party tomorrow."

"No problem."

To Gill's relief Isabel didn't protest, even though she'd been the one who'd insisted on this special celebration to honour Lani's fiftieth birthday and the new TV deal to serialise her books.

"I must change and get back to work. Superintendent Tyler's buggered off home."

"At the start of a murder case!" Isabel sounded scandalised.

"I'm not surprised," said Lani. "I saw him on the news bulletin earlier and thought he looked wrecked."

"What's he like?" asked Isabel.

Gill shrugged. "He wouldn't win any prizes for his sweet temper or charm but I think he's clever and everyone says he's the best SIO there is."

"I've seen him in Court and he's outstanding in the witness box," said Lani. "I'd guess he's a very intelligent man."

"What were you doing in Court?" demanded Isabel.

"Research of course. Don't worry they haven't caught me, I'm too smart."

Gill ignored Lani's frivolity. She said abruptly, "He was probably right to go home. He did look lousy. But that's not the point."

"What is the point then?" said Lani.

"I don't know if I can trust him."

"What do you mean?" Isabel's tone was sharp.

"Kerry Buller's a detective sergeant on his team and she

says he's a bastard who never gives a woman an even break."

"Are there any other women on the team?" asked Lani.

"Yes. Nikki Anderton seems to get on okay with him, but she's only a detective constable and she's graduate entry and about my age. Surely that must mean Tyler doesn't help women get promotion."

"Why don't you ask Nikki?" suggested Lani. "In fact why don't you suss out what the rest of the team thinks?"

Gill thought of the formality, close to hostility, she'd endured since she joined the team. "It's not that easy. Most of them are really standoffish with me. Kerry's the only one who calls me by my first name, the rest all call me Inspector, and one or two have actually called me ma'am."

Lani giggled. "It suits you. But have you considered maybe the others are stand-offish because Kerry's so pally?"

"What do you mean?"

"People are known by their friends. If the rest of the team aren't too keen on Kerry they're going to keep their distance from you."

"Kerry and I aren't friends," snapped Gill, then realised she was over-reacting because she had a suspicion Lani might be right. "But I will try and talk to Nikki."

She held out her hand to Isabel. "Come with me while I change. Lani, please stay and keep Isabel company."

"No problem." Lani picked up the TV remote. "I'll try and catch the News."

As they entered the large double bedroom at the back of the house Gill felt herself relax. This was the room that belonged totally to her and Isabel. Only people who knew their secret ventured upstairs to visit the cosy kitchen-diner. Downstairs they had two separate sitting rooms. It was there they enter- tained people who didn't know about their relationship. They had two front doors, labelled 12a and 12b.

Sometimes Gill wondered whether the secrecy was overdone, but Isabel insisted on it to protect her geriatric father from distress. It had been easy enough to keep their secret. They could go out together, as long as they weren't demonstrative and now caution had become a habit.

They'd been in love for twelve years but had only lived together for the last three, since Isabel's husband had died. Isabel had been too gentle to walk away from her marriage, and her husband had been a kind man. Not like Lani, who'd left her abusive husband years ago.

"Are you all right, love?"

Gill emerged from her thoughts. "Yes, I'm fine." She saw Isabel was picking up her dirty clothes and putting them in the washing basket. "You don't have to do that, Bel."

"I like to."

Gill wished she didn't have to go out again tonight. Isabel was so much her senior that, from the start of their relationship, they'd accepted it was likely, one day, Gill would be left alone. But now the swift eclipse of love in Stone Park clawed at her. She crossed the room and kissed Bel. "I do love you."

"I know." Isabel returned the embrace. "Come on, you've got work to do. It's no good complaining you don't get promotion if you don't put in the hours."

When they went back into the kitchen Lani was watching the television news. She turned troubled eyes towards Gill and said, "They've just given out the names of four of the victims. I've met Colleen and Sophie. Is Sophie going to be okay?"

"She should be. How well do you know her?"

"Slightly."

Gill knew she shouldn't talk about the case but she was certain Isabel and Lani were reliable and it was possible Lani knew things that would help. "There's a man who was shot as well. We haven't released his name because we haven't been able to track down a next of kin. It would help if we could get more information on him. His name's Joshua Fortune. Do you know him?"

She saw Lani's shock. "Oh God! Yes. Josh is a friend. We've taught together at creativity workshops. How bad is he?"

"He's seriously hurt. I'm sorry." Gill's professional instincts asserted themselves. "What's he like?"

"Talented, funny and kind, a lovely man."

"So you can't think of anyone who'd want to hurt him?"

"No..."

Gill picked up on the hesitation in her tone. "What are you thinking, Lani?"

"If you want to know about Josh, your best bet is to talk to Rhiannon Hughes, Sophie's mother. Rhiannon and Josh were in a relationship. They broke up about six years ago."

"Do you know why?"

"No. Josh didn't say much but it was clear he was desperately hurt and a few months ago he told me Sophie and her lover were making his life hell."

"In what way?"

Lani looked deeply troubled. "He said they were persecuting him."

Chapter 8

'*Light thickens and...night's black agents to their preys do rouse...*' Tyler jerked awake. Wrenching himself free of a dark, oppressive dream.

The time on his borrowed mobile informed him it was just before four a.m. He lay still for a moment, checking out how he felt. He decided he was much better, the mental fog had lifted and physically he'd be fine after a hot shower and decent breakfast. A memory intruded. He reached across to his bedside light; the switch clicked without offering illumination. He swore.

As he drew back he caught the shade with his hand and the lamp toppled and fell. He found his torch and turned it on. The china shepherd that formed the base of the lamp had been decapitated. Tyler surveyed the destruction with indifference. During their sixteen years of marriage his wife had furnished and refurnished the house to her capricious taste. Five years ago Vivienne had decided she no longer wished to retain Tyler or the house as part of the décor of her life. She'd packed eight suitcases and moved in with a boy young enough to be her son.

After her departure Tyler had carried on living in the house. His mood could best be described as stoic apathy. As things wore out or broke he replaced them or did without. But he'd rescued his books from exile in the loft and rehoused them in the drawing room on bookshelves he'd bought from the nearest shop.

He got up, stripped and showered. The icy water made him gasp but it sluiced any lingering cobwebs from his brain. As he dressed by torchlight he thought the clean clothes situation could soon become desperate. He'd have to phone an electrician as soon as possible. His household maintenance skills extended as far as changing a light bulb and no further;

somehow he'd never made time to learn these things.

He used his mobile to check with the Incident Room and heard that there had been no new developments. He decided to walk the three miles into work. A taxi would have got him there quicker and part of him felt guilty for wasting time, but he knew he needed the physical exercise and the mental space. At least he'd figured out where he'd left his car.

He stopped at an all-night stall and bought a sausage sandwich and mug of tea. He gulped down the tea then ate as he walked. The air was sleet-filled and bitterly cold. He thought of little Charlie, lost in the darkness, and hoped, against all reason, that he was still alive and being kept somewhere sheltered, and that he was not too hideously afraid.

The Serious Crimes Office was buzzing; everyone still working flat out. As he entered Gill Martin's office she looked up, surprise clear on her face. "Good morning sir. Are you feeling better?"

"I'm fine. Any developments?"

"Nothing major. No sign of little Charlie."

Tyler pulled up a chair and sat down. He wondered whether he'd called it right to put a total media blackout on Charlie's disappearance. Perhaps if they'd got the public looking they'd have found the kid by now. If only there was something to get hold of, some hint as to why this had happened and who'd taken that little boy.

"What about Sophie Hughes and Josh Fortune?" he asked.

"Sophie's still sedated but she's doing okay. And Josh Fortune's still alive." A slight frown creased Gill's forehead.

"What's wrong?"

"It may not be relevant, sir, but a friend of mine knows Josh Fortune. She said Josh and Rhiannon were together for some years and Josh was devastated when they split up. Recently Josh claimed Sophie and Colleen were persecuting him."

"Persecuting? That's a strong word. What did he mean?"

"I don't know but my friend said Josh Fortune's a thoroughly nice guy."

"That's all hearsay but we'll bear it in mind. Can your friend's account be trusted? Is she the sort of person who doesn't see faults in people she likes?"

Gill's face lit up in brief amusement. "No, Lani's not like that."

Tyler noted the unusual name and the certainty with which Gill spoke. He questioned neither. Again he thought she could prove an asset to his team.

"We need as many insights into these people as we can get. For starters what were Sophie and her lover doing in the park with her mother's ex-boyfriend?"

He paused and examined his last sentence suspiciously. To his relief, on close inspection it appeared to make sense.

"I'll ask Lani, sir, but I'm pretty sure she can't answer your last question or she'd have told me."

This time he indulged his curiosity. "I've never heard the name Lani before."

"It's a shortening of Alana."

"What else do we know about Josh Fortune?"

"As well as being a performer, he's a peripatetic teacher. One of his colleagues mentioned, wherever he was working, he was in the habit of eating lunch in a local park."

"Does that mean he goes to the park to eye up kids or just likes eating outdoors?"

Gill shrugged. "His DBS clearance is in order, for what that's worth."

There was a knock on the door and Stuart entered. "The team searching the allotment by the park have found something."

Tyler felt tension knot his stomach. "What?"

"A piece of wood, sir. A branch from a tree. It's got blood on it and a few hairs."

"Oh God!" Had the killer run out of bullets and battered

little Charlie to death? But, if so, where was his body? "What colour was the hair on the branch?"

"Fairish, sir."

"Charlie's hair is brown," said Gill.

"It's hard to tell the exact shade of the sample, ma'am. It's smeared with blood."

Tyler noted the formality of Stuart's tone and made a mental note to check Gill had a suitable working relationship with the team. "Where's this wood now, Stu?"

"With Forensics, sir. I told them you'd want it processed as top priority."

"You told them right."

"They're processing Charlie's DNA," said Gill. "SOCO took samples from his house."

Tyler nodded. "Remember this doesn't have to be Charlie's blood and hair. Someone else was there. They made the emergency call. Stu, get onto Forensics and make sure they match up the blood sample from that wood with all the other blood found in the park."

"Yes sir. I got a description of Daniel Peters, the artist who's been hanging round Stone Park, and he's got fair hair."

"I did better than that. As soon as I got in, I went to his website and printed off a photograph." Tyler held out a picture of a flaxen-haired, handsome, young man.

Gill flushed. "I should have told Kerry to get onto that. I'm sorry."

"No problem. You had enough to deal with." Kerry shouldn't have needed telling. He planned to point out to DS Buller it was time she stopped sulking about her failure to get promotion or he'd have her off his team. "Stu, print some copies off to pass around. And get someone to bring my car back from Stone Park."

"No problem, sir."

"Cheers." Tyler tossed the keys to him and he left.

Gill Martin looked puzzled. "Do we think Daniel Peters was at the park and he was the person who made that triple nine call, and then got clobbered by the killer? If so where's he gone? And where's Charlie? It doesn't make sense."

Tyler scowled at her. "Nothing about this bloody case makes sense."

Chapter 9

Gill tried to think of something to say or do to demonstrate that she was a pro-active and high-achieving DI. Nothing came to her.

The phone rang and Tyler answered it. Gill was irritated, after all this was her office.

Tyler said, "Yes speaking... Yeah, I'm fine... Thanks Nikki, I'll be right there." He put the phone down. "That was Nikki. Sophie's awake and we should be able to interview her pretty soon, so let's get moving."

"Moving sir?"

"Don't you want to hear what Sophie's got to say? I certainly do."

"Yes sir. But didn't you want me to go back to the Quantrulls?"

"The Quantrulls?" He looked puzzled, then she saw understanding dawn. "Putting you as FLO was a stop-gap. When I saw the way Kerry was reacting to them I couldn't leave her there. I'll get a junior officer appointed to support them as soon as I get back. Though God knows where I'll find a suitable one, we're stretched pretty tight."

For Gill that put a different slant on things. Perhaps Tyler didn't intend to sideline her. "I'd like to keep close contact with the Quantrulls. They're beginning to trust me."

She thought she saw approval in his face but he just said, "Fine. Now let's get moving. Sophie Hughes may be able to turn this case around."

"Yes sir." Gill jumped up and grabbed her bag and coat.

"You'll have to drive."

"No problem."

As they walked along the corridor she said, "Excuse me," and headed into the Ladies. Constant cups of coffee kept her alert but they were hell on the bladder.

Emerging from the cubicle she encountered Kerry, engaged in make-up repairs. "Hi Gill. Any joy?"

"Sophie Hughes is well enough to talk. The Superintendent and I are going to see if she remembers anything."

"You're honoured. I guess he needs a chauffeur."

Gill felt angry. Lani was right, she should never have allowed Kerry to get away with that sort of remark. She said crisply, "Don't talk about the Superintendent like that, Sergeant. Now get on with your work."

She stalked out of the cloakroom before Kerry could reply.

"I don't know what happened. I didn't see anything." Sophie's blue eyes were enormous and her pinched little face was as white as the dressing on her head. Her left shoulder was heavily bandaged. With her right hand she clung to her mother's fingers.

"That's all right, Sophie. Can you tell us what you do remember, please?" Tyler sat down on a chair beside the bed. His voice was gentle but Gill thought it was impossible to mute the strength and masculinity that were an intrinsic part of him.

"I remember everything! I just didn't see anything worth remembering!"

"Okay Sophie, try to relax. Shut your eyes and try to think back to being in the park. Now, tell us what you did see or hear. How were you sitting, you, Colleen and Josh?"

"Josh was on the left side of the bench; Colleen was sitting on the right and I was kneeling on top of her."

"Do you mean you had your knees on the bench and were sort of straddling her?"

Even as he spoke, Gill saw Tyler registering his mistake. The word 'straddling' was ugly. Worse it carried a sub-text of condemnation. Sophie turned her face away from him, tears trickling down her cheeks. Gill expected her mother

57

to protest or to make some gesture of comfort but Rhiannon stared at her daughter, her face unfathomable.

Gill felt a surge of indignation. Sophie was a victim not a villain. Tyler would be treating her differently if she'd been in a heterosexual relationship. She eased herself forward and crouched down so she wasn't towering over the bed. "Sophie, are you saying you were facing Colleen and didn't see anything?"

The softness in her tone brought Sophie's head round to look at her. "Yes."

"But you must have heard something?" As she spoke, Gill was aware of Tyler slipping out of his chair and stepping back to leave her in pole position. She knew she'd pay for this later but at least he wasn't shoving her aside to reclaim the questioning.

"Not really. Colleen and I were… talking."

"Tell me what happened, Sophie. Use your own words and take your time."

There was a long silence. Gill waited, afraid Tyler might try to hurry things along, but he was equally patient.

When Sophie started to speak her voice was younger and more childish. "Josh got up and started to walk away. Then he said, 'What the hell?' and jumped up on a bench. Then he jumped down and said, '*Get out of here.*' And Colleen started to argue. She said something like, '*You can't tell me what to do.*' Then she screamed and grabbed Sophie. She held so tight Sophie couldn't turn round. Then there was a bang and something punched Sophie in the shoulder. Sophie doesn't remember anything else."

Her voice trailed into silence. Gill struggled to assimilate not merely the information but Sophie's macabre way of delivering it. She glanced at Tyler and saw his heavy features were creased in a puzzled frown.

Rhiannon said quietly, "Sophie often used to talk like that. When things got hard she'd decide to be a spectator looking on." Her soft voice, with its lilting Welsh accent, seemed remarkably matter-of-fact.

Tyler bent down and muttered in Gill's ear, "See if you can find out about the time before the shooting."

"Did Sophie see anyone in the park before she heard the bang?" said Gill.

She received a look of incredulous indignation. "I'm not stupid. Don't talk to me like I'm a little kid."

Gill felt like she'd been slapped. She said crisply, "Did you see the children in the park? Two boys and a toddler?"

"No. But I think I heard them shouting."

"And did you hear or see anyone else in the park?"

"Only that man."

Gill struggled to stop her voice rising, "What man was that?"

"A man under the trees, taking photographs. I didn't really like him being there but I didn't say anything. Colleen hadn't noticed him. She'd have been angry. I hate it when Colleen makes scenes."

"What did this man look like, Sophie?"

"Fair-haired, not much older than me, quite nice looking. But don't you know? Haven't you spoken to him?"

"Not yet. We're still looking for him." Gill took the picture Tyler passed to her. "Is this the man, Sophie?"

"Yes!" Sophie's voice was shrill. "Was it him who killed Colleen? Could I have stopped it happening if I'd said something?"

Tyler answered quickly, "We don't know. He may have been hurt and wandered away. Can you think of anyone who would want to hurt you or Colleen?"

Eyes lowered she shook her head.

Tyler bent and murmured instructions in Gill's ear. She said, "Sophie, did either of you have another lover before you were together? Someone who might be jealous?"

"Colleen had a lover but she wouldn't hurt Colleen."

"What's her name?"

"Anita Coldstream. But she'd never hurt Colleen."

59

Gill moved on to the next of Tyler's low-voiced questions, "What were you and Colleen doing in Stone Park?"

Sophie didn't answer but Gill saw her stiffen. It was a risk but she decided to push the matter. "Did you know Josh would be there? Had you arranged to meet him?"

"Sophie didn't know." She silenced herself and, with an obvious effort, began again, "I didn't know. Colleen told me to meet her there. When I got there, I knew... but it was too late. I couldn't run away, not when Colleen wanted me to stay."

"Why did Colleen want you to stay?"

Sophie looked past Gill as if she hadn't heard the question. "Colleen wouldn't listen to me... she wouldn't believe me... she wouldn't stop it... she hated Josh so much." She closed her eyes. "I'm tired. I don't want to talk any more."

They trailed out, leaving Nikki with Sophie. To Gill's surprise, Rhiannon left her daughter and followed them.

In the corridor, Tyler said bluntly, "Rhiannon, do you know why Colleen and Sophie were meeting Josh in the park?"

"When you first told me where it happened I wondered about that. Colleen wouldn't usually leave the shop on a weekday. But now I can guess. Under her calm façade Colleen was a very tumultuous woman. She loved and hated passionately. She hated Josh and she'd do anything she could to torment him."

"Can you think of anyone who'd want to kill Colleen?"

Rhiannon opened her mouth then shut it again. Eventually she said, "No."

"What were you going to say first time round?" asked Tyler.

Rhiannon smiled. "I almost said, *'Apart from me?'* But I didn't because I realised how cheap it sounded."

"Would you have liked to kill her?" Gill thought Tyler sounded mildly interested rather than condemning.

"Sometimes, but I wouldn't have done it."

"Would Josh have liked to kill her?"

"Josh isn't the violent type."

Tyler didn't follow through. He seemed inclined to take Rhiannon's word for it. Irritated, Gill surged into the attack, "Even if he was pushed that inch too far? If a man's tormented, eventually he might break. Perhaps Josh killed Colleen and tried to kill Sophie and then attempted to kill himself."

Rhiannon stared at her. Her blue eyes looked deep and dark, like still water in a mountain lake. "If he was pushed too far, he might have killed himself. Possibly he might have lashed out at Colleen. But he wouldn't hurt Sophie and he'd never have harmed those two little boys. That's not a statement of faith, that's a statement of fact."

She turned on her heel and went back into Sophie's room.

As Gill followed Tyler out of the hospital he said, "About the way you took over the questioning, you played it well."

"Thank you sir." Praise was the last thing she'd expected.

She saw Tyler's swift gleam of amusement and knew he'd sussed out her thoughts.

Chapter 10

"Daniel Peters," Tyler repeated the name in a tone of savage frustration. They were back in his office and it was nineteen hours since Charlie had disappeared.

"Didn't his neighbours know anything?" asked Gill.

"It's the sort of village where nobody knows anybody until they've lived there for three generations. And Peters is an artist. Not the sort they like in Crossbrook."

"So what do we know, sir?"

"He was pretty successful until the last year or so. I gather he's had some sort of breakdown, which explains why he's reduced to doing sculptures for local parks." He rubbed the back of his neck and shrugged his shoulders, trying to ease tense muscles. "Anyone tracked down his ex-wife?"

"No sir. She's not at her flat. The girl who lives next door says she's off with her new boyfriend. By the way she's not officially his ex-wife yet."

"So where have we got to?" asked Tyler. A pile of newspapers had been left for his information on his desk, he registered the date and groaned inwardly. This didn't have much potential to be a happy birthday.

"The house-to-house enquiries turned up a few regular park-goers," said Gill. "They were shown the pictures. Nobody remembered seeing Colleen or Sophie there before but a few said they'd seen Josh Fortune. And there were several IDs of Dan Peters."

The phone rang. Tyler picked it up and snapped his name.

"It's Stuart, sir. I'm at the hospital. I was going to relieve Nikki."

"Yes?" Tyler felt greyness press down on him, he was sure he was about to hear Josh Fortune was dead. "Hang on." He switched to the speaker-phone. "Go ahead."

"An ambulance has brought in a man with head injuries. It's Dan Peters, and there's a little boy with him. I'm sure it's Charlie."

"Alive?"

"Very much alive. He's screaming the place down."

"How badly is he hurt?"

"He's not. At least the hospital staff don't think he is. They're having problems examining him, he's kicking and punching and throwing himself about. They're getting a consultant paediatrician to check him out."

Tyler knew he should feel relief, instead he felt numb. "Get Nikki down to keep an eye on Charlie and you stick with Dan Peters. How bad is he?"

"They're not sure yet. He's unconscious. He's got a head injury and he's close to hypothermia. He'd taken off his sweatshirt and jacket and put them on the kid to keep him warm."

"How did they end up at the hospital?" asked Gill.

"Apparently Peters phoned his wife. He was pretty confused but she tracked him down to this cottage where they once lived. It's derelict now. When she found them she dialled for an ambulance."

"His wife?" said Tyler. "But they're practically divorced."

"I don't know about that, sir, but she's here and fighting for him like a..." Stuart paused, clearly searching for a suitably descriptive word, "She's seriously scary."

For the first time since he'd started on this case Tyler felt a twinge of grim humour. "Scary wife or not, you stay with Peters. DI Martin and I will be along straight away."

"Yes sir."

Tyler put the phone down. "Come on."

In the main office he paused by Kerry's desk. "Get out to the Quantrull house and ask Jasmin and Ian Quantrull to accompany you. Take them straight to the hospital. Keep the radio turned off and ring me when you get close."

"Yes sir. What's going on?"

"You'll find out when you get there." Tyler saw the flicker of anger on Kerry's face. She probably thought he was paying her back for her insolence yesterday. Maybe he was. But he needed Gill Martin at the hospital and he was determined to keep this information on a need-to-know basis.

He set a fast pace out to the car park but Gill kept up with him. Give her due credit, the girl had staying power.

"Did you get any sleep last night?" he said.

"Not much, sir, but I'm okay."

"Make sure you take a break if you need it."

"Sir, was it necessary to be so harsh?"

"With your mate Sergeant Buller, you mean?" he said, deliberately obtuse. "She wouldn't like it if I was politer to her than the male members of the team."

"Kerry Buller's not a mate, sir. And I didn't mean you'd been harsh to her. I meant the Quantrulls. Surely they have the right to know we've got Charlie back?"

"Another half hour won't kill them. And we don't know for certain it is Charlie until they identify him. I want to make sure we've got maximum security in place before we let anyone know we've found him."

"You think someone could try and hurt him?"

Tyler shrugged. "If Daniel Peters is an innocent bystander, he and Charlie are the best potential witnesses we've got."

"But Charlie's a small child and he can't talk."

"We know that but maybe the killer isn't so well informed. I'm not taking any chances with Charlie's life."

When they reached A&E, Stuart met them at the door of the Visitor's Room that had been placed at their disposal. "Mrs Peters is in there, sir. She keeps demanding to be allowed to stay with her husband."

"I need to talk to her first. And I want to hear this message she says caused her to track him down."

"Here, sir. I told her we'd need to hang onto her phone."
He handed Tyler the mobile. *'Hannah... please help me...
I'm at our old cottage... I feel so ill...' a long pause and then,
'My head hurts.'*

Tyler played the message through twice then said, "I'll
talk to her. Stu, you get back to Daniel. Gill, check out how
Charlie's doing, please."

He shut the door on them, to Gill's clear annoyance and
Stuart's equally obvious relief.

Hannah Peters was a slightly built girl, no more than
five-two in height, with a cloud of soft brown hair. No
tough young cop should have classed her as scary but
Tyler understood Stuart's nervousness. The eyes she turned
towards him sparked blue fire and her white teeth chewed on
her lower lip, as if she wanted to bite.

"What exactly do you think Dan's done wrong?" she
demanded.

"We don't know exactly what Daniel has done. But he
must have witnessed something in Stone Park. And, for some
reason, he took away a young child."

"He didn't hurt him! Dan wouldn't hurt anyone. He was
concussed... confused. Daniel's not like that."

"Like what, Mrs Peters?"

She met his gaze defiantly. "Like you people are
implying."

Tyler noted she didn't reject her married title. He guided
her to a seat and said, "What is he like?"

She scanned his face and seemed to decide his question
was not frivolous or snide. "Controlled, non-violent,
passionate about his work, ambitious but thoroughly decent."

"Was the separation and imminent divorce his idea or
yours?"

She flushed. "Mine."

"May I ask why?" Tyler did not add 'when you're so
obviously crazy about the guy' but it was implicit in his tone.

The rose deepened to scarlet. "If I won't tell you, you'll

think Dan did something awful."

"Possibly."

"The truth is Dan was so passionate about his art, so deeply involved in it, I felt there was nothing left over for me. I thought I'd be happier with someone else. Someone who was focused on me." The bright colour drained leaving her ghost white. "Today it took one short phone call to convince me I was wrong. I should have picked up when he called. I could have talked to him. If he doesn't recover I missed my last chance."

"It's not your fault. If you're asleep you can't always get to the phone before the answer service kicks in."

Her colour flared again. "I wasn't asleep. I was screwing my new boyfriend."

By the look of things that was her ex new boyfriend. Tyler reviewed the best possible thing to say… or the least offensive. DCI Aron's favourite phrase was: 'I'm not here to judge you,' which always seemed to imply he had the right to do so if he chose. At last he settled for, "Thanks to you they got medical help before things got any worse. Hannah… may I call you Hannah?" She nodded assent and he continued, "I'd be grateful if you could fill in some background details. Daniel's twenty-seven, isn't he? Has he got any close family, apart from yourself?"

She looked doubtful. "He's got parents and four brothers but he hasn't seen them for years. They didn't like him choosing to do art. All his brothers are in the army."

"Dan seems well-off, not exactly a struggling artist."

"He inherited some money from his grandfather and put it into a commercial gallery. And he's a successful artist. He gets international commissions for his sculptures."

"I see. How long have you been married?"

"Six years."

"Do you have any children?"

"No."

"And your job is?"

"Nothing high-powered. A lot of temp work. At the moment I'm working for a travel agency."

"I'd have thought a girl like you would have a career in place by now." Tyler hoped she wouldn't think he was being patronising.

"It's funny you should say that. I've been thinking of going back to college and picking up some more qualifications. I married Dan when I was eighteen, a few weeks after I left college, and his work meant we were always moving round."

"Eighteen's pretty young. How did your family feel about that?"

Tyler had no idea what he was looking for, just hoping to get some sort of handle on Dan Peters and his life.

She shrugged. "My parents are old-fashioned working class. Even in the 21st Century there are people who think a girl's best career is to be married, especially if she can snare a guy with money."

Tyler conceded that could well be true. Of course, it was different when a rich bitch decided to marry her bit of rough; the way it had been with him and Vivienne.

"Hannah, can you think of any reason why Daniel should have taken Charlie away like that? Concussed or not it seems a strange course of action."

She looked troubled. "I can think of only one reason. He must have believed he was protecting him."

He didn't ask why Daniel had stripped the child. Stuart had told him Charlie had been soaked. And Daniel had endangered his own health by replacing Charlie's wet clothes with his own.

His phone rang. He answered and Kerry said, "There in five minutes, sir."

"Right." Tyler keyed off and got to his feet. "Hannah, thanks for your help. I assume, until the divorce becomes final, you're still Daniel's next of kin?"

She looked surprised. "I suppose I must be."

"Then I'll leave it up to you to decide whether to contact

his parents."

He met Gill in the corridor. "How's Charlie?"

"Not good. They're hoping his parents might break through the trauma, but they've got to be warned any approach has got to be calm and gentle, otherwise he could flip entirely. I've already warned Kerry to keep it cool."

She said the last words quietly as they reached the door to Charlie's hospital room. Kerry was waiting there with Jasmin and Ian Quantrull. Unshaven and crumpled, Ian looked like hell, but Jasmin was immaculate. The words of a 16th Century poet slid through Tyler's mind.

"Pardon sir?" said Gill.

"Nothing." He hadn't realised he'd spoken aloud. It embarrassed him.

Wrong-footed, he lost the opportunity to say the carefully prepared words that would lessen the shock to the parents.

The roars from inside the room started up again.

Ian Quantrull said, "Charlie!" He flung the door open and charged into the room.

Caught off balance, Tyler staggered.

Jasmin followed her husband. As they entered, the child stopped screaming. He stared at them, then he pressed back against the metal bars of the hospital cot. He looked like a baby rabbit trapped by predators.

Ian plucked him from the cot and hugged him. Jasmin moved slowly forward and reached out towards the little boy. A second's pause, when all hung in the balance, then Charlie stiffened in his father's grasp. He screamed and carried on screaming.

A nurse rushed forward but Jasmin pushed her away.

Tyler stepped in. "Please Ian, let the nurse have him. Move back, Jasmin, you're scaring him."

He was unprepared for Jasmin's fury. Eyes blazing she leapt at him, claws raking down his face. Her screams mingled with Charlie's.

Gill hauled Jasmin away and Kerry placed herself in

front of Ian Quantrull. Jasmin stopped screeching, started sobbing, and allowed Gill to lead her to a chair.

After a brief hesitation Ian passed Charlie to the nurse. The child's screams grew more penetrating.

"I'll call the paediatrician back down," said the nurse. She glared at Tyler as if it was all his fault, which he guessed, it was.

In the silence that followed, Kerry murmured, just loud enough for Tyler to hear. "Somehow I don't reckon that approach was calm and gentle enough."

Chapter 11

"How's it going then?"

Gill wondered why Kerry always seemed to be lurking when she arrived at work. Perhaps she had the Station entrance bugged. She was the sort of cop who liked to know all the gossip. Despite Gill's rebuke a few hours ago, she seemed friendly and eager for a chat.

"It's going okay, I suppose," said Gill. She'd spent most of the afternoon with Jasmin and Ian Quantrull at the hospital. "They've sedated Charlie and I've persuaded his parents to go home. The girl who helps with their kids is staying on overnight to look after Polly in case they need to go back to the hospital."

"Was there any more aggro?"

"No. They seem bewildered. Especially Ian. He's being very protective of Jasmin. He wouldn't let her stay at the hospital by herself."

"Probably scared she'll flip again and have a go at someone else. She bloody nearly had the Bossman's eye out."

Gill had only caught a glimpse of Tyler's face, the row of scratches sprouting tiny beads of blood, then he'd walked out of the room and left her and Kerry to supply damage control. "She was distraught."

"Yeah. Posh cows are the same as us common bitches when the claws are out."

Gill wasn't convinced she liked being rated with Kerry as a common bitch but the posh cow status didn't have much going for it either. To her surprise, Kerry had been really helpful after the incident, although her incisive questions about Jasmin's medical history had shocked Jasmin out of hysteria and into huffiness.

Remembering this, she asked, "Have you told the

Superintendent it's okay regarding HIV and stuff like that?"

"Yeah, straight off, as soon as I saw him."

"What have you been doing this afternoon?"

"Helping go through Colleen and Sophie's flat and Josh Fortune's bedsit."

"Anything useful?"

"Not that we could find. And I went with the Boss to the post-mortems. We've only just got back." For once Kerry sounded subdued.

"Ah, Inspector Martin! And you too Sergeant! What a fortunate coincidence. I was hoping to have a word with you."

Gill thought it was too fortunate a coincidence to be a coincidence at all. However one doesn't accuse the Assistant Chief Constable of laying in wait for female detectives. "Yes sir?"

"It's concerning the incident at the hospital this morning."

"Sir?" Gill played for time.

"A fracas involving the Quantrull family."

"Not a fracas, sir. A misunderstanding."

"Rather more than that. I've had a journalist on the phone, asking me whether Superintendent Tyler used callous shock tactics on this bereaved family, subjecting them to increased emotional trauma."

"It was nothing like that," said Kerry. "Jasmin Quantrull got hysterical. She was frightening the kid and when the Superintendent tried to reason with her she flipped."

"I see. Thank you Sergeant, that will be all." He waited until Kerry was some distance along the corridor. "Gill, you're not a permanent member of Superintendent Tyler's team. You're not bound by the same long-term loyalties that constrain DS Buller. Can you assure me there's no truth in this journalist's claim that, by Superintendent Tyler's orders, no-one warned the family Charlie had been found?"

Gill knew if she had concerns this was the time to voice them. Instead she said, "Superintendent Tyler wished

71

Charlie's discovery to be kept quiet until suitable security measures could be put in place. The child's safety was paramount. The parents heard him crying and pushed their way in before we could warn them."

The ACC looked sceptical. "I see. Thank you for your account of the matter."

The wisest course would be to accept her dismissal but she resented being put in the position of informer. "Forgive me, sir, but shouldn't you discuss this with the Superintendent rather than with his subordinates?"

The ACC's voice was icy, "Thank you for your advice, Inspector. I have already spoken to the Superintendent about this matter."

"Yes, sir." Gill knew she'd earned the snub. You don't intervene in a battle between gods.

As she entered the Main Office Kerry pounced on her. "Is the Lord High Executioner still out for Tyler's blood?"

Gill knew she was really asking whether Gill had snitched. "I told him Superintendent Tyler had acted for the safety of the child. I didn't expect you to stand up for him."

Kerry shrugged. "You know what it's like in a team. It's like a family. You might have your squabbles but you don't go loud-mouthing about 'em to the rest of the world." She grinned. "Anyway, if Tyler gets grief the chances are he'll share it, he's generous like that." She looked across to where Tyler had just emerged from his office. "Here we go. Talk of the devil and you hear the sizzle of his pitchfork."

"The what?"

"Pitchfork. When he's using it to cook sausages in the fires of hell."

"More likely giblets," said Gill, thinking that Tyler appeared willing to disembowel anyone that got in his way. He looked savagely bad-tempered and the scratches on his cheek glared vividly on his grim face. She glanced at her watch. "I wonder how long this will take."

"You got a date?"

"Not exactly. Just dinner at the Tudor House with some friends."

Kerry whistled appreciatively. "The Tudor House, very posh."

"It's a friend's birthday." Gill dropped into her technique of giving enough information to satisfy curiosity without letting anyone inside her life.

Tyler raised his voice, "Right, listen up you lot. This isn't a proper briefing. We'll do that tomorrow morning. But I thought I'd bring you people up to speed. As you know, we've got Charlie Quantrull back. He's under sedation but there's no sign of physical abuse or injury. Daniel Peters, the man who took Charlie away, is suffering from severe concussion and won't be fit to talk until tomorrow at the earliest. We've no way of being certain whether he was involved in the shootings or why he took Charlie, but all the medical and forensic signs indicate Peters was struck on the head, from behind, by someone using a tree branch. That was abandoned some distance away in the allotments. It's possible, in his dazed state, he believed he was safeguarding the child. We've recovered a camera from Daniel Peters' car. The photos give us a pretty clear idea of what was going on in the seating area a few minutes before the shooting."

He handed the pictures to a young uniformed officer who pinned them to the board. There was a long silence, then Luke said, "You don't get much more explicit than that."

The pictures showed three people on one bench. Sophie was straddling Colleen's lap, melting into her as they kissed. Beside them sat Josh Fortune, arms folded, staring straight ahead.

"It shows motive for Josh Fortune. You can see how angry he is," said Kerry, but she didn't sound convinced.

"But Sophie made it clear the killer wasn't Josh," objected Gill. "There are too many loose ends. And what about the boys? Why should Josh kill two innocent witnesses if he planned to top himself?"

"That's a good point," agreed Tyler. "I'm not sure I'd believe everything young Sophie says, but DI Martin did an excellent job of interviewing Sophie this morning, and Nikki has spent most of the day with her. When Nikki phoned me she said Sophie has kept her story consistent. The chances are it's fundamentally true. What did you reckon to her?"

The question was directed at Gill. It took her by surprise. "I don't think she was lying. But she's a disturbed girl."

"No argument there." Tyler turned back to the team. "Sophie gave us the name of someone who's definitely worth looking at. Anita Coldstream. She used to be Colleen's partner in both senses of the word. Now she lives in London. When she and Colleen split up, she kept a monetary interest in the shop. Apparently she was upset when Colleen wanted to buy her out. I've spoken to Colleen's lawyers and they tell me Colleen has left everything she possessed to Sophie. We don't know whether Anita was aware of that or not."

"You want Anita Coldstream brought in, sir?" asked Luke.

"I certainly want someone to talk with her. Kerry, are you up for a quick trip to the Smoke?"

"Sure sir."

"Take a uniformed officer with you. It's too late to catch Anita at her office, so check what she's up to and, if it all looks secure, make an appointment to speak with her tomorrow morning. Then you can get a few hours sleep. When you see her, ask what she was up to at the relevant time. She's a solicitor so tread carefully. I'll phone through and do the courtesy bit and warn the London force you're on their patch."

"Yes sir."

"I think that's all we can do for now. I suggest everyone gets a good night's sleep." Tyler got out a mobile and passed it to a young uniformed constable. "Thanks for the loan. I got a new one this afternoon."

He took a marker pen and wrote upon the board. "I've

kept my old mobile number, so this is for the information of anybody who hasn't got it. And, before anyone even thinks of it, I do not need it supplied to Chinese Take-Aways or Escort Services."

Hastily Gill recorded the number, then looked up to ask, "Sir, about the post-mortem results?"

"Tomorrow." The single word emerged as a snarl.

"Yes sir." She glared at his back as he returned to his office.

"He'll only go through the post-mortem results once, with the full team," said Kerry.

"Oh I see."

"He don't let on but he hates that sort of thing." She moved across to wipe away Tyler's number. "Leave it there and he'll be getting crank calls and expect me to use computer magic to track 'em down." She grinned at Gill. "You should be pleased we've finished early. You'll be able to get to your meal."

"True." Gill checked the time on her mobile. It was almost seven, so she'd have time to nip home and change. It would be good to have an evening free from murder and cops.

Chapter 12

As Tyler left he saw Kerry was still working. Hopefully that meant she was coming out of her sulky strop. He paused by her desk. "I'm off now. Keep me informed how it goes with Anita Coldstream." His stomach rumbled. It was a long time since his early-morning sandwich and he couldn't remember eating lunch.

Kerry must have heard. She grinned. "A word of warning, the canteen's doing their Pasta Surprise Bake. The surprise being no-one wants to eat the bloody thing. That means they've run out of chips. I'd get a take-away if I was you, sir."

"Cheers." Tyler didn't expect much of his birthday but he resented spending it eating a take-away in his cold, unlit house. "You don't know anywhere decent to eat, do you? Somewhere quiet. Not a cop pub."

"You could always try the Tudor House, sir." Kerry smiled brightly at him. "I hear it's pretty good."

The Tudor House was a glitter of sparkling chandeliers, gleaming silver and pristine tablecloths. Tyler was the only diner sitting alone. He knew that labelled him as a sad git without a social life. Well, socially, a sad git was what he was and there was no escaping it. He ordered steak, with treacle sponge pudding to follow and a bottle of wine. He'd walked here and he'd take a taxi home.

The restaurant was half empty. Not surprising at those prices and in the middle of the week. As he finished his meal a family party left, revealing a group of four women who were sitting quite near to him. A movement of withdrawal caught his attention and he focused on Gill Martin, seated at the far end of the table. She met his eyes and glared at him defiantly, then said something to her companions.

One of the women turned to face him. She smiled. "Good evening, Superintendent."

"Good evening."

"Would you like to join us? You're very welcome."

He felt his face heat up. The shyness he'd buried but never beaten overwhelmed him and he said brusquely, "Thanks all the same but I'd rather not."

She smiled again, then turned back to her party and the chatter revived. Tyler couldn't hear what they were saying but he found his gaze drawn back to them. The woman who'd spoken to him was plump and middle-aged. Her short brown hair was softly spiced with grey and she wore a dark-red dress. He thought she was aware of his scrutiny; again she turned towards him. As their eyes met he longed to go over and ask if he could change his mind and join them. He flushed and looked away.

When he surveyed them again he did so more cautiously. The girl sitting opposite the friendly woman must surely be her daughter; their hair was the same woodland shade, although the younger woman's held no hint of frost.

The other middle-aged woman was thin and had determinedly dark hair. She stood up, apparently proposing a toast. She raised her glass. "Here's to Mrs Robinson." The woman who'd smiled at him shook her head in laughing remonstrance.

Tyler's anger was overwhelming; so black, cold and vicious it was like a wave smashing over him, drowning all control. His chair crashed back and he covered the distance in four strides. "Can't you leave anyone's private life alone? I hope your joke was worth it, Inspector, because you're off my team."

He turned on his heel and left the restaurant. It was cold outside and he staggered as the wine hit his brain. He shivered. He'd have to go back to get his coat and pay his bill, but he'd sort out a taxi first. He sat down on a low wall and got out his mobile.

"You'll catch your death." The brown-haired woman approached, carrying his coat.

"Leave me alone!"

Undaunted she draped it round his shoulders. "The manager trusted me to bring your coat out to you. I told him you'd be back in a minute to pay your bill."

Tyler didn't know what to say and so he maintained a sullen silence.

"I'm sorry we upset you, but what exactly did we do?"

He tried to work out if she was in earnest. Her green eyes gazed back unwaveringly.

"It was that joke... that bloody song... I'm so pissed off with it."

"What joke?"

"Mrs Robinson. Don't pretend Gill Martin didn't tell you. After five years I thought it would have bloody well died down."

She rummaged in her bag. "One of the things we were celebrating was this."

He focused on the book she was holding: *Here's To You Mrs Robinson*.

"I write crime novels," she explained. "This is about a middle-aged, female PI. It was dramatised on TV recently and the publisher had to rush through a new paperback edition of the book."

Embarrassment overwhelmed him. He dredged words from the depths, "My wife left me for a kid half her age, a constable on my team. Everyone thought it was so bloody funny. No-one said anything to my face but everywhere I went someone seemed to be whistling or humming that bloody song... you know, from *The Graduate*." His voice wobbled on the last words.

"I don't think it's funny. I think it must have hurt you very much, and still does."

He stared at her, then thrust his hand hard against his mouth. Mockery had strengthened his bitter, self-absorbed control, but gentleness was undermining it.

After a minute he said, "I don't even know your name."

"Lani Scott."

Tyler remembered Gill Martin speaking of her the other day. "I'm Kev Tyler. Won't your friends be worried about where you've got to?"

"Probably. Is it a sign you're getting old when your kids start looking after you?"

He gazed at her. Despite the greying hair and the lines around her eyes and mouth, she was vibrant and youthful. "You're not old."

She smiled at him. "It's nice of you to say so, but it's my birthday. I'm fifty and a grandmother."

He thought how unusual she was. From thirty onwards, Vivienne had denied her true age. "It's my birthday too. I'm forty-six and I've got nothing to show for it."

"Nonsense. You've reached pretty near the top in your job."

For years he'd claimed that was enough but the depression that had been circling him forced him to say, "But it's not the best thing in the world, is it?"

She glanced back to where her daughter was standing in the doorway of the restaurant. Seeing her silhouetted by the light, Tyler realised she was pregnant.

Lani said, "No, it's not the best thing, at least not for me. But a good career's not the worst thing in the world either." She tugged him to his feet. "However, catching pneumonia on our birthdays ranks as pretty bad. Come back inside."

Chapter 13

Tyler allowed her to lead him back into the restaurant. In the doorway she said, "Everything's fine, Caz."

The girl smiled. "I assumed it was but Aunt Isabel was driving me crazy so I volunteered to come and look for you."

Lani laughed. "That's my girl. This is Kev Tyler. Kev, this is my daughter, Carys. Now come and join us."

Tyler hesitated. Walking away was always easier than returning, especially when you'd made a fool of yourself.

Lani had taken off her coat. Before he could frame a suitable refusal, she hooked Tyler's from his shoulders and hung up both garments. "Come on, Kev."

As they approached the table she slipped her hand through his arm and pre-empted all protest by saying brightly, "Misunderstanding sorted. It's Kev's birthday too and I've invited him to celebrate with us."

The dark-haired woman said, "Lani, you've no right to bring that man back here."

Tyler attempted to retreat, but Lani's grasp on his arm tightened. "I've every right to invite who I want to my birthday celebration. Kev, you already know Gill and this is my sister, Isabel. Bel, stop looking so sour, you'll turn the champagne into vinegar."

"Lani, how dare you bring that homophobic bastard to join us?"

"Homophobic?" Tyler echoed the word. He stared at Isabel then turned to look at Gill. They glared at him defiantly. Understanding dawned. He gazed helplessly at Lani. "I didn't..."

"I know that. For God's sake sit down, Kev. The manager's getting twitchy. I think he's expecting us to create another scene."

Tyler was grateful for the wording that didn't declare

him solely responsible for the recent contretemps. He accepted the chair Carys had dragged into place between her own and Lani's.

He saw Isabel's lips open and braced himself for another harangue but Lani got in first. "Isabel, shut up and turn your brain on. Until you told him, Kev didn't know Gill was a lesbian. He was angry because he misunderstood something we said and thought we were being lairy about his personal life."

"He didn't know? I told him? Oh Gill, I'm so sorry!"

Tyler mentally measured the distance to the door but he abandoned the idea of making a break for it. Lani seemed to be the sort of forceful woman who'd herd him back again. Anyway, he couldn't leave the situation with Gill Martin dangling until they encountered each other at work.

"For God's sake stop trying to turn this into the last act of Hamlet," begged Lani. "It's not that big a deal."

Gill and her lover turned their troubled eyes on Tyler. He felt spaced out but he recognised his cue. "I'm not interested in your private life. And you're not off the team. I'm sorry. I was angry. I thought you were getting at me."

The silence that followed these words seemed to go on forever.

Lani's voice was sharp with exasperation as she said, "Gill that's the best apology the poor man can give you and if you've got either sense or decency you'll say 'that's okay, sir, we're both tired and uptight.'"

Gill glanced at Isabel's rigid face, then she smiled at Tyler. "I'm sorry if you thought I was being nasty but I wasn't. Your private life's your own business and so's mine."

"If that's sorted, can we get back to enjoying ourselves?" enquired Lani.

Gill nodded and signalled to the waiter to bring another glass. She filled it with champagne and passed it to Tyler. "Cheers sir."

Lani leaned towards him and murmured, "Is that a good idea?"

"Probably not." With the sane part of his mind he knew champagne was unlikely to mix well with red wine but at the moment he didn't care.

Isabel proposed the toast, "To Lani, happy birthday and many more of them." She gave Tyler a sideways look, "And here's to Mrs Robinson."

Tyler raised his glass and drank.

As soon as the toast was over, Carys stood up. "I must go home. I promised I wouldn't be late. Does anyone want a lift?"

"Please." Gill was clearly eager to be out of the situation.

"Yes," said Isabel. "We ought to get home. We were later having dinner than I planned."

This complaint seemed to be directed at Lani. She glared at Isabel. "I warned you I was going to phone Gareth before I left."

Carys intervened. "I'm off. Are you coming Aunt Isabel?"

"Yes, of course." Isabel also rose. "Lani, are you ready?"

Lani glanced towards Tyler. Green eyes met amber. A question was asked and answered, so mutual it was impossible to separate the strands of the exchange. Without turning her head she said, "Thanks Isabel, but I'll stay on. Us birthday people want to celebrate, don't we Kev?"

"Before we get totally past it," he agreed.

"But Lani…"

"Isabel, get over it." The sharp note was back in Lani's voice.

Carys interrupted, "Come on Aunt Isabel, leave Mum to have fun." She kissed her mother, "Good luck with the book signing tomorrow."

"Thank you, darling."

Carys smiled at Tyler. "Happy birthday."

Tyler watched as they crossed the room to get their coats. He got the distinct impression Carys was ushering her aunt. He thought that it was very obvious that Carys was Lani's child.

Lani laughed. "Caz looks like a sheep dog making sure a recalcitrant ewe doesn't double back."

"What was all that about?"

"Call yourself a detective! That was Isabel trying to prevent her wild little sister from making an idiot of herself with an unsuitable man. But don't take it personally, Isabel considers all men as a sub-species."

"I gathered that. What I don't understand is why your daughter was encouraging you to put yourself on the line?"

He expected a light answer but Lani said seriously, "Caz makes me brave. She's the most empowering person in my life."

"I wouldn't have thought you needed encouragement to be brave."

"You know what they say about appearances?"

"Yeah." He knew how little of his true self he revealed and how exhausting it was to keep up his defences. Concern for Lani's safety made him say, "You shouldn't follow strange guys into dark car parks."

"You weren't really a stranger. I knew who you were."

"Who's Gareth?" He had no right to question her but he was desperate to know. Who was the man so important to her that she'd be late for her birthday dinner rather than miss out on talking with him?

"My son. He's spending a gap year travelling. At the moment he's in New Zealand." She grinned at him. "As you'll have gathered, Isabel doesn't approve. She's always been the 'life is real, life is earnest' type... Is your face sore?"

He realised he was fingering the gouges on his face.

"It's nothing. I walked into something."

"I read in the local newspaper about what happened at the hospital, or at least what the reporter said happened, which is probably a long way from the truth."

"It is."

He knew he couldn't tell Lani about it; he'd never discussed his cases with anyone who didn't have a right to know, but he was desperate to set the record straight. He didn't want her to think he was a bastard, at least not more of a bastard than he was. He gave her an abridged account of what had happened.

Lani listened quietly, her hand resting on his. He wound up dismally, "I meant to warn Charlie's parents but I got distracted."

"What distracted you?"

He felt embarrassed. "Just something I thought. Something bloody stupid."

Her hand slipped into his and squeezed. "Tell me."

"*'Still to be neat, still to be drest'*... it's a line from a poem."

"*'As you were going to a feast.'* Ben Jonson. Why were you thinking that?"

"I don't know. It came into my head the moment I saw Charlie's stepmother."

"Did you think she was taking it all too calmly?" asked Lani.

"Well if I did, I was bloody wrong. She was obviously on a knife-edge and I made her lose control. If Charlie ends up permanently traumatised it'll be my fault."

"That's nonsense and if you weren't so tired you'd know it without me telling you."

"It's what your mate Gill thinks."

"Gill knows nothing about kids."

"She knows as much as me then."

She looked at him, suddenly intent. "Kev, what's hurting you so much?"

Chapter 14

Tyler wondered how much of the list Lani was prepared to sit through. Today had been a marathon and the post-mortems hideous. But there was something else; personal and humiliating he couldn't lock into the drawer labelled *Crap at Work*.

"I got a birthday card from my ex-wife, the first card she'd sent since we split up five years ago. She wanted to rub in how happy she is with her toy-boy. They're going to have a baby."

He'd read the message, then screwed it up and threw it in the bin but the taunting words were etched inside his brain.

Dear Kevin,

I wanted to let you know that Gavin and I are expecting a baby very soon.

We're so incredibly happy. With all good wishes.

Vivienne

"Did you want children?" asked Lani.

"I wouldn't have minded. But Vivienne didn't want any, not when she was with me."

She put her arms round him. Her perfume was fresh, not overpowering like Jasmin Quantrull's and the similar flowery scent Lani's sister had worn.

He heard Lani say, "Thank you. Leave it there. I'll pour." A clink indicated a tray was being put down. The waiter with the coffee. He thought the way he'd behaved this evening, it was a miracle he hadn't been asked to leave.

He moved away. "Sorry. I must be more drunk than I thought."

"And exhausted and uptight and hurt by your bitch wife."

"I shouldn't be. We're divorced. It's over and finished now."

She shook her head. "Separation and divorce are a sort of

bereavement and if you don't mourn they fester inside you."

"Oh, so that's what hurts?" Tyler put his hand on the pain that was drilling through the mid-point of his chest.

"No, I'd guess that's indigestion. That was the Share-a-Sweet treacle pud you ordered." She rummaged in her handbag. "Chew these."

He put the tablets into his mouth. "Lani, are you single, divorced or widowed?" He was sure she'd have told him if she was in a relationship.

"I'm divorced and widowed. If you can be a widow after you've been divorced. I've never been too sure."

"I've never known anyone like you."

"In what way?"

"The way you came out into the car park after me. And the way you put your arms round me just now."

"I don't like misunderstandings and people hurting each other. And I've never seen a guy more in need of a hug than you were."

"You shouldn't take chances like that. Someone could take advantage." It occurred to him that she could be as drunk as he was.

She giggled. "You mean hugging a man within an hour of our first meeting could be misinterpreted? You know, I thought that myself, but I did it anyway. Never mind, I've never done it before and I'm pretty sure I won't do it again. And every crime writer should hug at least one top cop. It's an essential part of research."

He stared at her, uncertain at what level she was taking the piss. "What did your daughter mean about the book signing you had to do?"

She pulled a face. "I'm in the book shop on the High Street with my new book, *'Song of the Innocent.'* I'm not keen on crowds but, of course, if it's your event it's much worse if nobody turns up."

"*Song of the Innocent*," he repeated the title thoughtfully.

"It's about a group of children who band together to

kill their abusive grandfather. It's the darkest thing I've ever written and I don't know if it will come off or if my regular fans will hate it and I'll have to scurry back to my usual style." Then, with an abrupt change of subject, "Kev, there's one thing I really want to know."

"What's that?"

"Are there many top detectives who get distracted by Elizabethan poetry?"

He'd got nothing to lose in explaining. "I'm an English Literature graduate. Sometimes lines from poems arrive in my head."

Her eyes mocked him. "Kev, you admitted that as if it was a crime."

Tyler acknowledged the truth of that observation with a rueful grin. "It's not actually a crime but it's not the sort of thing you spread around."

"That's what Gill says about her relationship with Isabel."

"I reckon these days being a lesbian's regarded as less weird than reading poetry."

In the last twenty-five years, since he'd become a cop, he'd walked the line between two very different and potentially hostile worlds. His University tutor, disappointed at his refusal to work for a PhD, had made waspish comments about his ambition to emulate a character created by PD James. The few cop colleagues who'd sussed him out had been less subtle and a great deal more profane. But no-one had been as hurtful as his wife. He still winced at the memory of the dinner party, soon after their marriage, at which she'd led the laughter as she described his reading tastes to a circle of her friends. Looking back, he realised every movement of withdrawal on his part had provoked fresh acts of hostility on hers.

He hauled himself back to the present. "I've never talked to anyone like this before."

She smiled. "Don't worry, Kev, I won't tell anyone."

"I know that." He thought it strange how sure of this he was.

Chapter 15

It was after eight in the morning. Gill looked around the Incident Room and frowned. The briefing had been scheduled to start fifteen minutes ago, but one element was missing, a vital one. Gill crossed the room to Luke Warden, "Have you seen Superintendent Tyler?"

"Don't think he's in yet." Luke turned back to his paperwork.

Gill didn't know what to do. There were over twenty officers crowded into the room, obviously impatient to get on. There was none of the usual chatter, still less any hint of laughter; cops could joke about most things but not the slaughter of kids.

She wondered whether she should start without the Superintendent. Was he still in bed nursing a hangover? What time had he got to bed? And whose bed had he got to? Why did Lani have to make life so complicated?

"Haven't you started yet? For God's sake, I expect you to show some initiative." The words were snarled as Tyler strode past her. "Stuart, get my notes out of my office and let's get this show on the road."

The silence as he reached the Information Boards was instant and absolute. Tyler looked bilious and bad-tempered as he hurled words at them. Gill thought it felt more like a ram raid than a team briefing by the SIO.

"Right. There have been several developments in the night. The doctors reckon Daniel Peters should be able to talk to us this morning. Also the doctors have examined Charlie and they say there are no signs of physical or sexual abuse." He held out his hand for the file Stuart was offering him. His voice slowed slightly as he said, "The pathologist has completed the post-mortems and confirmed all the victims died from gunshot wounds. Ballistics have got back to us on the bullets. The gun used was a handgun that fired .45 calibre bullets but they can't be specific about the make or how many bullets it could fire."

Gill said, "How many bullets have we recovered, sir?"

"Six but that's no use unless we know how many bullets there were to start with."

"But all of the bullets hit, didn't they sir? SOCO couldn't find any others. Surely it must mean the killer's a good shot."

"Competent certainly but remember most of the victims were shot from close to. Forensic evidence indicates Josh Fortune was probably grappling with his assailant."

"What about forensic traces on his clothes?" asked Luke.

"His clothes were handled by a lot of people in A&E, they're still being checked." Tyler glanced round to see if there were any more questions, then continued, "Forensics are up against it, especially with Timothy falling into muddy water. That's buggered up a lot of trace evidence. They can't work out which group of people were shot first but they haven't found anything to contradict Sophie's limited version of events. However Sophie says she doesn't remember hearing any shots from the adventure playground."

He glanced at Gill, who said, "I'm not sure I'd place too much reliance on that. She's a self-absorbed girl, not the sort who noticed much until it affected her."

He nodded agreement, then said, "Thanks," as Nikki handed him a mug of tea. "Now on to the next move in the game. Sophie told us about Colleen's former partner, Anita Coldstream. She's a solicitor in her late thirties. She and Colleen were together for eight years and she took it hard when Colleen switched her affections to Sophie. I understand she made some threats, but people often scream they want to kill someone without meaning it. Anyway the person she threatened was Sophie not Colleen. Last night I sent Kerry up to London to talk to Anita.

Gill could see he was angry but his tone was level, "There was a muck up in communications and Anita heard we planned to interview her. She tried to top herself. She cut her wrists. Fortunately, Kerry thought there was something dodgy going on and got access to her apartment in time to save her. I was called in at a godforsaken hour to go up there. I've just got back. So I'd advise none of you to give me grief today."

His eyes met Gill's and she felt herself flush. "Do you think she's our killer?" she asked, holding his gaze.

"God knows. At least He may do. I don't. Kerry phoned me to say Anita Coldstream has discharged herself from hospital and she's agreed to accompany Kerry down here for questioning. They should be here in the next few minutes. Apart from that it's the usual slog. Stuart, you stay with Daniel Peters and don't let that wife of his prime him with what to say. I'll be along to talk to him as soon as I've seen Anita Coldstream. Nikki's staying on with Sophie and her mother and keeping an eye on Charlie. The detailed background checks on all of our victims and their families are complete but we're none the wiser. If we're assuming one or more of our victims was the intended target, we've got to work out which one."

Stuart said hesitantly, "Sir, it may be nothing, but I got the impression the boys weren't doing that great at school. But, like I told you, the teachers weren't exactly opening up to me."

"Okay. I'll check out the school when I get a minute. Gill, you spend as much time with Ian and Jasmin as you can and keep your ears open for anything that might help."

A phone rang. Luke answered it and said, "It's Kerry, sir. She's got Anita Coldstream in the interview room downstairs."

"Tell her I'll be with her in ten minutes. Right everyone, get moving. The ACC has assured the Media we're on the verge of a breakthrough, so we'd better make it happen."

As everyone dispersed he spoke to Gill. "My office."

Gill followed him, wondering if he was going to refer to

their meeting last night.

In his office Tyler sat down and gestured her to a chair. "We've been having fun and games with our London colleagues."

Gill felt a surge of relief that this wasn't personal. "What happened, sir?"

"As a matter of courtesy we informed the relevant cops in London about the state of play. The DCI saw fit to spread the word throughout her team. Anita Coldstream is very active in Gay Rights. One of the CID officers is a lesbian and a friend of Anita's. She called on Anita last night to warn her she was about to be interviewed."

Gill thought perhaps it was personal after all. "Who is this officer, sir?"

"Detective Sergeant Corder."

"I've never heard of her, much less met her, sir."

Tyler stared at her. "I never thought you had!" She saw his anger kindle. "This is me filling you in on the stuff I'm not telling the lower ranks, nothing else."

"I'm sorry, sir."

"So you bloody should be."

"How did Kerry suss out this tell-tale cop?"

Tyler gave a reluctant grin. "Kerry's the sort who gets her teeth in a thing and doesn't let go. She didn't like the attitude our colleagues were showing her, so she decided to wait outside Anita's flat. She saw the CID sergeant leave and got suspicious."

"That was smart of Kerry."

"Actually it was smart of the constable she'd got with her, Ryan Jones."

'You mean spirited bastard.' Even as Gill formulated the thought, Tyler said, "Kerry said Ryan noticed her car. Young Ryan's a car fanatic and I gather DS Corder's car is something special. Anyway, Ryan recognised the car as one he'd seen outside the police station. Kerry phoned through and got the owner's ID and that set alarm bells ringing. When

she couldn't get Anita to answer her door, she and Ryan broke in. They found Anita lying on her bed, dressed up like she was going to a party, with deep gashes on both wrists. They got her to the hospital and Kerry phoned me."

"What time was that, sir?"

"Around four this morning. I sent for a police driver and went straight up there and I've been soothing ruffled feelings ever since."

Gill tried to imagine Tyler as a diplomat and failed. "But they're in the wrong, sir. It's their detective sergeant that's behaved unprofessionally."

"That makes them even angrier. Their DCI has fought long and loud to get more women promoted in CID and this sergeant was one of her protégés." He shrugged. "It doesn't matter whose toes we've squashed. They'll get over it. But we're going to interview Anita Coldstream pretty soon and I want to know how to go about it."

"Yes sir?" Gill kept her voice calm but inside she was seething. She might have guessed he'd take advantage of his knowledge.

He met her gaze without bravado or embarrassment. "I need to know if Colleen was the intended victim and whether Anita Coldstream was responsible for what happened. I think your input could be useful."

He didn't say, 'Your sensibilities don't matter when we're investigating a murder case.' He didn't need to. Gill knew he was right. She was being over-sensitive because she felt vulnerable. "I'll do my best, sir."

He nodded. "Come on then, let's get on with it."

Chapter 16

Anita Coldstream was as white as the bandages on her wrists. Frail and elegant, she sat in her chair with a tightly controlled grace. There was an artificiality about her poise. Gill wondered whether it had its roots in her physical weakness or in her emotional instability or, possibly, in her awareness of her guilt.

As they entered, Kerry stood up and retired into the background. Tyler noted that she didn't leave. Trust Kerry to stick where the action was. He didn't tell her to get out; she'd travelled down from London with the suspect and her input could prove useful. He introduced himself and Gill to Anita and she acknowledged them with a nod. She'd not asked for legal representation, presumably she thought her own expertise was sufficient.

Tyler sat down opposite her. "Miss Coldstream, I'd be grateful if you'd tell us where you were on Tuesday between one and two p.m."

"At home, working on some papers."

"Can anyone confirm this?"

"No." Briefly her smile mocked him. "It will be up to you, Superintendent, to prove I was not."

He met her gaze stolidly. "Do you possess, or have you ever possessed, a gun?"

"No."

"Even though you lived in America for some years?"

"Even so."

"Please tell us about your relationship with Colleen Holebrook."

"That can be swiftly done, Superintendent. There has been no relationship for almost three years."

"And before that?"

"Before that we were lovers." Her voice was soft.

"And you were business partners as well?"

A gesture of dismissal. "I put money into her business."

"Wouldn't it be nearer the truth to say you helped her to set it up? Without you she wouldn't have got established, would she?"

Gill had to admit Tyler was good. His tone was just right, not overtly sympathetic but respectful, that of a top professional talking to one of his own kind.

Anita nodded agreement and he continued, "So what happened to separate you?"

The pale face twisted. "That little bitch got her claws into Colleen."

"Sophie Hughes? But Sophie was hardly more than a child when they first got together. How could Sophie out-manoeuvre a successful, clever woman like yourself?"

Anita glared at him and Gill thought he'd played it wrong, but it seemed her wrath was still directed at Sophie. "That's what I thought. It was what Colleen said to me, *'Love, she's just a child who has been betrayed by those who should have looked after her.'* By the time I realised she'd bamboozled Col with her tears and lies it was too late. But she never made Colleen happy, not the way she was happy with me."

"Have you had any other relationships since you and Colleen split up?"

"No." A single desolate word.

"You must have been angry when you realised Colleen wanted to buy you out of the business in order to leave it to Sophie."

It was one step too far. Gill saw Anita's lawyer's brain click into action. The measured words were cool, "It made no difference. Colleen had left me anyway."

"You never said you'd rather see the shop burned to the ground than let Sophie have it?" Tyler's voice was still level.

"People often say foolish things they don't mean."

"Like you'd rather Colleen was dead than with Sophie?"

94

"I never said that! I never wanted Colleen to die."

"No, it was Sophie you wanted dead, wasn't it?" The rapped out question made all the listeners jump. "You wanted Sophie dead, so Colleen would turn to you for comfort."

"No!" Gill watched as Anita struggled for control. "I don't have to answer any more of your questions and I'm not going to."

"As you wish, Miss Coldstream, but, if you're innocent, your best course of action would be to help us clear up this matter. I'd like permission for my people to search your house, car and office."

"I don't want people pawing through my things."

"If you won't give permission we've enough evidence to get a warrant. The threats you made against Colleen and Sophie give us grounds."

"You bastard!"

"That sort of abuse will get us nowhere. I'd prefer to settle the matter discreetly but, if you won't co-operate, I'll proceed in any legal way I can."

She pushed herself jerkily to her feet. "You'll pay for this, Superintendent."

"You mean the way Detective Sergeant Corder's paying?"

"Cheryl Corder? What have you done to her?"

He countered her question with one of his own, "Why did DS Corder come round to your flat?"

"She didn't." Anita Coldstream sat slowly down again.

"That's a lie, Miss Coldstream. She's already admitted it. You're an intelligent woman. You must have known we'd be talking to you. You didn't need DS Corder to warn you of that. What did she really want?"

She stared at him in blatant bewilderment. "I don't understand you. Cheryl is a friend. She came to comfort me."

"How good a friend? How far would she go for you?"

Gill thought Tyler's voice was like a dentist's drill, harsh and persistent as it probed into tender spots.

"I don't understand," repeated Anita. "What do you think Cheryl did for me?"

"I think she took something away for you. A gun, or maybe some bloodstained clothes. Like I said you're a clever woman but maybe, like a lot of clever people, you underestimated the opposition. Did we move too fast for you?"

"No! Cheryl did nothing wrong. She's just a friend."

"An expensive friendship. It's going to destroy her career."

"Cheryl did nothing wrong!" Her voice was ragged, close to a screech.

Gill lowered her eyes, hating to see this composed, intelligent woman fall apart.

Tyler carried on relentlessly, "In that case, I suggest you give us permission to search. The only thing that might help DS Corder is your full co-operation."

She looked at him with hatred. "Very well."

Tyler's voice powered down, "Why did you try to kill yourself, Anita?"

"You wouldn't understand."

"Try me."

With a visible struggle she regained self-control. She took a deep breath and sat back, hands resting on the chair arms. Everything about her declared the brittleness of her poise and how much it was costing her. "I didn't want to talk to anyone about Colleen. I didn't want to fight with Sophie about the business. I didn't want to sully the few good memories I had left." Her voice grew fainter, barely audible. "I'm so tired of living without her."

Chapter 17

"So what do you reckon?" said Tyler as he sat down behind his desk. His gaze turned from Gill to Kerry and back again to Gill.

"I'm not sure," she said. "But I believed her when she said she didn't want to kill Colleen."

"You're probably right. The question is whether she tried to kill Sophie and buggered up. That would be reason for her trying to kill herself. Kerry, what do you think?"

"I'd guess she could be ruthless. At the moment we're seeing her weak and vulnerable but I was talking to some of the cops in her district and they reckon she's as tough as they come."

"You happy to run with this? We need someone up there for the search of her flat."

Kerry flashed her cocky smile. "No problem, sir. We're not exactly flavour of the month since we showed up DS Corder's games, but I can cope with that."

"Try not to tread on too many toes but don't take any crap. You'd better get back up to London straight away." He stood up, muttered, "Back in a minute," and left.

Kerry grinned at Gill. "What's up with him then?"

"What do you mean?"

"If it was anyone but Tyler, I'd reckon he'd got a raging hangover."

Gill wondered why Kerry was asking her. Had someone spotted her and Tyler in the same restaurant last night? "What do you mean anyone but Tyler?"

"He doesn't drink, not in any normal sense. Even when he comes down the pub after a result he only drinks a pint and then switches to orange juice. But, give the devil his due, he's not mean, he always buys a couple of rounds."

Despite her cocky manner, Kerry had been keeping

an eye on the corridor beyond the open door, now she got hastily to her feet. "There's Alka Seltzer in my desk drawer. Dare you to offer him it." She left on the last words.

"You still here?" said Tyler as she passed him in the corridor.

"On my way, sir."

Tyler entered and sat down again. He scowled at Gill. "You got anything to add to 'I'm not sure'?"

That morning, as she was leaving, Isabel had said, *'Don't let that chauvinist bastard bully you.'* She bit down her instinct to apologise for not having all the answers. "I think Anita could have done it but she knows the burden of proof's on us."

"Yeah. She seemed confident we can't prove she had a gun. And, who knows? That may be the simple truth. It's not easy to bring one into the country illegally nowadays. You feel like making some coffee?"

Gill felt relegated to the status of tea lady, but she went and made instant coffee and brought it back to Tyler's office. She edged his mug onto a corner of his chaotic desk.

"Milk sir?"

"No thanks." Tyler sipped, then swore as the hot liquid burned his mouth. "Shut the door." She obeyed and he said quietly, "I need to talk about your personal life."

Gill sighed. The time had come to make her position clear. "I don't keep my relationship with Isabel secret because I'm ashamed of it. But my private life is my own business and nobody else's."

"And I want it to stay that way."

"What do you mean?"

"I want you to make sure it stays private until this case is finished."

She stared at him. For a moment she didn't understand, then anger swept through her. "I'm not DS Corder! I'm not a security risk!"

"If I thought you were you'd be off the team right now.

At this point in time, DS Corder has soured things for all homosexual cops and we've got enough pressure on the team as it is. This isn't the sort of case that makes it easy adjusting to a new DI and I want your private life kept quiet. Above all I need you focused. I don't want you to have to deal with the sort of aggro some arseholes will hand out."

There was a knock on the door and he yelled, "Come!"

Kerry reappeared. "Sorry to bother you, sir, but Anita Coldstream says she won't go back to London with us. Do you want us to push it?"

"No. Thank her for her co-operation and let her go. I've got some detectives on loan from other teams, get one of the girls to follow her."

"Yes sir. Would it be okay if I took young Ryan back up with me for the search? After all he's the one who spotted DS Corder's car."

Tyler scowled. "What do you think we're running, a rewards scheme for car fanatics? Okay, take him, but don't waste time faffing round up there."

"Yes sir." Kerry left, pulling a commiserating face at Gill from behind the shelter of the closing door.

Gill was sure Tyler was aware of the silent communication but he said, "Tell the cops guarding Sophie to keep alert."

"You don't think Anita would be crazy enough to have a go at her?"

"No but it would be bloody embarrassing if she did and we weren't ready. If she meant to kill Sophie and got Colleen, the lady may have nothing left to lose." He glanced at his watch. "I've got to get over to the hospital as soon as Stuart phones through. I don't want Daniel Peters to say too much until I'm there to hear it."

"Could I sit in on that, sir?"

"No. I need you back with the Quantrulls."

She knew she'd offered to stay in contact with the bereaved family but surely an hour's delay would make no difference? Resentment made her reckless. "If you don't want me in the loop, I'd rather go back to DCI Aron's team. I don't like the way you keep side-lining me."

"Side-lining you? I'm trusting you with the hardest job of all."

"What?" Gill's voice rose in sheer astonishment and she saw Tyler wince.

"Do you have to screech?" he demanded irritably.

"Sorry. But what do you mean about me having the hardest job?"

"It doesn't matter. It's just an idea that I'm not ready to share yet."

Gill wondered if this was the typical senior officer game; telling the troops they were indispensable to keep them in line. DCI Aron had used that technique and fooled no one, but Tyler wasn't Aron and any games he played he'd be good enough to win.

She reigned in her anger and forced herself to speak moderately, "Sir, I'd like to know what you're thinking that you haven't told us."

"I think a lot of things, most of them way off beam, that's why I don't share them until I've thought them through." His frown deepened. "I've learned the hard way. I've done it before, said something stupid and some wanker goes off half-cocked and acts on it."

Before she had time to think Gill found herself saying the unspeakable, "I'm not a wanker, sir, I'm a dyke, and I don't go off half-cocked."

Chapter 18

If nothing else Gill had the dubious satisfaction of shocking a Detective Superintendent who was widely held to be unshakeable. For a second Tyler's expression showed surprise, but this was swiftly replaced by a look of grim humour. "Thanks for that, Inspector, it's duly noted."

"Sorry sir." Gill couldn't believe she'd said that. Years of discretion blown away by one smart-arse remark.

"Don't be. I'm glad to see you can put yourself on the line." He must have read Gill's thoughts. "I'm the boss. I'm allowed to keep my mouth shut."

"Yes sir," said Gill in her demurest tone.

"And you can learn the difference between having your say and taking the piss out of the SIO."

"Sir, what's worrying you about the Quantrulls? I'll try not to let it prejudice me."

"It's nothing I know. It's just a thought that's been niggling at me all along. It fully hit me last night, in the restaurant, when Lani was talking about her new book." His voice was a shade too casual and he failed to meet Gill's eyes.

"*Song of the Innocent?* I haven't read it yet." Gill was surprised. He'd only just met Lani, surely he hadn't talked to her about the case?

"It made me focus on something. That first day, in the park, before we knew Charlie was the third child, I wondered if another child could have been responsible, but all along we've considered Tim and Barney as innocent victims. Last night it hit me... we don't know that for sure."

Gill stared at him. "You think the boys could be the killers?"

"It's possible."

"But Ian Quantrull swears he's never owned a gun."

"Certainly there's no record of any gun licence," agreed Tyler. "But that's true of everybody we know of who's involved in this case."

Now Gill knew what was wanted, she felt ready for action. "I'll see if I can have another less formal chat with the Quantrulls' nanny and the cleaner."

"Yeah, people who work in a household know a lot more than their employers realise. The trick is getting them to tell you what they know."

"I'll give it my best shot. But, if the boys did it, what happened to the gun?"

"That applies to just about anyone who was on the scene."

"It could still be the work of a random killer who's topped himself in some remote place and we haven't found his body."

"I don't reckon it's a spree killer. It hasn't got the right signature. I wish I could believe it. The best thing that could happen is for that phone to ring and someone tell me they'd found a dead killer, still clutching the gun, and he'd written a suicide note containing a full confession." He added peevishly, "Or should I say he-dash-she, in case the politically correct lobby are listening?"

"I think we're safe enough in here. Unless Kerry's bugged your office."

"Wouldn't put it past her."

He rubbed his forehead and Gill felt unwilling sympathy. He'd been stupid to drink too much last night but he was one of the best detectives she'd ever worked with. And it wasn't just the professional side of things. Lani was a friend and Lani liked this man. Gill wondered what Lani would want her to do in this situation but most of the answers scared her. Lani had a talent for spontaneity that Gill lacked. She decided on a lower risk strategy.

"Excuse me, sir." She went along the corridor to the water cooler, filled a plastic cup, then raided Kerry's desk.

She took the fizzing mixture back to Tyler and put it down in front of him.

For a moment he considered her through narrowed eyes, clearly alert for subtle insolence, then he picked up the cup and gulped the contents down.

"Okay," he said. "Convince me I'm wrong."

She sat down again. "I can't. There's a lot of sense in what you're saying. The kids weren't happy. They didn't get on with Jasmin and she didn't like them. I overheard her telling Ian he'd always spoiled them and she knew they'd end up in trouble."

Tyler scowled. "Not the most sensitive thing to say."

"There's a lot of stress in their relationship and Jasmin's the hysterical type."

"Tell me about it." He fingered the scratches on his cheek. "How neurotic is she?"

"It's hard to tell. Death by violence alters everything. Do you think the boys went on a killing spree and then topped themselves? Or did Tim go crazy? Barney was running away when he was shot."

"Maybe, when it came to it, he didn't fancy taking the final ride."

"But why attack Colleen and the others? If it was Jasmin they hated why didn't they kill her?"

"Who knows? Maybe they decided to kill the first adults they got a chance to blow away. When I say they, I really mean Timothy."

Gill nodded acceptance. Barney's body had yielded no traces of gunpowder on his hands or clothes but Timothy had fallen into muddy water and the forensic evidence had been compromised.

"Our forensic people are sure the hat we found beside the body was used to hold the gun," said Tyler. He rummaged through the papers on his desk, selected a report and handed it to her. "It belonged to Timothy, but that doesn't prove anything. Kids leave things lying around and anyone could have picked it up and used it to hold the gun."

"What about Tim's wound? Could he have killed himself?"

Again Tyler searched through the reports. "According to the pathologist the wound's, 'Not inconsistent with suicide.'"

"But Timothy was only ten. If he struggled with Josh Fortune, surely Josh would have overpowered him."

"Not if the first shot incapacitated Josh."

"But then there'd have been a transference of blood."

"We're waiting for the lab boys to come back on that."

"What about the school? They claimed Tim and Barney were ordinary boys. Surely there'd be signs if they were brewing up for a massacre?"

Tyler shrugged. "I know about that school. People spend a fortune to send their kids there because of its reputation. My guess is that they won't admit any of their kids were out of control."

"Do you want me to give them a go?"

"No. I'd rather you spent more time with the family. Then we'll both go to the school and overwhelm them with the majesty of the law."

"Fine sir." Gill felt relieved. She had no wish to tackle the staff of a snobbish private school.

"Gill, don't get carried away with this. We've got no evidence against Tim and Barney. I want this conversation kept between you and me. Imagine the sort of publicity we'd get if I'm wrong and it leaked out we were targeting two little boys, not to mention the pain we'd cause their family. If Daniel Peters isn't our killer it's possible he'll remember something that rules the boys right out of the frame."

His phone rang. He listened then stood up. "I'm heading to the hospital. Daniel Peters is fit to talk."

Chapter 19

When Tyler walked into Daniel Peters' room his first thought was that 'fit to talk' was optimistic in the extreme and calling him to talk to Dan was a waste of his time. He scowled at Stuart Farrell and prepared a tersely phrased rocket to deliver when there was no-one else listening in.

"Sorry, sir." Stuart must have interpreted his look. "I was going by what the doctor said. He keeps drifting in and out of consciousness."

Tyler had to admit Stuart was in a no win situation. If he'd waited too long he'd have been in even bigger trouble.

"I've got his wife's permission to record anything he says, sir."

"Fine, but we'll need his okay as well if we want to use anything he says in evidence."

Dan moaned.

"He's coming round again," said Stuart. "I'm sure he'll be able to talk soon."

Tyler suppressed a grin at this blatant attempt on Stuart's part to save his arse. "Let's give him a few minutes." He moved into the background and gestured Stuart to stay out of the way as well.

Dan groaned again and turned his head. Hannah approached his bed. "Dan." Tentatively she reached out and stroked his cheek.

"Hannah?"

"Yes, I'm here, Dan. You're going to be okay."

"Charlie... is he okay?"

Hannah glanced over her shoulder and met Tyler's eyes. "Dan, the police are here. They want to talk to you."

Tyler stepped forward. "Dan, I'm Detective Superintendent Tyler. Have we your permission to record this talk?"

Daniel looked surprised. "Yes... whatever... Charlie?"

"He's going to be okay. How did you know his name's Charlie?"

"He told me."

"Told you?" Tyler had assumed Charlie's only means of communication was screaming. "I didn't think he talked?"

"Not much. Just his name and 'Dad' but sometimes I thought he was saying 'Dan.'"

Tyler was tempted to follow through and try to find out why Daniel had taken Charlie away, but there were other, more urgent things he had to know and he wasn't sure how long Dan's strength would last.

"Dan, tell us what you remember about what happened in the park."

"The park?" He looked confused, as if groping for memories, at last he spoke, stumbling and hesitating. "The bench... three people... a girl... she had tear-drops painted on her cheeks... she was bleeding... the dead don't bleed... I read that somewhere... they'd been shot... did Josh do it?"

"Why do you think Josh did it, Dan?

"The gun... it was lying beside his hand."

"What? Are you sure of that?"

Dan didn't answer. The silence went on for so long that Tyler was about to give up, then Dan spoke again, "I picked up a phone... I dialled 999... but I couldn't speak... the words weren't there... like a nightmare... there was so much blood... the smell of blood and flowers."

They needed to take a break after that, but when Tyler resumed the questioning Dan was far more alert. It took a long, slow session of gentle questioning to piece Daniel's story together but in the end, combined with the information Tyler already had, a coherent picture emerged. To Tyler's relief, when Dan was taken back several steps, his memory seemed clearer, possibly intact.

When Tyler spoke of Dan's commission to create sculptures in Stone Park, he readily explained the way he always started work. "I like to watch people, see how they use the space."

"Were there many people using the park that day?"

"No, a lot less than usual. Just this guy, Josh, sitting on the bench. He often comes there for lunch. Is he dead?"

"No, but he's badly hurt. Do you know him, Dan?"

"No."

"But you knew his name?"

"She called him Josh... the woman... and he called her Colleen... and the girl... she called her Sophie." He shuddered. "Is Sophie dead?"

"Sophie's okay." Tyler noted he didn't ask about Colleen. "Tell me about the meeting between Colleen and Josh."

"She sat down beside him. It was strange, sort of pointed, when all the other benches were empty. There was a feeling of aggro between them. Then she came... Sophie."

"What happened then, Dan?"

"She sat on Colleen's lap. She didn't want to... Colleen told her to."

"We've seen the photos you took," said Tyler.

A flush mottled Daniel's white face. "I wanted them for a sculpture. I was going to ask permission, that's why I went back to the car, to get my business cards. And when I got back I found them..." His voice trailed away.

"Go back a bit Dan. How did Josh react when Colleen and Sophie kissed?"

"He didn't like it."

"Embarrassed?"

"I'm not sure. Embarrassed... angry... I don't know."

"So you went to your car. On either journey did you see or hear anything? Any screams or shots?"

"I don't think so... but I was thinking about the art I wanted to do."

"What about the two boys and the toddler? Did you see them at all?"

"Oh yes, I'm sorry, I saw them before Sophie came. They

ran past me to the playground. The little boy... Charlie... fell over in the leaves... I picked him up... And then I saw him on my way back from the car... hiding in the bushes... in a sort of den... I remember thinking it wasn't safe for a little kid alone quite near the lake... that I ought to tell his parents or someone." As he grew weary Dan's voice began to fade.

"What happened when you found Colleen, Josh and Sophie had been shot?"

"I couldn't find my phone... I'd left it in the car... and then I saw one lying at the top of a bag... I put in 999 but I couldn't speak... I managed to say something, then... I don't know... everything went black."

"What happened when you came to, Dan?"

"I... don't... know." Dan's face was slicked with sweat. He looked desperately confused.

"Did you see the other two boys after that?"

"No... I should have done... I should have checked they were all right. Are they okay? Did they see anything?" He must have read the answer in Tyler's face. "Oh God! Not those two kids as well?"

Tyler asked the question he knew would be used to discredit Daniel. "Why did you take Charlie away with you?"

"To keep him safe." The answer seemed sincere.

"And why did you undress him?"

"He was wet... and cold." Throughout his career Tyler had heard all sorts of crazy stories and he was beginning to believe this one.

"You're doing fine, Dan. Now, back to the gun. You're certain it was there when you found the victims?"

"Yes... I think so... I mean I was sure... but now you're pushing it... maybe I imagined it."

"No, that's fine." Tyler backed away from the subject. He was well aware that false memories could be planted in a witness' brain, where they became real memories, at least in so far as the witness was not deliberately lying. "When you regained consciousness did you see the gun?"

"No… I don't know… I don't remember it… but I don't remember much."

"And you've no memory of taking the gun away with you? If you've any thoughts on the matter please tell us, Dan. You're not in trouble but we need you to help us."

"I don't remember… I don't think I'd have touched it… I don't like weapons… my brothers… always… said I was… a wimp." His voice was slurring. "I'm sorry…"

"I'll leave you to rest now. Thanks Dan, you've been a great help. Stuart will stay here and if anything else comes to you, make sure you tell him."

Hannah bent and kissed Dan's cheek. "Back in a minute," she promised and accompanied Tyler to the door.

"What did he mean about not liking weapons?" he asked.

"Dan's family are all into hunting. They despise Dan for hating guns."

"I see." So Dan Peters had been brought up with weapons. Even if he disliked guns he must know how to use them. He smiled at Hannah. "Thanks."

"For what?" She looked surprised.

"For not being obstructive. For letting us ask our questions without interference."

"That was Dan's decision not mine."

"I know but I'd guess you were the sensible one within your partnership. The one who made the big decisions."

Her face grew sombre. "The trouble is that's a pretty dull thing to be."

He didn't deny it. In his experience the pragmatic breadwinners were the ones who were left plodding through boggy ground; the butterflies always found somewhere sweet to land.

He went upstairs to the small room beside the Children's Ward and felt profound relief when he realised Charlie wasn't screaming any more.

Gill was waiting outside the room. "Charlie's parents are with him. How's it going, sir?"

"Dan Peters rounded out the picture quite a bit, always assuming he can be believed." He drew her into an open space where they couldn't be overheard and gave her a detailed account of Daniel's interview.

She listened intently, not interrupting, which he appreciated. He'd come to find her in a conscientious effort to keep her in the loop, but now he was glad to have someone to take stock while he talked it through.

At last he asked, "What do you reckon?"

"If the gun was on the ground it explains why Dan Peters was hit by a branch and not shot."

"Maybe, but it would have been easy enough to have stunned him and shot him afterwards. Dan claims to have no memory of removing the gun but I'm going to get our people to take metal detectors out and check the area between Stone Park and the farm where Daniel and Charlie turned up."

"That's over ten miles of countryside, sir."

"Nothing else about this bloody case has been easy, so why should this be?"

Gill pitched her voice even lower. "If Tim and Barney were responsible, the gun would have been over by the adventure playground where they were found."

"Dan claims to have no memory of seeing the boys dead."

"Do you believe him, sir?"

"Yeah, I think I do, but that doesn't mean he didn't see them. After a shock like that the brain plays funny tricks."

"So what now, sir?"

Tyler sighed. He felt like shit, the result of too much wine and rich food and far too little sleep. "Now you stick with the Quantrulls and Kerry checks out Anita Coldstream. I'll speak to Sophie and see if I can find out anything else about Anita."

"Do you think Sophie knows anything worthwhile, sir?"

"I don't know. I doubt if she knows herself. But if she does I'm going to get it out of her."

Chapter 20

Sophie was sitting cross-legged on the bed. She looked young and vulnerable but Tyler did not allow that to soften his attitude. "Sophie, I need to know what happened between you, Colleen and Josh. I've heard some bits and pieces from people who were outside the game but now I want you to talk to me… you and your mother."

Sophie made a small, whimpering sound, indistinguishable as a word.

Rhiannon crossed the room and perched on the bed, her arm around her daughter. Sophie burrowed her face against her mother's shoulder.

"I think that's a no," said Rhiannon.

Tyler pulled up a chair and sat down. "I'm tired," he said quietly, "Very tired. And that makes me bad-tempered. Any more obstructive behaviour and I'll arrest everyone connected with this case and sit them in a cell until they get more co-operative."

"I didn't think you were going to let us off that lightly," said Rhiannon. "Come on, Sophie, tell the Detective Superintendent what he wants to know."

Sophie didn't move. Her face remained concealed.

"Very well, I'll start," said Rhiannon. "Josh lived with us since Sophie was seven until she was fourteen. Sophie's biological father walked out before she was born. Six years ago, Sophie dropped her bombshell. She told me Josh had been screwing her for months."

"And you believed her?"

Rhiannon met his eyes. "Josh denied it but I felt as if I had no choice. I couldn't be one of those women who ignore their daughters and call them liars when they tell them things like that. So I told Josh to move out. But no, deep down, I never believed her."

111

Tyler said nothing and, after a moment, she continued, "After that we all lost everything. Josh was gone and Sophie and I were far apart. Then, three years later, she took up with Colleen and, one day, she didn't bother to come home."

"And you and Josh never got together again?"

"How could I ask him to forgive the unforgivable? I haven't spoken to him for years. But I still go to his concerts, to watch him and be near him for a couple of hours."

Sophie pushed herself upright and stared at her mother, her blue eyes dominated her white face and she gnawed at her lower lip until a bead of blood appeared.

"Sophie, why were you and Colleen with Josh in the park?" said Tyler.

"To punish him," she whispered. "I did tell Colleen I'd lied... truly I did... but she wouldn't believe me. Colleen only liked things that were perfect. If I'd deceived her like that I wouldn't have been what she thought I was. It's hard to explain."

"What did Colleen do to punish Josh?"

"She kept finding out where Josh was likely to be and turning up there. Often she'd get me to join her. She liked showing him how happy we were. I begged her to stop."

Tyler looked at the glow in Rhiannon's eyes and thought, if Colleen had been the only person shot, he'd have had no hesitation in arresting her.

She read his mind. "You're right, Superintendent, there were times when I'd have willingly killed Colleen, but I'd never have hurt Sophie or Josh, not to mention those little boys."

He felt pretty sure that was the truth. He stood up. "Thanks for talking to us, Sophie. If anything else comes to mind let Nikki know and she'll pass it on to me."

Sophie said, "Did Anita kill Colleen?"

"We have no evidence she did. Do you think she could have done?"

"No!" Sophie gave a decisive shake of her head. "Like

Mum would never have hurt Josh, Anita wouldn't hurt Colleen. It was me she hated."

"Perhaps she was aiming for you."

To his surprise she thought it through calmly. "But why should she do it like that? Anita's the sort of person who plans things. If she'd wanted to get rid of me she wouldn't do it in a way Colleen would know about and never forgive. She'd do it so she could comfort Col."

It was a valid argument, one Tyler had thought of for himself, but he didn't have Sophie's knowledge of the people involved. "Thank you, you've been very helpful."

Sophie shook her head. "It's not enough. I'd do anything to alter what I've done."

Tyler was halfway across the car park when he heard his name, "Kevin!"

He stopped, then wished he hadn't. There were only two females who called him Kevin and this was not his mum. Reluctantly he turned and said. "Hello Vivienne."

As she tottered across to meet him, he thought her heels were unsuitable for an enormously pregnant woman. She looked old and raddled despite her heavy make-up. Her new husband was lurking in the background. He seemed ill at ease.

"Kevin, you look terrible."

He thought there was no concern in her voice; more a kind of smugness, as if she was glad he was having a rough time. He squashed down the retort that she looked pretty ropey herself and said, "I'm on a tough case. What are you doing here?"

"I've been for a check-up. Everything's perfect. I'm so glad we saw you. I wanted to let you know how happy we are."

"Yeah, you said on that card you sent me. Good luck with everything."

She stepped nearer and her heavy perfume engulfed him.

"We'll let you know when the baby arrives. You're still at the old house, aren't you? You haven't moved on?"

"Whatever." He shrugged and walked away from them. He thought, if Vivienne still felt so vindictive towards him, she couldn't have moved on very far herself.

Chapter 21

Family Liaison Officer was never an easy job and it was one that DIs rarely had to undertake. Gill hoped, after this, she'd never have to do it again. She felt desperately sorry for them: Ian Quantrull, so distraught he was barely functioning, and Jasmin, hiding behind her mask of studied elegance. How would they cope if Tyler's suspicions turned out to be true? And how could she make sure no hint of what she was thinking appeared for them to see? She had to admit Tyler was right, it would have been easier if she hadn't known.

She escorted the Quantrulls out of the hospital by a basement route, in the hope of avoiding reporters. The media interest was swirling around them like a hurricane.

As Gill drove them back to their house, Jasmin said, "We haven't seen that Superintendent today. Is he still on the case?"

"Of course he is. Superintendent Tyler has a lot of different leads to follow up. It's my role to look after you. That's why I'm spending so much time with you."

Gill was appalled at the stiffness of her tone. She sounded almost hostile. Did she really dislike the Quantrulls? The answer hit her: if the Quantrull boys had done this dreadful thing then surely their parents must, at some level, be to blame.

She continued, picking her words carefully, "As SIO on a difficult case like this, Superintendent Tyler has to deal with many strands of the investigation and his priority is… and always has been… to make sure Charlie's safe."

"You mean he thinks somebody could still hurt Charlie?" Ian croaked the question. He leaned forward and Gill could smell the whisky on his breath.

Gill thought he was over-playing the horrified surprise. Surely he realised this was a possibility? Unless Ian had reason to think the killers were dead? Or he was so submerged in grief and booze he couldn't think at all?

"Keeping Charlie safe is our priority," she repeated.

The cops on guard duty cleared a path through the reporters and opened the gates, and Gill drove through.

In the hall they were met by the young nanny who said, "Mrs Quantrull is here."

"Oh God!" exclaimed Jasmin.

"They were her grandchildren," snapped Ian.

"Oh I know, darling. I didn't mean to be unkind. But it's all so awful and she's bound to blame me."

Ian led the way into the drawing room and Jasmin followed. Gill slipped in after them even though it was not tactful or polite to eavesdrop on family grief.

The woman seated in the drawing room was thin, grey and stiffly elegant. She was holding Polly on her lap. The baby was gurgling happily and Gill got a brief impression of tenderness on the elderly woman's face. Then she looked at her son and daughter-in-law and the gentleness was replaced by rigorous self-control.

Jasmin darted across the room and kissed the woman's cheek. "Thank you for coming, Mother." She scooped the baby from her mother-in-law's lap.

The older woman looked enquiringly at Gill and she introduced herself.

"Good afternoon, Inspector. I am Elizabeth Quantrull. Tell me, have you made any progress?"

"We're pursuing many lines of enquiry."

The grey eyes were disconcertingly shrewd. "That sounds like soft soap, Inspector. The sort of line you spin to placate grieving relatives."

"I'm sorry. I know it can sound like that, but it's the truth. This is a very complex and confusing case and we're following many different strands. We cannot share any information until the time is suitable."

She expected one or all of the Quantrulls to protest they had the right to know, but Ian broke in to say abruptly,

116

"Mother, if you'll stay with Jasmin, I'll go into work. There's a lot to sort out."

Jasmin looked indignant but Ian's mother said, "That will be quite in order, Ian." Her shrewd eyes assessed his drink-fuddled face. "You shouldn't drive. Allie, would you drive Ian to work?"

The nanny had been lingering by the door. "Of course, Mrs Quantrull."

"Thank you, dear. Ian, your father's lawyers will be in touch with you later today. The boys' deaths change things."

Ian's lips were tightly compressed and Gill wasn't sure if he was holding back on tears or anger. He left the room and the home help followed him. A minute later Gill heard the sounds of departure.

Jasmin said, "I'm going to lie down."

Her mother-in-law held out her hands. "Leave Polly here. I'll look after her."

"No, I'd rather keep her with me." Jasmin clutched the baby tightly to her breast.

She left and Gill was alone with the older Mrs Quantrull.

"Please sit down, Inspector. You must find us sadly ill-mannered but perhaps, in your profession, you are accustomed to that."

"When people are bereaved they react in many ways, Mrs Quantrull."

"That is undoubtedly true. I understand from Allie that Jasmin assaulted a police officer last night."

Gill was tired of providing damage control on this but she said quietly, "It was an unfortunate misunderstanding. Superintendent Tyler is a fine detective and he's working extremely hard to solve this case."

"Jasmin does tend towards hysteria." Mrs Quantrull sounded neither excusing nor condemning, but as if she was stating a rather tedious fact.

"Is that why your son has gone into work? To get some space?"

117

For a moment Gill thought she'd pushed her bluntness too far but Mrs Quantrull nodded. "Possibly. My son loved his first wife, Melissa, very much and her death has been an abiding grief to him. He loved Timothy and Barney, and now he has lost them too. He is... distressed."

"And you must be too."

The grey eyes surveyed her coldly, then Mrs Quantrull said, "You are a perceptive young woman."

"Mrs Quantrull, the only way we can solve this case is by knowing everything we can about the people involved. Most of it will be irrelevant and we'll forget it the second the case is solved. But we do need to know. Ian and Jasmin have been too distressed to talk to us. Please, would you tell me about Barney and Tim?"

Mrs Quantrull was silent for a while. At last she said, "A few years ago they were an ordinary, happy family. Ian and Melissa and their three boys. Then Tim caught meningitis. While he was still very ill, Melissa was diagnosed with an extremely aggressive cancer. She died within two months. Tim recovered and there were no extreme physical side effects, just a slight clumsiness when he was tired. But he had changed. I've never been sure if that was caused by the disease or by the loss of his mother."

"In what way did Tim change?"

"He was difficult sometimes. He has... had a quick temper. He gets that from his father. Barney was like Melissa, gentle and caring." Mrs Quantrull removed a tissue from her handbag and dabbed her eyes.

"When did Melissa die?"

"Over three years ago. When Tim was seven and Barney eight and Charlie just a baby. Two years later Ian met Jasmin." As she made the last statement Mrs Quantrull's voice was neutral.

"Forgive me for asking this but, before this tragedy, did Ian and Jasmin get on well?"

"My son does not believe in divorce."

"I see." Gill thought that what Mrs Quantrull did not say spoke a lot more clearly than what she'd said. She pushed her luck a bit further, "How did Tim and Barney take their father's second marriage?"

"Not well. Tim was especially angry."

"Was Tim ever violent?"

"No! He's... he was just an unhappy, confused, little boy."

That was as far as Gill dared to go. No way could she ask Mrs Quantrull whether the family owned a gun. She tried a different track. "What did you mean when you said to your son that the boys' deaths changed things?"

Mrs Quantrull dabbed her lips with her tissue then replied. "Edward, my late husband, decided, unwisely in my view, to settle his remaining money on his four grandchildren. He divided the money between Tim, Barney and Charlie and the child Jasmin was expecting, that's Polly."

"I see. What happens now Tim and Barney are dead?"

"It all goes to Charlie and Polly."

"And none to you or Ian?"

A glint in the grey eyes reproved insolence but Mrs Quantrull replied. "My husband left me a suitable income to ensure I can live comfortably. He created a successful business, which he gave to Ian. He then proceeded to make a second, even larger fortune, which he left to his grandchildren. My husband believed Ian was more likely to make a success of the business if he didn't have a safety net." There was an acerbic note in her voice that made clear her opinion of this scheme.

"And how did Ian feel about that?"

"We have not discussed the matter."

Again Gill knew it was time to back away but she imagined herself returning to Tyler and talking vaguely about 'fortunes,' and him enquiring sarcastically exactly how long was a piece of string. "When you say a lot of money, how much do you mean?"

119

Mrs Quantrull smiled. "A good point. There was a time, when my husband and I started out, when a hundred pounds would have seemed like a fortune. When they came of age, Timothy and Barney would have both had around two million pounds. That means Charlie and Polly will now get four million each."

Gill swallowed and tried to appear nonchalant. She said, "Mrs Quantrull, would it be all right if I looked round the boys' rooms?" The over-worked SOCOs would check the house through at some point but they were busy elsewhere and Gill needed to find out more about the children now.

Again she was aware of the shrewdness of Elizabeth Quantrull's gaze. "Of course, if you think it will help. Allow me to show you the way."

She escorted Gill upstairs and left her to her work. As soon as she was alone, Gill pulled on crime scene gloves and started to look through the children's toys and clothes.

Both boys' rooms were full of football gear and computer games. Gill thought it was the normal sort of stuff she'd associate with kids on the verge of adolescence. Nothing screamed Child Monster or, for that matter, Mini-Millionaire.

"What are you doing in Timothy's room?"

Gill jumped and turned to face Jasmin, who was standing in the doorway. Aware of her gloved hands she felt awkward. "Your mother-in-law said it was all right to look round."

"Do you think Timothy did something bad?"

Gill felt chilled by the indifference of Jasmin's tone. It was strange how she looked both fragile and invulnerable. She'd changed her outfit of this morning and now wore pale green trousers and a white silk top.

"Why do you ask that, Jasmin?"

She shrugged and came into the room. "I know he's dead but the truth is Timothy was a strange little boy. Ian spoiled them all but especially Timothy, because he'd been so ill. He'd had meningitis and it affected his brain."

"In what way?"

Jasmin looked down at her hands and didn't answer.

"Jasmin, please, if you know anything you must tell us. You know something about Tim's behaviour, don't you? Something that worried you."

Jasmin's fingers pleated the delicate material of her top. Without looking up she said, "You won't tell Ian I told you about this?"

"No."

"Timothy liked to hurt things. They won't talk about it, Ian and his mother and Allie, but Barney had a rabbit and Timothy broke its neck."

Gill winced. Many violent criminals started off by hurting animals. "In that case why did you allow him to take Charlie to the park?"

"Timothy didn't mind Charlie. It was Polly he hated. Polly and me. I never dared leave Polly alone with Timothy, the only time I did he started touching her." She shuddered.

"What do you mean touching?" Gill's stomach clenched with pity and disgust but she felt a tingle of excitement, this was why Tyler had placed her here.

"Sort of stroking. I don't want to talk about it."

"What about Barney? Did you worry about him too?"

Jasmin looked surprised. Gill wondered if this was the first time she'd considered Barney as a person in his own right. If so the thought processes didn't take her far. "Barney was good at looking after Charlie. I'll miss Barney." She sounded surprised at this thought. "You must think I'm an awful person?" Tears trickled down her face.

"It's been a dreadful shock."

"I suppose Ian's mother told you I wanted to send the boys away?"

Gill masked her surprise. "Why don't you tell me your side of it, Jasmin?"

"I wanted them to go to boarding school. I thought it would be good for Timothy. And I couldn't live with the fear that one day, when I wasn't looking, he'd hurt my little girl."

"I see. When…" Gill was interrupted by a baby's cry.

"That's Polly!" Jasmin fled.

Gill closed the door and went swiftly and methodically through the drawers. She moved on to the bookcase and the rack of computer games and DVDs. Tim's taste seemed to run to fantasy and horror but she guessed that was true of many boys his age. She tried the toy cupboard. There was mainly sports gear on the top shelves but lower down there was a box of toy cars and a selection of Action Man figures and vehicles. She turned them over as a matter of routine, then paused, suddenly tense. She picked up a red-haired, fashion doll, dressed in white shorts and blue bikini top. Its arms and legs were bound with parcel tape. Its face had been melted away.

Chapter 22

"Blood! The earth will have blood! The Pentannual Circle is closing. Rich, red blood soaks into the Place of Sacrifice. We offer the blood of the innocents to the Sacred Oak."

"George, if you don't shut up you'll get yourself put away again. Luke, get him out of here." Tyler rubbed his aching forehead and waited while the sergeant hustled George Crosby out of his office and handed him over to an uniformed constable.

"You got any more loonies who want to waste my time?" he asked when Luke returned.

"Sorry, sir. I know it sounds like nonsense but George Crosby's obsessed by the old oak tree and he's been violent before."

"No alibi for the time of the shootings?"

"No. He says he doesn't even know where he was."

Tyler sighed. "When did they let George out of the mental hospital?"

Luke consulted his notes. "Ten days ago. They make him take his medication so he gets more or less sorted, then they let him loose and the cycle starts again."

"If it was a knife job or a beating I'd put George at the top of my list. But give him a gun and I reckon he'd fire the whole lot in one go. It sounds crazy but I think the Stone Park shootings were too restrained for him. But there's one scumbag noticeable by his absence. Why the hell haven't you brought Brian Purvis in?"

"He's got an alibi. At the time of the shooting he was at Saltern Museum, giving a talk to the local history society."

"He was what! Are you taking the piss?"

"While he was in prison, Purvis studied history, got a degree and wrote a book about legends or some such crap.

Now he goes round talking about it."

Tyler scowled. From all he knew of Purvis it sounded like a con. "I'll see him myself."

His phone rang. "Tyler."

"It's Sergeant Ellis on the Main Desk, sir. Sorry to bother you but there's a Ms Corder down here at reception who wants to see you. She says she's got information and she'll only talk to you."

"Have her brought to my office." Tyler noted wryly that DS Corder had chosen not to mention her rank. "Luke. I need you with me for this interview."

"Yes, sir. Sir, I don't mean to be nosy but are you okay? You're looking pretty wiped."

"Bit of a stomach upset." Tyler knew it was probably all over the Station that the Super had a hangover. An encounter with the ACC in the corridor had resulted in a rebuke about the standards of appearance expected of senior officers.

"That's hard luck, sir," said Luke. "Probably those lousy airline meals."

The door opened and Cheryl Corder was escorted into the room. She was a slender, pretty woman, her brown hair cut into a silky bob.

"Sit down, Sergeant Corder. Luke, you stay."

"I'd rather he didn't," she protested.

"And I'd rather he did. You've already screwed up your own team and your own DCI and I'm damned if you're going to play the same game with me."

A flush touched her white cheeks but she didn't argue anymore.

"What do you want Sergeant?" He felt no sympathy for her. He was uncertain whether she'd been corrupt or stupid and he didn't care, in his mind both were unforgivable.

"There's something I have to tell you. I should have told you this morning but I wasn't thinking straight."

"What is it?"

She clenched her hands and spoke in a rapid monotone.

"When I saw Anita yesterday she gave me a parcel to post."

"And did you post it?"

"Yes."

"How large a parcel was it?"

"About shoe box size and quite heavy. She'd put a lot of postage on it."

Tyler was startled. If his suspicions were right, Anita Coldstream had been unbelievably brazen and given a cop the murder weapon to post. But why go to such lengths if she planned to top herself? "Did you see who it was addressed to?"

She nodded. "Jennifer Marlowe. She helps run a women's refuge, but this was addressed to her house."

"Do you know anything about this woman or the refuge?"

"Not really. I've met her when we've been following up complaints about domestic abuse."

"Do you know if Anita had any special links with her?"

"Anita's involved with a lot of Women's causes."

"And can you remember the address or any part of it?"

"It was North London, a place called Stanmore."

"Right. It might be a good idea if you were out of communication for the next few hours."

She flushed. "I won't contact her again."

He allowed his scepticism to show.

"It was different before. I felt sorry for her. I was bloody stupid."

Tyler knew he had no grounds to hold her and, if he did, he'd cause a lot of aggro with the London force. Trust seemed to be his only option.

"I can't offer you any favourable treatment because of this."

She met his gaze. "I don't expect any."

As Luke was escorting her out of the building, Tyler's mobile rang. He answered it quietly; attitude required more energy than he had left.

125

"Kev, it's Lani. Thank you for the flowers, they're beautiful."

"I'm glad you like them." He was glad he'd made time to go into the hospital florist and order the flowers. Also he was glad he'd put his mobile number on the card. Above all he was glad she'd phoned him. He was startled at how pleased he felt about that.

"They're perfect. I'm especially grateful they're in a basket. Flower-arranging is one of the many talents I don't possess."

He laughed, then gasped as pain knifed through his head.

"Are you okay, Kev?"

"Yeah. Just a bit fragile. How about you?"

"Fine. I'm waiting for a taxi. I think I said last night, I've got a book signing at the Landowne Bookshop until six this evening. That's not as nerve-racking as radio or TV, but any public appearances aren't my favourite thing."

"Tell me about it." Tyler spoke with more fervour than he'd intended.

"Do you get nervous when you have to give statements on TV?" asked Lani.

"Every time."

"You cover it well."

"Sometimes I reckon I cover it too well."

Miraculously she seemed to understand. "Do you feel cross when people say, 'It's easy for you. Doing that sort of thing comes naturally'?"

"Yeah." Tyler felt a welling up of all the bitterness he'd suppressed during a thousand conversations with people who thought they knew him when they hadn't got a clue. There was a knock on his door. "Lani, I'm sorry, I've got to go."

"Of course. I didn't mean to hold you up. Thanks again for the flowers."

"No... I mean thank you."

As he put the phone down he was aware of a sense of loss. He should have asked Lani if she'd see him again. If

126

only he hadn't been interrupted. Deep down he doubted if he'd have had the guts to anyway. A small, mocking voice of honesty taunted him, *'And live a coward in thine own esteem, letting I dare not wait upon I would, like the poor cat i' th' adage.'* That lightened his mood. Trust Shakespeare to have the right words for everything. One day he'd go on the Internet and try to find out what the unfortunate cat had done or failed to do.

Chapter 23

Late that afternoon, when Tyler entered her office, Gill thought he looked even more knackered than earlier. He sat down opposite her. "Any developments?"

"I think you may have called it right, sir."

His air of weariness deepened. "Timothy?"

"Yes. At least it seems possible."

"Okay, what have you got?"

Gill took him through all the evidence against Timothy Quantrull. Tyler's expression was harsh but she was beginning to read him and she saw despair beneath the mask.

"The mutilated doll and dead rabbit add up to a seriously disturbed boy," he said.

"Yes sir, but I can't work out where he could have got the gun."

"You can get just about anything on the street if you have money and know where to look. It's a question of whether these kids did know and if they had access to their inheritance or if it's all locked in this Trust. Anyway, we'll have to find out more about Tim and Barney."

Gill glanced at her mobile, checking both messages and time. "I guess it's too late to tackle the school today?"

"Yeah. For God's sake stop fiddling with that phone and concentrate!"

"Sorry sir." She bit back her resentment at his rebuke. Isabel had often complained that she checked her phone with obsessive frequency.

"I want to see how the Anita Coldstream side of things pans out before we stir up aggro in that school."

"What's happened with Anita Coldstream, sir?"

"Detective Sergeant Corder came to see me this afternoon. She told me she'd posted a parcel for Anita."

"The silly bitch!"

"Anita or Corder?"

"Probably both, but I meant Corder."

"Yeah. The parcel's addressed to Jennifer Marlowe. She helps run a Woman's Refuge. It'll probably arrive at her home address tomorrow morning. Luke's checked her background and she's pretty well clean. She had a caution for assault but that's it."

"Who did she assault?"

"An abusive husband who'd forced his way into the refuge."

"And she got cautioned?"

"Yeah, the arsehole husband was a cop. Kerry's staying there while we sort out the relevant paperwork and I want you to go up first thing tomorrow and join her. Kerry might need a senior officer, someone with a bit of clout. We aren't exactly popular up there."

Gill nodded. "I'll be up there early. This assault Jennifer Marlowe was cautioned for, did she use a weapon?"

"A frying pan." He said it straight-faced and Gill wasn't sure whether he was entirely serious or had a slyer sense of humour than she'd credited him with.

She sighed. "This case gets weirder every day."

"More like every hour. You wishing you were back with DCI Aron?"

Gill thought Aron wasn't the sort of SIO anyone wanted to return to. "No, but I hate this case. It's such a tangle. I feel as though we'll never sort it out."

"Tell me about it, and you haven't met George Crosby yet, or heard him ranting about blood sacrifice."

Gill shuddered. She'd heard gossip about George Crosby in the Incident Room. "Does he know anything about the shootings or is it total crap?"

"He's a badly disturbed guy but there's no escaping the fact that, a few years ago, there was some seriously nasty stuff happening around those lunatics."

Gill wished she'd listened more attentively when Tyler

had first spoken of it. "Please could you tell me about it again, sir?"

"There's this guy called Brian Purvis. Somehow he attracts people who're searching for something to fill their lives. He's about my age but he always had a group of kids hanging round him. They weren't the usual yobs. These kids were looking for some sort of cause, and they'd do anything Brian told them, including violence. Does that sound crazy?"

"No. Some people have that sort of personality. If they're unscrupulous and manipulative they can do a lot of harm."

"Purvis is unscrupulous and manipulative all right. He's a bloody sociopath. He's turned respectable, thanks to the prison education scheme, but I'd lay odds he's still playing the same games just with a different twist."

"Prison? He was the one who got banged up for assault?"

"That's right. An archaeologist called Philip Henderson wanted to lead a University dig in Stone Park and Purvis campaigned to stop him. When non-violent protest didn't work Purvis moved on to vandalism and death threats and assault."

"It's unusual for that sort to do their own dirty work."

"Yeah, possibly that's why Purvis screwed up. George Crosby, his chief heavy, had gone crazy and landed himself in hospital. So Purvis had to get his own hands dirty. Two days before the dig was due to start he beat up Henderson. It was a vicious assault and we put him away for attempted murder. If you ask me, the sentence he got was light. I always felt there was more behind what he did, something we were missing, but maybe that's me being paranoid. Brian Purvis wasn't a character I took to, even by the standards of our usual customers." Tyler stopped speaking and rubbed his hands across his face.

"Why don't you go home, sir?" Gill hoped Tyler wouldn't interpret this as an attempt to usurp his authority.

"You sure? I'd like to call it a day but you must want to get home yourself."

"No, I'm fine. I made sure I got an early night last night."

Too late she realised how self-righteous that sounded. She saw a spark of anger in Tyler's eyes; it kindled and took hold. "You needn't tell me I shouldn't have been out last night. I know the SIO on a case like this doesn't have a right to any personal life."

He hauled himself to his feet and slammed out of the room.

Gill felt as though the roof had fallen in. That was not the way to win friends or influence people. The last thing she wanted was to piss off her SIO. Getting a reputation as a difficult second-in-command wouldn't do her career any good at all. When she thought she'd worked out the right thing to say, she went in search of him. He wasn't in his office so she tried the Incident Room. Again no Tyler but Luke Warden was there.

"Luke, have you seen the Superintendent?"

"He's gone down to see Inspector Rowner to finalise the last details of the house-to-house. He said he'd only be a few minutes." He looked over her shoulder to the office door. "Oh hell, that's all we need!"

She turned and saw the ACC approaching. He looked like a peevish god of war who was wondering where some inefficient subordinate had stored his thunderbolts.

She took a deep breath and went to meet him. "Sir, what time would it be convenient for me to brief you on the developments in the Stone Park case?" This was high-risk strategy but it was worth taking a chance.

His look of displeasure deepened. "I instructed Superintendent Tyler to do that."

"The Superintendent's not well, sir. I think it's food poisoning."

"Oh I see. He should have informed me of that. This is a very high-profile case."

"I'm sure a good night's sleep is all he needs to set him right, sir."

"That's what he said yesterday."

"But he didn't get a good night's sleep. He had to go up to London in the early hours. With your permission I'll leave instructions that I'm to be called if there are any developments tonight."

"Very well, Inspector. I'll see you in my office in half-an-hour."

He left and Gill hurried downstairs to lurk in the corridor where Inspector Rowner had his office. It was essential she caught Tyler before he reported to the ACC The adrenaline had stopped pumping and she was afraid she'd screwed up. He was already pissed off with her and now he'd be furious that she'd been so presumptuous.

Ten minutes later Tyler emerged from the office. He saw her waiting for him and looked surprised. "You after me?"

"Yes sir. About before, I'm sorry, I didn't mean to sound critical."

"No, it was me. I copped because I was already blaming myself. I can't seem to get a grip on anything since I got back."

She took a deep breath. Sir, I've seen the ACC. He's happy for me to brief him for the Media. I told him you'd got food poisoning." She waited for the executioner's axe to fall.

Instead, he grinned, "On the assumption that P.G. Wodehouse was right when he said alcohol's a food? I'll be off then. Thanks."

Chapter 24

Tyler locked his car and walked along the street. He thought this was one of the craziest things he'd ever done. He hesitated, on the point of turning back.

'He either fears his fate too much, or his deserts are small, who dare not put it to the touch to win or lose it all.' Those words by a 17th Century soldier-poet had always been a personal touchstone. If you didn't have the guts to take a chance, you didn't deserve to win. It would do no harm to glance through the bookshop window and see what sort of turnout she'd achieved.

As he peered inside he felt disappointed for her. Only five people queued by the central desk. He pushed the door open. At least he could buy a book to cheer her up.

A shop assistant moved to intercept him. "I'm sorry, sir, I'm afraid the queue to see Lani Scott is closed but you can buy a signed book from the sales point over there. We've got copies of her new book and the one that's just been televised."

"Oh… I thought there weren't many customers."

"At five-thirty the queue was all round the shop. She's very popular. It's the TV programme that's done it, that and her being local."

"I see. Thanks." Tyler turned to leave. He'd buy one of her books tomorrow, at the moment he was focused on not intruding when she was busy.

"Kev! Don't go!" Lani disentangled herself from books and admirers and hurried across to him.

He felt a rush of pleasure at the warmth of her smile, then he saw the curious stares of the on-lookers and wished he'd smartened up for her.

"Were you really sneaking away without saying hello?"

"You're busy."

"Not really. Please, don't disappear, unless you're in a

133

desperate hurry. I'll be finished in ten minutes."

"I don't want to get in your way."

"You won't."

Tyler followed her to the table and the shop assistant provided him with a chair.

In fact it was twenty minutes before she finished. Her last customer was a young disabled man and she put everything on hold to follow his slurred speech.

Not wanting to stare at the poor guy, Tyler picked up a paperback from the piles on the table and opened it at random.

'Look before you leap.' That's what her mother used to tell her. But Mother never mentioned that if you stop and look, the chances are you won't leap at all.

She wonders what he'd make of her if she walked in there, smiled at him and said, 'Hi, I'm Elinor Robinson and I've got a proposition for you.'

She's overwhelmed by the certainty he'd think her a tart... or worse, a lunatic.

She walks away.

Then she stops.

She reminds herself she's no longer a fat mess. She's an attractive woman. At least as attractive as she's ever going to get.

She's going to do it. She's going to go for it.

For once in her life she's going to reach out for the thing she wants.

She turns round, heads back along the street, pushes the door open and walks up to him. She switches on a glowing smile. 'Hi, I'm Elinor Robinson'.

The last customer left and Tyler closed the book and put it back onto the pile.

Lani smiled at the manager. "That went well. Thanks for your help."

"Thank you," he said. "Did you say you needed to phone for transport home?"

"I'd meant to call a taxi but now I hope my friend will give me a lift. Do you mind, Kev? Carys has borrowed my car."

"Of course." Tyler was grateful for how easy she was making it.

She put on her coat and gathered together her things. The manager let them out of the shop and Tyler led her to his car.

As they drove, she said, "I'm sorry. I ambushed you into driving me."

"No. I mean I wanted to." He cursed himself for the rough tone and the clumsiness of the words. He felt as awkward as a kid on his first date. "Lani, do you fancy coming out for a meal?"

He saw her look sideways at him. "I'd love to..." He knew there was a 'but' coming and braced himself for rejection. "But why don't we go back to my place and eat?"

Ruefully he accepted that was reasonable. He shouldn't have asked her when he was in this state. It had been a long day and everything he was wearing felt stale.

They drove in silence until they reached her block of flats and she directed him into the tenants' underground car park. As he pulled into her parking bay she said, "Kev, you aren't taking your work home with you, are you?"

"What?"

"It smells like you've got a dead body in those bin bags on the back seat."

He was glad it was too dark for her to see his embarrassment. "It's my washing. My electric's gone off. Tonight, when I got home, it hit me I'd got no clean clothes left. I meant to take it to the laundrette. I'm sorry about the smell."

"How long since the electric died on you?"

"It was while I was in the US. This case started before I could get it fixed and I haven't had a minute to call my own. Some of the washing was still damp. That's probably

135

the stuff that stinks."

"Probably. What have you been doing about cooking?"

"I've been eating in the canteen, the food there's not that bad." He was afraid she'd think he was a dirty slob and added hastily, "I've been showering and shaving at work. It's clean clothes that are the problem. I'll nip into a supermarket and buy some shirts and stuff on my way home."

She clambered out, opened the back door of the car and grabbed a bin bag. "You bring the other two. I'll do your washing."

"I can't ask you to do that!"

"You didn't. I offered." She walked away still holding the bag.

Mesmerised, he hauled the other bags out of the car, followed her to the lift and up four flights. Her flat was bright, modern and wonderfully warm. At her command he dumped his bin bags in the kitchen. He thought ruefully it was as well she'd turned down his offer of eating at a restaurant. He still felt bloody awful.

"The cloakroom's on the right, Kev. Second door along."

"Cheers." Apparently he must look as bad as he felt.

"Come into the living room and sit down."

Obediently he followed her, removed his coat and sank into the embrace of the most comfortable sofa in the world. "Are you sure you don't mind doing this?"

"Of course I don't. You look shattered. Why do you think I suggested eating here?"

His wits deserted him. "You mean you did it because you thought I looked tired?"

"What did you think I...?" Her voice trailed away and Tyler saw bright colour burn into her face.

He didn't know why she was embarrassed but he hastened into apology, "I'm sorry. I know I look scruffy." He ran a hand over his dark stubble. "I forgot how early it was this morning when I shaved."

Lani's awkwardness vanished. "Kev, you idiot, I'd be

136

proud to be seen with you anywhere."

"That's more than the ACC would. When he saw me early this afternoon, he booted me off this evening's TV interview. Said he'd do it himself."

"Good. Let him have the stress for once. Was he arsey because you'd got a hangover?"

"He didn't seem sure whether I'd got a hangover. I'm not much of a drinker as a rule and the team rallied round. Gill told him I'd got food poisoning."

Lani giggled. "Treacle pud poisoning."

"Can we change the subject? I don't want to think about that pudding."

"In that case do you feel up to eating now or would you rather leave it for a while?"

"Whenever you like."

He saw the shrewd look she gave him. "Back in a minute." She went into the kitchen. After a few minutes she returned and handed him a glass. "Drink this."

He obeyed. The liquid was thick and tasted of peppermint.

Lani said briskly, "I'll sort something later, when you feel more up to eating. I'll shove some washing in the machine, then I'll shower and change. I won't be long."

Left alone Tyler wondered at what point his life had got so totally out of control. The trouble was he didn't know what moves Lani wanted him to make. She'd given him no sign she wanted anything warmer than friendship... or had she? He'd never been good at reading the signals women gave off.

The row of bookcases took his attention. It was a selection after his own heart, a large sprinkling of the classics of English Literature and a solid shelf of poetry and plays, several art books, history and psychology. There was also a lot of crime fiction, one genre he tended to avoid. He hunted for Lani's own books, but didn't find any.

He spotted a pile of new paperbacks on a side table. It was the book that Lani was promoting: *The Song of the Innocent*. He picked one up and opened it at random.

'Grandfather's cat was a lazy old creature. It rolled onto its side and watched as they approached. It showed no recognition of advancing danger.

The others watched as he slipped the rope around its neck. A slipknot. He'd got a book out of the library and practised until he was sure he could always get it right. He tossed the rope over the tree branch and hauled the cat to dangle in the air. Its legs flailed. It writhed. It made a tight sort of noise, the sort of sound you'd expect a strangled thing to make. The sound was drowned by Gemma's high-pitched laughter.

It took a long time for the cat to die.

He got it down. The small furry body was limp in his cradling hands. It had taken longer than he expected. Next time it would be easier.

Death wasn't so special. It was nothing except the absence of life.

But the eyes of the dead were different. Sort of glazed and blank.

He looked up, staring into the middle distance. He wondered if, to others, his eyes looked dead, the way they looked when he was seeing through them from inside.

Chapter 25

Lani returned wearing cord trousers and a vivid pink, fluffy jumper. Tyler thought she looked incredibly soft and warm, impossible to believe she could write such searing stuff.

"Are you feeling better, Kev?"

His headache had eased and, for the first time in that long day, he didn't feel sick. "Yeah, I'm good."

"I'll sort some dinner."

"I didn't mean to push you into cooking for me."

"Freezer to microwave is hardly a big deal."

She disappeared into the kitchen and he picked up the book again and opened it a few pages from the end:

The blue eyes were wide-open and a half-smile played on the softly curved lips. It was impossible to read the thoughts behind the angel's mask.

"Why didn't they put them back together again?... They're so clever... They know all sorts of things... Surely they could mend people if they really tried. It's not my fault... I'd like to go home now..."

He closed the book and stared at the cover: a black-and-white image of a young boy holding a rope and fashioning a knot. His mind was filled with thoughts of the Quantrull boys. He could imagine Timothy thinking things like that.

Lani returned five minutes later carrying two half-pint goblets full of a clear, sparkling liquid. For a second Tyler felt worried.

She smiled at him. "Last night champagne, tonight lemonade, that's life."

"I'm sorry to be such a misery." He was dismally aware that the impression he was making on this second meeting was little better than the first.

"Kev, it's okay. Sit down, relax, stop worrying and make yourself comfortable."

"What, all at once? I'm a guy, I don't do multi-tasking."

She stuck her tongue out at him but the beep of the microwave cut off her retort.

They ate sitting on the sofa, trays on laps. They chatted about books and music, and their silences were as comfortable as their words. The chicken was warm and tasty and he felt better when he'd eaten.

"That was good," he said.

"It's one of Caz's meals. She's setting up a small home-catering business. That's why she's had to pinch my car while her van's off the road."

"Perhaps she could help me fill my freezer when I've got the power sorted." He remembered that first evening he'd got back, wading through his kitchen where his fridge and freezer had leaked. Strange how it was the small things that made a situation unbearable.

After they'd eaten, Lani made an enormous pot of tea. As they drank it Tyler said, "Lani, could I ask about your book? The one about the children."

She looked surprised. "Of course."

"Do you do a lot of psychological research? How do you know what turns a child into a killer?"

"I don't. I just think myself into that person's head. In that book the children hate their lives. Because of this they've separated fantasy and reality and withdrawn into another place. At one level they really believe what they've done is still redeemable and that the dead can be resurrected."

"I'm sorry, I haven't read it, just flipped through." He hoped she wouldn't feel offended.

"That's okay. It's the last thing you'd want to read at the moment. In the book three children bond together to eradicate their abusive grandfather. But, having done so, they find murder is addictive. Soon they're punishing those around them for the slightest perceived crimes, until they start to devour themselves."

Tyler shuddered. "Remind me never to annoy you."

She laughed. "Don't worry, I'm a theoretical murderer."
Then, suddenly serious, "A lot of what I write appals me, at
least with part of my mind. But that's the way those kids felt
when I was channelling it through my imagination."

He drank his tea in silence then roused himself to say,
"Sorry, I'm being lousy company."

"If this is what you look like when you feel a bit fragile,
I'd hate to see you when you feel really crap."

He grinned at that. "It's not just the hangover. It's this
case. There are too many victims and way too many potential
suspects. It's a mess. And it feels so nasty. It's a long while
since I felt so... outraged as when I saw those two dead boys.
My last DI used to get really choked up when it was kids
who were killed, but he's a father and grandfather. I always
thought it was different for him but this time I felt the same
way."

She reached across and rested her hand lightly on top of
his. "There's a wonderful poem about the holocaust that says
we're all parents when children die."

He stared at her in blank astonishment. "You mean
Richard Burns? I've never met anyone else who knows his
work."

"Burns is one of my favourite modern poets." Lani
giggled suddenly. "I told Isabel I was having problems
getting a copy of one of his books and she went out and
bought me the complete works of Robert Burns. She was so
pleased with herself, I didn't have the heart to tell her that
Richard Burns was totally different."

That made him laugh, then he asked a question he'd
never dared ask anyone before, "Lani, do lines of verse keep
appearing in your head?"

"Of course they do." She sounded surprised that he'd
asked; as if to her it seemed quite normal. "That's what words
are for, to help people make sense of things and express
feelings they can't sort out in other ways."

"I'd never thought of it like that." He'd always considered

it a bizarre sort of weakness on his part. It made him feel better, even though he still didn't intend to share his thoughts with anyone, except perhaps Lani. He looked at her hand, still resting on his and thought, *'Let me not to the marriage of true minds admit impediment.'* He didn't say the words out loud. He wasn't ready for that leap... not yet.

"It's probably good that, after all you've seen, you can still feel outrage." He felt grateful to Lani for steering the conversation back to the safe ground of crime.

"I guess. The truth is, I was already pissed off. I hated that US conference."

"You must have been to hundreds of conferences. Why did this one get to you?"

He despised himself for moaning. "You don't want to listen to me whinging."

"Yes I do. You need to stop brooding about it. And I can always use it as research."

"Cheers. You'll probably land me on a CIA hit list, if I'm not there already."

Lani squeezed his hand. "Tell me."

He started slowly, stumbling slightly as he tried to correlate details and explain them to her. The conference had centred on juveniles and their increasing propensity towards violent crime. Tyler was one of the low-profile delegates; he was there to listen, learn, and carry the word back to Britain.

He was no great drinker and not the most sociable of men, and he'd found the hospitality that surrounded the conference claustrophobically lavish. He'd spent increasingly long periods of networking time cloistered in his room. He'd downloaded more books onto his Kindle than he usually had time to read in a year.

The subject matter of the conference had been terrifying. He was appalled by the knowledge that there were small children going out with guns. Like the angel-faced six-year-old who'd shot her baby-sitter because the woman wouldn't let her watch TV.

Suddenly, talking to Lani, he found it possible to pinpoint the truth behind his depression. "It all seemed so hopeless. I kept thinking how the hell can we change anything when we're not addressing the real issues involved?"

"You can't," said Lani briskly. "The trouble with you is you've got delusions of grandeur. Face it, Kev, you're a cop, that means you're one of society's dustbin-men. You get to clear up the crap."

It wasn't the most elegant definition of his vocation but Tyler found it curiously comforting in its simplicity.

"You're afraid the Quantrull boys did the shootings, aren't you?" She added hastily, "You don't have to answer that if you don't want to."

He did want to answer. He wanted someone to tell him it was his imagination working overtime. After all it would be a major coincidence to go to a conference on juvenile crime and return straight to a case of children committing murder.

"Yeah, that's what I've been thinking, but I want to be convinced I'm wrong." He was shocked at how desperate he sounded. He hadn't realised he felt like that.

"I can't tell you you're wrong. You've got the evidence and you're much better at analysing it than me."

"It's the thought of those kids being so full of rage and hatred."

"A lot of kids are. Haven't you got some dark places you never want to revisit? Some memories of humiliation or injustice? I know I have."

"Yeah. But most kids don't turn into killers."

"Most of us apply the brakes or have them applied for us. But for some the opportunity to lash out appears at the wrong time and they do something that sets Fate on a rollercoaster."

He scoured wearily at his eyes. "I'm worried, Lani. My team's stretched too thin. They've given me reinforcements but the core team are trying to run in too many directions and they can't keep up this pace for long."

"I know. Isabel said Gill's going up to London tomorrow

143

morning. And, before you think it, Gill wasn't being indiscreet, Bel didn't know any more than that."

It was clear Lani was carefully excluding any hint of question from her tone; perversely that made Tyler more willing to confide. What he'd said about his team was true for him, he couldn't keep up this pressure without some form of release.

In broad strokes, naming no suspects' names and giving few details, he told her what Gill and Kerry were going to do in London the next day.

He finished up by saying, "Kerry's on a high. She thinks we're going to recover the gun tomorrow. But I'm not so sure. It doesn't make sense. Our suspect's smart enough to have ditched the gun straight away. Anyway why give it to a cop to post?"

"Maybe she wanted to set her up."

He stared at her. "That's a point."

"It's no good worrying about it tonight. You'll find out tomorrow, if and when the parcel turns up."

"It better had. I can't spare Kerry for much longer. She may get on my nerves but at least she gets through the work." He saw Lani's half-smile. "What's funny about that?"

"Nothing. You just proved me right."

"About what?"

"Gill was wondering why you put up with Kerry when she gives you so much grief and I guessed it was because you valued the way she did her job."

"Yeah. You need a lot of dimensions on a team to cover as many bases as possible. And it doesn't do for a team to get too cosy. You need a bit of sand... in the... works."

He stumbled over the last words. Exhaustion was sweeping over him in drowning waves. "I'd better go."

"You don't have to leave."

He hesitated, uncertain what she was offering and painfully aware he was too exhausted to fulfil the most minor sexual fantasy. "You don't have to... you can't want me here when I'm wrecked." To his horror the protest came out as self-pitying.

She glared at him. "Kev, I've got a perfectly good spare bedroom. I'm not offering sex or romance or anything like that, but I thought friendship would be nice. The ball's in your court. It's up to you whether you'd like to stay or not."

Ridiculous to feel disappointed that friendship was the only thing on offer, when a friend was the thing he'd longed for most.

"I'd like to stay. I didn't mean to be ungrateful."

"I know you didn't. Kick off your shoes, undo your collar and get comfortable."

He obeyed, relaxing into her maternal bossiness. It felt strange to be treated like a child. Not that he'd ever had much of a chance to be a proper kid. Her Man of the House, that's what Mum used to call him. Until his step-dad appeared on the scene.

He tried to recall the anger and resentment he'd felt then. But he couldn't. It was too long ago and he'd buried it too deep.

Chapter 26

Gill and Kerry followed the postman up the path as he rang the bell.

A woman opened the door as far as a security chain would allow.

"Parcel for you, love. Too big to fit through the letter box."

"Oh... thank you." The woman released the chain and opened the door. The postman left and the woman looked at Gill and Kerry. "Can I help you?"

"Mrs Marlowe? Jennifer Marlowe?" Gill showed her ID and introduced herself and Kerry. "May I ask, are you aware of the contents of that parcel?"

"No." Mrs Marlowe shifted the parcel, holding it away from her.

"May I?" Gill reached forward and took it from her hands.

"Be careful, in case..."

"In case of what, Mrs Marlowe?"

"In case it's something dangerous."

Gill waved to the figures waiting outside the gate. "Are you willing for these officers of the Firearms Unit to open this package?"

"Yes of course, but I don't understand."

"Perhaps we could go inside while these officers do their job."

Leaving the Firearms Officers to it, the woman allowed Gill and Kerry inside. It was a pleasant, suburban semi and Gill thought Jennifer Marlowe fitted it well. She was plump and grey-haired, wearing jogging trousers and a fleece top. She didn't look like the sort of woman to receive guns through the mail. But then she didn't look like a woman who'd assault an abusive man with a frying pan.

Kerry said, "What are you afraid of, Mrs Marlowe?"

"Last year one of our helpers had a home-made bomb posted to her but, fortunately, it didn't go off. The police couldn't get enough evidence to prosecute."

"Have you had any dodgy parcels before?"

Jennifer Marlowe shuddered. "Only once. But that was at the refuge. Lobbed over the wall. A man whose wife had left him, kidnapped their oldest daughter and threatened to kill her unless his wife came back. To prove he was serious he sent her severed finger to the refuge."

"Bastard!" said Kerry.

"Yes. I must admit that time the police were good."

"DI Martin, do you want to look at this?" The firearms expert called from outside.

Gill and Kerry went to where the package was lying on protective plastic sheeting, its wrapping peeled away and its contents laid out beside the box.

Gill stared down and then looked at Kerry, whose expression mirrored her own. Recovering quickly, Kerry grinned at her. "Over to you, Gill. It's your job to tell the Bossman what we've got."

Gill pulled a face at her. She returned to Jennifer Marlowe to check out some facts. These established, she went outside, to a secluded corner, and got out her phone. Her first call, to the office, was answered by Luke who informed her Tyler wasn't in yet. Gill hesitated, uncertain whether to ring his mobile. She didn't want to wake him if he was sick but he needed to be told about this development. She keyed in his number.

"Tyler." To her relief he sounded okay.

"Sir, it's me, Gill. We've opened the parcel Anita Coldstream sent to the refuge woman. It isn't the gun, it's a load of jewellery."

"Jewellery?" Tyler sounded as astonished as she and Kerry had been.

"Yes sir. It looks valuable, and there's a printed note,

'TO BE SOLD AND USED FOR THE REFUGE.' I guess Anita selected the jewellery she wanted to wear while she topped herself and sent the rest to be used for refuge funds. She probably thought they'd play it clever and keep quiet."

"If Anita had that package ready to post, she must have planned to top herself all along. It was nothing to do with DS Corder's warning that we wanted to speak to her."

"That's what I thought, sir."

"And you reckon Jennifer Marlowe's okay?"

"I think so. Kerry did a background check last night. She's a nurse who took early retirement. Married with grown up kids and grandchildren."

"What's she got to say about her involvement with Anita?"

"She says she knows her quite well. Anita has done a lot of legal work for the refuge and she advises abused women at a drop-in centre that Jennifer helps run. She and Anita have had lunch together a few times."

"What about Colleen, did she know her?"

"No. She said Anita didn't talk about her private life."

"So we've got nothing on Anita?"

"No sir." Tyler knew as well as she did that their search of her flat, office and car had produced nothing.

"Okay. I'd like you back right away. I want you to visit the boys' school with me."

"I'll be as quick as I can, sir." Gill keyed off and went back inside.

"Was Tyler mad about that package?" demanded Kerry.

"No. He was fine about it."

"Jesus, that's a bad sign! You watch it, Gill. If the bastard's being reasonable it means he's waiting for a chance to sneak up on you."

"I've told you before…" She saw Kerry was grinning. She smiled back and realised she was beginning to feel like part of Tyler's team.

Chapter 27

When Gill rang off, Tyler put his mobile down and stretched cautiously, assessing how bad he felt today. It was a pleasant surprise to find he was okay.

There was a knock on the door and he called, "Come in."

"Good morning, Kev. I was just going to wake you. It's almost half-past-eight." Lani entered carrying a giant mug of tea.

The last memory he had was of sitting on the sofa. "What the hell? How did I...?" His top half was bare and he resisted the temptation to look under the duvet and see if the bottom matched.

She laughed and he knew she'd read his thoughts. "You were so tired. I thought you were going to end up spending all night on the sofa. But about one o'clock you stirred enough to get in here and into bed." The mischief deepened. "Don't worry, you undressed yourself. Your clean clothes are here."

"Thank you."

"You're welcome. I'll be out for a lot of the day. I'll give you a spare key in case by some miracle you get away earlier than me."

Things were moving too fast for Tyler to get a grip on them. "Are you sure you don't mind me coming back here?"

"If I minded I wouldn't have offered. Unless you want to, there's no point in going back to your house until you've got your electric sorted. You've got enough to contend with, trying to solve this case."

As soon as she left he checked under the duvet. He was still wearing boxers.

He drank the tea and had a quick shower. As he shaved he thought it was luxury to feel warm, clean and smart and not have to grope around in the half-light. Lani had prepared a cooked breakfast and he ate the lot.

Lani was checking papers and inserting them into her briefcase.

"What are you doing today?" he asked.

"The Further Education College have asked me to take Josh Fortune's Empowerment by Creativity class. It's short notice but the students are lovely. They won't worry if I recap my usual stuff."

He was ashamed to realise he didn't know what her usual stuff was and now didn't seem to be the time to ask. He stood up to leave. "Do you need a lift?"

"No, I'm fine thanks. It's only a few minutes walk." She smiled at him. "Have a good day."

"You have a good day too and thanks for everything." He clamped down on an impulse to kiss her goodbye. It seemed a natural thing to do, but she'd stated the ground rules and that wasn't in the bargain.

Back in the office, he busied himself with his mound of paperwork. There were detailed reports on everyone they knew to be involved in the case, and he spared a grateful thought for Gill, who'd obviously spent yesterday evening collating it all. In the information about the adults, he found nothing to indicate they were capable of such violence.

The Quantrull family solicitors confirmed Ian's father had left a large sum of money to be divided between his four grandchildren. Now the money would be split between Charlie and Polly. Ian Quantrull was the executor of his father's will and administrator of his children's fortunes until they came of age. Other less formal checks had revealed that Ian's firm was floundering. Of course that didn't make him unique, or even incompetent. In the present economic climate many firms had sunk without trace. All the same, Tyler wondered if there was any way Ian could use the boys' inheritance.

He moved on to the file recording the assault on Philip Henderson, the archaeologist who'd wanted to excavate in

Stone Park. It was five years ago and he needed to refresh his memory. Tyler had just returned to the area and was building up his present team. He recalled how grateful he'd been for the local knowledge and common-sense of his DI. Roy had been supportive in every way, especially when Tyler's marriage had ended so humiliatingly. He was worried about the way Roy's health had failed and knew he should make time to visit him; but Roy wouldn't expect that while this case was on.

Tyler turned back to the file. He remembered the important facts but the fine detail had faded. Henderson had been attacked just after ten at night, in the quiet suburban road where he lived.

During his hunt for promotion, Tyler had accepted positions that took him all over England but this was his native town and he'd started his working life here. He couldn't remember a time when Purvis hadn't been there, at the edge of the cops' vision, but they couldn't nail him. He was one of those people who got someone else to do their dirty work. George Crosby was the usual fall guy, and he'd been the initial suspect in the assault enquiry. His coat had been discovered abandoned at the scene and it was stained with Philip Henderson's blood. 'Too good to be true' had been Tyler's first thought at the time, although George was so disturbed anything was possible.

But Tyler's gut instinct had been right; George wasn't wearing his coat that night. George was being rushed to hospital, having been discovered staggering along the road, sullying the respectable middle-class pavements with his own blood. His psychotic state had hit rock bottom and he'd slit his wrists.

Tyler wondered why he'd instinctively thought of respectable, middle-class pavements. This truant memory jogged him into going back to check on reports of the incident. The Good Samaritan who'd dialled 999 was a PE teacher at St Ignatius' School. He'd just finished refereeing a five-a-side, indoor football match. George had been five miles away from the road where Philip Henderson was assaulted but very close to Stone Park. Tyler swore softly. What the hell was it with that place?

Brian Purvis also had an alibi but it was made up of his young followers, the kids from his area, over whom he exercised a corrupting influence. Tyler had worked like crazy on the Henderson assault, taking out a lot of his domestic frustration in checking and rechecking each small lead, and talking to the kids who swore Brian hadn't left his house; and, in the end, Purvis' alibi had unravelled.

One of the kids had broken ranks and stated how, on the night in question, Brian had got them all stoned. But this kid didn't like cannabis, so he'd only pretended. He'd seen Brian leave the house and return. And he'd been curious enough to shadow Brian and watch while he hid a pair of boots in the garden shed of the house next door.

The bloodstained, steel-capped boots were swiftly recovered. The middle-aged couple who owned the house were clearly bewildered and dismayed. They rarely used the shed and it had been taken over by their young daughter, Sarah, who was one of Purvis' followers. Tyler's team and the forensic experts did a thorough job tying the boots to Purvis and to the Henderson assault and Purvis was sent down.

But there was more than that. The boy who'd turned against Purvis was Ryan Jones.

Chapter 28

It was mid-morning when Tyler was summoned to the ACC's office. He felt bleak amusement when he saw how relieved his senior officer looked that he was smartly dressed and alert. "Good morning, sir."

"Good morning, Kev. I wasn't sure if you'd be in today."

"I'm fine now."

"DI Martin said you were suffering from food poisoning?"

"Something certainly disagreed with me."

"Well as long as you're better. This case is attracting a lot of media attention."

"We are making progress, sir, but at the moment we're still gathering information and trying to evaluate it."

The ACC frowned. "I don't understand precisely what you mean."

"It's like with Anita Coldstream." Swiftly Tyler out-lined their investigation of Colleen's ex-lover and how promising a suspect she had seemed. He finished up with, "She may be the killer but we haven't got any evidence."

"Yes," said the ACC thoughtfully, "I see."

"The same could be said about half-a-dozen other suspects. And it could be someone we haven't even seen or heard of yet. There weren't many people about that day."

He remembered Lani saying, *'It's so scary. Caz could have been there with Jack. Or I could have been. I often take him there.'*

He shivered when he thought his only view of Lani might have been of her lying dead in Stone Park. "Usually the park's full of small kids but that day there was a charity party in the Town Hall and most of the under-fives were there. Charlie would have been if his little sister hadn't been ill."

The ACC looked horrified. "You mean we could have

had a massacre of toddlers?"

"It's possible. Or maybe, if the park had been full, nothing would have happened. Sir, we need a criminal psychologist who has expertise in the study of child killers."

"You've decided the Quantrull boys were the prime target?"

Tyler cursed his own inaccuracy. "No. Sorry sir. I meant someone who specialises in studying children who have killed."

The ACC stared at him. "Oh God! Not those little boys?"

"I don't like it, sir, but it's a possibility that has to be faced."

"We have to be very sure before we even consider making such an idea public."

"I know. If the psychologist says I'm wrong I'll be glad to hear it but, with respect, I must remind you that you insisted I attended that US conference. You said I should find out the way American crime culture had gone because we're only a couple of steps behind." He stood up. "If you'll excuse me, I need to get moving. I've got other lines of enquiry to pursue."

Back in the Main Office he went straight to Luke Warden's desk. "I reckon it's time I had a chat with Brian Purvis."

"Shall I ring his house and check he's there, sir?"

"No, we'll chance it. With any luck we'll catch him unawares."

As they were leaving, a respectful voice said, "Superintendent Tyler."

Tyler turned to confront PC Ryan Jones. "Constable." The kid looked like a hopeful puppy and he pushed out further words, "DS Buller said you did well in London. I'm glad you were useful."

"Thank you, sir. Sir, I heard you talking about Brian Purvis." Tyler scowled. "I'm sorry, sir, I didn't mean to listen in. It's just I know him. I used to live a few doors away from him. I thought maybe I could help."

"How do you feel about Brian Purvis?"

The boy hesitated. "A lot of people down there think he's wonderful. There's plenty who'll tell you the cops fitted him up. Ever since he got out of prison and wrote that bloody book everyone acts like he's a bloody genius." He coloured and said, "Sorry, sir."

"I've heard worse. But that wasn't what I asked. What do you think of him?"

"I never liked him much, sir." Tyler continued to look steadily at him and he muttered, "Well not for a long while."

"Do you really think you can contribute anything or do you want to enjoy the show?"

By this time the boy was scarlet but he said, "I thought it might unsettle him. If one of the kids who used to hang round him was there to bust him, it might give him a jolt."

"Why did you hang round him if you didn't reckon him?" asked Luke.

For the first time he failed to meet their eyes. "There was a girl... Sarah. She lived next door to him. She thought he was wonderful."

With a quickening of interest, Tyler remembered Sarah had been the girl who'd tried to cover up Purvis' involvement in the assault. Recent reports on Purvis indicated that Sarah was now living with him. Ryan Jones could be the wedge that drove Purvis and Sarah apart. "Okay, convince me."

"No-one down that road has a good word for the police. That was Purvis' doing. My mum had to move house because things got so bad for her, there wasn't a day without broken windows and graffiti and dog shit through the letterbox. I was scared one day they'd burn her out."

"And you think you're going to make it better by going in there with us?"

"I don't think it can make things worse, sir."

"What do you reckon the Duty Sergeant's going to say if you bugger off with CID again?" enquired Luke.

The boy indicated his civilian clothes. "I'm off duty. I only came in with some paperwork that Kerry... DS Buller... asked me to bring back from London."

Tyler knew he should tell the boy to run away and play but it was possible Jones could show him some way of getting through Purvis' defences.

"Luke, I'll be ready in five minutes. Jones, you come with me."

He led the way to his office. "Okay Ryan, I know you gave evidence against Purvis five years ago. Now I want to know why? Is it some spite against him because of this girl? I don't need vendettas buggering up my case."

"No sir! I mean I liked Sarah. But I didn't speak out against him because of that."

"Why then?"

"Well actually it was you, sir."

"Me?" Whatever Tyler had expected it hadn't been that.

"Five years ago you gathered together all the kids who'd been with Brian and told us about how some people wanted power over other people. And you said other people had rights. They had the right to live without being hurt by someone like Brian Purvis. You made me see the way he manipulated people, innocent people like Sarah and vulnerable people like George Crosby. I realised you were right."

And three years later he'd joined the police force. Tyler wondered why everything always turned out to be his fault. Out loud he said, "Okay, you can tag along."

Chapter 29

"Come in, Superintendent." Brian Purvis flung open his front door. "This is a great pleasure. I've often wished to see you again, to thank you."

"Thank me? Why would you think you had any reason to do that?" As before when dealing with this man, Tyler felt as if he was walking along a tightrope.

Purvis smiled at him. "You were the man who, unwittingly I know, set my feet on the Path to Higher Things." He shut the door to the sitting room but Tyler had glimpsed a group of young people gathered there.

"I heard you were pretending to be an academic, nowadays. What are you teaching those kids in there? How to make a writing career out of attempted murder?"

Purvis shook his head reprovingly. Tyler had to admit the bastard had weathered well. He was tall and handsome, there were no lines on his face and no hint of grey in his thick dark hair.

"Superintendent, I'm saddened to see you are still so bitter and so prejudiced. Is there no way I can convince you I'm innocent of harming that poor man?"

Tyler opened his mouth to reply that nothing could make him disbelieve what he knew was the truth but Purvis' attention had left him, his smile slithered past Luke Warden and fastened on Ryan Jones. His voice took on a deeper, warmer note, "My dear Ryan! It's been so long I hardly recognised you. Imagine, little Ryan, grown up and serving the Community."

Tyler cursed himself for bringing Jones here and giving Purvis the chance to jerk another cop around.

To his surprise Ryan responded with a dazzling smile. "Hi there, Bri. Good to see you haven't changed. Even though you've got older and put on weight. I'd guess being banged up with all the other scum does that. Still, like I said, in all that matters, you're the same old Bri that used to bore the shit out of us when we were kids."

As a display of sheer insolence it was superb. Tyler watched as Purvis' smile became rigid. "What do you want, Superintendent? I'm a busy man. I have engagements to teach and to sell my books all over town and many worthy people rely on me."

"You know why I'm here. I want to know about Stone Park."

"As I told your sergeant, I know nothing about the events in that unhappy place."

"What? No insights to offer? I thought that book you were peddling was all about the Stone Park oak?"

"One small chapter only. It is true I have traced the growth of superstition and legend that surrounds that mutilated symbol of the past, but it is only one of the haunted, mysterious places in Saltern that I have written about. But here, please accept this, so that you may discover for yourself the innocence of my writings." He picked up a slim, A-4 sized, hard backed book from a pile on the hall table and held it out to Tyler. "It will give me great pleasure to think of you reading it."

Tyler looked down at the proffered book and read the title, *Shades of Saltern*. The cover illustration wasn't the Stone Park oak; it was the shell of a church, roof and one wall gone. Photographed in black and white, the shadows looked sinister. Tyler recognised the building. The Church of the Holy Innocents. Bombed in the Second World War, it was a wreck but the Local History Society had campaigned to prevent its demolition.

Reluctantly Tyler took the book. If he refused, Purvis would have scored. He'd have to do a pile of paperwork to legitimise this 'gift' so that it could not be termed a bribe. On the other hand, he'd be interested to read it. Know your enemy was always a good rule. "I'll read it with great care.

It'll help me figure out how your mind works."

"I'm flattered." Purvis' smile did not waver but Tyler was sure he'd picked up on the sub-text. "I intend to make such landscapes the theme of my PhD paper. I have a great fancy to hear you call me Doctor Purvis."

One good thing about knowing a scumbag was baiting you was that it removed the temptation to expose yourself. Tyler smiled with a falseness that matched Purvis' own smirk. "The best way would be to get yourself banged up again and get it on the state. I'd be pleased to oblige you and I've got plenty of colleagues who feel the same. Have you seen George Crosby recently?"

"Poor George. I have little in common with him now."

"So you've no idea why he should have referred to Sacrifice of the Innocents and how the oak in Stone Park needed blood?"

"None at all." Purvis turned as the door opened. "Sarah, we have visitors."

"So I see." The girl was young, blonde and pretty. She glared at them. Her hostility intensified when she looked at Ryan Jones. "Brian, I've ironed your shirt and fetched your suit from the dry-cleaners. You must eat before you go."

Purvis stretched out his hand and stroked her cheek. "Dearest Sarah, my practical Martha and my visionary Mary in one exquisite woman."

Behind him Tyler heard Ryan's sharply in-drawn breath. He felt sorry for the boy but he must have known what he was letting himself in for. Or perhaps he hadn't known, hadn't realised Sarah was now Brian Purvis' lover.

"Sarah, I'm Detective Superintendent Tyler of the Serious Crimes Team."

"I know. You're the bastard who fitted Brian up."

He ignored this. "Do you live here, Sarah?"

Her colour flared. "Mind your own business! I'm over eighteen and I can live where I want."

Purvis intervened, "Sarah's parents moved away, so now

159

she lives here with me."

"I see." Tyler chose his words carefully. The girl was already hostile and instinctively he knew that wasn't the way to get information out of her. "Sarah, I'm sure you've heard about what's happened in Stone Park. I'm the senior officer investigating that dreadful crime. Two of the victims were children. I was hoping Brian could help us find out who killed them."

He saw her gesture of protest and continued hastily, "Brian has a lot of influence and people tell him things. If someone's gone crazy we've got to stop them before they decide the Sacred Oak needs more blood."

He put all of his persuasive powers into this speech and was gratified to see her hostility lessen. "None of Brian's friends would do anything like that…"

"How about George Crosby? He's had some pretty bad mental health problems."

"I suppose… yes, I suppose George…" She wrenched her gaze away from him. "Brian, you must get ready, otherwise you'll be late."

Tyler hadn't got far but he knew that it was time to call it quits… at least for now. "We'll be in touch." Despite his initial show of welcome, Purvis hadn't let them get further than the front hall.

In the street, Tyler said, "Luke, take your car down the road and park. Might be worth keeping an eye open to see if George Crosby turns up to talk to Purvis. I'll get someone to relieve you as soon as I can."

"No problem, sir. But do you really think he's tied up with the Stone Park killings?"

"Probably not. It's even possible he's going straight. Chances are I loathe the bastard so much I'm making something out of nothing."

"Sir, may I stay with DS Warden?" asked Ryan Jones.

"Keen aren't you? Yeah, you can stay, as long as you do what you're told without any argument. What can you

160

tell me about Sarah? Apart from the fact you fancy her. I've already worked that out."

Ryan ignored Luke's laughter and said with creditable dignity, "She's twenty, the same age as me. We were at school together. She's an only child and her parents were quite old when they had her. They're very conventional and strict, and they were really upset when Sarah tried to cover up what Brian had done. They took it so hard that her dad took early retirement and they moved right away to Pevensey. It's a village on the East Sussex coast."

Tyler was puzzled. "Surely they took Sarah with them? She can't have been more than fourteen when Purvis was sent down."

"Yeah, but when he got out, he whistled and she came running. There was nothing her parents could do. She was eighteen by then." Ryan sounded bitter.

"Well just make sure your feelings don't get the better of you. See you later, Luke. I'll walk to the High Street and grab a taxi."

"You heading back to Stone Park, sir?" asked Luke.

"I'm off to the kids' school. Why?"

"The forensics team have finished and uniformed were wondering how much longer they should secure the park."

Tyler's instinct was to keep a guard on the place until the case was solved, but that could mean forever. "We need someone there in the day to keep off sightseers but, subject to the ACC's approval, I don't see the need to keep anyone there at night."

"That'll please the uniformed lads. They hate being there… said the place felt evil."

Tyler scowled. "I've had enough supernatural garbage for one day. Any cops that start going psychic and talking about evil places will wish they hadn't if I hear them."

Tyler walked briskly, enjoying the exercise. As he strode along he phoned Gill Martin and arranged to meet her outside the school. He passed Colleen's dress shop, closed and shuttered, and wondered what Sophie would do with the business. Further along the High Street he took a taxi. His appointment was at two-thirty and he had no intention of being late.

The taxi dropped him off in the road beside Stone Park. Walking towards the school he spotted Gill, sitting in her car with her laptop open. He tapped softly on the side window and she jumped, then smiled and released the central locking. He slid into the front passenger seat and she said, "Lost your car again, sir?"

"Something like that. Any joy with Anita Coldstream?"

"It's like we thought. She says she wanted her jewellery to be used for a good cause, without getting tied up in litigation. The only jewellery she kept back were gifts Colleen had given her."

Tyler sighed. "I reckon she's moved from front runner to a long way back."

"Yes sir. Have you had any luck?"

"I've spent my lunch hour talking to Brian Purvis, which isn't my idea of luck. Speaking of which, if you look to your right you'll see George Crosby who used to be Purvis' second-in-command."

"The big guy with a face like a gorilla who's talking to himself?"

"Don't knock it. George has to talk to himself, no-one else will listen. Now why the hell's he going into Stone Park?"

"I don't know, sir, but I can find out. He doesn't know me."

"Okay but keep your distance, he's a seriously deranged man."

"I will." Gill slid out of the car and then paused to say, "There's a spare sandwich in the glove compartment if you're hungry."

"Cheers." Tyler watched her vanish in the direction of

162

the park and then investigated the glove compartment. The first thing he found was an elegant silk scarf. As he pulled it clear its perfume made him think of Jasmine Quantrull. He realised it belonged to Isabel; who'd worn the same heavy, flower-drenched perfume the evening he'd met her in the restaurant. Further exploration revealed a ham and salad sandwich. As he ate he thought there were advantages in having a civilised DI. The last time he'd been in Roy's car the only food available had been a carton of abandoned, mould-furred fish and chips.

Gill returned and said, "He wanted to go and touch the oak. When our guys told him to bugger off he got quite nasty but they managed to send him on his way."

"God knows what's going on in that poor bastard's mind. Thanks for the sandwich."

"You're welcome. Is there anything new on the house-to-house or the forensics?"

"We're still waiting on forensics but the house-to-house hasn't turned up anything. It's a drain on manpower, so Reg Rowner and I have agreed to call it a day. Hardly anyone seems to have been out and about, apart from that neighbour of the Quantrulls who called round to deliver the church magazine and got no answer."

Gill nodded. "Jasmin said this woman always stays for hours so she didn't answer. The woman said she knew someone must be in because she heard Polly crying."

"You spoke to the neighbour yourself?" He was impressed by her thoroughness.

"I thought I ought to, as she'd been wandering around the neighbourhood at the time. She wasn't a good witness. The sort who gets an idea in her head and won't budge."

"How do you mean?"

"She insisted the paper-boy had already been past, even though the evening paper hadn't been delivered and the kid didn't get out of school for another two hours."

"What made her think he'd been there?"

"She couldn't give any reason. According to the newsagent she blames everything on the paper-boy. She gave me an earful about the kid and when I said I couldn't arrest him for cycling over her grass, she told me she didn't know what the police were coming to."

Tyler grinned. "One of the *'Bring Back Dixon of Dock Green'* Brigade?" He glanced at his watch. "Time for that bloody school."

"It's a miserable looking place. I can't imagine why anyone would want to send their kids there, much less pay to do it," said Gill.

"Yeah." Greatly daring, he ventured into the realms of literature, although not poetry. "Dickens described the doors of Newgate Prison as looking as if they were made for the express purpose of letting people in, and never letting them out again." He eyed the grim, four-storey building. "Talk about the happiest days of your life! I've seen Remand Homes that looked more inviting."

Chapter 30

Their appointment had been diverted to the Headmaster's secretary and there was no sign of the Great Man himself. Tyler declared this was inadequate. Their subsequent progress through the school hierarchy was slow. Gill admired the patient determination with which Tyler dealt with the tangle of red tape. It seemed, in St Ignatius' School, the Headmaster was not only more powerful than God but a great deal less accessible. At last they battled through.

Dr James Rowanbridge, PhD was a tall, harsh-featured man of about Tyler's age. Tyler shook hands and sat down. Gill felt uncomfortable. The place was overwhelmingly male-dominated. Instinctively she moved into the background to maintain an observer's role.

"I'm grateful for your time, sir, and I don't wish to waste it," said Tyler. "Still less do I wish to waste my own. We need to know the truth about Timothy and Barnabas Quantrull and that includes their behaviour in school. We also need information about their relationship with each other, their family and their friends."

The Headmaster regarded him coldly. "These things cannot be relevant. I would prefer the School not to be involved."

"The children attended this school; that means it is involved. And, in this enquiry I'm the person who decides what's relevant. Anything I discard will be forgotten and anything I keep on board will be used as tactfully as possible." An implacable note crept into Tyler's voice, "But if I have to waste time and manpower forcing people to co-operate, the chances are the Press will hear about it."

There was a moment's silence then Dr Rowanbridge said, "I anticipated these questions and have made enquiries of my staff."

"And?" said Tyler.

Dr. Rowanbridge spoke reluctantly, clearly measuring his words, "In the past year there has been a degree of disruptive behaviour centred around the Quantrull boys."

"What sort of disruptive behaviour?"

"It's not easy to be specific. It was mainly in their attitude. There was a falling off of work standards; some insolence; aggressive behaviour in the playground and other matters of that kind. I must admit I found it rather ironic that Timothy was frequently getting into fights when he was excused from physical contact games because of the illness he suffered some years ago."

"Were both of them aggressive?"

"Mainly Timothy, but Barnabas tended to follow him into trouble, often in an attempt to extricate him from the consequences of his misdeeds. Timothy was an exceptionally clever boy but he lacked self-control."

"And Barney?"

"He was a quieter child and not outstanding in any way."

His tone was dismissive. Gill saw a glint in Tyler's amber eyes but his manner was still moderate as he said, "You've had a lot of experience of children, Dr Rowanbridge. Why do you think the boys' behaviour had deteriorated?"

"I cannot answer that. They were approaching adolescence, never an easy time."

"Do you think they were capable of extreme violence, sir?"

For a second, Gill was appalled at the chance Tyler was taking. It was crazy to show what they were thinking about such a sensitive case. But of course the Headmaster wanted adverse publicity even less than the cops.

"I don't know. Are you thinking...?" Dr Rowanbridge's question trailed away.

"I don't know." Tyler echoed the same words. "Thanks for your co-operation, sir. I'll need dates, times and details of the skiving and other incidents."

"I will give instructions to have a list compiled."

Tyler handed him a business card. "I'd be grateful if it was on my desk first thing tomorrow."

Dr Rowanbridge pursed his lips but said, "I'll do my best to oblige you."

"Thank you. And I'll need a list of Tim and Barney's friends and any teachers who had day-to-day dealings with them. One of my officers will have to talk to them, so I'll need permission from their parents, unless you happen to be in *loco parentis*."

Dr Rowanbridge's air of displeasure deepened. "I will consider your request."

"It's essential."

"I hope I can rely upon your discretion. You cannot comprehend the qualities we instil in our pupils: strength, leadership, power, the ability to forge ahead."

Tyler's reply surprised Gill. "My brother-in-law came here and I've seen from him what sort of people this school turns out."

"Your brother-in-law?"

"Alexander Mabberley."

"Alex Mabberley! Good Heavens! We were at this school together nearly forty years ago. He was the year above me. Let me see, he'd be forty-nine now if he'd lived. And, of course, his three sons were at school here at the time of the tragedy."

Gill saw the shock on Tyler's face. He couldn't have been more stunned if the headmaster had hit him with the antique axe that hung on the wall behind his desk. She said hastily, "The Superintendent doesn't like to talk about it, sir."

"Of course. I understand." He shook hands with Tyler with more warmth than formerly and showed them to the door. "If you don't mind waiting a few minutes I'll instruct the boys' Form Tutor to compile a list of their close friends and I'll get the rest of the information to you as soon as possible. I'm sure you can be trusted to safeguard our reputation as

167

carefully as Mabberley would have himself."

As they waited in the secretary's office, Tyler was silent and preoccupied. Gill picked up a school prospectus and studied it but, from behind its glossy pages, she kept a protective eye on him. When the secretary returned with the list, it was Gill who accepted it. There were four names: Jonathan Tuckerdale, Robert Bruce-Williams, Nigel Bartell and Henry Dovedale. At the moment they meant nothing to her but she'd have to get to know them. Any one of them could have the key to what had been going on with Tim and Barney.

Gill and Tyler walked in silence back to her car. Once they were seated she asked, "You okay, sir?"

Tyler drew a deep breath. "Yeah. Thanks for covering for me. I didn't see that one coming."

"But didn't you know your brother-in-law was dead?"

"No. My wife and I are divorced."

"But it was all over the news. I remember the headline in the local paper, *'Prominent Local Family Wiped Out In Plane Crash.'*"

He stared at her. "Did you say family wiped out?"

"That's right. Alexander Mabberley, his wife and their three sons. Their private plane crashed while he was piloting it."

"When was this?"

"About a year... maybe fourteen or fifteen months ago."

"I was on a long extradition trip around then."

"I'm sorry. It must have been an awful shock, hearing it like that."

"Too right it was. I'm sorry about the kids but I hardly knew them and I couldn't stand Alexander or his wife." He leaned forward, suddenly alert. "There's George again. Pull over will you?"

Gill obeyed and watched as the tall, stooping figure shambled towards them. He was muttering and tears were pouring down his cheeks.

"The poor old sod," she said.

"Sod but not old. George is only in his mid-thirties."

"But he looks at least sixty!"

Tyler shrugged. "There are a lot of things that can age a person, grief, pain, ill-health, drugs, homelessness, but you throw mental sickness into the boiling pot and you've got the real ageing formula. I'll have a word with him." He clambered out of the car. "You can go on back to the Station if you like. I can get a taxi."

"No, I'll wait for you." Gill thought if anything went wrong, she didn't want to explain she'd abandoned him with a loony outside that famous death spot, Stone Park.

She watched as he walked up to George Crosby and spoke to him, then drew him to sit on a low wall that bordered the entrance to the park. She couldn't hear what they were saying but she could see George doing most of the talking. He kept moving towards Tyler as the Superintendent edged away. At last Tyler got to his feet. He took out his wallet, removed a banknote and handed it to George, then he walked back to the car.

"Get anything, sir?" asked Gill.

"Just a face full of saliva." Tyler rummaged in his pocket, produced a wad of tissues, wiped his face and then moved down to blot his shirt. "You always know how near the edge George is by the amount of spray. The poor bastard's pretty bad today. I think he's due for another trip to the mental hospital. I'll get someone to ring through to Social Services and ask them to keep an eye on him."

"I saw you give him money."

Tyler glared at her and she waited for the thunderbolt to fall, but he said quietly, "He's been chucked out of his lodgings. Not that I blame his landlady. I mean George isn't the sort of thing you'd want loose in your house when he's having a funny turn. But ten quid will get him a hot meal. He'd been round to his friend Brian's but with him charity begins with Number One and finishes there as well."

169

Gill thought there must be a Biblical quote in that but she was pretty sure Tyler had endured enough assorted religions for one day.

She changed the subject, "You know how it worried me that the killer must have had some experience with guns?"

"Yeah?"

"While we were waiting for that information, I was reading the school prospectus. They advertise marksmanship as one of their sports activities."

Tyler stared at her, his amber eyes intent. "I should have guessed. Oh God, it makes sense, doesn't it? Not just a couple of kids on a killing spree but a couple of kids who were trained in marksmanship."

Chapter 31

Tyler had got it planned. This evening he'd take Lani somewhere special to eat. He'd show her he could behave like a civilised human being.

He turned the key in the door and called, "Lani, it's me."

He heard the sound of laughter from the kitchen then Lani appeared leading a toddler. "Hi Kev, you're nice and early. Or is this just a break and you've got to go back to work?"

"No, I'm finished for the night, all being well. But I can go off somewhere if I'm in your way."

"Of course you're not. This is my Jack. Darling, this is Uncle Kev."

"Unc Kev." The child's face was screwed up with concentration as he processed this new name, then he gave an enchanting smile and said, "Dinner."

"Just a few more minutes," said Lani.

"Grandma, Unc Kev dinner," said Jack, obviously determined to make his point.

"Of course Uncle Kev's staying for dinner. You happy with pasta, Kev?"

So much for dreams of a sophisticated evening to impress the lady. "That's great."

They ate at the table. Not dinner party manners but the sort that set a good example to a child. The sauce was not very spicy but that was more than compensated for by the pasta dinosaurs.

"How did it go today?" he asked Lani.

"Good. The students were upset about Josh so we made him a tape of messages and songs. Would it be all right if I dropped it into the hospital tomorrow?"

"Of course. He's still sedated but they say he's holding his own."

171

"I'm glad. How was your day?"

"Weird. I'll tell you about it later. As long as you don't mind me off-loading?"

"Of course I don't. I want to know anything you can tell me."

Tyler felt ashamed. "It hit me this morning, I don't know what you teach."

"I'm part of a therapy by creativity programme, which makes it sound a lot posher than it is. It's trying to help people to step beyond the stuff in their lives that's pulling them down and use their experiences to write or sing or dance or paint or sculpt." She leaned across and wiped Jack's mouth. "All right, darling, you can get down now."

"Grandma peep-bo," said Jack.

"Please," said Lani.

"Please Grandma."

She smiled at Tyler. "Excuse us. This may take some time."

The game seemed to involve Jack and Lani both putting their heads under an ornate embroidered throw and demanding loudly to know where the other was. At irregular intervals one of them would emerge with a loud shout of 'Peep-bo!' Sometimes both would appear at the same time, which occasioned much giggling and a tickle fight.

The ring of Lani's phone summoned her. She answered, then covered the receiver, "Kev, can you keep an eye on Jack? It's business."

"Sure." Tyler hoped he didn't sound as terrified by the prospect as he felt.

She took the phone into the bedroom and Jack fixed Tyler with a firm eye. "Unc Kev peep-bo."

Actually it wasn't difficult. Not once he'd shelved his inhibitions. Tyler discovered that almost-three-year-olds are wonderfully non-critical, they don't think you're making a fool of yourself even when you are.

He emerged from a vigorous tickle-fight to see Lani

smiling at them. "Okay Jack, time to get ready to go home."

She went through a departure countdown as sophisticated as preparations for a lunar lift off, although Tyler suspected astronauts weren't told, "Now come and do a wee before we go."

While Lani supervised Jack in the cloakroom, Tyler wandered round restoring toys to the box in the corner. A scrapbook caught his eye: '*My Book about me and my Family. Jack's book.*' Smiling he opened it and flicked through, then he stopped and stared. The page featured '*Mummy and Grandma when Mummy was at school.*' Carys was in her early teens but she was more easily recognisable than Lani. In this picture she was a drably dressed, podgy woman with nervous eyes and a deprecating smile. Feeling like a Peeping Tom he shut the book and thrust it deep into the box.

Lani and Jack appeared dressed for the outdoors. She said, "Thanks for tidying up, Kev. I should make him do it but, when he's tired, it's a struggle. Jack, say thank you to Uncle Kev."

"Thank you Unc Kev."

Jack put his face up and Lani said, "He's offering you a kiss."

Tyler bent and kissed the soft cheek. How could anyone deliberately hurt a child?

They left and Tyler had a shower and changed his clothes. Contact with George Crosby had made him feel sad and soiled. Then he cleared the table and loaded the dishwasher. It was strange, this feeling of domesticity. Even when he'd been married it hadn't been like this. Vivienne had received an allowance from her parents and she'd employed a cleaner who'd done the washing and ironing, also a gardener twice a week and called in people to do decorating and DIY. Viv had arranged flowers and she'd cooked occasionally, extravagant, exotic dishes. She'd held dinner parties, loathsome affairs with people who bored him. But there were other occasions when she'd cooked just for him. Tyler had always associated

Vivienne's intimate dinners for two with a demand for something he couldn't afford or wouldn't wish to do.

Forty minutes later, when Lani returned, he was sitting, reading Purvis' book and finding it heavy going. Concentrating, he didn't hear her until she entered the room. Caught unawares he looked up and smiled. "I'm glad you're back."

She laughed at him. "And I've been away so long. What's that you're reading?"

"It's called *Shades of Saltern*." He raised it so she could see the cover. "It's about…"

"I know what it's about. I've read it. I had to for work. The man who wrote it came into College to give a talk and I had to introduce him and field the questions afterwards. Why are you reading it? It hardly comes under the category great literature although a lot of the purple prose should be considered a crime."

Tyler grinned. "Like you, I'm reading it for work. I'm looking for clues to send the author down for another long stretch."

"Sounds like a plan. It's a pity he can't do prison time for massacring the English language. I've never waded through so many over-used adverbs and adjectives in my entire career." Then, suddenly serious. "Do you think Brian Purvis is connected to what's happened in Stone Park?"

"I don't know. Instinct says he's got something to do with it, but the only connection I've got is him writing about the oak in this book. What did you think of him?

"Too slimy for my taste and too keen on trading on his image as a poor, wrongly-imprisoned, misunderstood victim. And, apart from the style, I don't like the reactionary tone of it. Nothing is to be altered or investigated or even renovated."

"You're right." He wondered what he had done to deserve a woman with such insight. He found himself saying, "Lani, why me?"

She didn't play games or pretend not to understand. "I

174

think it was because of your intelligence."

"My what?" Of all the reasons he'd considered that hadn't been in his reckoning.

"I told you I'd seen you in Court. I'd seen plenty of other cops give evidence but you were different. It was as if you could out-think the lawyers. You were usually several steps ahead of them."

He stared at her, astonished and half-horrified. "That makes me sound as bad as the bloody lawyers."

In her smile he could see indulgence, affection and amusement, but no reassurance he wasn't as bad as the barristers. It hit him that she was as intelligent as he was and a lot more intuitive. There were few people in his life for whom he'd felt that ultimate respect.

"And then," she continued, "I met you and we seemed to get along. We laugh at the same things. That's what's so special about you, you know when I'm joking."

Tyler thought it would have been nice if she'd fancied him for his looks, sex appeal and sophisticated charm but he hadn't really believed that and to be valued for his intelligence and sense of humour was better than the reason he'd thought most probable. "I thought you were being kind because you felt sorry for me."

She stared at him, her expression comical in its surprise. "Detective Superintendent Tyler, has anyone ever mentioned you've got serious problems with your self-esteem?"

In that moment, he realised Lani had seen right through him. Through the tough-guy image. Through the veneer of ambitious, unyielding cop to the central insecurity and the socially shy man. "Most people say I'm an arrogant bastard."

"Of course they do. What's the point of protective camouflage if it's transparent? Are you the oldest in your family?"

That question surprised him. "Yeah, I'm the oldest of four."

"I thought you might be. Are your parents still alive?"

"Mum is. Dad died when I was nine. Mum got married again when I was fifteen."

He remembered the disorientation of that adjustment. He'd spent over six years acting as his mum's 'Man of the House' and then he'd been relegated back to kid status.

"I see."

"What do you see?" Whatever Lani saw was likely to be too much.

"A hard-worker and high-achiever. Everyone around him expected a hundred per cent all the time and he expected it of himself and still does."

He remembered his mum's words when he got a B for his O-level Chemistry. *'What went wrong then? You didn't work hard enough did you? Too busy reading poetry.'* The success of his nine 'A' grades had turned sour when she said that.

"How did you know?"

"Typical profile of a high achiever with low self-esteem. A lot of them were kids who were brought up with the words *'Only ninety-nine per cent? What went wrong?'*"

He wasn't sure if he hated being so transparent or if it was wonderfully restful. "I haven't seen my family for years. Mum loathed Vivienne. She thought she was a posh, snobbish bitch."

"And was she wrong?" enquired Lani.

"No. And Viv said Mum was an intolerant, overbearing old cow and she called it right as well."

"Poor Kev, stuck in the middle of two warring women."

He desperately wanted to kiss her. To avert the danger, he lurched into speech, "The only thing they agreed about was I should quit being a cop."

"Why?"

"Vivienne wanted me to join her father's firm and Mum thought it would be a safer life for me. My dad was a cop. He had to take early retirement after a gang of drunks gave him a kicking. His kidneys packed up and he was only forty when he died."

"I see."

Tyler leaned forward on the sofa, hands clenched, shoulders tense. "Mum did try to keep in touch until Viv made it so bloody unpleasant it became impossible."

"Well Vivienne's not between you anymore."

"Yes she is. I never told Mum that Viv had left. I thought she'd say 'I told you so.'"

Lani stared at him. "As I said, you have serious issues with your self-esteem."

"And I thought I was a bloody thick bastard."

"That is a credible alternative explanation."

He grinned but said, "At least I found out today why Vivienne decided to have a baby with her new guy when she hated the idea with me."

"Okay, tell me why this stupid woman with incredibly poor taste is now pregnant?"

"Her brother died last year in a plane crash, and his kids died as well."

"You mean they're having a child to provide an heir for Vivienne's father's firm?"

"I know it sounds crazy but it's the only reason I can think of."

"That poor little sod!"

He was puzzled, then he realised she meant the baby. He sighed.

"Worrying isn't going to help, Kev. It's not your problem."

"I know." To change the subject, he asked, "What were you like as a child?"

"Awkward, ordinary and overweight," came the prompt reply. "And clumsy, shy and stubborn. While Isabel was beautiful and good at everything. My parents found me a disappointment."

He was silent, not knowing what to say.

"That's why I got married halfway through my teacher training course. I was living at home because Dad wouldn't

177

pay his part of the grant and I was desperate to get away from my parents. It was a selfish, wicked thing to do... and stupid when David was so like Dad. He had to have control of everything... and everyone."

"Did he hurt you?" It was implicit in her defensive body language.

Lani looked down at her hands and, with a visible effort, controlled their nervous movements. "It was mainly psychological domination. He wasn't physically violent very often and then he went in for shaking and pushing rather than anything too extreme. But yes, he made us afraid."

"The bastard!"

Lani's determined brightness flickered. "Of course, if he was violent, he'd say it was our fault for provoking him. He'd claim he couldn't control his temper."

"That's nonsense!"

"I know. But I didn't have the courage to break free until I had to."

"Why did you have to?" Tyler spoke with careful gentleness.

She gave a wavering smile. "I realised that Caz and Gareth were growing up to be like me. They didn't believe they were beautiful or loveable. So I took them away. I went back to teaching and got us a very grotty flat. It wasn't easy."

Tyler was silent, uncertain what to say.

She looked at him cautiously and said, "Do you think I'm horrible?"

"God no! Why should I?" He supplied his own answer, "Because of Vivienne leaving me, you mean? I didn't blame her for going. We had nothing in common and I was hardly ever there. What I hated her for was the vindictiveness, for running off in the most public way she could and making me look like an idiot at work."

"David said I'd ruined his life," whispered Lani. "He died six years ago. He killed himself. He left a note saying it was all my fault."

Surely, in such circumstances, a hug is permitted between friends? Tyler put his arms round her. "It wasn't your fault. He sounds like the sort of guy who always had to blame somebody else. Anyway, you got through it. You didn't let him break you."

"No, but it was a close run thing." She wouldn't meet his eyes. "I was a total mess for quite some time."

Tyler remembered the picture in Jack's album and Lani's description of Mrs Robinson regaining her life after being a 'fat mess.' He hugged her even tighter.

After a moment, she smiled at him. "It's over. And I've got my kids and Jack. I'm going to make a cup of tea."

He followed her into the kitchen. She was dressed in jeans and a baggy jumper. No make-up, no jewellery, no pretence, the real thing through and through.

"Would you like a cake, Kev?"

"Please."

She picked up a tray and held it out for him to take his choice. He gazed, entranced, at the medley of chocolate cup cakes decorated with clowns' faces made from Smarties and coloured icing. Many of the faces were skew-whiff.

"Jack and I had a baking session," she said, rearranging a few sweets that had slithered off the side in a torrent of chocolate icing. "He took a lot home with him but he wanted to leave some for us."

"They're all different."

"Of course. No two clowns have the same make-up."

He selected a red-nosed clown with green eyes and orange hair. "Aren't you having one?"

"I shouldn't but I'm going to."

"Why shouldn't you?"

"Too fat already."

"Lani you're beautiful!" The words reverberated around the kitchen.

She turned to face him, her expression incredulous. In her preoccupation she tilted the tray and all the cakes slithered dangerously to the side.

He leapt forward to save them. He righted the tray and they stood, both clutching it, staring at each other.

Lani broke the silence, "You see, I told you I was clumsy. I'm always breaking things." Her voice was breathless but she made a good try for casual.

All those years of reading poetry and when he needed a good line of love poetry his mind was a total blank. "You don't break people," he said. "You put them together when they're falling apart."

She stared at him. "Oh Kev!"

Tyler saw tears glimmering in her eyes. He felt an overwhelming rush of tenderness surge through him. And something else, a desperate sexual urge. He felt his flies taking the strain and didn't dare look down to see how obvious it was.

He said huskily, "Lani, you know that agreement we made? Just friendship, no commitment or anything?... I wondered?... Is it possible?... Would you mind?... Could we change the rules?"

She moved towards him. He was astounded by the radiance in her face.

"Kev darling, it's our game. We can change anything we want."

Chapter 32

"Incredible!" Tyler didn't mean to say the word out loud but the feeling hit him the moment he opened his eyes. Nowadays it was rare for him to feel more than the mildest surprise. It occurred to him that he'd been so afraid of being hurt he'd encased his emotions in armour, a protective shell that kept him safe... and lonely.

She was curled into a soft curve, facing him. Now she opened her eyes and smiled at him then shuffled closer and raised her face for a kiss. It was early, ages before he had to go to work. He wondered whether Lani could be up for it again. He placed a tentative hand on the inside of her thigh. There was no doubt about her response.

Love making over, they lay, holding each other. He smiled down at her. "I've been longing to do that since that night in the restaurant."

She laughed back at him, her green eyes alight with mischief. "I can do better than that. I've been lusting after you since I first saw you in Court."

An hour later, dressed and sleek with satisfaction, he went through to the kitchen. Lani was there, preparing to cook breakfast, but she turned as he came in. "Kev, there's something we need to talk about."

He felt a shiver of fear. Her embarrassment warned him this was something she found hard to say. He should have known it was too good to be true.

"What is it?" Dread made his voice harsh.

"It's about contraception. At my age I know it's not likely I'll get pregnant but it's not impossible. I'll get the Morning After Pill today but we'll have to use condoms until I get sorted with the Pill."

He stared at her, speechless with relief.

She must have misunderstood his dazed expression.

"That's if you want us to carry on. I understand if it was a one-night thing. For God's sake say something, even if it's 'Goodbye.' I promise I won't throw the frying pan at you."

He pushed out clumsy words, "I want this to last."

Her flustered look turned to happiness. She crossed the kitchen and kissed him.

After an enjoyable few minutes, he said, "You don't need the Pill, I had the snip years ago." Her enquiring look pushed him into explanation, "I told you Viv didn't want kids. She decided the Pill wasn't good for her, so we went to condoms but we must have slipped up and she got pregnant. She had an abortion. She made me feel like the whole thing was my fault so I agreed to have it done. Even the posh private clinic her parents paid for weren't keen. I was only thirty-one."

Lani hugged him. He felt the movement of her lips as her face pressed against his shoulder.

"What are you saying?"

She pushed away slightly. "I was ill-wishing the bitch." She must have seen his shock. "I don't mean bad things for her baby, but I hope she has an excruciatingly painful labour and afterwards everything sags and she looks really old."

He started to laugh. "And she gets so bad-tempered that she takes it out on the toy boy the way she used to do with me. You don't need to worry about us doing it unprotected. After Vivienne left, I realised she'd been screwing round, so I got myself checked out. I haven't been with anyone since we split up."

No time, no energy, no confidence to make a new relationship. Too wary to go for one-night-stands or paid sex, he'd seen too many cops bugger up that way.

"I didn't need to ask, I knew I'd be safe with you. I'm okay as well. No-one but David, and he didn't sleep around."

There was something else he wanted to know. "When I asked what you'd first seen in me you said it was my intelligence but this morning it sounded as if you'd fancied me from the start?"

"Of course I did."

He asked again, "Lani, why me?"

Her green eyes were alight with mischief but she said seriously, "When I first saw you, giving evidence in Court, you took my breath away. I stayed there just to watch you. You look so tough but there's so much beneath the surface. You must know you're a very sexy guy."

"No." As a self-image that was totally new to him.

Chapter 33

"The Bossman's on top form." Kerry sounded pleased and Gill wondered if she'd misread the team dynamics.

"I guess he's over the jet lag and food poisoning."

"Yeah," said Kerry, cynicism dripping from her voice. "You're looking good too. What did you do last night?"

Gill stiffened. It was time to renew the firewall around her private life. "I managed to put in a session in the gym." Not to mention a training run, despite the cold and dark, and an intimate evening with Isabel.

Throughout the briefing Tyler was crisp, succinct and totally on the ball, but it was undeniable that no satisfactory progress had been made. Gill was aware of the Criminal Psychologist, a slim, brown-haired woman, who sat in the background quietly taking notes.

At last Tyler dismissed most of the officers. Only his own team and the psychologist remained. He said, "This is Dr Tremaine. She's going to see if she can shed any light on things. I want it clearly understood that what's said isn't to go any further."

He outlined his suspicions of the Quantrull boys, then said, "Dr Tremaine, would you like to take it from here?"

She moved to the front of the room. "Thank you, Superintendent. I've looked at the evidence and I can't make any definitive statements on the subject. It's quite possible that the two boys, with Timothy as the leader, committed these crimes. There's plenty of reasons for their aggression: a disturbed home background: the loss of their mother; a father who drinks too much; and an unsympathetic stepmother."

"Charlie's far behind the usual development of a child his age," said Tyler.

"I'm arranging for access to his health records," said Dr Tremaine. "There can be many reasons for delayed development but it could be the result of stress or abuse at home. As for the older boys, from all you've told me, they definitely had problems. I'm especially concerned with the mutilation of the doll and the story the stepmother told DI Martin about Tim killing the rabbit. Did anyone check it was true?"

"I phoned the family vet," said Gill. "He confirmed the boys' pet rabbit was put to sleep after Ian brought it in with a broken back, but Ian had said it was an accident."

The psychologist nodded acknowledgement. "Thank you, Inspector. I wonder, is there any sign of Internet communications indicating the boys had violent interests or that they were being groomed by a person with violent intentions?"

Gill saw Tyler's expression. It mirrored her own thought of, *'Oh shit!'*

"Not that we've found," said Kerry. She flashed Tyler a cheeky grin. "The Superintendent gets me to check out the computer side of things. The parents gave permission for me to check the computers in the house. The boys only had games computers, no Internet access. Some of the games are quite violent but I've seen a lot worse. Ian Quantrull said he doesn't keep a computer at home."

"That's right," agreed Gill. "Although occasionally he'll bring a laptop from the office. Jasmin was going... saying she didn't like him working from home."

The psychologist said, "Were you about to say that Jasmin was 'going on' about her husband bringing work home?"

"Yes." Gill felt uncomfortable.

"Does Jasmin 'go on'?"

"I suppose she does, but it's not so much nagging as a sort of little girl whine."

"And how does Ian respond?"

"At the moment he's pretty shut off from everything. She's burying herself in their baby girl and he's drowning himself in drink."

"What I want to know is why a family like the Quantrulls don't have Internet for their kids at home," said Tyler. "Gill, can you try and find out, please?"

"Yes sir." Gill mentally scheduled another 'casual chat' with Jasmin.

"And we've still got to check the computers at the school," continued Tyler. "With any luck we'll get to them today. You got any thoughts for us, Doctor?"

"It's difficult, Superintendent. If the gun had been found *in situ* it would have made life a lot easier. For that matter it would help if we could be sure the killer removed the gun. As it is, the absence of the weapon could indicate an organised killer or a very disorganised one, or its removal could be nothing to do with the killer. I presume, if you believe the Quantrull boys did the shootings, you are assuming Daniel Peters must have removed the weapon?"

"He may have, I wouldn't say must."

"Do you think he's telling the truth?"

Tyler shrugged. "He's got no record of violence or any sort of crime."

"And what do you think of his art? I found a great deal of it extremely sensual."

Gill thought it was another *'oh shit, we should have thought of that'* moment, but Tyler said, "Sensual certainly, but nothing perverted in it that I could see. Not that I'm an expert and I've only seen the catalogue pictures of his work."

Dr Tremaine persisted, "There's a pattern of behaviour where violent rage can give way to remorse, that would account for the phone call to the emergency services. The breakdown of his marriage may have sent him over the edge. He was a high-profile artist. People in the public eye find it hard to cope with humiliation."

Gill was aware of tension in the room. Tyler's own marital breakdown had been played out in the most humiliating circumstances for all his subordinates to see. None of the team was looking directly at him but everybody was aware of him and nervous about his response.

His tiger-eyes were hot but his voice was ice. "Even if his wife walking out on him had turned Dan Peters into a violent killer, it doesn't explain how or why he hit himself over the head with sufficient force to cause severe concussion. Psychological theorising is fine but only when it's taken in context with physical evidence."

Their eyes locked. The psychologist looked away first.

Tyler's voice lost its challenge. "There's also Brian Purvis and George Crosby. Purvis has got an alibi but he's a manipulative bastard who could still be behind everything. In that case, the person who pulled the trigger is probably George Crosby. He's got a history of violence and mental illness and used to do Purvis' dirty work."

"I read the reports you sent me. Because they've both been in prison we've got a lot more details about Purvis and Crosby. I'd say together they made the perfect machine to maximise violence and damage to the community. Purvis is the planner and, as you say, he's manipulative. Crosby is a creature of misguided conscience, a man with sincere but dangerous beliefs."

There were imperfectly smothered sounds of derision from the team. Tyler glared them down. "Do you reckon Crosby or Purvis could be behind the Stone Park shootings, Doctor?"

"It's possible. If Crosby did it there will have been a reason but it may be so bizarre no-one would recognise it. But Crosby has always used hands-on violence. I think the killings were too remote for him and there'd be no thought of concealing evidence."

"So that would be where Purvis came in?"

She nodded, clearly approving his reasoning. "Yes, but I think Purvis would require a reason for his massacre. I mean a real reason, one that made sense to you or me. Are Purvis and Crosby still in contact with each other?"

"As far as we know, they do still see each other but not

often. It's always George going to Purvis' house," said Luke. "There's no way to tell if Purvis sends for him."

Tyler pulled a book from his pile of notes and said, "Purvis wrote this book about haunted places in Saltern. There's a section about the oak in Stone Park but he doesn't appear to be saying more about it than the rest of the places. It's flowery and over-written but I can't see anything sinister in it. Just a lot of emoting about saving the remains of the old oak and other endangered, historical sites... what he calls spiritual places. I'd be grateful for your opinion."

As he passed it to the psychologist, Gill saw the cover. She started to her feet. "May I look at that, please?" She took it and stared down. "I'm sure the Quantrulls have a copy of this book. I saw it on Ian's desk in the room he uses when he works from home."

"And that takes us where exactly?" said Tyler.

It took Gill a moment to realise he wasn't being snide. He was as uncertain of its significance as she was herself. "It's probably just a coincidence. Purvis has been selling them all around Saltern. His main market's going to be here."

"Nevertheless I'd like to read it through," said Dr Tremaine. "It may give me some further insight into Purvis as he is now." She held out her hand and Gill gave it to her, meekly, feeling rather like she was back in Junior School.

Tyler grinned at her and she knew he'd seen her embarrassment. "Check out anything you can about the Quantrulls buying it, Gill. It may mean nothing but any links need looking at, however tenuous. Doctor, in your opinion, is it possible a random killer wandered into Stone Park, shot five people and hit Dan Peters over the head then went again without leaving a trail of carnage anywhere outside the park?"

"It's possible but highly improbable. This doesn't have the hallmarks of a random killing. A long-distance killer would have hidden in the bushes and picked off one or two victims; a spree killer would have run through blazing away."

"What about the weapon?" said Tyler. "A handgun's not the usual tool for a random massacre."

"I agree. I've been through what we know about all the adults involved in the shooting. Partnership difficulties aside there's nothing to indicate that Daniel Peters, Joshua Fortune or Colleen Holebrook were liable to commit such a crime. Sophie Hughes is more interesting. She's a girl whose emotional development has been retarded by her own actions and those of the people around her."

"Sophie's growing up pretty fast right now," interposed Nikki.

"That proves nothing," said Dr Tremaine with a thin-lipped smile.

"Sophie couldn't have been the shooter, it's physically impossible," said Tyler.

The psychologist nodded. "I think, Superintendent, you're probably right and we should concentrate on the Quantrull boys. Although I would recommend you keep a watch on Purvis and Crosby."

"I've already given the orders on that." Tyler sounded surprised it needed to be said.

Chapter 34

The psychologist left and Tyler abandoned formality. He moved to sit on a desk, feet on a chair, and stared gloomily at his team. They gazed back equally glumly.

"No need for you to practise your funeral faces. Just because the psychologist thinks I might be right, it doesn't mean I am. There are plenty of other options than the kids."

"If it was the kids, are we going to be able to prove it?" asked Luke.

"We're going to have a damned good shot at it. The biggest step forward would be to prove they had the gun and where they got it from."

"And where it went after the shooting," said Gill. "Sir, do you believe Dan Peters' claim that he doesn't remember anything about seeing the boys when they were dead?"

"I'm giving him the benefit of the doubt. We've got no physical evidence to counter his story. The only blood on his clothing belongs to Josh and himself, and Dan could have picked up Josh's from the ground. What worries me is whether, if Dan's memory comes back, he'll decide to keep quiet. He must realise he's a soft target and if we find the gun with his prints on it, he'll be in the shit even if he's innocent. But if he stays co-operative, as soon as he's well enough, I want to set up a cognitive interview."

"You plan to take the poor bastard back to Stone Park?" Even Kerry sounded shaken.

Gill was shocked at Tyler's ruthlessness but she was also interested. Cognitive interviewing involved placing people in a situation that would stimulate their memory and then asking the right questions in the right way. She'd done some basic training in cognitive techniques when she'd updated her training in interviewing witnesses but DCI Aron hadn't believed in cutting edge and she had a lot of skills to make up.

"If they agree to it, I want Dan and Sophie back in the park as soon as possible," said Tyler. "And I want Sophie dressed the same as she was that day."

"That's not a problem," said Gill. "We've got the clothes for the re-enactment."

Today they planned to reconstruct the arrival of the victims at Stone Park. No-one had any great hopes of it being much use. No witnesses had come forward to say they'd been near the park at the relevant time, so it seemed unlikely it would jog anyone's memory. Still, the press coverage could help someone remember some previous incident that the witness had not connected with the victims. Even a long-shot was worth trying and it was a good idea to keep the newsboys sweet.

"Have you got any idea when Dan will be up to it?" she asked.

Tyler shrugged. "The bulletins from the hospital say Dan and Sophie are making good progress and Josh Fortune is hanging on."

"If he shows any sign of consciousness we can wheel him and his life-support machine into Stone Park for a cognitive interview as well," muttered Kerry.

"Shut it." Luke's words were backed by a murmur of agreement from the team.

Tyler ignored this interlude. "Nikki, you fancy making some coffee?"

"Sure sir." Nikki got up and went across to the kettle.

"Kerry, thanks for covering our arses about the chat rooms," said Tyler.

Gill knew Kerry had come through when the chips were down but she should have flagged up her information. She'd deserved, and probably expected, a rebuke.

Kerry turned red. "Sorry sir. I should have let you know I'd done those checks."

"That's okay. I should have asked." His eyes met hers in a level, searching gaze and she looked away, suddenly becoming engrossed in the papers on her desk.

Gill thought, 'He's bloody clever and he knows how to get the best out of his team.'

Nikki offered Gill a cup of coffee. Her back to Tyler she pulled a mischievous face. "Typical of the Boss, expecting more of himself than he does of anyone else."

"What are you muttering about?" he said.

She smiled at him. "Just checking I've made the DI's coffee the way she likes it."

Tyler gave her a suspicious look but said, "Okay, lets get sorted. Kerry, you run with the Internet angle. Check whether those boys had any other access to it. Be tactful, we don't want anyone to know we're looking at the kids in that sort of way."

"Yes sir. The school may be sticky though."

"Point out we can only be discreet if we have full co-operation. The words *'tabloid newspapers'* seem to work quite nicely."

Kerry grinned at him. "Neat sir."

Tyler's answering smile reminded Gill of the Wolf inviting Three Little Pigs to a sausage supper. "I'm always delighted to piss off people like Dr Rowanbridge."

He gulped his coffee. "Gill, stay with the Quantrulls. We need to know what's been going on inside that house. Nikki, see what you can get out of Sophie and her mum. Stu, you stick with Dan Peters. Luke, I hate to break it to you..."

"Don't tell me. I'm to stay with the Purvis and Crosby angle?"

"Afraid so."

Luke grinned. "And I hate to break it to you, sir, but I'm not good enough for George Crosby. I got in at six this morning and he was already waiting downstairs. He doesn't want to see me. It's you he's set his heart on and he's prepared to wait all day."

"That's all I need. You reckon he's got anything worth listening to?"

"If he has it's too mixed up in all that blood of the sacrifice and innocent bones crap for us to get to it."

"It's my own fault. I shouldn't have encouraged him yesterday. We can't leave him sitting in reception. It'll piss off uniformed and the chances are some Press boys will get hold of him and print a tarted up version of his ramblings."

Gill had an inspiration. "Is the psychologist still around?"

She saw by the gleam in Tyler's eyes that he knew what she was thinking and approved it. "She should be. We've given her a small office and the up-dated files to read. You reckon she should have a chat with George?"

"Well if anyone needs a psychologist it's him. And maybe she could make some sense out of all that sacrificial stuff."

"Cheers Gill. Luke, fix that up will you?" He stood up. "I'm heading for the hospital. I plan to touch a lot of bases today."

"Which angle are you working on, sir?" asked Gill.

"All of them." He threw the words over his shoulder as he left.

Gill gathered together her things and headed for the car park. To her surprise Nikki fell in step with her. "It's good to see the Boss back on form," she said.

Gill was certain there was a reason for this remark, but she didn't know whether Nikki was trying to find out something or tell her something or both. She hedged her bets. "I'd always heard he was one of the best SIOs around."

"Not one of the best, he's the absolute best, but I'm prejudiced."

"Really? I was told he wasn't keen on promoting women, that he saw them as glorified tea ladies."

"With respect, ma'am, that's rubbish."

Gill was irritated by the formality of her reply. "Not entirely. You're the one who always makes the drinks."

"Too right I do. No-one in their senses wants to drink

anything Stu has made. Anyway I can do two things at once, which means I don't lose count of the number of spoonfuls I've put in a cup if I'm listening to what's going on. You shouldn't believe everything Kerry tells you, ma'am."

"For God's sake cut out the ma'am! I didn't get much choice about who to listen to. Until the Superintendent came back no-one else would talk to me."

Nikki paused. She seemed to weigh Gill up. "If you want the truth, we were being careful. Recently there's been a lot of people playing politics with our team. It's been getting the Boss down, always having to watch his back. We knew he didn't want to go to that conference in the States."

That surprised Gill. "Did he tell you that?" Complaining to the lower ranks was not in her reading of his character.

"Of course not. But we know he's not a conference sort of guy."

"What's this got to do with how arsey you were to me?"

"We were suspicious when Roy went off on leave so suddenly, just after the Bossman was sent to America. We thought the ACC was pulling a fast one."

"What sort of fast one?" They'd reached their cars but Gill wasn't quitting now.

Nikki shrugged. "Going behind the Super's back to land him with a new DI."

"I don't play politics. I just do my job." Gill hadn't realised how angry she was until she heard her own tone. "Roy Brent had personal reasons for going on leave."

"I know. He had a health scare. The Super told us yesterday. He had to have tests for prostate cancer but it looks like he's okay."

"I'm glad."

"Yeah, poor old Roy. We used to wind him up about needing to pee every few minutes." She grinned suddenly. "The Boss spotted the way we were with you. He told us the police force wasn't a democracy and we'd work with any senior officer we were assigned to."

194

"Thanks for that. It's nice to know I'm only getting co-operation because Superintendent Tyler told you to."

"Actually we'd already decided you were okay. You helped carry the Boss until he was over his jet lag and you began to suss Kerry out… eventually."

Gill ignored the mischief in the final word. "What's with Kerry? Why the attitude?"

"She was pissed off because the Boss refused to back her promotion application. He told her she had to mature before she'd be ready to make DI. But of course, being Kerry, she decided it was sexual prejudice."

Gill was still annoyed enough to say, "She told me you were still a constable because the Superintendent's prejudiced against women officers."

This won an answering spark of anger. "There are times when Kerry really pushes her luck! The reason I'm still a constable is because I've had three kids in the past seven years. Not many senior officers would have kept me on their team."

Gill opened her mouth to protest but Nikki steamrollered over her, "I know you're going to say there are rules safeguarding the rights of women with young families. But in reality a senior officer can make it impossible to do the job. I was with a SIO like that when I had my first baby, and she was a woman. The Boss has given me more than my rights. He'd probably say it's because he likes a variety of life experiences and knowledge on his team, but the truth is he's a decent guy and there aren't many of those in the top ranks of the police."

"Not that many in the lower ranks either."

This won a reluctant laugh. "That's true. Sorry. I didn't mean to sound off at you, but there are times when Kerry makes me mad."

"You two got nothing better to do than gossip?" Tyler strode past them.

"Sorry sir. Just chatting about our favourite senior

officer," said Nikki cheekily.

Tyler paused and turned to stare at them. Gill braced herself for the rebuke that was sure to come. He grinned. "I'll tell DCI Aron you were talking about him," he said.

Chapter 35

When Tyler got to Dan Peters' room Dan was out of bed and sitting in a chair. "Good morning, Superintendent."

"Morning. How are you feeling?"

"All right. How's Josh? And Sophie? And Charlie? No-one will tell me anything. You're the boss aren't you? You can let me know what's going on."

Dan's voice was jagged and his hands were fidgeting incessantly with a fold of his dressing gown. Tyler shelved his plan to suggest a cognitive interview.

"They're all doing okay," he said non-committally.

"I'd like to see Charlie. Would that be possible?"

"I don't know. It's up to his parents and the doctors. I'll ask if you like." Tyler thought it might be interesting to bring Dan and Charlie together and observe what transpired.

"Thank you."

"Dan, I know you don't remember much about the time after you were hit, but do you know if Charlie said anything?"

"I don't think so. Only his name. I kept asking him until he told me that. And I told him my name and that I'd keep him safe. Apart from that he only said Dad, over and over in a sort of chant. But sometimes I thought he was saying Dan. I keep going over it in my mind but I'm not sure. My head was aching so badly and I kept throwing up. I'm sorry. All I really remember was trying to keep him quiet."

"Why was that Dan?"

"I thought someone would come after us and kill us." The shudders racked his body and his breathing came in gasps.

Hannah put her arms around him. "It's over. Try not to think about it anymore."

She glared at Tyler, defying him to continue the questioning. He smiled at her and made an 'I quit' gesture with his hand. He had no intention of alienating helpful witnesses or of driving a sick man into hysterics.

Dan said shakily, "I can't just not think of things. I need to know the truth."

It was a viewpoint Tyler could relate to and respect, nevertheless he said, "Yeah but your wife's right. You need to know how to pace yourself. It's no good trying to force yourself to remember, you'll just end up a lot sicker than you already are. I had a bad concussion a few years ago and it was surprising how depressed I was afterwards. It felt like everything had drained away, all my energy and self-confidence, even the ability to think coherently. It took several months before I was normal again."

Over Dan's head Hannah gave Tyler a grateful smile.

"I hate not being in control," complained Dan.

"I know but there's nothing you can do. Try to rest and let your wife take charge."

"She doesn't need encouraging. She's too bossy as it is." The words were not light-hearted enough but it was a brave effort.

Tyler was surprised when Hannah followed him out of the room. "The doctors are talking about discharging Dan in the next couple of days, as long as he's got someone to look after him at home, but I think it's too soon."

Tyler considered. Witnesses often remembered better when they were relaxed in their own homes but there was a more pressing consideration here. "As far as we're concerned, it's easier to protect him in hospital."

"You really think he's in danger?"

He could see she was scared but she was a girl with courage and he might need her help. "I don't know. I don't know what he saw, or what the killer thinks he saw, and unfortunately Dan doesn't know either. We'll do our best to protect him."

"Thank you." She smiled at him. "And thank you for what you said about concussion. We both needed to hear that."

Tyler nodded and turned away. Memory was heavy upon him, which was his own fault for awakening it. His concussion had happened over nine years ago, when he'd been stationed up North. He'd been hospitalised by a thug wielding an iron bar. He'd spent eight days in hospital, but the following weeks were total hell as well. Physically they'd been dominated by headaches, nausea and the inability to concentrate; emotionally by a fog of grim despair.

Of course they'd sent him home to recuperate. In his fourth sick week, when he was feeling terrified he'd stay like this forever, Vivienne suggested it would be better if he moved back to his rented flat in Leeds. She had more important things to do than look after him. After all, it was his own fault. If he'd taken the office job her father had offered him, he wouldn't have been injured and caused them all such inconvenience.

Tyler saw the point of her arguments. Apathetically he'd allowed her to drive him back up North, drearily grateful she hadn't insisted he took the train.

Officially their marriage had lasted another four years, but, looking back, he knew it had died then.

Chapter 36

As soon as Tyler entered Charlie's room he felt the change in atmosphere. The toddler was snuggled deeply into his father's lap, sucking at Ian's finger and apparently half asleep.

Ian Quantrull was haggard. He looked like a man who was trapped in Hell but, in response to Tyler's quiet greeting, he managed a brief contortion of his colourless lips.

Tyler moved a chair and sat down opposite to Ian. "How's Charlie doing?"

"Calmer." He nodded to the finger trapped in Charlie's mouth. "He used to suck my finger when he was a baby."

"Painful now he's got teeth."

Ian made a faint movement of dismissal, too slight to be even the beginning of a shrug. "Pain doesn't matter... not physical pain." The bloodshot eyes seemed to be looking past Tyler, not focusing on anything in the room. "They let me see my boys today. They advised against it but I needed to."

Deep inside himself, Tyler winced. No parent should have to remember those ruined faces. "DI Martin would have gone with you. Or I'd have done it, if you preferred a man."

"I wanted to go alone. I didn't drive. Allie took me."

"Allie?"

"Our nanny. My mother seems to have appointed her as my minder. Jasmin isn't pleased. She says Allie's there to help her and she ought to be sorting stuff in the house. I don't know what she's fussing about. She prefers looking after Polly herself, and no-one's going to care if the house is dusty, not until the funerals."

Tyler thought that Ian was speaking at random, his words floating above the dark realities, like scum on dead water.

"There's nothing to say, is there Ian? *'I'm sorry'* is totally inadequate."

"I know. It's what I said to Barney and Tim. *'I'm sorry…*
so sorry.' It's pathetic, useless, more of an insult than an
apology."

"Why should you apologise, Ian?"

"It was my job to keep them safe. Have you got kids?"

"No."

"When Barney was born I was so scared. He looked so
little I was afraid to pick him up. My wife… my first wife…
used to laugh at me. With Timmy it was different. He seemed
tougher. We thought he was a survivor, that he'd come
through anything. And now I've got to sort out their funerals.
They'll be buried with my father. He's got *Rest In Peace* on
his gravestone. Rest! For God's sake, my boys were never
bloody still!"

'Rest in sweet peace, and, asked, say here doth lie Ben
Jonson his best piece of poetry.' The poet's eulogy for his
first son echoed hollowly through Tyler's mind.

The tears were coursing down Ian's face. Tyler opened
the door and spoke to the cop on guard duty, "Are any of Mr
Quantrull's family around?"

"The older Mrs Quantrull is down the corridor, sir."

"Go and get her. I'll stay here." Tyler waited by the door
until the cop returned, followed by a tall, grey haired woman
and a plump, pleasant looking girl. So this was Mrs Quantrull
Senior and, at a guess, Allie the nanny.

He held the door open and they entered the room. The
girl went straight to Ian and lifted Charlie out of his arms.
Ian didn't protest but Charlie gave a little snort and opened
his eyes. Tyler braced himself for a fresh bout of screams but
the child cuddled against the young woman and went back
to sleep.

Mrs Quantrull pulled Tyler's abandoned chair close to
her son and sat down. She rested a hand lightly on his and
waited until the sobs turned into shuddering hiccups. She
removed a pack of tissues from her handbag. "Wipe your
eyes, Ian, and blow your nose."

201

Shakily he obeyed. She poured him a glass of water and said, "Drink this." As he did so she turned an enquiring gaze on Tyler. "You are a police officer?"

"Detective Superintendent Tyler." He saw her consider the scratches on his face and waited for her to protest at the distress he'd caused both her daughter-in-law and son.

"I'm Elizabeth Quantrull. Thank you for looking after my son, Superintendent." His surprise must have been obvious because she continued, "I believe this is the first time he has cried. Stoicism is all very well but it can be an over-rated quality."

"Yes ma'am." This from a ramrod straight, old woman, who looked as if she'd never succumbed to emotion in her life.

She must have caught the dryness in his tone. She gave him an enchanting smile and said, "One of the disadvantages of self-control is that people batten onto it and then revile you for being insensitive."

She turned back to Ian. "That's better, dear. Now you must go and wash your face and have something to eat. You can be of no use to Charlie if you faint from lack of food. Would you like me to come with you to the canteen?"

"No! Stay here with Charlie. Please. Promise me you won't leave him."

"I promise." She looked at Tyler. "Superintendent, I wonder...?"

"If Mr Quantrull will let me I'll keep him company."

Tyler didn't like using his genuine sympathy for the guy to pump him, but it went with the territory. If you couldn't cope with feeling like Judas you shouldn't take on the bloody job.

Chapter 37

Gill and Tyler met by chance in the hospital corridor, Tyler with Ian, Gill accompanying Jasmin and Polly and a newly arrived visitor.

"Maurice, I wasn't expecting you," said Ian. Gill thought he didn't sound pleased, but he was so clearly wrecked normal standards could not apply.

"Of course I came, as soon as I could." The newcomer gave a sympathetic smile.

Gill met Tyler's questioning look and said, "Maurice Walton, Jasmin's brother. Mr Walton, this is Detective Superintendent Tyler. He's leading the enquiry into your nephews' deaths."

"They weren't his nephews," said Ian.

"Poor Ian, this must be hideous for you." Maurice Walton stepped forward and engulfed him in a hug. Ian Quantrull was a tall man but Maurice Walton was larger in every way. *'Big, blonde and gorgeous'* was the way Gill would have summed him up if she'd been into men, and if his unctuous manner hadn't irritated her.

Ian said stiffly, "Thank you for coming, Maurice. Perhaps you can help Jasmin. I'm not being much use to her at the moment."

"Of course I'll look after Jassy." He put his arm around her. She shrugged him off and stepped clear, burying her face in Polly's downy hair.

They returned to Charlie's room. Ian and Jasmin were in front, with Maurice Walton between them. Tyler and Gill dropped back until they couldn't be heard by the grieving family.

Tyler said, "Ian didn't seem pleased to see him, did he? What about Jasmin? Did she know her brother was coming?"

"I don't think so. He turned up just as we were leaving

for the hospital and she looked shocked when his taxi pulled up at their gate." She hesitated. "I thought she looked upset, almost afraid, but that could be my imagination."

"Before the brother turned up, when you were chatting to Jasmin, did you get anything about the kids?"

"Lots of incidents where the boys behaved like little thugs. She doesn't want Ian to know she's told me. I think, whatever they did, he was protective of them. Jasmin said they regarded her as the wicked stepmother. However I did find out one thing. According to Jasmin they removed the Internet from their home because Tim kept going on inappropriate websites. Jasmin said he liked the violent ones. The crunch came when they found him on one that described how to make bombs."

Tyler raised his eyebrows. "Interesting."

"What about you, sir? Did Ian say anything?"

"That's a completely different story. The way Ian tells it they were ordinary kids. Just a bit wild. They missed their mum and weren't happy with his second marriage."

"What about the trouble at school?"

"He said they didn't like the school and he shouldn't have sent them there in the first place. It was his father's idea and he'd paid the fees. Nothing but the best for his grandsons. Like you put in your report, Jasmin wanted them to go to boarding school but the boys hated the idea."

"How did Ian feel about it?"

"I don't know. He was crying. He's been doing a lot of that today."

Gill heard the tension in Tyler's voice. "Tough day, sir?"

"Known ones I've enjoyed more. Dan Peters asked if he could see Charlie. The doctors say okay and Ian's agreed to it."

"How's Jasmin going to take that?"

"God knows." He raised his voice, "Ian, have you told your wife what we've decided?"

Ian turned to Jasmin. "They're going to bring the chap

over who found Charlie. He wants to check Charlie's all right. The police will be here all the time and there's no need for you to make a scene."

She shrugged pettishly. "You'll do what you want. You always do. I won't be there. I'm not letting him near Polly. I can't understand why you want to turn that paedophile loose on your only remaining son."

At Tyler's invitation, Gill went with him to fetch Daniel. They were quite a procession: Dan in a wheelchair with a porter to push him; Tyler, Gill and Hannah alongside; Stuart in front and the police guard behind.

Ian, his mother and Allie were awaiting them in Charlie's room.

Daniel stood up. "Hello Charlie."

Charlie peeped cautiously from the shelter of Allie's arms then he pushed himself free of her grasp. "Dan," he said. His chubby arms twined around Dan's neck.

On the way back Daniel was frowning and preoccupied. Tyler muttered, "I hope this hasn't been too much for him. We don't want him to have a relapse."

Gill was surprised at Tyler's humanitarian attitude. She must have let her scepticism show because he said curtly, "I need him to remember everything as soon as possible."

"Yes sir."

Her non-committal tone didn't fool him. He glared at her. "I know you all think I'm a bastard because I want him to do a cognitive interview but if you can think of another way to sort this case I'll be glad to hear it."

"I don't think you're a bastard." 'Driven' was the word that sprang to mind.

They found the corridor blocked by cleaning trolleys. One of the guard cops went and checked. "There's been some kind of spillage, sir. They're going to be a while cleaning up. It would be quicker to cut round the outside."

Tyler swore beneath his breath but there was little choice. They went round the side of the hospital. A boy on a bicycle went screeching past. A van driver slammed his door with a fierce crash. In that moment it sounded like a shot. Instinctively Gill leapt forward and Tyler flung himself to shield Daniel. Clearly embarrassed he straightened up. "Sorry I..."

"He's hyperventilating!" Gill spoke over him, hearing Dan's struggle for breath.

"Get him inside fast!" roared Tyler. He grabbed control of the wheelchair and bundled Dan into the building.

Daniel's panic attack was not serious. It was swiftly dealt with by medical staff but it took a lot out of Dan and quite a bit out of his bodyguards.

They left Dan in bed, sedated. Outside his room, Tyler rubbed the back of his neck and flexed his shoulders. Gill sympathised, the strain was getting to her as well.

"Stu, you won't be needed here until Dan surfaces, so check in with Kerry and see if she wants any help. Gill, you'd better get back to the Quantrulls."

"Yes sir." Gill no longer felt sidelined. She was sure this was where the action was.

Chapter 38

Before heading back to the office, Tyler went up to Josh Fortune's room, cradling the faint hope that they'd say he was near to regaining consciousness. The police guard seemed relieved to see him. "A woman brought a CD for the victim, sir. I said I'd check whether it was all right to pass it on."

"What sort of CD?"

"She said it was from his pupils... songs and messages, that sort of thing. Mrs Hughes came out and spoke to her, but I wouldn't let anyone take the CD in without your permission."

"Did you get this lady's name?"

"Yes sir, Mrs Scott."

To Tyler's annoyance he felt his colour rise. He'd forgotten that Lani had asked his permission to bring it in. "Yes, that's okay."

He took the CD and went into the room. Rhiannon and Sophie were both there. That surprised him but he didn't comment. "Lani Scott, who's taking some of Josh's classes, sent this," he said.

Rhiannon smiled. "I know. I spoke to her. She said if anything could impel him to get out of his sick bed and come back to work it was hearing what they were doing to his songs."

"How's Josh doing?"

"Better. They're keeping him sedated but they say his heart seems to be getting back in rhythm. I think they're cautiously optimistic."

"That's good." He longed fervently for Josh to recover consciousness and tell them what he'd witnessed in Stone Park.

He went back to the office to a mountain of paperwork. The details about the boys had come from the school and he went through them. Their school offences were all minor incidents and their behaviour indicated unhappy kids but it didn't scream 'Murder' at him. He went along the corridor to talk to the psychologist.

She greeted him pleasantly and supplied him with a cup of excellent coffee from a giant flask. "I've spent some time with George Crosby and I agree he's a severely disturbed man."

"Did he have anything to do with the murders in Stone Park?"

"I doubt it. In fact he seemed to think it was a waste. All that blood could have been directed at the sacred oak if the rituals had been properly performed. He seemed to feel the oak would be angry at the sacrilege and would exact retribution."

Tyler had a vision of the stump of the oak uprooting itself and prowling the park. A ludicrous image, but it made him shiver. "Sounds like George has lost it again. I'll get someone to contact his social worker and see if she can arrange to have him sectioned."

The psychologist peered at him over the top of her reading glasses, her look was disapproving. "A convenient solution for the authorities but not necessarily the best one for George Crosby."

"Better than hanging round Stone Park ranting about blood."

"Perhaps if you were to talk to the man again yourself. You seem to have made a great impression upon him when you spoke to him yesterday."

"You're the psychologist, not me."

"I'm also a woman. George wouldn't respect me. Are you familiar with his background, Superintendent?"

"Remind me." It was a long time since Tyler had checked out George Crosby's early file and knowing he should have done so added an edge to his voice.

"He comes from a professional, middle-class background,

but there were no women in his life as permanent carers. His mother left when he was a small child. His father was bitter and poisoned George's mind. George despises women. He respects men. Men like you and Brian Purvis."

"Don't put me in the same category as that sleazy bastard!"

Dr Tremaine made a gesture of apology. "I meant no comparison. But I believe George would open up to you."

"If he can't tell me about the shootings I haven't got time to deal with him."

"Very well, Superintendent. I have had a quick look at Brian Purvis' book. I found nothing significant in it. The section about Stone Park does not stand out. It confirms my initial impression of him as a man who lives by self-aggrandisement. He's not as clever academically as he appears to think he is but he'd make an excellent spin-doctor."

"Yeah, that's the way I've always thought of him. Thanks for checking it out. Now I want your opinion on this information from the Quantrull boys' school."

"Certainly. I'll read it now if you have time to wait. Help yourself to more coffee."

He did so and waited while she read the reports through. At last she said, "It's clear the boys were unhappy but there's little sign of the sort of behaviour that results in running wild with a lethal weapon. However if they were in possession of the gun, it could have been a crime of impulse."

"Is that likely?"

"Not without some sort of provocation from the adults in the park."

"You think Tim Quantrull would have needed a reason to shoot three unknown adults? He couldn't have done it out of pure rage?"

"I don't think so but there are no absolutes in this. This report doesn't indicate they were particularly violent children. Timothy was involved in a few fights but they sound like childish scraps. The only really sinister indications are the mutilated doll and what their stepmother told DI Martin about their use of the Internet added to Timothy's behaviour to the baby, and killing a pet rabbit, that's especially significant."

"Yeah, I know."

"If the boys had attacked their stepmother, I'd think it was a cut-and-dried case. But we're talking about shooting strangers. And the gun indicates planning."

"Yeah," said Tyler wearily. "It all comes back to the gun. Where did it come from and where the hell did it go?"

"Possibly it came from criminal connections made via the Internet before their parents prevented access to it, but I have no theories about where it disappeared to afterwards. You'll be interviewing the boys' school friends and maybe they can shed light on the matter. Would you like me to go with you?"

"I won't be doing it myself, not yet. That would give the whole thing too high a profile and show we're focusing on the boys. I'm sending Stuart Farrow to talk to their friends but I'd be grateful if you could suggest what sort of questions he should ask and listen in to the interviews. And I'd be even more grateful if you kept a low profile."

She smiled. "Don't worry, Superintendent, That's not difficult for a woman at St Ignatius' School."

Tyler returned to his paperwork until Luke Warden knocked on his door. "Sir, you won't believe this, but that bastard Purvis is here."

"What? Of his own volition? Or has someone pulled him in?"

"He's got that girl with him, the one that was with him in his house. The cocky bastard's come to make a complaint."

Tyler stared at him, hearing but not believing. He slammed to his feet. "Let's see if we can give him something to complain about."

As Tyler entered into the waiting room he saw Purvis looked smug but Sarah was white and tear-stained. "Right

Purvis, what are you complaining about?"

Purvis gave his smooth smile. "Superintendent, I'm not complaining for myself. I have become inured to police brutality. But Sarah must be protected from that infatuated youth who is obsessed with her."

"What?" Tyler leaned his clenched fists on the table and glared at Purvis.

"Ryan Jones. Such a nice boy before your forces of evil corrupted him. He has been stalking Sarah, phoning her and hanging round the house. This harassment must stop."

Tyler felt a cold anger that made him long to smash something. Wasn't this case difficult enough without a lovesick prat of a kid buggering it up? He looked at Sarah and saw her shrink before the fury in his eyes.

"Are you saying Ryan Jones has been bothering you, Sarah?"

She wouldn't look at him. "I want him to stop," she whispered.

"Are you making an official complaint, Sarah?"

She shook her head.

"In that case, I'll have a word with him. I'm sure he didn't understand you were already spoken for." He saw her wince and was glad of it.

"Really Superintendent, I must protest!"

He met Purvis' eyes and held the gaze. "I wouldn't advise you to protest too loudly. I know you, Purvis. You're a liar and a bully, a manipulator and a hypocrite. You're also a violent criminal. And one day you're going to take another step too far outside the law and I'm going to have you and you'll be back inside."

He turned and walked away. Luke Warden caught up with him and he snapped, "I want Jones in my office now."

Chapter 39

It was over two hours before Ryan Jones could be retrieved from his duties and dispatched to Tyler's office but Tyler's mood hadn't softened.

The boy had obviously been warned he was in trouble. He stood to attention, pale but stubborn-looking. Tyler let him wait for three minutes, timed exactly, although he appeared to be concentrating on his paperwork.

At last he looked up. "I received a complaint about you this afternoon."

"Sir."

"I don't enjoy receiving crap from nasty little scrotes that I am trying to bang up. You will stay away from Brian Purvis and Sarah. Is that understood?"

"Sir, I only wanted to talk to her…"

"Is that understood?"

"Yes sir."

"I'm not having you contaminating any case I can make against Purvis. Nor do I wish Purvis to set his thugs on you. George Crosby alone could take you apart."

"George isn't so keen on Purvis anymore, sir. Sarah said…"

"Nor do I want any backchat. Get out of here."

As the boy obeyed, Tyler knew that he shouldn't have let his temper overtake his instinct to enquire. Driving a wedge between Crosby and Purvis could reveal the truth behind a lot of crimes. He opened his mouth to call Jones back. His phone rang.

"Kev, it's Roy. I know you must be up to your eyes in this new case but have you got a few minutes to talk?" His old DI sounded tentative, almost nervous.

"Hi Roy. Yeah of course I've got time. I've been meaning to phone you. How are you doing? Any idea when you'll be back with us?"

"That's what I'm phoning about."

The conversation went on for a while. By the time they'd finished it was too late to summon Ryan Jones back.

The day plodded relentlessly onwards. Mid-evening Tyler managed to get his team together, only Gill was absent, still at the Quantrulls' house. Over take-away pizza, they exchanged notes. Kerry had got nothing useful from the school computers or the ones that belonged to Tim and Barney's friends. Consequently she was snapping and snarling at everyone. Stuart had got nothing from the Quantrull boys' school friends. He said the psychologist was going to get her notes in order and report to Tyler later on. Luke, still dealing with Purvis and Crosby, was morose. Nikki was subdued.

Tyler was depressed by the conversation he'd had with Roy, although he knew his decision to retire made sense.

"Sorry I'm late, sir." Gill entered. She looked tired but cheerful. "Thank you, Nikki," as Nikki handed her a slice of pizza.

"You haven't missed much," said Tyler. "Have you got anything to report?"

"Not much, but it was Purvis' book I saw on Ian Quantrull's desk, and more to the point, Tim had given it to him. There was a message on the flyleaf: 'To Dad, love Tim.'"

"Interesting," said Tyler. "Not conclusive but indicative. It's possible that's where he got the idea of staging a new death scenario at Stone Park. Well done, Gill."

That cheered him up. As she settled in, Gill's work was getting better every day. He decided to sound her out and see if she wanted to stay on as his DI. If so, he'd set an official request in motion.

He returned to his office. The psychologist dropped in to confirm Stuart's information; the interviews with the boys' friends had been inconclusive but there were one or two angles she wished to consider and she'd come back to him.

After she left, he got on the phone and started to chase reports. He attended the meeting with the Media, then skimmed through notes of the team's work during the day, ready to sift and incorporate them into the next morning's general briefing. It occurred to him that he'd been so thorough because he needed to prove to himself he wasn't skiving off. For the first time in years, there was somewhere else he'd rather be.

The main office was quiet. Only Kerry was still at her desk, working at her computer. "What are you up to?" he asked.

"I'm trying to trace ways the boys could have bought that gun."

Tyler though that was e-bay with serious attitude. "Don't work too late."

She flashed him a cheeky grin, reminding him of the old Kerry before she started on this long-term sulk. "No problem, sir. When I've got my teeth into something I like to stay with it till it's sorted."

"Fair enough. Goodnight."

"'Night sir." Her attention was back on the screen before he'd left the room.

As he started across the car park, Tyler caught sight of a lanky figure, sitting on the ground beside the exit. The last thing he needed was another chat with George.

A group of cops came past, heading for their cars. Tyler tagged on beside them, shoulders hunched against the driving rain. Once in his car he timed it so the exit was clear. He caught a scrabble of movement as George clambered to his feet but by that time Tyler was accelerating away. Tomorrow would do for George.

Outside Lani's flat he felt nervous. What if everything wasn't as good as last night? What if she didn't want what he was hoping for? Come to that what was he hoping for?

"Hi Kev." She came into the hall to greet him. "Have you eaten?"

Another pitfall. Should he have let her know he was eating at the office? "Yeah, I had a take-away with the team. I'm sorry. You didn't wait for me, did you?"

"Of course not. Would you like a drink?"

"No, I'm good." He went into the sitting room and subsided onto the sofa.

She followed him and sat down next to him. "Bad day?" she asked.

"Long and disjointed but not particularly bad." He pulled her closer and she snuggled up to him. He noticed the DVD player was on although the television screen was blank. "What were you watching?"

"One of Josh's concerts. I thought you might not want it on right now."

"I'd like to see it. I ought to know more about him."

Obediently she switched the television on again.

Josh looked so different when he was moving. And he moved well. He had a gravel-based voice, harsh compared with the beauty of his words. Tyler guessed his work would be defined as Folk Rock. "If he survives, I wonder if he'll perform again."

"Perhaps, even if he can't perform, he'll be able to write songs." Lani sounded sad.

"Lani, where do we go from here?" That question had been haunting him all day.

The miracle continued. She understood what he was asking and her rueful smile showed she'd been thinking the same thing. "Very slowly and very carefully."

"Is that slow and careful as in screwing on our third meeting?"

She pulled a face at him but answered seriously, "The last two nights, when I heard your key in the lock, my heart lifted. I don't ever want it to be like it was with David."

"You mean when you heard him coming your heart sank?"

"Right through the floorboards. There are going to be

times when we both need space as well as the times we need company."

He was astonished that their views matched so perfectly. He smiled at her. "I know. But I hope tonight's not one of those times you want space?"

Laughing, she jumped up and pulled him to his feet. "Let's go to bed," she said.

Chapter 40

The sound of Tyler's mobile jerked him awake. Lani switched on the bedside light. 4.25 a.m.

"Sir, it's Kerry. I'm at Stone Park. We've got more trouble."

"What sort of trouble?"

"Another death, a guy. But this time it looks like suicide."

His first thought was Ian Quantrull. There was only so much a person could endure. But Kerry would have said if it were Ian. "Who is it?"

"We don't know yet. There's no ID. Middle-aged guy, unshaven, wearing blue jeans and a black duffle coat. Looks like a down-and-out. Uniformed found him a few minutes ago."

Tyler felt a jolt of recognition, swiftly followed by a stab of guilt. "Ask around the uniformed guys, see if anyone knows George Crosby. It sounds like him. I'll be there in a few minutes. There's no need to drag the rest of the team out tonight."

He rang off and scrambled out of bed. He saw Lani's anxious eyes and outlined what had happened.

"Could he have been responsible for the shootings? Is that why he killed himself?"

"I don't know. I didn't think so, but now I'm not sure. He wanted to talk to me but I couldn't be bothered with him. Perhaps that's what he wanted to tell me."

As he flung his clothes on, it occurred to him that this would be a convenient solution for the powers that be. At least if they thought the real killers were dead. No shock and outrage about what our society was coming to; no extra grief for the parents; no embarrassment for a prominent local school. Let sad, mad George take the blame and everyone would be happy. Apart from George, and he never had been happy, so why should he expect anything different now he was dead?

As he finished shaving, Lani appeared with a mug of coffee.

"You didn't have to get up."

She smiled at him. "No problem."

He was unaware of his tension until she said gently, "You can't save every damaged person in the world."

"But this one I might have. The chances are they'll blame it all on him. It's a convenient solution."

"But you don't think it's true?"

"No, I don't think so. But does that matter? I mean as long as the real killers are dead and not going to hurt anybody else?"

She said slowly, "It feels wrong."

The knowledge that it felt just as wrong to him made him sullen. He was a cop. Clear-up rates and a good result were what had to matter.

He drained his mug and turned to go. She stepped in his way, raised her face and pulled his head down to kiss him.

He felt a surge of gratitude that she'd refused to let him leave her while he was encased in his dark, destructive mood. He thought how brave of her that was, swiftly followed by how much he wanted her. "I'm sorry, I shouldn't have taken it out on you."

"It's okay. I'll make you suffer the next time my editor pisses me off. Take care, Kev."

"Don't worry, I'll be fine. For all we know this may not be George."

"You called it right, sir," said Kerry. "It's George Crosby. Sorry to drag you out. I should have spotted the likeness from the photo on the Incident Room board. One of the uniformed guys recognised him straight off."

"Yeah, poor old George." They were huddled in the pathologist's tent, which had again been pitched beside the

218

ancient oak. They were cold and wet and the presence of George's body didn't improve matters.

"Uniformed found the rest of his stuff in a carrier bag, dumped in a bin," continued Kerry. "SOCO are checking it out."

Tyler spoke to the pathologist, "How did he die?"

"As far as I can tell at present, he slit his wrists, sat down and bled out." The pathologist looked at George's body and shook her head. "A sad, lonely way to go."

Tyler felt a mixture of pity and anger; it combined to clog his throat. He swallowed and said, "Who found him and when?"

"The cops who were detailed to check out the park found him at 3.45," said Kerry. "I was still in the office so I came straight out. The weapon's here. It seems like he used a kitchen knife. SOCO have bagged it."

Tyler nodded. He knew George wasn't his responsibility but a deeper instinct insisted that it isn't right simply to walk away, not from the sick and vulnerable.

Again he looked down at the corpse. So white, so still. It seemed as if he'd pressed his wrists against the ground, offering his lifeblood to the oak. "You're sure it's suicide? Are there hesitation marks?"

The pathologist shook her head. "No. I wondered about that but everything else seems natural."

"Yeah." George had known no doubts. He'd wanted to die. That should have lightened Tyler's burden of guilt but it didn't seem to help in any significant way.

Chapter 41

"Is that it, sir? Case closed?"

Gill was glad Luke had asked that question. When the SIO looked as grim as he did now, she preferred to leave it to a more established member of the team.

This morning Tyler was very much the senior officer. Gill thought that he was not standing on the dignity of his rank, he was retiring within it, as if it was a bullet proof, semi-transparent booth. Unlike previous occasions, he hadn't relaxed when he was alone with his team. His eyes were narrowed and his mouth tightly set.

"I'd like to hear your opinion on that, all of you. Was George Crosby responsible for the shootings in Stone Park? And did he kill himself in a fit of remorse?"

There was an uncomfortable silence, much as though Tyler had asked who'd like to be first to try out the guillotine. Gill knew she had to speak, although good sense warned her to keep quiet. "Sir, did Crosby give any hint of his motivation when you spoke to him the other day?"

Tyler stared at her, stone-faced. "I don't know."

There was a pause and Gill wondered if he was going to leave it like that.

He continued, "I keep trying to remember what we talked about, but he was rambling and I had other things on my mind. He talked a lot about the Sacred Oak and sacrificial blood and the bones of the innocent. He seemed to feel if enough blood was offered to the oak it would grow again or some weird idea like that."

"That sounds like the ramblings of a man who could be responsible for the killings, doesn't it sir?" said Kerry, her tone more warily respectful than Gill had heard it before.

"Maybe."

"But you're not happy with it?" Gill felt like they were

walking on eggshells, knowing that there was razor wire beneath.

He shrugged. "I got the feeling George thought the sacrifice of those kids near his sacred oak was an Act of God, whatever god he worshipped. But I didn't get the impression he'd... facilitated it."

Nikki said, "Was Crosby's death definitely suicide, sir?"

"The pathologist thinks so and the psychologist reckons it has a totally different imprint to the murders."

"In that case we're still looking, the case isn't closed," said Kerry briskly.

"Yeah, until the powers that be decide otherwise," agreed Tyler.

"There's one thing I don't understand, sir." Kerry still sounded uncharacteristically hesitant.

"What's that?"

"The uniformed guy who identified Crosby told me he'd been one of the cops who'd turned him away from Stone Park the other day. He said they'd searched Crosby and his bags and he'd got no weapon on him. So where did he get that knife from?"

No-one could fault Tyler's self-control but Gill saw a tightening of face muscles already tense. Suddenly she knew what he was thinking.

"From the description of the knife it was a top range kitchen tool," she said. "Even in the street market that sort of thing would cost at least twenty pounds."

"They don't have that brand in the market," said Nikki. "You're talking seriously expensive."

"You're certain of that?" said Tyler sharply.

"Yes sir."

Gill felt glad Tyler didn't have to live with the fear that the poor bastard had used his handout to buy a weapon to top himself. "Could he have had it all along and hidden it somewhere?" she asked.

"Maybe." Tyler sounded unconvinced.

"You don't think so, sir?"

"I think he'd regard that knife as too important to leave it lying round. Remember he'd been thrown out of his lodgings and hadn't got anywhere permanent to live. That knife must have seemed special... almost a sacred symbol..." Tyler made an impatient gesture and stumbled to a halt.

"Part of the ritual, an instrument of the sacrifice," said Gill.

Tyler flashed her a grateful look then said with his normal briskness, "I want to know where George got that knife."

"We've kept up the surveillance on Brian Purvis' house and George went there yesterday afternoon," offered Luke.

"We'll follow that up later." Tyler made it sound like a promise of revenge. He turned his head as Ryan Jones entered. "Yes?"

"I'm sorry sir. I saw this letter downstairs. Apparently it was left for you yesterday evening at the desk." The boy sounded nervous but he met Tyler's glare. "I recognised the writing. It's George Crosby's. I thought it might be relevant."

Gill noted, with approval, that Ryan was holding the edge of the envelope through a clean piece of folded paper.

Tyler pulled a pair of plastic gloves out of his pocket and put them on before he held out his hand. As the boy turned to leave, he said, "Stay here. I might need your input. What did you make of George Crosby?"

"He was strange, sir. As kids we laughed at him but we were scared of him too."

"Are you surprised he killed himself?"

"No sir, not really." Ryan's face was screwed up in concentration. "I think the only thing I'd have found hard to believe is if he'd topped himself in an unobtrusive way."

"Right." Tyler looked at the sealed envelope, his expression a mixture of reluctance and distaste. He opened it, removed the single sheet of notepaper and read silently.

Gill thought how hard it must be for him to do this with an audience.

"It's George Crosby's suicide note." He sounded like

he'd been gargling with sand.

He held it out to her. She too pulled on gloves to hold it. It was a surprisingly literate letter in a stylised sloping hand. "May I read it to the team?"

He nodded and she read out loud:

Dear Mr Tyler,

I hoped to speak to you and thank you for what you've done for me but I understand that you are a busy man.

I wanted to tell you that I understand what you told me about no-one having the right to sacrifice anybody except themselves. I wish someone had explained it to me before. However the Sacred Oak still requires its homage of blood and bones.

Your servant

George Crosby

PS. I tried to tell Sarah but she would not listen to me.

You are one of the truly great spiritual leaders of the world.

Not even the last sentence caused a ripple of amusement in the team. Not with Tyler watching them, his face like stone.

"That makes it pretty clear it was suicide but there's no confession to the Stone Park killings and I still want to know where he got the knife. Gill, take over please." Tyler turned and left.

"I suppose it's genuine?" said Kerry. "It seems well-written for a guy like George."

Ryan Jones sounded apologetic. "I'm pretty sure it's for real. Like I said, I recognise the handwriting and George was at Uni before he went crazy."

"Even with the evidence of our expert witness, we need to get this letter authenticated and dusted for prints," said Gill. She smiled at Ryan to take the sting out of her words.

"I'll pass it on to SOCO." Stuart came forward with an evidence bag and secured the letter.

"Thanks Stu. And I want to know exactly when it was delivered, who received it and whether it was left by George himself."

"I asked and the officer on duty didn't remember anyone delivering it," said Ryan. "But George was hanging around a lot all yesterday. They were pissed off about him cluttering up the place."

"Thanks, Ryan, you've done well. That's all for now." She waited until the young constable had left before she continued. "Okay folks, carry on digging. If the Superintendent doesn't need me with him, I'll stay focused on the Quantrulls. Kerry, carry on with your computer research. Nikki get down to the hospital and check on all the victims, please. Stuart, see if the psychologist has any angles she wants you to follow up. And Luke, you stay looking at Brian Purvis. It would cheer up the Boss if we could nail him."

Warden nodded. "It'd make my day too."

The officers dispersed and Gill made two mugs of instant coffee and took them through to Tyler's office. The door was open and she went straight in.

Tyler was staring out of the window with more attention than the view of the station dustbins merited. Gill wondered about him, this tough-looking, curt man who pretended he didn't care at all and probably cared too much.

She said quietly, "I've made you a coffee sir."

She saw the tense shoulders brace, then he gave a shuddering shiver, turned and said, "Cheers Gill. Are there any biscuits? I'm starving."

Chapter 42

'If the bastard doesn't wipe that smirk off his face I'm going to do it for him.'

"Pardon sir?"

"Nothing." Tyler hoped he'd not lost it so totally that he'd spoken out loud, but if he hadn't Gill must be reading his thoughts. Neither scenario seemed particularly desirable.

Brian Purvis was assuring them he was devastated by poor George's death but they must be comforted by the thought that George was happy now. At intervals a smile wafted over his face, as artificial and cloying as cheap air freshener.

Tyler scowled. "George visited you yesterday. You've known him for years and yet you claim you'd no idea he was planning to kill himself?"

"Alas no. Poor George. He told me you had been talking to him, Superintendent. I do not know what you said to him on that last fateful day." Again that slimy smile. "But I do not reproach you. You must examine your own conscience to decide how far you led him into self-destruction."

Tyler considered whether it was worth wrecking his career for the satisfaction of knocking Brian Purvis into hell. He decided it probably was, but Gill Martin had stepped in his way.

"I wouldn't have thought you were the one to preach about conscience, Brian, " she said. "After all, you've never taken responsibility for your actions, never said you're sorry and never admitted a mistake." The contempt in her tone brought angry colour flooding into Purvis' face.

She glanced over her shoulder. "We're wasting our time, sir. You can't get the truth out of a man who's too thick to know when he's lying."

"Yeah, you're right. Brian, we need to talk to Sarah and

check out the house."

"Do you have a warrant?"

"Of course." Tyler removed the warrant from his pocket and held it out.

Purvis' unctuous manner slithered away from him. "Get on with it then."

Luke Warden displayed a photograph of the knife, stained with George's blood. "Did this knife come from your kitchen?"

"How the hell should I know? I'm not the cook… I mean I'm an academic."

Tyler managed a fair imitation of Gill's dismissive tone, "What you mean is you've never done a hand's turn in your life."

"Except when you were inside," amended Luke, and Tyler thought he too had learned from Gill's example.

Purvis scowled. "I have to leave. I have a lecturing engagement." He picked up his document case and moved towards the door.

Tyler blocked him. "I'll check that case out first."

Purvis muttered about police harassment but he surrendered the case without protest, which told Tyler there was probably nothing in it he wanted to hide, although Purvis was a master of the double bluff. The case contained lecture notes and copies of his book.

"Okay, you can go." They had no grounds to hold him and he didn't believe Purvis would run away; he had too snug a set-up here.

They found Sarah in the kitchen. She was dressed in a brown coat and blue hat and scarf.

"We'd appreciate a word, please Sarah."

"I can't stop. I'm going out."

"This will only take a minute. You've heard what happened to George Crosby, haven't you?"

She nodded, like a puppet jerked by strings.

"We're trying to trace George's movements yesterday

and establish where he got the knife that was used to kill him."

Her lips were blanched but she picked up on the phrasing. "Used to kill him? But he killed himself, didn't he?"

"That's for the Coroner to decide. It would help if we could find out where and when he got the knife. Do you recognise this?" He held up the picture and she grew even paler. Again that mechanical gesture of her head. "It's one of ours. Part of a set." The words came as a breathy whisper.

"May I see the rest of the set, Sarah?"

She nodded towards a cupboard. Gill opened it, delved deep, and revealed a knife block with one slot unoccupied.

"When did you notice the knife was missing, Sarah?"

"A few minutes ago. When I washed up after preparing Brian's lunch."

"And what did you think when you saw it was gone?"

"I don't know… I didn't think… I was afraid…"

Afraid George had stolen the knife in order to kill himself? Or afraid Brian had given him the knife and urged him towards suicide? Or worse?

"Were you here when George came round yesterday?" Tyler spoke softly; one wrong word and the girl would be in hysterics, which might tell them something, but nothing admissible.

Again the nod, followed by a whispered, "Yes."

"Did you speak to him?"

"A bit." She glanced at her watch. "I must go. I'll be late."

"We'll give you a lift."

"No!" She wrenched the back door open, ran into the garden, grabbed up a bike, jumped onto it and left. As she went through the back gate she wobbled violently, but gathered momentum as she reached the road.

"Shit! " said Tyler. "We've got no grounds to stop her but I hoped to get more out of her than that. I tried my best not to scare her."

"She was terrified already. Excuse me, sir. I'll see to this." Gill also left through the garden door at a run.

Tyler thought it was good to have a second-in-command he could trust to take the initiative. He hadn't realised how lethargic Roy had been in the past year. Or maybe Tyler himself had become too dominant.

"Do you reckon she thinks she can catch a bike on foot?" asked Luke.

Tyler grinned. "Wouldn't put it past her."

"Yeah." Luke watched Gill as she sprinted along the road. "And she's got a pretty fit arse, especially when she runs."

Chapter 43

Gill settled into an easy pace behind Sarah as she cycled through the town. At first she took it gently, keeping her distance, satisfied with keeping her within sight. She was confident in her own ability and sure the only way she'd lose Sarah was by pulling a muscle if she ran full speed before she'd warmed up enough. Sarah did not look back, except when she stopped at traffic lights. Then she looked over her shoulder, scanning the traffic behind her. Gill dropped to an inconspicuous walk but Sarah hardly glanced at the pavement; all her attention was clearly on whether she was being followed by car.

They travelled four miles across the town; skirting the shopping centre and heading, Gill was pretty sure, for the railway station. It had been built in Victorian times and was situated on the edge of town.

Gill was enjoying herself now, running well within her powers. Her smart, work trousers weren't as comfortable as her running gear but it was a bonus that she'd happened to put on her most comfortable, leather trainers.

The wrought iron canopy of the station came in sight and Gill put on a sprint. If Sarah had pre-purchased her ticket she could board the train and leave before Gill had bought hers. It would be crazy to lose her now.

The luck was with her. There was no queue at the ticket office and, hanging discreetly back, she heard Sarah ask for a return to Pevensey. As soon as Sarah went onto the platform, Gill bought her own ticket, asking for the same place, although she hoped she wouldn't have to travel all the way. According to the station bulletin board the first train seemed to stop everywhere and it required two changes to get to Pevensey. She didn't want to consider Tyler's reaction if she spent all day on a trip to the seaside.

The train pulled in and she got on it further down than Sarah. She waited until it was in motion then made her way through the carriages. "May I join you, Sarah?"

The girl looked startled but she did not object.

"It's okay you know, Sarah. No-one's going to tell Brian you talked to me."

The slender fingers wound in and out of the straps of the small rucksack she was holding on her lap. "He'd be so hurt, so angry. He'd think I was a traitor like Ryan and…"

"And George? Is that what you were going to say? That Brian thought George was a traitor?"

No answer. Gill saw tears welling in Sarah's eyes. "Did you like George?"

"No, not really, he scared me. But I hate the thought he killed himself like that."

"Did you see George when he came round yesterday?"

"Yes, for a little while. George kept saying he wanted to speak to me but Brian sent me out. He knew George made me feel uncomfortable."

"Did you hear anything of what George said, Sarah? It's important we establish what he was thinking."

"Not really, just a lot of ramblings about sacrifice and his new mentor."

"New mentor?" queried Gill, discomfort prickling down her spine.

"Brian told me George had fallen under an evil influence."

"And what do you think he meant by that?"

"That policeman, the one who framed Brian."

Gill decided to take a chance. She'd had enough of the cajoling, elder sister tone. "Come off it, Sarah, you know better than anyone that Superintendent Tyler didn't frame Brian. Brian was guilty of that assault and many other crimes but he's not man enough to admit it."

For a second she thought she'd pushed the girl too far. Sarah gave her a swift, startled look then said, "That's what

Ryan said."

"Ryan was right. And that was a lousy trick you played on him yesterday."

"It's better for Ryan if he stays away."

"Maybe. But it might be better for you if you'd let him help you."

"Ryan can't help me, no-one can, and he's just a kid."

Gill stared at her. She felt exasperation and pity, tinged with contempt. How the hell had the girl turned out like this?

"Why are you looking at me like that?" Sarah sounded scared.

"I was thinking Ryan's a lot more grown up than Brian Purvis is, or ever will be. But you're right about one thing, Ryan doesn't need you screwing up his career. So why don't you tell me about it and see if I can help?"

"No-one can help me. When you've done something there's no undoing it, however much you want to."

Gill said nothing and after a minute Sarah asked, "What did you mean when you said Brian wasn't grown up?"

"I think that deep down you know what I mean. How old is Brian Purvis?"

"Forty-seven." Sarah flushed guiltily. "At least that's what Ryan told me. Brian won't talk about things like age."

"That makes him a year older than Superintendent Tyler. And yet Brian Purvis has got practically no lines on his face while the Superintendent has lots. That's because Brian doesn't care about anyone enough to worry about them. He doesn't take responsibility. Nothing's ever his fault, is it? There's always someone else to blame: the cops or you or Ryan or poor old George. It doesn't matter who, the only rule is Brian's never at fault."

Sarah gazed at her piteously. Gill didn't believe in telepathy but something made her say, "Sarah, what's scaring you? Is it to do with George and his visit yesterday?"

There was a long, finely balanced silence, then Sarah said, "About the knife. I wondered how he knew where those

231

knives were. We only bought them a few days ago and they were in the cupboard. So how could George have known?" She sprang up. "I've got to change trains here. Please leave me alone. Don't follow me anymore. It would upset my parents it they knew the police were questioning me."

Gill rose to her feet and let her pass. "Take my advice, Sarah, stay with your parents and keep clear of this mess."

She stayed on the train until the next station. There she got off and phoned Luke Warden to pick her up.

She had to wait some time before Luke arrived. "Sorry about the delay." He grinned at her. "The speed you run, you could probably have jogged back in half the time."

Gill settled herself in the passenger seat and returned his grin. "I would have if I'd known you were going to take this long. Still not to worry. It gave me time to write up my notes about what Sarah said. I got the feeling that her doubts about Brian Purvis are beginning to get to her. With any luck we may be able to turn her and get some useful information."

"About time she put her brain in gear. Not that I'd believe much she told me without proof. Still Purvis isn't our priority at the moment. Something's come up at our end too. That's why I had to take the Boss back to the Station before I picked you up."

"Anything useful?"

"Might be. The psychologist wasn't happy about the attitude of one of the kids she and Stuart interviewed yesterday, so they decided to give him another go. Apparently he's told them something important enough for Stuart to drag the Boss in to listen to him. I just hope it's good." He pulled a face that was more eloquent than words.

"For Stuart to risk that today it must be pretty big."

"It'd better be or we'll be scraping Stuart off the office walls. With the Boss this strung up, low profile's the only safe thing to be."

"We've all had a rough few days, especially the Superintendent."

"Yeah. Though yesterday he seemed fitter than I've ever seen him look."

Gill guessed that gossip about Tyler's private life was running like wildfire around the team. She was glad they'd reached the car park and she didn't have to reply.

As soon as she entered the Main Office, Kerry said, "Gill, the Bossman wants you in the kids' room."

Gill hurried along to the special room that they kept for interviewing children. Tyler was there with a young, anxious looking man and a dark haired, plump schoolboy.

"Come in Gill. Robbie, this is Gill Martin, she works with me. Gill, this is Robert Bruce-Williams, a friend of Tim and Barney, and this is Mr Fenton, one of his teachers. He's here because Robbie's parents work in America."

Robbie and his teacher made inarticulate sounds of greeting. They both looked very nervous. The psychologist was sitting discreetly at the edge of the room, where she could see Robbie but he'd have to turn to look at her.

Tyler was sitting on a low seat and keeping his voice soft. It was clear he was trying to be as non-threatening as he could. "Robbie was telling me he's a boarder at the school and sometimes he'd go to tea with Tim and Barney. Rob, tell Gill what you were telling me, about what Tim showed you."

"A handgun." The boy's voice was squeaky but he answered readily.

"How did you know it was a handgun?"

"I've seen them in the States, sir."

"Why did Tim show it to you, Robbie? What brought the conversation round to guns?"

The boy looked at his teacher. "Please sir, do I have to say?"

Fleetingly the young man's eyes met Tyler's, then he cleared his throat and said, "Answer the Superintendent's question, Robert."

The boy took a deep breath and launched into speech. "I'd told Tim about how my dad let me fire his gun when we were in the States and he said that was nothing and he'd got

233

his own and I said I didn't believe him and so he got it out. And please don't tell my dad I told you about him letting me fire the gun. He said I wasn't to tell anyone, especially not my mum. She won't even let me do shooting lessons in school."

"Don't worry about that, Robbie. Where did Tim store the gun?"

"A toy cupboard. Underneath a lot of Action Man stuff."

Gill said, "Did you see a doll in with the Action Man stuff? A doll with red hair?"

The way the colour blazed into Robbie's face and his shifty look were answer enough. "We didn't mean any harm. It was just pretend."

"Whose idea was it to do that to the doll?"

He wouldn't meet her eyes. "Tim's. He was into that sort of stuff."

Tyler looked at Gill enquiringly, obviously trying to work out whether she wished to carry on. She made a small, negative gesture and he took back the questioning, "When did they show you the gun? How many weeks ago?"

The boy frowned as he thought this through. "I don't know, sir. It was after the summer holidays. When I got back from the States."

The teacher said, "There'll be a record of the date of any visits in the school log book. All the boarders are signed in and out."

"Thank you." Tyler turned back to Robert. "Did Tim or Barney say where they'd got the gun?"

"No. They wouldn't. They said it was their secret."

"Do you know how many bullets it had in it?"

Now that the worst confession was over, the boy had steadied. "Tim said that it had nine bullets. But then he fired it, so there'd be eight after that."

"Tim fired it?" Tyler managed to make the question sound casual.

"I told Tim I didn't believe it was a real gun. I thought it might be a replica. So we went out to the allotments and Tim fired it at a shed."

Gill's eyes met Tyler's and they shared the same urgent thought: as soon as the interview was over, they'd get SOCO straight over to the allotments, to check the sheds and find any bullets for comparison with the fatal ones.

"How many bullets were fired, Rob?" asked Tyler.

"Just one. I wanted to try but he wouldn't let me have a go. He said they hadn't got any more bullets and it would be a waste."

"I see. And did they say what they wanted the rest of the bullets for?"

"No, not really."

"What do you mean, Rob?"

Robbie shrugged. "Tim said he liked to have it, liked to know it was there and one day he was going to use it and they'd be sorry then."

Tyler leaned forward. "Who did he mean, Rob? Who'd be sorry?"

Another shrug. "Anyone who pissed him off."

There was a brief silence, then Tyler said, "Thank you, Robbie. We'll get you a drink and some biscuits and then we'd like you to look at some pictures of handguns, to see if you can narrow down the weapon."

"Cool."

"That will be all for now." Tyler stood up abruptly and strode out of the room.

Robbie stared after him. "Is he cross with me?"

"Of course not, Robbie. He's busy," said Gill.

The lie was feeble and Robbie's expression made this clear. Irritated, Gill spoke bluntly, "We don't think killing's cool."

The boy's plump face turned pink and tears filled his eyes. "I didn't mean it was cool that Tim and Barney are dead. I think it's awful someone stole their gun and shot them with it... but..."

235

Gill thought, 'But you're ten years old and this is the most exciting thing that's ever happened to you and for the first time you're centre stage.'

"Thanks for your help, Robbie. I'll send an officer to look through the pictures of guns with you."

She stepped into the corridor just in time to see Superintendent Tyler punching hell out of a wall.

Chapter 44

"How did that reconstruction you were doing yesterday work out? Any results?" demanded Dan Peters.

Tyler was glad to see Dan looking better but he didn't appreciate his interest in the details of the case, much less an interrogation the moment he walked into his room. "No results," he said curtly. "I see you're on the mend."

"The doctor says I should be out of here today or tomorrow."

Tyler glanced at Hannah's anxious face. "Are you willing for us to fix up suitable accommodation, Dan?" he asked.

"A safe house you mean? Now I really do feel important." Despite the levity, there was a tremor in his voice. Tyler realised that Dan was aware of the danger and concealing his fear behind a joker's mask. "It's a pity I can't remember anything to make it worthwhile for you, Superintendent."

"There's time yet. It's possible that, quite unexpectedly, a light will click on in your mind and you'll remember seeing someone or something."

Tyler pulled up a chair and sat down. The oak at Stone Park was again sealed off, so he had to decide whether a cognitive interview in the seating area was worthwhile.

"Talk to me about what happened, Dan. Shut your eyes and tell me anything that comes into your mind."

Dan obeyed. "One thing I'm sure of, the park was unusually empty. As a rule you get lots of pre-school kids there after lunch."

"There was a big charity party at the Town Hall."

"Was there? That was lucky, otherwise it might have been a lot worse."

"You've spent a lot of time in Stone Park recently. You must have seen most of the regular park-users?"

"I suppose so."

237

"Tell me about them. You said it was usually busy at that time of day?"

"There were usually mums with their kids, unless the weather was really bad. There aren't many old people on Monday lunchtime. It's half-price day for the over-sixties at the local Chinese takeaway. One of the old ladies told me that."

"Had you seen any of the people who got shot before that day?"

"Just Josh. He was in the park a couple of times a week, always lunch time."

"Did he ever speak to anyone?"

Dan took longer to think this through. "Not really. Maybe 'Good morning,' if anyone walked past. Do you think Josh was the target?"

"I don't know."

Recently Tyler had realised that Josh was vulnerable in other ways than his private life. Part of his work was with disturbed adults and, as a peripatetic teacher, his complete client list was proving hard to compile. And he was a performer, that made him vulnerable to lunatic stalkers. Above all, he was the only victim who was known to be a lunchtime regular at Stone Park. Tyler wondered whether Josh had ever taught George Crosby. George must have undergone most types of therapy in his time.

He refocused on Dan, who was waiting patiently for his next question. "And you'd not seen any of the others before?"

"I'm not sure about the boys. They could have come after school. There were often kids playing football but I don't remember those two particularly."

"What about Charlie?"

"If he'd come before with his mum I don't think I'd have noticed him. It was him being there with his brothers that got my attention. And seeing him later in his den."

"And the two women, Sophie and Colleen?"

"I'm not sure about Colleen. Sophie I'm sure I'd never seen before."

Tyler glanced at Hannah to see her reaction to Dan's certainty.

Her smile was wry as she said, "Sophie's beautiful, is she?"

Dan met her eyes with a hint of defiance. "She's extraordinary. So vivid. When I saw her I thought I might…"

"Might what, Dan?"

His voice was savage, "Might do a decent piece of artwork again, even without you."

She looked startled. "I can't believe I made that much difference to your art?"

"Can't you?" He turned back to Tyler. "I'm sorry, I can't help you. I'd give anything to remember. Not just to solve the case, but for myself."

"I'll bear that in mind."

Tyler's tone held a reservation and Dan picked up on it. "What are you thinking?"

"I don't want to send you over the edge again, like when you heard that door bang and it sounded like a shot."

"It wasn't a shot, the gun was on the ground." Dan answered automatically then stared at Tyler in bewilderment.

"Then what panicked you?" Tyler thought back to those few moments outside the hospital. "There was a bike. I heard the swoosh of tyres. Is that what you heard, Dan?"

"It could have been. I'm sorry. I'm not sure."

"We'll check it out."

Tyler remembered a neighbour of the Quantrulls thinking the paper-boy was around. The chances were the Quantrull boys had bikes. So did some of Brian Purvis' followers. As well as Sarah's, he'd seen several bikes chained up outside the house.

As he recalled all the tyre tracks in Stone Park he had a bad feeling that SOCO weren't going to see the funny side of this.

Chapter 45

The hospital café was serving early lunches. Tyler paid for his fish and chips and looked for somewhere to sit. A small table had one occupant, Jasmin Quantrull, with Polly sleeping in a pushchair next to her. Tyler said, "May I?"

She nodded but he thought she seemed nervous. He realised she was looking at the scratches her nails had made on his cheek.

"I hope you don't mind the smell of fish and chips?" He thought ruefully it didn't mix well with her heavy, floral perfume.

"No, that's all right." She moved her coffee cup over and helped him unload his tray. "I'm sorry about what happened the other day."

"That's okay. I didn't mean to startle you. Things happened a bit too fast."

"I was so worried about what that paedophile had done to Charlie."

"We've got no reason to think he's a paedophile."

She looked stubborn. "Ian shouldn't have let him near Charlie yesterday. I hate to think of him being in the same building as Polly."

Tyler decided that reasoning with Jasmin wasn't going to work but he wanted to keep her talking. "Well the chances are Dan will be going home today, so you won't have to worry...." He broke off as a young man approached his table. "Morning Gavin."

"Sir." His ex-wife's second husband looked embarrassed. "I was hoping to see you. Viv wanted you to know. We had a little boy last night. She said to give you this." He handed Tyler a photograph of a blotchy, crumple-faced baby. Tyler hoped he didn't expect him to say the kid was beautiful. He turned the photo over and saw a message:

To Kevin,
Perfect happiness at last,
Regards from Vivienne, Gavin and baby Alistair.

"Congratulations." Tyler shoved the picture into his pocket. He had a strange, breathless feeling, like he'd been bruised inside. All that mattered was no-one should see he'd been hurt, not this jumped-up boy, nor Jasmin, who was obviously listening.

"I'm surprised she didn't go to a private nursing home." Ridiculous to feel she'd had the child here just to piss him off.

"This hospital's got the best maternity facilities but, of course, she's got a private room. I must get back now."

"Give Vivienne my congratulations."

Tyler watched him walk away, then turned his attention back to his lunch.

"Are you all right?" asked Jasmin.

He forced a smile. "Fine." He changed the subject. "Is Ian with Charlie?"

"Yes, he spends all his time there. And when he's off with his mother making funeral arrangements, Allie's with Charlie. No-one seems to think about me and Polly."

Tyler thought she was a whingy little cow but he said, "You must be glad your brother's here."

"Oh yes." She picked at her nail varnish.

"What's wrong, Jasmin?"

She gave a swift smile. "How quick you are. I'm afraid…"

"What are you scared of?" Tyler put his knife and fork down. It was hard to get the right tone with a mouth full of chips.

"We were in Spain last year, staying with Maurice, and I know Maurice had a gun."

For a moment Tyler thought she was accusing her brother of the shootings, then he understood. "Has he still got it?"

241

Her eyes looked wide and frightened. "I don't think so. I asked him and he said it had gone missing. He said one of the cleaning women must have taken it but I know he doesn't believe that. And I remembered how excited Timothy was when Maurice showed it to him and how much he wanted one."

"You think Timothy took your brother's gun?"

"I don't know. I wondered. We didn't come back with the boys. Ian had to get home to sort out a business deal. Tim and Barney came back later."

It was the explanation Tyler had been looking for; nevertheless he was sceptical. "Two kids wouldn't be able to get a gun through airport security."

"They didn't come back by plane. They sailed back. Maurice has a friend who owns a yacht."

Tyler suspected security checks on private boats might be less stringent than at airports. They were probably focusing on drugs or illegal immigrants rather than young children smuggling handguns.

"Jasmin, do you think Timothy had emotional problems?"

She met his eyes, her own brimming with tears. "He was a difficult boy. I was afraid to leave him with Polly, even for a moment, I thought he might do things to her."

"What sort of things, Jasmin?"

"Bad things."

"Do you think Tim could have been responsible for what happened in Stone Park?"

"I don't know." The words were a whisper, hardly audible above the café clatter.

Someone dropped a pile of trays and Tyler winced. "It's noisy in here."

"I don't mind noise. It's silence I hate."

"Really?"

"For a lot of my childhood I was deaf. I had an operation when I was thirteen so I could hear again."

Tyler wondered if he'd misjudged her and the whining

242

lilt in her voice was due to her childhood deafness rather than her personality. "It must have been strange at first, being able to hear again?"

"It was. Everything seemed so loud."

"Was it scarier than being deaf?" He was interested enough to divert from more relevant questioning.

She smiled at him. "You're the first person who ever asked me that. I suppose in a way it was."

"It must have been hard for you."

She made a dismissive gesture. "All my life I seem to have been surrounded by silence, staring into the shadows, waiting for the slightest movement, watching them shift and change. It's strange when you know you're screaming but you can't hear a sound."

For some reason her words revived the feeling he'd had in Stone Park from the moment he'd seen the dead children. The poetry of the First World War had always had a special resonance for him and now the words of Isaac Rosenberg, the most humble of soldier-poets twisted through his memory, *'Earth has waited for them, all the time of their growth, fretting for their decay.'* He hunted for the logic behind the image, trying to pin it down.

"How's that man who was shot in Stone Park?" Jasmin's question pierced his reverie.

He hauled himself back to the noisy café. "He's still unconscious."

"If he wakes up, I wonder…" She stopped as her brother approached.

"Good afternoon, Mr Walton," said Tyler. "Won't you join us?"

"No thank you. I just came to check my sister was all right."

"Maurice, he knows about the gun," said Jasmin.

"You told him?" Maurice sounded reproachful.

"I had to."

Tyler stood up. "If you're not here to eat, perhaps we can

243

have a word outside, Mr Walton?"

"Certainly."

To Tyler's relief, Jasmin remained in the café. He didn't fancy provoking another of her hysterical outbursts.

"Tell me about this gun you had, sir."

"It was an Astra…. I had it in Spain, for protection."

"And you showed it to Tim and Barney? You let them play with it?"

"Yes. You look disapproving, but I was brought up in the country and the good old country sports involved guns. We were all taught to shoot when we were children and it never did us any harm."

Tyler elected not to argue this. "What did you think of Tim and Barney?"

"Nice enough boys but my sister found them difficult."

"Before this tragedy did Jasmin and Ian get on all right?"

"Of course."

"And have you got any proof this gun was stolen?" Tyler watched Walton's assurance evaporate.

"Are you accusing me of lying? For God's sake! I was in Spain when these shootings took place and I can prove it."

Tyler kept his voice non-confrontational, "I'm glad to hear that. You may be required to."

Chapter 46

Rhiannon looked exhausted but, when Tyler entered Josh's room, she greeted him with a radiant smile. "They say he's improving."

"That's brilliant." Tyler had already checked out Josh's progress with the medical staff but he acted like the news was fresh to him. It seemed likely that Josh would regain consciousness within the next two days. The question was how badly he'd be impaired and whether he'd remember anything. Tyler hoped he would. One identification was not a lot to ask of life.

Sophie was also in Josh's room. She was dressed, although her arm was in a sling and there was a large sticking plaster on her head. She said timidly, "Superintendent, have you found out who did it?"

"We've got ideas but no real evidence." Tyler hesitated, uncertain whether to make his next request.

"Why are you looking at me like that?"

"There's something you could do that might help, but it may be too much to ask of you or Daniel Peters."

"What is it?"

"I wondered if you'd consider going back to where you were shot, wearing clothes similar to the ones you were wearing that day and talk through what happened before the shootings, to see if it brings any buried memories to the surface?"

She hesitated but only for reasonable thinking time. "I'll do anything I can to help."

The door opened and the guard cop said, "Mrs Scott's here with your suitcase, Mrs Hughes."

Rhiannon said, "Thank you." She met Tyler's startled gaze and explained, "Josh's friend came by earlier to see how he was doing and offered to get me some stuff from my house. I didn't want to leave the hospital in case he regains consciousness earlier than the doctors think he will."

Tyler was bombarded by conflicting emotions. He wanted Lani to stay clear of all this crap and he wanted his relationship with her to stay private, but he had to respect her kindness to a friend in trouble. He didn't want to see her because he was prickly and tense, but he wanted to see her because she was the only person who could make him feel better. Whatever. He couldn't lurk in here. He followed Rhiannon into the corridor.

Nikki was close behind him. "I'll have to check the case. It's just a formality."

"Of course." Lani handed her the suitcase and showed no offence as she searched it.

"Thank you so much," said Rhiannon. "Lani, this is Detective Superintendent Tyler."

"I know."

Tyler realised Lani too was struggling for a foothold in this slippery situation. Clearly she didn't want to embarrass him in front of his junior officers. He smiled at her and said, "Hi, Lani."

"How are things going, Kev?"

"Could be worse." He remembered the thought that had occurred to him earlier. "Lani, do you know whether Josh works with any disturbed people? The sort who could have become obsessed with him?"

"We both work with people with mental health problems but I'd have told you if I'd known of anyone like that who posed a risk. Josh is more adventurous in his client groups than me. We overlap on therapy for depression, bereavement and trauma, but he has lots of people I don't know about."

"Does he work with kids? Perhaps ones who'd had a bereavement?"

He knew she'd interpreted the subtext but she said simply, "Josh works in Adult Ed. I'm pretty sure he's not qualified to work with kids."

"Thanks." He turned to Nikki, "Tell Sophie I'll be in touch about the cognitive interview."

As he left ITU his footsteps slowed. Lani caught up and walked along with him. "Are you okay?" she asked.

"Yeah, just pissed off."

"So it was George Crosby in the park?"

Tyler nodded. "He left a suicide note saying how I'd inspired him to sacrifice himself to the sacred oak."

"Oh Kev!" Then fiercely, "It wasn't your fault. When people are mentally sick they latch onto things and twist them."

"You don't understand." As the words left his mouth he remembered Lani's ex-husband had committed suicide. "I'm sorry!"

She said crossly, "This is impossible. I wish I could get you somewhere private."

"So you could slap me?"

"So I could hug you, you idiot."

"I don't deserve to be hugged."

"It's not a question of what you deserve, it's what you need." She moved close enough for her arm to touch his. "Think of this as a hug."

The way his body was reacting it seemed to think that slight contact was a full-blown seduction. "Don't tempt me or I might jump on you here and now."

She grinned at him. "I'm up for that."

"I'm in enough trouble as it is. I've already had a sticky session with the ACC. He more or less told me SIOs should not encourage loonies to commit suicide but, if they did, they should go for illiterate ones who couldn't leave embarrassing notes."

"For God's sake Kev, stop beating yourself up."

They had reached the stairwell and were heading down. He put his arm around her, ignoring the possibility of security cameras, then he pulled the photograph Vivienne had sent him from his pocket and handed it to her.

247

She looked at the picture, then turned it over and read the message. Tyler saw her lips tighten. "Will you let me deal with this?"

"Willingly. You're not planning to organise a hit, are you?"

"Nothing so crude. I assume you're not worried about keeping our relationship secret, apart from at your work?"

"Of course not." He felt uncomfortable. "I'm not ashamed of our relationship but I feel sort of vulnerable."

She led the way to the hospital flower shop and ordered a magnificent bouquet, the sort that claimed attention. She selected an ornate card and wrote upon it in a flamboyant hand:

To Vivienne and Family,

Congratulations. Hope that you're as gloriously happy as we are.

All good wishes from Kev and Lani.

PS. Don't worry if we're out of touch for a while.

We're off to France as soon as Kev can get some leave.

"Are we?" he asked, reading over her shoulder.

"Gloriously happy? Or off to France?"

"France, of course."

"We can be. Isabel and I share a holiday house there."

She got out her credit card and he protested, "You can't pay for flowers for my ex."

"Trust me."

She waited until they were clear of the shop to explain, "This way if Vivienne sends her new husband down to find out who paid for the flowers, she won't be able to kid herself you were bluffing about your new relationship."

"But why should she?" Vivienne's manoeuvres had always been a mystery to him.

"The way I read it Vivienne likes knowing you're alone. To put it crudely, she likes rubbing your nose in it."

"So you send her a big bunch of flowers that all her visitors are going to notice?" Tyler began to understand.

248

"That's the idea. They say, *'What lovely flowers. Who sent them?'* and go across and read the card. And, for pride's sake, Vivienne has to keep a smile on her face."

"You're a ruthless woman, Lani."

"Yes, but you're safe. I'm on your side."

As he walked her to her car, she said, "I'm out tonight. As Gill's so busy, Bel asked me to go to the theatre with her, but if you need me phone through and I'll cancel."

"That's not in the bargain. You can't give up your evening out for me."

She wrinkled her nose. "It's no major sacrifice."

"Why? What are you going to see?"

"*Othello*. Call me shallow but I prefer *Twelfth Night* or *Much Ado*. The language is great but Othello was such a self-centred, stupid man."

"Aren't we all?" said Tyler ruefully.

Chapter 47

Sophie looked beautiful and fragile in duplicates of the clothes that held such bitter memories. Her hands were shaking as she painted silver tear-drops on her pale cheeks.

She draped a glittering scarf around her shoulders then gave Tyler a pathetic smile.

"Is that it?" he asked. "As close as you can get?"

"Yes." She sat down in the wheelchair to be pushed to the police car.

Her mother kissed her. "Do you want me to come with you?"

"No, you stay with Josh. I must do this alone." Her painted lips trembled into a smile. "Sophie's a big girl now. All grown up."

Tyler had surrounded the park with uniformed men to act as guards and to head off sightseers and reporters. Two of the cops who'd done the mock up yesterday were seated on a bench to represent Josh and Colleen.

Sophie got out of her wheelchair and passed the place where Dan was standing. Tyler heard him catch his breath and saw him shudder.

Tyler nodded to the technicians who were recording the scene and they started up their equipment while he gently talked Dan back into that day.

At his discreet signal, three suitably dressed boys, cops' kids borrowed for the occasion, ran past. Tyler hadn't expected much of this part of the interview but Daniel frowned and said, "Why the hat?"

"Tim's stepmother said that he was wearing it. We found it at the scene."

"He wasn't wearing it when I saw him."

"Fair enough." Tyler might not be an expert on kids but he knew they took their hats off when their parents weren't looking.

He signalled to Sophie and she approached the bench. Self-consciously she knelt, embracing the woman cop as she had Colleen.

All the time Tyler asked gentle questions, probing Dan's memory. At first Dan answered hesitantly but, when prompted, he raised his camera and took shot after shot. Then Tyler walked him along, talking him back. "Now you're returning to the car. What do you see?"

"Nothing, just the bushes and the sky getting darker all the time."

"What do you hear?"

"Some bangs. They're a long way off. I think someone's car's screwed up."

"How many bangs?"

"...Three... One then two more close together."

"Do you hear anything else?"

"Voices... maybe... I'm not sure... some sort of shout... a man's voice."

"What's he saying?"

"...I don't know..."

"Okay, move on." They reached Dan's car. Tyler said, "Is there anyone around?"

"No."

"What do you do?"

"I put my camera in my pocket... don't want to seem pushy... grab my business cards and head back." Dan's hands were shaking but he matched the actions with the words. "The car backfires again... three times I think... it makes me jump... it sounds near but I can't see a car."

Tyler guided him back into the park. "You're in a hurry. What do you see?"

"The kid in the bushes. It isn't safe leaving him there. He could run out of the park onto the road or end up in the lake."

"What do you hear?"

"Just the wind and the rustle of the leaves."

"Okay. You're back at the benches." Tyler led Dan

251

towards the most harrowing part of the interview. He was pushing the boundaries in a way that few cops would care to go. The reconstruction of the death scene was painfully accurate. They'd offered Sophie a substitute for this but she'd refused and was lying on the ground beside the pretend Josh, in a pool of fake blood.

He heard Dan's breathing go haywire. "What do you see, Dan?"

"Colleen, shot through the throat... she's lying back... there's blood on her shirt... Josh and Sophie on the ground... the gun's by his hand... there's so much blood... that glittery scarf is filling up with it."

"And what do you do?"

"Try to find my phone... it's not there... must have left it in car... I see one... pick it up...I have to phone for help... but I can't... I drop it... I kneel in the blood to get it... but I can't talk... all that blood... and the noise."

"What noise?"

"Josh. He's sort of gurgling, like he's gargling with blood."

"Move on past Josh. Come on, Dan, move on. What else can you hear?"

"Nothing. Just the person on the phone asking me questions. I try to tell them but I don't make sense. Then the ground comes up and hits me." He focused on Tyler. "No, wait!... Just before that I heard a shush... like a moving bike."

His legs buckled and Tyler got an arm round him and helped him to sit down on the bench. Stuart and Hannah hurried to join them.

"That's enough. Let's wrap it up," said Tyler. To get Dan to re-enact finding Charlie and taking him from the park would be pushing him too far.

The woman who'd taken Colleen's place attempted to assist Sophie to her feet but she shied away from her. Nikki came forward and helped Sophie stand. Nikki's eyes met Tyler's and she shook her head.

Shakily, Sophie approached Daniel. He said, "Are you all right?"

She nodded. "Are you?"

"I will be." They shared shy conspiratorial smiles, like survivors of a holocaust.

Dan leaned back against Hannah's supporting arm. He looked worried.

"What's wrong, Dan?" asked Tyler.

Anxiety became irritation. "The smell was wrong," he said petulantly.

"What did he mean the smell was wrong?" demanded Gill.

Tyler shrugged. They were back in his office and his desk seemed to have grown a fresh crop of paperwork. "I don't know. Probably nothing. A cognitive interview is the same as an ordinary one, there's a lot of garbage to sort out for everything that's worth focusing on. You have to be careful with the cognitive game. You can put ideas into a witness' mind or you can push a vulnerable witness too far. I nearly did that with Dan."

"The doctors say another night in hospital and he'll be fine. At least we've got the order of the shootings. The kids were shot first, assuming the man that shouted was Josh."

"That ties in with Sophie's first statement. She said Josh yelled 'What the hell' and then told them to get out of the park."

"It's a pity you couldn't do a cognitive interview with Sophie at the same time."

"Nikki was dealing with Sophie. Not that she got much. Sophie was preoccupied by hating the aggro between Colleen and Josh and wishing she'd never lied about him."

"Is Nikki trained to do cognitive interviews?"

"Of course she is. I like my team to put in a lot of training. You happy with that?"

"Yes, sir."

"Roy's confirmed he's retiring so, if you want to stay on, I'll be glad to apply for your permanent placement."

"I'd like that, sir. Thank you." Despite the moderate words, Gill's smile lit up her face. "Do you want a hand with this paperwork?"

"Too right I do. I've got a close encounter with the Media tonight. They're running a documentary on spree killers and the ACC insists I go along."

"But we don't know Stone Park's a spree killing. In fact the chances are it's not. What are you going to tell them?"

"As little as possible. That programme's built its reputation on slagging off cops."

They worked in silence through a pile of personal background checks and witness statements. Gill opened the file containing the latest Forensic reports and looked up. "I've got something."

"The age of miracles isn't over. What is it?"

"The report on Josh Fortune's clothing. They've found a hair on his jumper and they've matched it to Timothy Quantrull's."

"So Josh was in physical contact with Tim?" That turned a lot of theories upside down and Tyler wasn't at all sure where it fitted in.

"Apparently. But Josh's clothing was potentially contaminated in A&E, so this wouldn't stand up in Court." Gill shrugged. "Not that there'll be a court case if it was Timothy."

"Tomorrow I want a proper search of the Quantrull house. No more faffing around." He glanced at his watch. "I'd better smarten up."

"Look at it as your chance to achieve instant stardom, sir."

"Ha bloody ha." He took himself off to shave and change his shirt.

Chapter 48

Gill sent out for pizza and ploughed on through the paper-work. Just after eight, Kerry opened her office door and said, "The Bossman's on."

Gill joined Kerry and Luke in front of the computer that Kerry had set up to watch and record the programme. On screen Tyler looked even bigger and tougher than he was in real life. He parried questions about the progress of the investigation, putting a positive spin on it that impressed Gill, who knew it wasn't true.

"So Superintendent, are you near to an arrest?"

"I believe we are near to a conclusion."

Gill saw the interviewer think this through.

"Would you care to elaborate on that statement?"

"No thank you."

Tyler allowed the questioner a glimpse of his tiger smile and Kerry remarked dispassionately, "Jesus, he's a seriously scary guy."

"Then I'm surprised you push your luck with him the way you do," said Luke.

"Superintendent, can you tell us about the new death last night in Stone Park?"

Tyler looked even grimmer. "A mentally ill, homeless man was found dead there early this morning. We're still investigating his death."

"Do you suspect foul play?"

"As I said we're still investigating the circumstances of his death."

"Isn't it true that you knew this man well?"

"As a police officer, I meet many people in this town, including the mentally sick and homeless. Perhaps you should make mental health care the subject of your next documentary."

"Well done you lairy sod," commented Kerry as the interview wound up.

"Thought you hated him," said Luke.

"Not half as much as I hate bloody reporters."

Gill half-listened to their banter, half to the documentary.

They had moved away from Tyler and on through descriptions of recent spree killings. Gill thought the programme must be grinding to an end and felt relief Tyler had got through it so well. She stood up to go back to her desk.

"And now some news just in. Katerina Gibson, a freelance journalist, has discovered that Daniel Peters, whom police have described as a witness in the Stone Park case, is a suspected paedophile. Peters, aged twenty-seven, is known for his erotic sculptures of children.

A reputable source has informed Katerina that Peters abducted three-year-old Charlie Quantrull from Stone Park. Charlie, the brother of the two murdered schoolboys, was discovered by police the next day in an isolated, derelict building, in company with Peters. Charlie had been stripped of all his clothes. This disclosure is especially disquieting when the police are relying on Peters as a vital witness in their enquiry. Police conduct must be further questioned when this programme has discovered that, yesterday, they allowed Peters access to Charlie in his hospital room.

Speaking to us from the small village of Crossbrook, where Daniel Peters has been living for the past year, Katerina tells us that feelings are running high. Parents in Crossbrook must be especially perturbed tonight, now this potentially dangerous man has been released from hospital to return to their quiet community.

Unfortunately Detective Superintendent Tyler, the Senior Investigating Officer in this case, has already left the studio and we are unable to obtain an explanation from him."

"Unfortunately my arse," said Kerry, kicking a waste bin across the room. "Those bastards made sure the Bossman was clear of the place before they spread their filth."

For a moment Gill was speechless with outrage. At last she said, "For God's sake! They've got no shred of proof to back their accusations."

Luke shrugged. "It packs in the punters, that's all they care about. Anyway they've twisted the facts but they haven't said anything that can be proved to be a lie. Don't you remember Katerina Gibson? She led the *Name the Paedophile* Campaign in the local press a few years ago."

"You mean the one who incited a mob who burnt out a paediatric nurse? I'd have thought she'd have learned her lesson."

"Not her sort. They go to ground for a while then pop up again as lairy as ever. Are you going to let the Boss know what's happened?"

Gill hesitated. The chances were that Tyler hadn't heard about this development. Kerry was right, the programme makers had almost certainly waited until he'd got clear of the studio because they wouldn't want to hear his forcible rejection of their claims. She could phone him on his mobile but the last thing they needed was for the SIO to crash his car because he was driving recklessly.

"No. Time enough for that when he gets back. Thank God Dan Peters is still safely in hospital. Luke, phone down and ask uniformed to tell the car patrols to do a few sweeps past his house. If feelings in the village are running high, some bastards may trash it. Kerry, ring through to Stuart and warn him what's happened. But if he's in with Dan make it tactful. Dan's been through enough today."

Kerry grinned at her. "You know me, Tact's my middle name."

"Now I thought it was Attitude," said Luke as he picked up his phone.

When Tyler joined them he looked tired but alert. "What's going on?" he demanded as he walked in the door.

Again Gill was startled by how sharp he was.

"Don't tell me it's nothing. I knew something was brewing the second I walked in the Station."

"There's plenty wrong, sir." Swiftly she told Tyler what had been going down and Kerry played the relevant section of the recording she'd taken of the programme.

Gill had not expected exclamations, Tyler was not an exclaiming sort of man, but she was surprised there was no visible reaction to her news. Then she realised that all his emotions were harnessed to serve his formidable intelligence.

"So how did this bitch reporter know all that stuff?" They stared at him and he elaborated, "About Charlie being undressed and where Dan had taken him. That was on a need-to-know basis."

"And how did they know Dan was supposed to be released from hospital today?" said Gill.

"I want a word with Katerina Gibson," said Tyler.

"She won't tell you the identity of her informant," said Kerry.

"Oh I think she will." His voice was soft and menacing.

"Do you think there's a leak in this team, sir?" Gill was horribly aware of her new-girl status.

She knew he'd spotted her insecurity. "No. I trust all my team."

His mobile rang. He listened and said, "Yes sir, I've heard. Right." He keyed off. "The ACC has been watching television and he wants to see me now."

"Oh shit!" said Kerry.

"Yeah, didn't sound like he was a happy man."

Twenty minutes later he returned.

"Okay, sir?" asked Gill.

"I've had meetings I've enjoyed more. Still, he's agreed we should interview that bloody reporter."

Kerry's phone rang. She answered, "DS Buller... oh shit! Okay, we're on our way."

She put the phone down. Her face was white. "Sir,

258

we're needed at Crossbrook. It's urgent. Uniformed and the paramedics are on their way."

Tyler was already moving. As Gill ran to keep up with him she heard him say, "Paramedics? Who's hurt? Not Dan Peters? He's still in hospital."

Kerry sounded breathless. "They said a gang of thugs are trying to kill a cop."

Chapter 49

For once there were no complaints about the speed of Kerry's driving. Tyler, in the front passenger seat, kept his mobile on. He'd instructed that all information was to be relayed straight to him and he passed it on to the rest of his team.

"The squad car's there." Then after a suitable pause, "He's alive."

"Who is it?" asked Gill.

"Hang on." He snapped a question and waited, everything about him tensed to cracking point. The reply was what he'd expected. "It's Stuart."

"Sweet Jesus!" The car swerved. Kerry brought it back under control. "What's he doing out there? He's supposed to be at the hospital."

"I'd guess he went to get Dan's stuff to speed up the move to the safe house."

"But... oh Christ he didn't know! I got through to the guy outside the hospital door and told him to be careful in case someone made a try for Dan. He said Stuart wasn't around at that moment but he'd let him know. I'm sorry!"

"We'll discuss it later." Tyler forced himself to speak moderately. "Now concentrate on driving, or the whole team will end up in A&E."

Lit by the lights of the police cars, the scene outside the house was macabre. In fact it was multi-coloured. For a second Tyler thought he was seriously losing it. Whatever. He'd got no time for a mental breakdown now. Before the car had stopped he was out of his seat and sprinting across the grass to kneel beside Stuart. Under the oxygen mask the boy's face was puffy and bloodstained, his eyes were closed and his breathing laboured.

"How is he?"

"He's had a nasty beating," said the paramedic. "We don't know how bad the internal damage is."

At the sound of Tyler's voice, Stuart opened his eyes and made a feeble gesture towards the oxygen mask. The paramedic removed it and Stuart muttered, "Sorry sir."

"You haven't done anything to apologise for. The ones who'll be sorry are the bastards who did this. Any idea who it was?"

"No sir... I'm sorry..."

"Rest easy, Stu. You're going to be fine." He crossed to the patrol cops. "You were first on the scene?"

"Yes sir. We found DC Farrow lying here. The young lady was kneeling beside him."

"Young lady?" Tyler followed the constable's gesture and saw Hannah seated on the ground. Gill had already reached her. He strode over to them. "Hannah are you okay?"

She looked up and nodded, staring at him with shock glazed eyes.

"What happened?"

Gill said, "Hannah's just told me, sir. Like you thought, she and Stuart came to get some stuff for Dan. Stuart was putting the perishable food in the dustbin when Hannah heard shouting outside. She looked out the window and saw a gang of six to eight people attacking Stuart. They were calling him a pervert and a paedophile. Hannah dialled 999 then she went after the thugs and drove them off using spray paint from Dan's studio."

Which explained the bizarre look of the garden. Tyler sat down beside Hannah and put his arm around her shaking shoulders. "Well done and thank you."

Her voice was unsteady. "I was afraid, but I was angry too. I didn't think they'd run away like that."

"That sort are usually cowards."

"Especially when you brand them," said Gill.

"Yeah." Tyler's eyes went to the traces of bright blue and yellow paint. "We're going to get them, Hannah. We'll round them up if we have to kick down every door in this bloody village."

"But why did they do it? I don't understand."

He didn't have time to go into it now. "We'll talk about that later. I want you to go back in the ambulance with Stuart and DI Martin." He drew Gill aside. "I'm sorry but I need a senior officer to go back with them. Get Nikki down to keep an eye on Stuart and double the guard on Dan's room. When you get free ring my mobile and I'll tell you where I need you."

"Should I tell Hannah that we think they mistook Stuart for Dan?"

"You can confirm it if she asks. The chances are she'll work it out. They're the same sort of age and build and both fair-haired, and Stuart was making himself at home in Dan's house."

He waited until the ambulance was loaded, snapping commands into his phone about the manpower he required.

"That's going to leave us a bit stretched for a Saturday night," said Luke. "Not that I'm arguing."

"I'd advise you not to. The clubbing yobs can have free reign for once." Tyler glanced across at Kerry, still unusually subdued. "Kerry, what do they say on that CSI programme you're always on about?"

For a moment, her habitual cheekiness showed through. "Tonight this is the only crime scene in town," she quoted.

"Precisely," said Tyler, "So get on with it."

Chapter 50

The reporter pushed a strand of blonde hair out of her eyes and glared at Tyler. "I won't reveal my sources and you've no right to keep me here."

"You're sure you don't want to co-operate?"

"Certain. I've been here an hour and now I'm leaving." She stood up.

"I was hoping you'd say that." Tyler purred the words. He waited until she was within touching distance of the interview room door and said, "DI Martin, arrest her please, incitement to violence will do for starters."

"What?" The reporter swung round to face him. "I want my solicitor."

"Of course. But you'll have to wait in the cells. We need our interview rooms for your co-conspirators. They're being more informative."

This at least was true. The large number of police drafted into Crossbrook had shaken that smug little village out of its superiority. Hannah had aimed shrewdly, pointing at the thugs' eyes, where balaclavas and scarves didn't protect. There were five paint-stained suspects in custody and the cops were still knocking on doors.

"I haven't got any co-conspirators. I haven't done anything wrong."

Tyler stood up. "DI Martin, get her booked in please." He smiled at the reporter. "It's ironic. You'll be the only reporter not putting in a story about the Crossbrook raids."

Gill waited until the reporter had been processed and led away, then asked, "Do you think we'll be able to make it stick, sir?"

"Probably not but we've got enough that she won't be able to sue us. All it needs is one of those thugs to swear Katerina Gibson incited them and we've got her. But the main thing is to find out the name of her informant. First thing tomorrow, I want you checking exactly who knew what and who they told."

"Yes sir. May I ask why?" Tyler heard the reserved note in Gill's voice.

"Whoever told that journalist about Dan knew a bloody sight too much. And the other day, the local newspaper published the story about Jasmin going for me within a few of hours of it happening. I don't believe it's one of my team, so that means it's someone else connected with this case. I reckon someone out there is jerking us round and I want to know who."

"Ian Quantrull knew about Charlie being undressed; Jasmin asked about it in the hospital on the day Charlie was found. And I'm sure Ian's realised that we're looking at Tim and Barney as the possible killers."

"And he's throwing diversions in our way? Yeah, that's possible. Nikki's got a contact at the local paper. I'll tell her to find out who fed them the story about Jasmin scratching my face. In the meantime, I've got to go and talk to some friendly reporters. What's so funny?"

"When you said 'friendly reporters' I thought of those adverts that tell you to *'top up your friendly bacteria'*."

Tyler grinned. "By friendly, I mean that some of them owe me a favour and a lot know I'm not a good person to piss off. Fortunately Stuart's a bit of a hero. He got a commendation for dragging a kid clear of a burning car when he was in uniform. The Press Office is playing that for all it's worth."

"Have you heard anymore about how he is, sir?"

"Pretty battered but they reckon he'll be okay. When I've finished with the Media I'll head over to the hospital to see him. You get on with the interrogations. I'll be back as soon as I can."

The corridors were deserted. All available officers were on the streets, either maintaining order amongst the clubbing kids or raiding houses in Crossbrook.

"This place is dead," said Tyler. "The ACC's getting us more manpower from other forces as soon as possible. I reckon I've used up my quota of reinforcements for the rest of my career."

Tyler had just parked at the hospital when his mobile rang. He didn't recognise the caller's number and answered with a cautious, "Yeah?"

"Sir? Superintendent Tyler? It's Jones, sir, Ryan Jones. I'm sorry to ring you like this…"

"Okay, Ryan, calm down. Tell me what's wrong."

"It's Sarah, sir. I know what you said about staying away from her but she phoned me. She's in Stone Park and she needs me, sir."

"What do you mean needs you?"

"She said there was something she had to find out. That she thought she could do it alone but now she knows she can't. She's scared sir. I've got to help her. But I wanted to tell you because, if anything goes wrong, I wouldn't want you to think I'd gone behind your back, and…" there was a moment's panting hesitation, "I'm scared too."

"Where are you?"

"Outside Stone Park, sir. The entrance near the school."

"Stay there. I'll come straight away." There was no answer and he repeated, "Ryan, stay there."

"She's scared, sir. She needs me."

Tyler cursed and headed for the exit. He was delayed by the checkout barrier, and had to find a machine to buy a token for his two-minute stay. He drove through the town centre, slowing to avoid the drunken kids hanging around the clubs. He put his foot down as he hit the quieter streets.

When he arrived at the entrance to Stone Park, Ryan was not in sight. Tyler got out of the car, then hesitated. He keyed in Gill Martin's number and got her answer service. "Gill, it's Tyler. I think there may be more trouble at Stone Park. Could you and Luke come along here straight away? Make it low profile and discreet. I could be making an idiot of myself."

He pocketed his mobile and his torch and moved into the park.

The tree-lined paths were shadowed. A half-drowned moon lurked sulkily behind thick clouds. The only sounds were Tyler's soft footsteps and the occasional rush of water as he brushed against a rain-laden branch.

"No!" The anguish in the young voice spurred Tyler to speed. Now he could hear a struggle not far away. He identified the direction of the fight and ran towards it.

Chapter 51

It was like a clip from a Fifties' movie, all black and white and shades of grey. Two men struggled beside the lake. They were unevenly matched; one taller and bulkier than the other. There was a sound that blended between scream and gasp. The slighter one doubled over. A shove from his opponent staggered him into the lake.

Tyler sprinted towards the scene. His brain had abandoned thought but, somewhere in the depths, panted the words, *'No more. No more deaths.'*

The remaining man turned to meet him. Tyler couldn't see his face but instinct told him who it was. "Purvis!"

He glimpsed the movement of a hand headed towards his guts. He lunged sideways to avoid it and felt red-hot stinging slice down his thigh. He clenched his fist and hit out. One hefty blow that held all his pent-up rage. Purvis went down. Tyler didn't see the weapon but he heard the tinkle of metal skittering along the ground.

He pulled his torch out of his pocket. Purvis was sprawled and still. His eyes were shut and he was rasping for breath. Tyler didn't know how badly he was hurt and didn't care. The victim in the water claimed precedence.

He dragged off his coat and dropped it. Then, cursing his own incompetence, he bent to retrieve his mobile phone. He kicked off his shoes and waded into the ice-cold water. His torch beam arced through the darkness. Waist deep he paused and keyed in 999. He thought his voice sounded remarkably crisp and clear, although it echoed eerily in his head. "This is Detective Superintendent Tyler. Get police and paramedics to Stone Park, the south side of the lake. Officer down." He was certain the man in the lake was Ryan Jones.

He shoved the phone into his breast pocket and carried on looking. Fortunately this was the shallowest part of the lake, the water no more than five feet deep. There was something by the bank. A body. He struggled to it and wrestled it onto dry ground. He was feeling faint now and sick, although surprisingly his leg didn't hurt that much. He was shaking and the torch beam kept veering off. He steadied it. The body was lying on its face, ominously still. That light hair didn't belong to Ryan. He dragged the helpless form onto its back. In the torchlight, Sarah's face was bleached lime-white, her eyes were open and her throat was cut.

'I can't do it. I can't go in that bloody lake again.' Helplessness swept over Tyler. He looked down at Sarah's body. The blank eyes stared up. Ridiculous to think the dead can accuse.

He pushed himself upright, shoulders hunched, like a man forcing against an immense weight. He staggered back to the water and plunged in. His sight was blurred. Everything seemed distorted. Time was running in slow motion, which wasn't fair when time was running out for Ryan. It wasn't fair. Life wasn't fair. Death wasn't bloody fair.

At first he thought the lake was cloaked in fog. Then he realised it was his weakness. He couldn't see. He couldn't hear. He flailed through the water, using the only sense he had left. When he touched flesh he hardly registered it. In fact he recoiled, repulsed by the cold limpness. Then he realised and grabbed at it before it slipped away. A hand. He followed through, feeling along the arm and dragging the body to him, cradling it, head above water. For a moment, his vision cleared. He saw Ryan's blanched face.

Tyler headed for the bank; or at least where he reckoned it should be. The mist in his head was thicker than ever and he'd lost his bearings. Lost everything except the need for haste. One step, then another, Ryan's limp body cradled to him. Surely he should have hit the bank by now? He stumbled. As he went down he tried to shove Ryan upwards. Water filled his mouth and his nose. He regained his tenuous balance and came up spluttering. Now he knew that he was done. His leg wouldn't hold him anymore and, despite the numbing cold of the water, it hurt like hell.

If he released Ryan, he might stand some chance of making it himself. He tightened his grip.

Life was a bitch. Just when you thought you'd got something good, Fate screwed it up for you.

Again his leg gave way. This time he went right down. He swallowed a lot of water, but as he surfaced he saw the bank. It was only a couple of yards away. Fuck Fate! He wasn't going to die that easily. Not now, when he'd got someone to live for. And he wasn't going to fail. He dragged Ryan towards solid ground.

There was sound, distorted but recognisable. The sound of running feet. The sound of voices. Someone tried to take Ryan away from him. He held on. "It's okay, sir. It's me, Gill. Luke and I have got him. You can let go."

He obeyed, slowly because each muscle took an age to unclench. He knew he should hurry, knew there was stuff he had to say. "Ryan... think... Purvis... stabbed him..."

"It's okay, sir. I can hear the ambulance."

A different voice... Nikki. "Come on, sir. We need to get you on dry land."

Nikki should be at the hospital, keeping an eye on Stuart. He'd meant to visit Stuart. He muttered, "How's Stuart? I should have seen him."

"Don't worry, sir. With the run on cops they're having, they'll probably put you in the same hospital bed."

That was Kerry, close beside him. That meant the whole bloody team was here splashing round in the lake. Who the hell was taking care of all the work?

"Ryan... is he...?"

"Gill and Luke are taking care of him. Let's get you out the water."

Tyler found himself being manhandled onto the bank. The jolt as he was deposited on the ground wrenched a protest from him, half whimper and half blasphemy.

"You hurt, sir?" He'd never heard Kerry sound so concerned.

"My leg. Purvis with his knife. The bastard hasn't got away?"

"No, he's here, out cold. And there's a girl's body. What the fuck's been going on?"

"Purvis." The world swirled round Tyler and he felt violently sick.

"How bad's your leg, sir?"

"I don't know."

"And you still went into the water after Ryan?"

"Twice… I went in twice… I found Sarah first."

"Jesus, talk about more balls than bloody brains!"

In some dim recess of his mind, Tyler knew that Kerry's remark was insolent and insubordinate. He'd have felt better able to deal with it if Nikki hadn't been removing his trousers. "What… you… doing?" Every word was a mountain to toil up.

"Checking your leg… Oh shit!"

Chapter 52

"I'm fine. It's just a scratch."

"A scratch that needed twelve stitches and only just missed the femoral artery." Gill struggled to moderate the sharpness of her tone. Tyler was acting like a macho idiot but it was clear he was deep in shock; his face was slush grey and his eyes were fever bright.

The hospital was overstretched and Tyler was still in an A&E cubicle. He was lying on the comfortless, narrow bed, a blanket wrapped around him; shivering violently.

"How's Ryan?" he demanded.

"Still in surgery. His mum's here."

"I ought to see her."

"Not tonight. I've spoken to her. She's holding up okay. You need to rest." The doctor had been eloquent about the loss of blood, the risk of infection and the amount of dirty water Tyler had swallowed.

"I didn't get to see Stuart." His fingers plucked at the blanket.

"Stuart's doing fine. He'll probably be back on duty before you are."

"I'm not going off duty."

More macho crap. Again Gill didn't argue. She was still cold, although she'd dried herself and changed her clothes for the spare ones she kept in her car. "Sir, what happened tonight?"

"Ryan phoned me. He said Sarah needed to see him and she was scared. I told him to wait for me but he didn't. That's why I phoned you."

She stared in horror. "What would have happened if I hadn't checked my answer service?"

"You always do. Every few minutes you check your phone." He gave a shaky grin. "It's bloody annoying but it came in useful tonight. But I didn't expect you to pull the whole bloody team off their duties and come charging to the rescue."

"Luke and Kerry were there when I got your message. I don't know if they'd have obeyed a direct order to stay out of it but I doubt it."

Tyler gave a non-committal grunt. "So how did Nikki get in on the act?"

"One of them must have phoned her. You can't blame them. They're your team."

"I suppose I should be grateful Stuart didn't hi-jack an ambulance and nip down to Stone Park to join the action."

Gill decided to abandon the subject while she was still marginally ahead. "What happened in the park?"

Tyler ran a hand across his face. The struggle to rally his thoughts was painfully obvious but his account was brief and coherent.

"How many times did you hit Purvis?" She couldn't conceal her tension.

He stared at her. "Once."

"And what did you hit him with?"

"My fist. Why?"

"They say he's in a bad way. He's got a broken neck and they're not sure he's going to make it."

There was a drawn-out silence. At last he said, "That's inconvenient. Internal enquiries are a total pain. Anyway, I'd rather the bastard came to trial."

Again Gill decided it would be politic to move on. "What about the spade, sir?"

"What spade?"

"There was a spade in the grass, near to Sarah's bike."

"I didn't see it." He was silent, a brooding frown upon his face.

Gill gathered up her courage. "Have you called Lani?"

The frown deepened. "It's late. No need to bother her."

"She'd want to know and there's a good chance it'll be

272

all over the news."

She saw him waver. "My mobile's buggered. The water got in it. That's the second one in a week."

Gill got out her phone, keyed in the number, handed it to him and withdrew.

Three minutes later, when she ventured back, she thought Tyler looked less burdened. He returned her phone. "Thanks. She's coming in. Have you contacted Isabel and let her know you're all right?"

He sounded embarrassed. Gill wasn't sure if that was because of the nature of her and Bel's relationship or because he was uncomfortable when talking about personal lives.

"Yes, I've already called her."

A nurse pulled back the cubicle curtain. "There's a lady asking for Mr Tyler."

For a bewildered second, Gill thought even Lani couldn't get to the hospital that fast, then a small, anxious-looking woman walked purposefully into the cubicle and said, "Mr Tyler? I'm Moira Jones, Ryan's mum."

Gill pulled a chair forward. "Please sit down, Mrs Jones." It was a weird reversal of the usual breaking of bad news.

Ryan's mother perched on the edge of the chair and spoke directly to Tyler, "I mustn't stop above a minute. I wanted to tell you Ryan's out of surgery. He's still in a bad way but they say he's got a good chance of recovering. That's thanks to you. If it hadn't been for you he'd have been a goner like that poor, stupid, little bitch who led him on."

She must have seen the protest on their faces. "I know I shouldn't talk ill of the dead and whatever she did she's paid for it, poor girl. But why couldn't she have stuck to my Ryan instead of running after a man old enough to be her dad?"

She stood up. "I must get back to Ryan. I'm sorry, ranting on like that. I don't know what you must think of me. I don't usually act like this."

She left abruptly. Neither Gill nor Tyler had managed to say a word.

Tyler lay back on his pillows, the grey shade had deepened in his face. "Everything she said was true and yet, emotionally, Sarah was just a child. Like a shoot that's been nipped off before it can grow the way it should." He wiped the back of his hand across his lips and glanced around uneasily, as if trying to locate something.

"Have you lost something, sir?"

"No, I..."

The curtain was pulled back and this time Lani stood there. She looked pale and anxious. She gave Gill a swift smile then settled on the edge of Tyler's bed and hugged him, crooning words of comfort.

Gill slipped away and returned to work.

Chapter 53

"I'm sorry." Tyler muttered his apology.

"What for?"

"For scaring you, for dragging you out in the middle of the night, for... oh, for being useless."

"Stoopid." Her tone made the insult a caress.

He tried again. "How about for throwing up on you?"

"You haven't."

"Not yet but it's liable to happen at any moment and I can't find a bowl."

"Hold it for just one second." She whizzed into the corridor and returned with a pile of cardboard bowls. "Now go for it. The nurse told me you'd been swallowing half the lake. It'll show those germs if you vomit them up again."

That made him laugh, with immediate consequences. She steadied the bowl and was comfortingly practical.

"I'm sorry," he said again, when the worst was past.

"So you should be. Attempts to gain sympathy by half-killing yourself can stop."

She removed the bowl and got out a packet of wet wipes to sponge his face.

"You're amazing."

"Why?" Her gaze went to the wipes. "Oh I always carry these. Grandson's bum or lover's puke, men of all ages are a messy breed."

A young doctor came in. "That's good. Otherwise we'd have had to give you something to clear your stomach."

Tyler glared at him with watery bloodshot eyes. Then another wave of sickness overwhelmed him.

Through his misery he could hear the doctor apologising about the lack of vacant beds and Lani asking if she could take him home. By the time he was able to rejoin the conversation it had all been sorted out.

An hour later he was lying in Lani's bed, aching all over and drowsy with painkillers, grateful the sickness had passed.

Lani slid into the bed, carefully avoiding his injured leg, and snuggled close to him.

Again he said, "I'm sorry."

"What for this time?"

"I didn't want to phone you, not at first."

"Why not, Kev?"

"The thing is I've been on my own so long. Even when I was a kid, if I was hurt I'd go somewhere private to hide. When I was little I had these boxes stored under my bed and I'd pull them out, crawl in and pull them back again so no one could find me."

"We could get under the bed if you'd feel more at home there."

He gave a shaky laugh. "Lani, stop fooling. You know what I mean."

"Of course I do." She hugged him even closer. She was warm against him and, for the first time since his plunge into the lake, he wasn't shivering.

When she spoke again her voice was hesitant, as if she feared to presume too much, "Would I do as a private place, Kev? A place where you could crawl away to hide?"

"'*A fine and private place.*'" Too late he recalled what the poet was describing as a refuge, which proved you shouldn't try quoting love poetry when your temperature is sky-high.

Lani laughed. "'*The grave's a fine and private place*', but not yet. We've got a lot of living to do first."

It was just after nine when Tyler woke and found Lani lying beside him, watching him.

"How do you feel?" she asked.

"Not bad." She looked quizzical and he admitted, "I ache a bit and my leg is bloody sore." Actually it was bloody agony but he wasn't admitting that, even to Lani, to whom he'd revealed more of himself than he ever had to anyone before. He followed that line of thought. "I never thought it would happen to me."

Lani looked surprised. "Being wounded in the line of duty? I'd have thought that had happened before?"

"I meant falling in love." Even as he spoke he couldn't believe he was actually saying that.

She smiled at him. "Go on, say it."

"Say what?"

"*'Even so quickly can one catch the plague.'*"

"You reckon that would go with *'The grave's a fine and private place'*? I may not be the greatest romantic hero in the world but I do know that when you're in a hole you ought to stop... digging." His voice trailed away on the last word.

"Kev, what's wrong?"

"Digging. Why take a spade?"

"Pardon?"

"Someone had left a spade in the park. Why would they? What do you do with a spade?"

"Dig a hole or maybe bury something."

"Or dig something up." He pushed the bedclothes aside. "Lani, I'm sorry but I've got to get back to Stone Park."

Chapter 54

'There's dedication to duty and there's sheer bloodymindedness.' The words were in Gill's head but she didn't say them. Telling Tyler he was being an idiot wasn't the way to get him to see sense. However she did say, "What are we doing here, sir?"

"Digging."

That was obvious. A group of archaeology students, under the direction of a thin, eager man, were grubbing around the base of the old oak. Tyler sat in a canvas chair and watched them, like the director of some cut-price film.

Gill had been working all night. She hadn't expected this Sunday to be a day of rest but neither had she anticipated spending the morning standing in Stone Park trying to ignore the glares that DCI Aron kept directing at her as he and his team worked on the area by the lake. It was Aron's job to investigate Ryan's wounding and Sarah's death. Gill forced her mind into autopilot, refusing to think of Sarah. She wouldn't dwell on the girl she'd talked to on the train. She wouldn't try to work out whether she could have said or done something to make things turn out differently.

Gill wondered whether Lani had tried to dissuade Tyler from out-reaching his strength. When Gill had seen Lani, a couple of hours ago, she'd shown no obvious disapproval. She'd driven Tyler to meet Gill, helped him out of the car and passed him a walking stick. She'd handed Gill a folded camp chair and said, "He shouldn't stand for long."

"He shouldn't be here at all."

Lani shrugged. "He says there are things it's important to dig up."

A few minutes later the archaeology team had arrived.

Gill tried again, "Why are they digging, sir?"

"Someone brought a spade with them last night. I'm sure

it wasn't Ryan, he'd no idea Sarah was going to summon him. That leaves Brian Purvis or Sarah."

"DCI Aron thinks that Purvis brought it to bury Sarah after he'd killed her." Gill knew that was nonsense and Tyler's look of irritation confirmed this.

"Purvis is a sociopath not an idiot. He wouldn't bury a woman in an active crime scene. I don't reckon he planned to kill Sarah here. I'm not certain he planned to kill her at all."

"But why are we digging under the oak?"

"Because it's where Purvis doesn't want anyone to dig. He hasn't wanted them to look under this oak for at least the past five years." He nodded towards the lead archaeologist. "That's why he attacked Henderson rather than let him excavate here. The rest of the area was dug up to lay the surface for the children's playground but not the bit around the oak."

"In that case, shouldn't you have got Scene of Crimes to do this, not a load of kids from the University?"

"Do you seriously think the ACC's going to give me any more SOCOs to follow through a crazy hunch? Especially on a Sunday. The overtime budget's already sky-high. These kids are doing okay. They often ask archaeologists out to war zones to excavate the killing fields. Anyway Henderson deserves a chance to look at this site."

"But what do you think they'll find?"

She'd lost Tyler's attention. "Stephen Aron seems to be heading our way and, by the look of him, he's out for blood."

"Well he can't have yours, you've lost too much already."

As DCI Aron drew near he scowled at Tyler. "What the hell are you doing here?"

Gill saw Tyler stiffen. "Good morning, Chief Inspector." His voice was softly menacing.

It was clear Aron had read the danger signals. "Good morning, Superintendent. Excuse me, but should you be here?"

"It's my crime scene."

279

"I'm in charge of investigating what happened here last night."

Tyler scowled. "That was beside the lake. I'm in charge of the investigation into the death of the Quantrull boys and that happened here."

"The ACC told me you'd be taking sick leave."

"Then the ACC got it wrong. I don't go on sick leave because of a scratched leg. Now bugger off to your crime scene and let me concentrate on mine."

Tyler's tone had progressed from curt to downright churlish. DCI Aron flushed and walked away. Gill felt Tyler had behaved badly, which was a pity when she was on his side.

He glared at her. "You treating me to silent disapproval again?"

"No, but I was wondering how high your temperature is?"

For a second the hard look persisted then he shrugged. "Pretty high."

"Why don't you go home?" Gill insinuated a persuasive note into her voice. "Think about a comfortable bed and no need to pretend you're okay when you're not."

The amber eyes surveyed her with a glint that might have been temper, humour or fever, then he grinned. "Don't try to manipulate me. I've been fitted up by world-class experts."

Despite the smile, Gill knew he wasn't joking. She wondered if he was talking about rival cops or his bitch wife. "I'm sorry. I wasn't trying to fit you up."

"I know. I didn't mean that. I'm not saying things the way I should."

"Then why not go home?"

"Because this case needs finishing properly. And you haven't got the clout to do that. Although, after last night's fiasco, I'm not sure I have either."

"Is there anything I can do to help?"

"Yeah, you can go and smooth down Stephen Aron. If

necessary, lay it on with a trowel about how bloody sick I am."

"I'll do my best."

Gill had covered half the distance between the oak tree and the lake before she realised Tyler had played her. It wasn't the easiest of tasks to soothe the damaged dignity of your last senior officer who'd just been insulted by your present SIO. And DCI Aron was a man who took swift offence and was jealously mindful of his rank.

"Superintendent Tyler asked me to apologise for him, sir." Aron's offended expression didn't relax and she continued, "The Superintendent isn't well, sir."

Still no softening. She'd worked under Aron for over a year and had experienced his ability to sulk. She knew it would take time and patience to placate him and this morning she was out of both. To hell with politics. "Excuse me." She turned to leave.

"You've changed your allegiance very quickly, Gill."

So that was in the boiling pot along with everything else? Of course, she should have guessed, Aron was jealous of Tyler. She turned back to face him. "No sir. My primary allegiance is to the Police Force."

She could imagine Tyler's scorn if she tried to spin him that line, but Aron fell for it and she could see him acknowledge the propriety of her words.

"Many people find Superintendent Tyler challenging to work for," he said.

"Yes sir." Gill was able to agree wholeheartedly.

"And the murder of children is always hard to deal with." Aron had three daughters whom he adored. It was the best thing Gill knew about him.

"Yes. It's a very demanding case."

Aron shivered. "It's getting colder. We'll soon be finished here. The ACC requested me to come out personally and tie things up quickly."

That made Gill uneasy. How could she convince Aron

to look beneath the surface of the case? "I'm sure the ACC appreciates how good you are with detail, sir. It would be disastrous if Purvis' lawyer claimed Ryan Jones had killed Sarah in a fit of jealousy."

Aron looked startled. "Yes, of course you're right."

"And it would be worse if the media decided we were trying to cover for one of our own."

She saw surprise turn into alarm. DCI Aron had always been paranoid about his reputation. He said fretfully, "Superintendent Tyler shouldn't be here. What's he looking for?"

"I'm not sure, sir." Gill couldn't say that Tyler was looking for whatever Sarah or Purvis had intended to dig up, that would put it firmly back as Aron's investigation.

Aron seemed gratified by her admission of ignorance. "Better get used to being left out of the loop, Gill. Not many senior officers are as considerate as I am."

"No sir, I'm sure that's true." Gill kept her voice muted and her eyes demurely down. "Excuse me sir." She set off briskly back towards the oak.

"What's so funny?" demanded Tyler as she rejoined him.

That startled her. "I'm not laughing."

"No, you're smirking."

Gill was pretty sure that she wasn't, at least not outwardly. Tyler saw too much.

"You sorted with DCI Aron?" he asked.

"I think so."

"Good. It won't help your career to piss him off."

"Me piss him off?"

"Yeah. He doesn't like it when officers are willing to transfer away from him, especially to my team."

Gill wondered if Tyler had sent her to talk to DCI Aron for his own ends or hers and whether it really mattered.

"Thanks for coming out, Gill, but you'd better get back to the office. This is my game and there's a lot of other stuff to do."

Gill was almost out of the park when a shout summoned her. A young archaeologist came puffing up behind her. "You're needed back there urgently."

She turned and ran back, arriving at the oak just ahead of DCI Aron and his sergeant. The archaeology students had drawn back into a semi-circle, their faces were solemn and their manner subdued. Tyler and the senior archaeologist were standing close to the excavation looking down into the hole.

"What have you found?" she demanded, then saw the tiny bones lying amidst the roots. "Oh God!"

"Yeah," said Tyler. "We've found what Sarah came here to dig up."

Chapter 55

Dear Ryan,

I hope you won't ever read this because if you do I will probably be dead. I know that sounds crazy but if I die or disappear you'll know what to do to set things right.

It started when we were thirteen. You were my best friend and Mum kept going on about how I should be careful because boys wanted things from girls, and somehow that made it hard for me to stay being friends with you. Brian had always been there, next door, ever since I could remember. I used to call him Uncle Brian and that's the way I thought of him, as a friend of Mum and Dad's. Then one day he kissed me. He saw I liked it and he made love to me. It was brilliant to feel so special. Then I got pregnant and Brian was angry. He told me he'd be sent to prison because I was too young. So we kept it secret. Mum and Dad never knew. I had the baby and Brian took it away. He said it was being adopted by people who had wanted a baby for years. I knew it was the sensible thing to do but nothing was fun anymore. I wanted my baby back. Then Brian went to prison. And Mum and Dad and I moved away. I was lonely and I didn't know what to do with my life. When Brian came out of prison, he came and got me. He said I should live with him, so I did.

When I saw you the other day, I wanted to be friends again but Brian wouldn't let me. He made me complain about you to your boss. I'm sorry I did that.

George wrote me a letter. He sent it to my parents' house and I went to collect it. He said Brian killed my baby. They sacrificed it in Stone Park and buried it under the Sacred Oak. I don't want believe it, but I know it's true. Tonight I'm going to Stone Park to dig. I think I'm brave enough. I know I've got to be. Brian looks at me so oddly,

I'm sure he suspects. I'm sure he made George kill himself. If Brian killed my baby I want to make him sorry. I want him to be as unhappy as I am.

Love from Sarah

Tyler laid down the crumpled and tear-stained letter, preserved in a transparent evidence bag and turned to DCI Aron. "That seems to cover everything. You say she sent it to Ryan at his mother's house?"

Aron nodded. "Yes. Although, to be accurate, she put it through the door. It must have been sometime yesterday evening but Mrs Jones was visiting her sister and, of course, she went straight to the hospital and stayed there all night with her son. She only discovered it an hour ago when she nipped home to get some things she needed, then she brought it straight to us. I must say, it makes things nice and neat." Tyler thought Aron sounded smug. He'd arrived in Tyler's office bright and early in order to gloat over the fact that he'd cleared up his case within twelve hours, while Tyler was still struggling with his triple murder.

"I wonder if Purvis heard her on the phone talking to Ryan, or if he already suspected she was up to something," said Tyler.

"I doubt we'll ever know. It's a well-written letter. You wouldn't think an intelligent girl would fall for a con-artist like Purvis."

Tyler grunted non-committally. 'Uncle Brian' had been corrupting Sarah since she was a child and the secret pregnancy and loss of her baby had dried up something inside her before it was fully formed. "Did you recover George Crosby's letter to Sarah?"

"No. It's probably been destroyed. Still we've got Purvis on attacking you and PC Jones and probably on killing the girl as well. And the chances are he won't live to come to trial."

Tyler saw Aron assessing him and shrugged. "Better him

than me and Ryan Jones."

"Too right." The response was so prompt that Tyler wondered if he'd been mistaken about Aron winding him up. "We've got the knife. It's from the same set George Crosby used to kill himself. It's with the lab boys now, being tested. If Purvis does recover we don't need any smart barrister claiming young Jones killed the girl out of jealousy and you're lying to protect him."

"Thanks Stephen." Tyler was glad he didn't have to point it out. He hadn't expected Aron to show that much imagination.

"Kev, how did you know Sarah's baby was buried there?"

"I didn't know, I just..." Tyler searched for a more professional word than 'guessed.' "There had to be a reason for Purvis being so desperate to stop Henderson excavating. And there was that book he wrote. It was all about not doing anything with certain sites in Saltern. The bastard's cunning, he hid his tree in a forest." He saw that Aron looked bewildered and wondered if it would improve things if he explained that Chesterton had said he who wishes to hide a leaf should hide it in a forest. On the whole he thought it probably wouldn't help.

"I suppose Purvis was the baby's father?" said Aron. "It would really muck up our case if it turned out to be Ryan Jones."

"Sarah's letter names Purvis but we'll need DNA confirmation to keep things watertight if it comes to Court."

"Jones is going to be okay, isn't he?"

"They seem to think so." Tyler's mouth had a wry twist as he remembered the eager youngster that first day in the park. *'It was lucky I caught you, sir.'* At the time Tyler had wondered what sort of luck that was.

"Are you all right, Kev?"

"I was thinking it's less than a week since this bloody case broke."

"It's been a rough week for you," said Aron. "And there'll have to be an enquiry about whether you used undue force on Purvis."

"Cheers for that." Tyler wished Aron would make up his mind whether he was being supportive colleague or pain-in-the-arse. His phone rang. He listened to the terse request without surprise, put the phone down and said, "I've got to see the ACC"

Aron's satisfaction deepened visibly. "I expect he'll order you to go on leave."

Tyler knew Aron really meant 'suspend you'. "Maybe he'll give me a commendation for saving Ryan Jones' life," he said, and watched the smugness fade from Aron's face.

Half an hour later, as he limped back from the ACC's office, Tyler thought the interview could have gone much worse. He hadn't been suspended. He hadn't even been ordered to go on sick leave. Of course neither had he been offered a commendation. In fact the ACC had enquired why, if there was any trouble going, Tyler always managed to be in the thick of it. However he'd agreed that, unless Purvis died, Tyler could stay on the Stone Park case, if he was certain that he was fit enough. Tyler thought his, *'I'm fine,'* had been one of the largest lies he'd ever told.

"Sir." Luke fell into step beside him. "Nikki phoned to say her contact on the Saltern News reckons the person who phoned in the story about the trouble at the hospital was a woman, but she refused to give her name."

"Could have been anyone," said Tyler, "Jasmin, Allie, old Mrs Quantrull or any of the nurses. Another lead bites the dust."

"Now for the good news, sir. One of the guys who assaulted Stuart is ready to talk."

"Yeah?"

"He doesn't fancy going down for trying to kill a cop. He says the reporter was encouraging them to go to the cottage and attack the paedophile."

Tyler didn't ask what persuasions Kerry and Luke had used to get this statement. At the moment, Police and Criminal Evidence regulations didn't worry him. All he wanted was enough leverage to make the reporter talk. "Good work, Luke. I'll…"

"Sir." This time it was Gill who hurried to meet him. She looked excited but she spoke quietly, "DCI Aron's team have found the gun."

"Where?"

"In the bushes at the edge of the park, on the allotment side of the lake."

"No way!" Luke's voice rose in protest and Tyler frowned at him. Obediently he lowered the volume but not the emphasis, "I oversaw the search and we couldn't have missed the gun. Not if it was on a straight line between the shootings and the footpath."

"It's okay Luke. I wondered when that gun was going to stage an appearance. In fact I was thinking it was overdue." Tyler turned back to Gill, "Any details about it yet?"

"Only that there's one bullet left in it and it matches the type Maurice Walton told you had been stolen. Not that there's any proof Walton's was the gun used in the shooting until they've rushed through the tests."

"It will be," said Tyler.

"DCI Aron plans to ask Maurice Walton to come in and talk to him."

Tyler thought ruefully he couldn't complain about that; he'd stuck his nose in Stephen Aron's case and now Aron was returning the compliment. "Where's Walton now?"

"At the hospital visiting Charlie."

"Right. Gill, you stay with me. We're going to have a chat with Walton. Luke, you get back to that journalist. Get the name of her informant and where she got the details about Dan and Charlie. Remind her how hard they come down on people who shield child murderers. Let Kerry lead the interview and she can be as abrasive as she wants."

"You mind if I hide under the table, sir?"

Tyler realised his junior officers were joking with him, the way they used to. It had been one of the things that had made his team unique but recently they hadn't risked the mildest quip. He grinned. "Personally I'd suggest wearing riot gear."

Chapter 56

Guided by Tyler into a secluded hospital waiting room, Maurice Walton received the news about the gun with protestations of horror. "You mean the boys did it, Superintendent?"

"You knew them, Mr Walton. Do you think it's possible?"

"I suppose it must be. Jasmin told me how violent Timothy had become. She was afraid he'd hurt Polly."

"How well do you know Ian?" Tyler hoped if he kept probing some light would emerge.

"Hardly at all. I've always done my best with him for Jasmin's sake but we've got nothing in common."

"Are you and Jasmin close?"

"Of course we are. Our mother died when Jassy was a little girl. It was left to us to bring her up, my father, my elder brother Andrew and myself."

"You're quite a bit older than your sister, aren't you?"

"My father was in his fifties when she was born and Andy and I were in our early teens. She was such a pretty little girl. Of course we adored her. I suppose we spoiled her."

"That's natural, especially considering her disability. Did she go to a special school for the deaf?"

"No. We didn't want to expose her to that sort of place. She was educated at home. A tutor came in once or twice a week. Anyway that's long past. The operation was successful and she's perfectly normal now."

Tyler wondered if anyone could be normal after a childhood like that but he didn't challenge Maurice. "Your father and brother are both dead now?"

Walton nodded. "When Jasmin was fifteen. There was an accident. My father's car went off the road. He and my brother were killed. It was only chance that I wasn't with them. An unexpected phone call saved my life."

"Fortuitous. How did Jasmin cope?"

"She was deeply distressed and wanted to get away. She went off to boarding school. Jasmin's highly-strung and imaginative, one might say over-imaginative."

Tyler inspected the bait that was being dangled in front of him and refused to bite. "Did this fatal accident happen in Spain?"

"No, in North Yorkshire. We had land up there."

"Farming?"

"Yes and grouse shooting."

Startled, Tyler met Gill's eyes.

"I can't imagine Jasmin as a country girl," she said.

Maurice Walton smiled. "On the contrary she was a great one for shooting and riding to hounds. I miss the country life but the Yorkshire climate is too harsh for me. I suffer from a heart condition. This tragedy has been very hard on me."

"It's been hard on a lot of people." The self-conscious pathos of Walton's manner irritated Tyler but he kept his tone mild. If Walton was going to have a heart attack he could do it while Aron was questioning him.

"Thanks for your help, Mr Walton. That's all for now, but we need you to go to the Police Station and identify the gun."

"Very well. I've got plenty of time this morning. Ian and Jasmin wanted to spend time at home together, so I came here, but Mrs Quantrull won't let me near Charlie."

After Walton left, Gill said, "I know it's likely Tim and Barney stole the gun from his Spanish villa and smuggled it into England. But what happened then?"

"Either our original scenario was correct and Tim did the shootings. Then a member of his family somehow got the gun back and later planted it in order to cover for Tim. Or, more likely, Tim pinched it from Walton and someone appropriated it from him. That widens the field: Ian, Jasmin, Mrs Quantrull or the nanny. Or it could be any of the school kids Tim showed off to, but they couldn't be the shooters, they're accounted for in class."

"We haven't had confirmation that Walton was actually in Spain, have we?"

"No, he claims he was in his villa but he hasn't got live-in staff and the Spanish police haven't found anyone who can swear to seeing him. He's got friends with boats. It's possible he got over here undetected."

"But why should he kill the boys?" Gill answered her own question. "The money?"

Tyler shrugged. "It's never wise to forget about money, especially that amount."

"But Maurice wouldn't inherit."

"His niece would."

"Do you think Jasmin and her brother are in collusion?"

"It's possible. Although, if so, I don't know what game Jasmin was playing when she tipped us off about the gun."

He saw Gill frown as she tried to work out the permutations. "She must have known we'd not give up until we found it. And when we did, it would lead us straight to her brother. Better to say it had been stolen before we came to ask. Or perhaps it's simply that they're both ratting and hoping the other gets the blame."

"True. Maurice was eager to sow seeds of doubt about Jasmin's reliability as a witness. Not to mention dropping into the conversation that she's good with guns."

"Yes, but, if the motive is money, the killer could as easily be Ian."

"To save his business, you mean? In that case he must have intended Charlie to die in Stone Park as well and planned to dispose of Polly at some later date."

Gill shuddered. "It's monstrous. He wouldn't do it."

Tyler thought of the man who'd wept for his dead boys and mourned his failure to keep them safe. His instincts told him Ian's grief was genuine but he'd known many people who could feign sorrow and some that truly felt it when it was too late.

"I don't think so either, but it's possible. Especially if he was thinking of starting another family with a third wife."

"Allie? I got the feeling she's in love with Ian but, as far as I can see, she was very fond of Ian's boys. If she or Ian wanted to kill someone, Jasmin should have been their target."

"Why kill anyone? What's wrong with good, old-fashioned divorce?"

"Ian doesn't believe in divorce, sir. His mother mentioned that. In fact, what about Mrs Quantrull? She could have planned to kill off all her grandchildren to rescue the family business for her son?" Gill read the answer on Tyler's face. "I know. It's ridiculous."

"It's not impossible. She's got no alibi. She says she was at home alone at the time. But I can't see her being the killer. Ignoring love and morality, she's a woman in her late sixties. I doubt if she'd have the physical strength or speed."

"I guess I'm getting desperate."

"Desperate! You're talking to the guy who had young Robbie's whereabouts checked in case he was double bluffing and he'd nicked the gun. And, before you ask, he was in school at the time, alibied by a maths teacher and his class."

Gill sighed. "We've gone round the entire Quantrull family and got nowhere."

"I know." Tyler grinned at her ruefully. "Any idea what game we're playing? Ring o' roses or Blind Man's Buff?"

Chapter 57

Gill followed Tyler as he limped along the hospital corridors towards ICU. She wondered if she dared offer him a supporting arm or whether it would be bitten off. "What now, sir?"

"I need to know if Josh Fortune shows any signs of surfacing. We need his evidence now. We're running out of time."

Gill tried not to let her concern about Tyler show. The last twelve hours had possessed an out-of-control feeling. Everything had a macabre sense of unreality and she was beginning to fear he was losing his grip. "I checked that, sir. He should regain consciousness within the next few hours."

"That's likely to be too long."

"What do you mean?"

"One of the guys guarding Brian Purvis warned me they're getting the results of the tests they've done on him pretty soon. If he's brain dead, they'll turn off the life support, and if he dies they'll take me off this case."

"I see." Common-sense told her it would be a good thing for Tyler to be sent on sick leave before he totally killed himself but without him she wasn't sure this case would ever be sorted. She didn't want her first case on Tyler's team to be a failure and, more important, she wanted justice for Tim, Barney and Colleen. Unfortunately Tyler was right, without Josh Fortune's evidence, she couldn't think of any way to discover the truth. She sighed.

"My sentiments exactly," said Tyler. "I keep wondering what was in Dan's head when he went on about the smell of blood and flowers. I even went back to the park to check if I could smell any flowers in the area where Josh and the others were shot but it was no good."

Gill smiled. "Pity we don't have any flower sniffer dogs." They had them for explosives, drugs, blood, dead bodies and stuff like that, but nobody had seen any reason for a canine floristry unit.

He grinned back at her. "Well I'm not going to put in a requisition for a sniffer dog called Fleur. The A.C.C thinks I'm pretty near certifiable anyway. But I still think that blood and flowers is significant. In cognitive interviewing smell is a primal sense that could release a lot of memories."

Gill nodded, all laughter draining out of her. "I know. My mother died of bowel cancer seven years ago. She was so ashamed of the vile smell in her room that she sprayed perfume everywhere to try and mask it. It didn't work. In fact the smell from the colostomy bag mingling with the scent was horrible. Even now, when I smell that particular perfume it makes me feel sick and I'm back there in that hospital room... Sir, are you all right?"

She had reason for her concern. Tyler was doing a creditable imitation of a pillar of salt; assuming Lot's wife had been grey-white and totally immobile.

He came to himself with a shudder and glared at her. "Of course I'm all right. I've thought of a way I might get a quick result, but I'll need your help."

For years Gill's career strategy had been to keep her head below the parapet, and yet her answer came without hesitation. "Of course, sir. What do you want me to do?"

One thing Lani and Isabel had in common was they'd do anything requested of them by those they cared about and not ask why. It took less than half an hour for Bel to get across town and meet Gill in a quiet street outside the hospital grounds.

When Gill saw Bel the tension inside her snapped and, for the first time in their relationship, she hugged her in a public place and followed up with a kiss.

"It's all right, darling." Bel's voice was tender.

Gill managed a watery smile. "Yes, I know. I'm sorry. It's been so horrible. That poor kid, Sarah, and everything."

"Is Superintendent Tyler all right? Lani told me he'd been injured."

"He's still just about on his feet. Is Lani worried about him?"

"She didn't say much, which means she's worried sick. Gill, remember if there's anything I can do, please tell me. I really want to help." She opened her bag and handed Gill a small bottle. "I brought what you asked for."

"Perfect." Gill's phone rang. She answered and the ACC demanded, "Inspector, are you with Superintendent Tyler?"

"No sir." Gill felt relief that she could answer honestly.

"Do you know where he is?"

"No, I don't know exactly where he is." This time she was accurate without being truthful.

"It's essential I speak to him."

"It's possible he's gone off duty, sir." Gill told herself anything was possible.

"I see. Of course." The ACC sounded relieved. "Thank you, Inspector."

"I'll be in the hospital for a while, sir, and my phone will be off." As Gill keyed off, she met Isabel's wondering gaze. "What's wrong?"

"You've changed. You're not as cautious as you used to be."

"Nor are you."

"That's true. I'm sorry."

Gill wondered whether she was apologising for present recklessness or for all the years of stifling caution. She smiled. "Don't be. I like it."

In the hospital entrance Gill encountered Kerry Buller. "Kerry, what are you doing here?"

"Needed to speak to the Bossman. Luke and I tossed for who should come and who should hold the fort."

"I gather you won."

Kerry's cheeky grin flashed out. "I always do. I've got a

296

lucky pound coin."

Gill wondered if it was weighted to fall always heads or always tails. "Are you here because you've got a result with that reporter or because you're skiving?"

"You wanna watch it, you sounded just like the Bossman when you said that. Yeah, we've got a result and I thought we'd better get it to him straight off."

"He said he was going to check on Ryan and then go down to see Stuart." Gill led the way along the corridor. "I hope you've got good news because he doesn't need anymore of the other sort."

"Yeah, poor sod. Is he okay?"

"Bearing up." Gill eyed her quizzically. "I thought you hated him?"

She had the satisfaction of seeing Kerry blush. "I was mad at him for not backing my promotion. I guess I forgot what a bloody good cop he is and how he always comes through for us when things get tough."

"Let me guess. He's taking the flak for you screwing up about warning Stuart?"

"Yeah. As if he hasn't got enough grief on his own account."

"I hope he gave you a bloody good bollocking."

"Don't worry, he did, but he couldn't kick me harder than I've been kicking myself." Kerry quickened her step as Tyler came out of the Intensive Care ward. "Have you seen Ryan? How's he doing?"

"Getting there. The doctor didn't want him to know about Sarah's death, not until he's stronger, but he woke up remembering seeing her body, so his mum and I had to tell him."

"How did he take it?"

"Quietly." Tyler looked drained. "Why are you here, Kerry?"

"The reporter has come through with her story but it's a bit complicated."

"Okay, tell me."

"The reporter says her informant contacted by phone. It was a man, not a woman like the one who called the local newspaper about what happened in the hospital. He told her Dan Peters had kidnapped and abused Charlie. He gave his name as Ian Quantrull. It's what these vultures dream of, an inside sexual abuse story from the dead kids' dad. She checked him out and he knew lots of details about the boys and their lives and he suggested she phoned him back on the Quantrull house phone. It's ex-directory but that doesn't stop a reporter from checking and she said it was definitely their phone. Anyway, when she phoned back he spun her the story about Dan Peters being a paedophile and how the cops weren't doing anything."

"I hear a 'but' coming any moment now," said Tyler.

Kerry grinned at him. "But we checked out her story."

"And she was lying?"

"No." Kerry sounded gleeful. "She'd been had. At the time she was phoning her snitch at the Quantrull's house, Ian Quantrull was definitely here at the hospital. I called her a liar and she got mad and produced a recording of the phone call."

"Maurice Walton?" said Tyler.

"We'd guess so, but neither Luke or I have ever heard his voice."

"Where's Walton now?"

"Down at the Station. DCI Aron wanted to speak to him."

"Contact Luke and tell him, when DCI Aron's finished with Walton, he's to interview him. If necessary he can arrest him because I want that interview on tape. Then get the two recordings to the speech specialist to compare. And make it quick. Go on Kerry, get moving. You've done a good job, both of you. Tell Luke I'm impressed."

Kerry sprinted away and Gill wondered whether Tyler's plans had altered since he'd received this information.

Apparently not. "Come on, Gill, let's get on with it."

They found Dan and Hannah in Stuart's room. Stuart was in bed, propped up with pillows. He was bruised and battered, his breathing shallow because of his cracked ribs. Hannah looked like a white-faced little ghost. Dan was fully dressed. He seemed much fitter than the day before. He grinned at Tyler and said, "My turn to visit the sick."

"How are you, Stu?"

"Okay sir. How are you?"

"I'll live. Dan, are they discharging you today?"

"Yes." His voice lost its determined brightness. "I get a safe house and cops to protect me. I hope they don't believe what they hear on TV or they might decide to throw me to the mob."

Tyler responded to the unspoken plea. "Dan, I promise I'll do my best to clear you of this garbage."

"Thanks, but some shit always sticks. No matter how unfair it is."

Tyler didn't deny it. He looked at Gill, command clear in his eyes.

"Excuse me a moment." She went into the corridor, got out the bottle Isabel had given her and sprayed herself liberally with perfume.

She moved quietly back into the room and stood behind Dan. For a few moments he was unaware of her then he stiffened. He began to shake. He span round to face her.

"That's it," he whispered. "That's the smell. When I was kneeling beside Josh and Sophie... there was so much blood and suddenly it smelled like flowers."

Chapter 58

The police guard was still in place outside the Quantrull house. They confirmed that Ian and Jasmin were inside.

Tyler knocked on the door. It took some time for Ian to open it. They followed him into the drawing room. The curtains were drawn and the room was in shadow, lit only by an elegant, Art Deco lamp.

Tyler wondered if Ian was too drunk to be fit for questioning. His eyes looked dead, as if all the light had drained out of them.

He sat down opposite Ian and said, "Where's Jasmin?"

"Resting."

"Ian, we need to talk."

"Go ahead." Ian's voice was as indifferent as his gaze.

"Did Timothy steal a gun from his uncle's house?"

A long silence then, "I think so."

"Do you know what he meant to do with it?"

"No."

"Did he plan to kill someone with it? Did he want to hurt Jasmin?"

"I don't know."

"You lied to us, Ian. You told us you didn't know about the gun."

"I didn't know. Not until yesterday."

Tyler leaned forward. "What happened yesterday, Ian?"

"I came home unexpectedly. It was late…"

"What happened?" Tyler prompted him.

"I let myself in and I heard Maurice and Jasmin in here, talking. He sounded hysterical but Jasmin was calm. She told him he shouldn't have allowed Tim to steal the gun and he'd be prosecuted as an accessory."

"What else did she say, Ian?"

"She said she'd got it back from the park. She said she'd

300

done it for Maurice, to save him from blame, and he must throw it in the lake where it wouldn't be found for a long while."

Tyler realised why the gun had been abandoned in such an obvious and clumsy hiding place. Last night, by the time Maurice got there, the lake had been occupied by murdered girls and wounded cops. He must have panicked and dumped it in the bushes.

"Ian, did Jasmin say how she got the gun back from Stone Park after the shootings?"

"No. I thought he'd ask her that, but he didn't. I guess he was too scared to think."

"Scared?"

"Of the position he'd got himself into. Maurice is all front. He's got no guts at all."

"What did you do then, Ian?"

"I went upstairs to my room. I had to think. I was so afraid Tim had shot all those people, then his brother and himself."

Tyler couldn't imagine how appalling that fear had been.

"Then I thought it through and knew it wasn't Tim."

"Do you know who it was?"

"I've got no proof." For the first time Ian wouldn't meet his eyes.

"Why wouldn't you leave Jasmin alone with Charlie for the last week?"

Ian looked surprised, thrown off balance by this shift in questioning. "I don't know. I had a feeling. And Charlie seemed terrified of her."

"Tell me about Tim and Barney."

"They were good boys but they'd been hurt and they were angry. Angry with me ever since…" His voice wavered into silence.

"Ever since you married Jasmin?"

"Yes."

Tyler couldn't remember ever feeling sorrier for

301

anyone than he felt for this man; nevertheless he carried on questioning. "What about Allie?"

"Allie? Allie's kind."

"Are you and Allie lovers?"

"No! I wouldn't. I'm married to Jasmin." There was a long silence then he continued. "I felt so lost after Mel died. Then I met Jasmin. She was so beautiful and so different."

"Then she got pregnant?"

"Yes. But I shouldn't have married her. I could have looked after her and Polly without that. It's all my fault."

"Did you think of getting a divorce?"

"I couldn't do that. If you make a bargain you ought to stick to it."

Tyler thought principles were a good thing but sometimes they could cost way too much. "Ian, do you think Jasmin shot Tim, Barney and the others?"

Silence then a slow nod of the head. "I think I knew when I thought about Tim's hat."

"What about the hat, Ian?"

"Tim kept it in his bed. It was a reminder of his mum... she made it for him. But it didn't fit him anymore. He wouldn't have taken it to the park."

Tyler thought that must be the cruellest act of all, to take a child's comforter and use it to shield the weapon of his death.

The sound of the front door opening made them all turn their heads, then Maurice's voice calling, "Jassy? Ian? Anyone at home?"

Chapter 59

"I'll see to him, sir." Gill didn't want to leave at this vital stage of questioning but she couldn't allow Walton's arrival to make Ian's flow of confidences dry up.

She went into the hall where Walton was hanging up his coat. "I've got a few questions for you, Mr Walton. If you don't mind coming in here?" She opened the door to the dining room and gestured for Walton to enter. Then she opened the front door and said to the two constables on duty, "I need one of you with me."

As she entered the dining room she thought how strange it was that, despite the central heating, the room felt bleak. A few petals had dropped from the white, hot house roses and lay, curling at the edges, on the polished, oak sideboard.

She nodded to the constable to stand by the door and said, "Please, sit down, sir."

"Of course, Inspector." He smiled at her. "Or may I call you Gill? After all you're here so much you're almost part of the family."

"Inspector will be more appropriate, sir." His smarmy smile made her flesh creep.

She took a seat opposite him, removed a small recorder from her pocket, placed it on the table and switched it on. "Maurice Walton, I am arresting you for perverting the course of justice." He gaped at her as she spoke the words of the official warning and warned him that she was recording the interview. This was the biggest risk she'd ever taken in all her police career and she prayed it didn't backfire. The team was already in hot water without her turning it up to boiling point.

"You can't arrest me! I haven't done anything!"

"You disposed of the murder weapon... a weapon that belonged to you. And you made false allegations to the Press, impersonating your brother-in-law. The reporter recorded you and her recording is being compared with ones we've taken of your voice. Your time's running out." There were situations when a hint of melodrama worked.

He clutched his chest. "I'm not well. My heart."

Gill looked him over. He was pale but not blue about the lips or gasping for breath. She took her mobile out of her pocket and said, "If you are unwell I can stop this interview and phone for medical aid. It will give us time to interview Jasmin and get her story. I'm sure she'll tell us all about your involvement in the crimes."

"No! I'll talk to you now. I wasn't even in the country when the boys were killed. It was Jasmin. All Jasmin!"

"You're saying that Jasmin killed Timothy and Barney and Colleen Holebrook and wounded Josh Fortune and Sophie Hughes?"

"Yes, it was Jasmin."

"But it's your gun, not Jasmin's. Are you claiming she stole it?" The more scepticism she showed the harder Walton would work to convince her.

"No, Timothy did that. They were all staying with me last summer, but Ian had to go back to deal with his business and Jasmin went with him. They left the three boys and the nanny there for another week. I didn't realise until they'd gone but Timothy must have stolen it then. I know you're not supposed to say bad things about the dead but Timothy was a nasty, evil brat."

Gill kept her voice and expression neutral. "What do you think Tim wanted with the gun?"

Walton shrugged. "To hurt someone. Jasmin thought he wanted to kill her."

"Do you expect us to believe a ten-year-old boy could steal a gun and smuggle it out of Spain and into this country?"

"Timothy and Barney didn't go back by plane. The nanny flew with Charlie but the two older boys went with a friend of mine who owns a yacht. If you berth at a marina, the chances are that no-one will even check. They certainly wouldn't be searching a kid in case he was carrying a gun."

"So how did Jasmin get hold of it?"

Another shrug. "I don't know. I'd guess she went through the boys' rooms. She did that pretty often. Like I said, you couldn't trust the cunning little buggers."

Gill saw the constable make an instinctive gesture of protest at these harsh words. She gave him a swift, hard glance to warn him to keep quiet.

"So, did Jasmin tell you about killing the boys?"

"Yes. She sent them to the park. She told them to stay in the play area by the tree, not to go in the bushes or near the lake. That way she thought she'd find them quickly, she knew she wouldn't have much time." The words were spilling out of him, stumbling over each other in his eagerness to tell his tale. "Then she put on Timothy's clothes and got on Barney's bike and rode to the park. She found the two older boys in the play area, so that was all right, but Charlie wasn't there and that man heard the shots. He stood on the bench and shouted. He saw her."

"And so she shot them?" Gill was torn between sick horror and amazed triumph at getting a full account of the crime. Jasmin wouldn't be able to wriggle out of it now and nor would her treacherous brother, even though, at any moment he was liable to stop panicking and call his lawyer.

"She had to. She'd gone too far. She couldn't leave witnesses. She told me she got a bit flustered when it went wrong. She dropped the gun on the ground beside the man, then she heard someone coming and hid in the trees. When he was bending over the guy on the ground she hit him."

"What did she hit him with?" Gill didn't want to interrupt the flow but she needed all the collaborative detail she could get.

"A piece of wood... a branch or something."

Gill nodded. So far this hung together perfectly. "Then what did she do."

"She remembered she had to leave the gun next to Timothy, so she picked it up again. She cycled off and looked for Charlie all over the park but she couldn't find him. Then she heard the sirens and realised they were heading towards the park. So she gave up on Charlie and cycled home. She was almost home when she realised she'd forgotten to leave the gun. It was too late then, so she got inside and hid the gun and changed and put the clothes in the washing machine."

"Where did she hide the gun?"

"I don't know. But later she got scared you cops would search the house again. That's why she made me phone the reporter, to put you off the scent. She was certain the Superintendent suspected her."

"Why did she think that?"

"He said something about Charlie being terrified of her. That scared her so much that she completely lost it and went for him. So she made me take the gun and get rid of it. She told me to throw it in the lake, but when I got there the park was full of cops, so I threw it in the bushes. It wasn't my fault." To Gill's amazement he actually sounded aggrieved. "You won't really charge me with anything will you?"

Gill thought, if she had her way, he'd be charged at least with accessory after the fact, but, at the moment she wanted to keep him talking. "That's not my decision. My superiors will decide about that, but the more you co-operate the better."

"I've told you everything I can."

Except the most important thing of all. "Why did Jasmin want to kill her stepsons?"

"I told you that. To stop them killing her. Ever since she had Polly she's been obsessed with the fear that the boys would get rid of her and start to abuse Polly."

"Abuse? You mean sexually?" Gill stared at him. Amongst all the anger, hurt and cruelty, this wasn't something she'd seen coming. Why would Jasmin think that?

Chapter 60

Tyler waited until the door closed behind Gill then turned back to Ian, determined to keep the questioning on track. "You said Jasmin is different. What do you mean?"

"I thought it was because she'd been deaf when she was small. But these last few weeks, I've become pretty sure something else happened when she was a child."

Tyler identified the feeling that had been nudging at his mind every time he'd met Jasmin. He should have recognised the signs, the watchful eyes in the tense, still face and the wary, placating childishness. "You mean she was abused?"

"She had another brother, Andrew. She'd never talk about him. Lately I've wondered…"

Tyler thought that might explain why Maurice Walton had alerted the Press to Dan's alleged activities as a paedophile. Did he hope to exorcise some belated guilt for not helping Jasmin... or for doing something worse? Or was it simply that Walton was looking for a scapegoat? Dan Peters or Ian Quantrull, it didn't matter as long as he was off the hook.

Ian must have taken his silence for disbelief. "I've got no proof. It was just some things she said." He paused, obviously summoning his thoughts. "About three weeks ago, she and Allie were talking about what fun it would be to dress Polly up in pretty clothes. Allie said about a dress she'd been given as a birthday present and how disappointed she'd been because she was a tomboy and would rather have been given football boots. And Jasmin started to talk about her sixth birthday. I don't know if I can get you to understand this… I'm not sure I understand myself. Sometimes, when Jasmin gets caught up in what she's saying, it's as if she forgets she's talking out loud. It's like the stuff inside her head and what she's saying get mixed up. Anyway, she said she'd thought her brother Andrew had got her a dress because he told her to take her clothes off. Then she stopped speaking and she looked... I don't know how to explain it... full of pain."

"I see." Tyler remembered Jasmin talking about her deafness and watching the shadows and how she hadn't been able to hear herself scream.

"It sounds like nonsense." Ian was apologetic. "Just my imagination."

"I don't think so. Was there anything else?"

"It's nothing. Just something that happened soon after the baby was born."

"Run it past me anyway."

"My mother came to spend the day. As a rule Mother and Jasmin don't get on but Mother was being really kind. She said that Polly was going to be beautiful, like her mummy. Jasmin went white... she simply drained of colour... then she grabbed up Polly and ran upstairs. I went after her and found her in her bedroom, kneeling on the floor, holding Polly so tight I was afraid she'd hurt her and crying hysterically. I knelt down beside her and put my arms around them and begged her to tell me what was wrong, but all she'd say was, *'She mustn't be beautiful. She mustn't be beautiful. It's dangerous. Beautiful people get hurt.'*"

Tyler thought that explained just about everything. "Why do you think Andrew was the one who abused her, rather than Maurice or her father?"

"Partly because of what she said about the dress and partly because once, a long time ago, she was complaining about Tim and I was saying he didn't mean any harm, and she said, *'Fathers never believe their sons have done bad things. Even when they're told. Like my father and Andrew.'* Maurice is a slimy bastard but I don't think he'd do that. Apart from anything else, I don't think he'd have the guts."

"It doesn't take much in the way of guts to assault a little girl."

"Yeah, but it does to face her now she's grown up."

"Fair enough. How did Jasmin feel about Tim, Barney and Charlie?"

"She never liked them. I was so stupid. At first I didn't realise. She wanted to send them away... Tim and Barney to boarding school and Charlie to a special nursery. I refused. If I'd agreed my boys would be alive."

"You can't blame yourself for not seeing the future."

"I was so bloody stupid." He caught his breath on a sob. "I should have realised. Two weeks ago she found Tim stroking Polly's hair, quite gently, not hurting her, and she went crazy. She started screaming he was evil."

"Perhaps that's because he'd killed Barney's rabbit." Tyler felt like the Devil's Advocate.

Ian stared at him, clearly puzzled. "He didn't. Not the way you make it sound."

"What happened to the rabbit?"

"Tim was clumsy. It was because of the meningitis. The rabbit twisted in his arms and he dropped it. It broke its back and the vet put it to sleep. Tim was upset, they both were, but Barney knew Tim didn't mean to do it. I wanted to get them a new pet, perhaps a dog, but Jasmin said no, she didn't like animals making a mess."

Just one more thing Tyler wanted to clear up. "There's a book, *Shades of Saltern*, did Tim give that to you?"

"Yes. The chap who wrote it came into their school to talk about Local History. Tim thought the legends about the oak tree were cool." He choked on the last words. "I wonder if that's why she chose that place to do it."

Tyler thought it certainly added to the false case Jasmin had built against Tim.

The door opened and Gill slipped into the room. She looked tired and her lips were set in a grim line but there was an air of suppressed triumph about her too. Her eyes met Tyler's and she gave a barely perceptible nod.

So that was that. The beginning of the end. "I need to talk to Jasmin."

"She's in her room, lying down. I put the radio on. She didn't like silence."

As he took in those last words, Tyler felt a stab of urgency. "Gill, could you check on Jasmin, please?"

He listened, all senses strained, as she ran up the stairs. A door opened. She said Jasmin's name. Repeated it in a shriller tone. Then she shouted, "Call an ambulance."

Ian looked at his watch then smiled at Tyler. "You're too late. But don't feel bad about it. We all were. Over twenty years too late to save Jasmin."

Chapter 61

"An overdose of sleeping pills… her own prescription. We were too late. They've been in her for too long. The doctors say it's a matter of hours." Tyler lowered his voice to tell Gill this. Ian was sitting on the other side of Jasmin's bed in ITU.

Ian must have caught the words. He repeated what he'd said before, "We were all too late to save her." The grey shade in his face deepened and he leaned forward, head resting in his hands.

Tyler felt sick with a new fear. "Ian, you haven't taken anything, have you?"

A ghost of a smile. "No. I wouldn't. There's Charlie and Polly. I'm all they've got. But I'm so tired."

"Go and rest."

"I can't leave her to die alone."

Tyler wondered whether that made Ian a bloody saint or a bloody idiot. "I'll stay with her. Go and see your kids." What did that offer make him?

"If you're sure. Just for a few minutes." Ian staggered to his feet.

"And don't tell anyone anything unless you've got a lawyer in place."

Ian gave a twisted smile. "I bet there aren't many cops like you."

He left and, at a nod from Tyler, Gill accompanied him.

He sat back, glad to be rid of Ian's suffering presence. It was two hours since they'd reached the hospital. For Gill, it had been two hours of intensive sorting out and tying in the threads. For Tyler, two hours of enforced inactivity. The ACC had caught up with him and told him that, regardless of what happened to Brian Purvis, he was to go on sick leave. Tyler had not protested, but even if his official role was curtailed, he planned to see the case through to the end.

Gill returned from escorting Ian and sat down next to him.

"Did she do it herself or did he give them to her?" she asked.

Tyler shrugged. "We'll never prove it wasn't suicide."

"He must have known. He spoke about her as if she was dead before I went upstairs."

"I didn't hear him," Tyler spoke with emphasis.

After a moment, Gill said, "You're right, sir, I didn't hear anything either."

"Even if Ian did know, we can't prove he gave her the overdose. If you want to pursue the poor devil for assisted suicide you can do it without me."

"No sir. He's been through enough, and he's all those kids have got."

"Where is he now?"

"He collapsed just after he got to Charlie's room. The doctors say he's near to total breakdown."

Again Tyler thought of the hell Ian had endured in this past week. Alongside the grief for Tim and Barney must have come the creeping horror of realising what Jasmin was capable of. And the fear for Charlie. How could he ever leave him alone with her?

He said irritably, "Where's her brother? Did you send word to the Station?"

After Gill had finished questioning Walton, she'd sent him to the police station in the custody of the uniformed officer.

"Yes. They offered to drive him here to be with her but he refused. He says he's too ill to cope with more strain." Gill's tone was heavy with sarcasm. "I think he hopes, if Jasmin dies there won't be enough to charge him with."

"We'll see about that." Tyler's voice was grim. "You said you gave him all the proper warnings and told him you were recording him. That should be enough to convict him. You did a bloody good job. Well done."

"Thank you. Sir, do you believe Ian knew instinctively that Jasmin wasn't to be trusted with Charlie?"

"Yeah. I reckon people develop the instincts they need. After his first wife's death, Ian did more or less everything for those boys."

"I suppose you're right. By the way, Josh Fortune's surfaced. He's very weak but he managed a short statement. He said he heard the shooting in the adventure playground. He thought it was kids messing round, then he heard a scream. So he jumped up on a bench to have a look."

Tyler groaned softly.

"Are you all right?"

"Just thinking how it all comes down to the sort of people they were."

"What do you mean?"

"Jasmin was a schemer. She'd kept that gun and, when she decided to kill, she put all the safeguards in place. She chose the day of the Charity Party and phoned Ian to check he was still at work. I wouldn't mind betting she suggested to the boys they went to the adventure playground."

"She did," said Gill. "Her brother told me that."

"Then it went pear-shaped because the boys had dumped Charlie in their den and she couldn't find him. And Barney screamed. And there was a man in the seating area; a man who wasn't the sort who'd walk past on the other side."

"So if Josh hadn't attracted her attention, none of the adults would have been shot?"

"I don't know, but I think she'd planned to kill the boys and leave the gun in Tim's hand. She'd got her story ready and backed up very cleverly with proofs. All the evidence against Tim was fed to us by her."

Gill nodded. "The lab reports came back on the gun. The only recognisable prints were Tim and Barney's but there were some smudges made by gloves."

"She probably burned them. The first time we were there I noticed the log fire."

"It's incredible she could plan it all so coldly."

Tyler thought it was easy to be cold when you are dead. And Jasmin had been dead inside for years. "The trouble with planners is, when it starts going wrong, it unravels completely. If she'd used that last bullet to kill Dan, Josh would have died before help got to him. Chance is a funny business, isn't it? What did Josh say happened after the boys were shot?"

"A cyclist hurtled towards him and dismounted. He saw the gun and tried to grab it. He remembers wanting to shield Sophie but not much else. He may remember more when he's stronger."

"Did he give a description of the killer?"

"A small figure in a blue anorak, wearing a balaclava. He couldn't see the features but he's sure it was a woman and, like Dan Peters, he smelled her perfume. Of course it didn't come out as coherently as that. It took Nikki a long while to get it out of him a few words at a time."

"Have you found the clothes?"

"We've put a new search team through the house. There's a blue anorak in Tim's wardrobe, freshly washed. And there's mud from the park on Barney's bike. Of course the kid probably rode it there a hundred times himself, but Forensics are checking for traces of blood."

Tyler thought it was obvious when you knew how. "What better disguise than Tim's clothes? That's how Tim's hair got transferred to Josh. She's a small woman, the only adult in that household who could have worn Tim or Barney's clothes."

"So that neighbour who called was right about there being no-one in."

"Seems likely, but she must have noticed something subconsciously about the bike, which accounts for her newsboy fixation. When Jasmin saw the Parish Magazine on the mat she must have known the woman would have knocked, so she incorporated it into her alibi."

314

"There's something else, sir. We've found where the gun was hidden. She kept it in the baby's cot, underneath the mattress, between it and the envelope sheet. They found the imprint of it in the mattress. Imagine doing that."

Tyler said nothing. Given the motive, the hiding place seemed appropriate.

"How could she hate the boys so much?" It seemed as if Gill had picked the word 'motive' from his mind.

"Because she was afraid." Tyler struggled to keep impatience out of his tone. "She knew Tim hated her and he'd stolen the gun. He probably wouldn't have used it but we don't know for sure. And ever since Polly was born, Jasmin has been afraid Tim or Barney would hurt Polly, like Jasmin's brother did her."

"But why?"

"There's no logic to it. Call it post-natal dementia or the effect of early sexual abuse. I'd guess it was aggravated by poor little Tim's hatred."

"But she'd have shot Charlie too!"

"A bullet's remote. That must make it easier. I guess she didn't use the last bullet on Dan because she was saving it for Charlie." He tried to imagine the terror Charlie had suffered as he'd cowered in that den.

"But why did she want to kill Charlie?"

"Perhaps the fear he'd grow up and abuse his sister. Or one day he'd start speaking and he'd remember what he'd seen." He shrugged. "Or maybe it was simply about the money."

Tyler saw the revulsion in Gill's face as she stared at Jasmin.

"She doesn't look like a monster," she said.

"No." With her red hair softly curling on the white pillow, she looked like a Pre-Raphaelite heroine. "Gill, you've done a good job. It's up to you and the rest of the team to finish off the details. The ACC tells me Purvis is likely to pull through, though he may be paralysed." Tyler thought wryly that, in the prison hospital, Purvis might well get his doctorate. It made no difference; he'd never get out of prison to flaunt it.

"I'm glad he's going to make it. I mean I'm glad for you."

"I don't reckon I'll get much fall-out. The ACC tells me Stephen Aron's putting together a fireproof case." He grinned. "The only question is whether I can cope with Aron spending the rest of our working lives boasting how he saved my career. You'd better get on now."

"Yes sir." In the doorway she hesitated, "Shall I phone Lani for you?"

"No." He saw her concerned expression and forced himself to explain. "I've already called her. She'll come and get me as soon as it's over."

"Is there anything else I can do, sir?"

"No." Then suddenly, "Yes, there's one thing. What's the name of that perfume? The one she always wears." It was still there faintly, just a hint in the air, holding its own against the smells of the hospital room.

"It's called Gathered Flowers."

"Thanks. I wondered."

Gill left and he hauled her chair across and rested his leg on it. He hoped he had enough strength to see this through. This close to her, the perfume was more obvious. *'But one night or another night, will come the gardener in white, and gathered flowers are dead, Yasmin.'* What a fool he'd been not to recognise a perfectly decent omen until it was too late. That reminded him of the words that had distracted him the day they'd got Charlie back. *'Still to be neat, still to be dres't, as you were going to a feast. Lady it is to be presumed, all is not sweet, all is not sound.'* In the moment he'd thought that he'd had the key to the crime within his hands, but even if he'd realised it, feelings were useless without proof to back them up.

Without her make-up she looked much younger than he'd seen her before. He listened to her harsh breathing and wondered if she was aware of anything. She'd said she hated silence and hearing was the last sense to fail.

There was little he could talk about that was removed from crime and guilt, so he repeated over and over again, "Polly will be fine. She'll have a happy life."

They were empty words. A promise he couldn't keep. But he believed it was what Jasmin needed to hear. He was still saying them when he heard the change in her breathing and the faint death rustle in her throat.

Epilogue

Charlie knew he must be quiet. As still and quiet as a mouse. The way he'd been so many times before. But this time it was all right. He wanted to stay like this, curled up in Daddy's lap.

Daddy had one arm around Charlie, the other cradled Polly. He kept saying the same thing. "You're safe now, Charlie. It's okay. You're both safe."

Charlie didn't know what that meant, but Daddy said Charlie was a good boy. Not a bad, bad, wicked boy, the way she'd said.

Daddy was crying. He kept on crying and saying they were safe.

Charlie reached up and, with one small finger, traced the trail of his father's tears.

Poetry Credits

1.) Chapter 1. Isaac Rosenberg. (1890-1918.) Break of Day in the Trenches.

2.) Chapter 4. William Shakespeare. (c.1564-1616.) King John; Act III, scene 4.

3.) Chapter 4. Bible. New Testament. Mark; chapter 10, verse 14.

4.) Chapter 8. William Shakespeare. (c.1564-1616.) Macbeth; Act III, scene 2.

5.) Chapter 13. Ben Jonson. (1572-1637.) Epicoene, or the Silent Woman.

6.) Chapter 22. William Shakespeare. (c.1564-1616.) Macbeth; Act I, scene 7.

7.) Chapter 24. James Graham, Fifth Earl and First Marquess of Montrose. (1612 to 1650.)

8.) Chapter 25. William Shakespeare. (c.1564-1616.) Sonnet 116.

9.) Chapter 36. Ben Jonson. (1572-1637.) On My First Son.

10.) Chapter 45. Isaac Rosenberg. (1890-1918.) Dead Man's Dump.

11.) Chapter 53. Andrew Marvell. (1621-1678.) To His Coy Mistress.

12.) Chapter 53. William Shakespeare. (c.1564-1616.) Twelfth Night. Act I, scene 5.

13.) Chapter 61. James Elroy Flecker. (1884-1919). Hassan's Serenade.

14.) Chapter 61. Ben Jonson. (1572-1637.) Epicoene, or the Silent Woman

COMING 2015

Karma and the Singing Frogs

A Mia Trent Scene of Crime Novel

27135685R00194

Made in the USA
Charleston, SC
03 March 2014